Shadows of Revenge

Shadows of Revenge

Ken R. Abell

RESOURCE *Publications* · Eugene, Oregon

SHADOWS OF REVENGE

Resource Publications
An Imprint of Wipf and Stock Publishers
199 W. 8th Ave., Suite 3
Eugene, OR 97401
www.wipfandstock.com

ISBN 13: 978-1-62564-093-2
Manufactured in the U.S.A.

Scripture taken from the HOLY BIBLE, KING JAMES VERSION, Public Domain.

For my brother Rob, who long ago and faraway ran the trails
with me from Sugarloaf Hill to Scout Point and beyond,
mostly staying one step ahead of trouble.

&

For Anita Irene, who was stuck with me in a breakdown lane
on the outskirts of Tucumcari. We passed the time brainstorming
characters and storyline found on these pages.

&

For our sons and grandchildren. May they sooner rather than later
determine their true worth, and always know the power
of second chances and new beginnings.

&

For a couple Kansas Brethren who gave me lifetime encouragement
in low moments; a legendary buffalo hunter in Abilene
and an old-time rock and roller in Salina.

Contents

Acknowledgments

THANK YOU TO BARBARA JUNE for wisdom she shared with me on October 1, 1972 when I was seventeen. The sentiments expressed then have been woven into my worldview and became an integral part of this story.

Many thanks to Kathi Ellicott for having a keen eye and a patient heart—not to mention an encouraging way that is always expressed in a can-do attitude. Her school marm skills were successfully put to the test in this manuscript, for which I am extremely grateful. She is also the originator of the finest recipe for salsa available anywhere in the free world.

Thanks to an Ojibwe brother from many moons and miles ago. He was taken to his reward far too soon—before he departed planet earth, he reminded me about truths regarding the Creator speaking through creation. He told me that nature is where God's voice can be clearly heard by those who desire to listen.

Also by Ken R. Abell

Nonfiction
An Ordinary Story of Extraordinary Hope

Fiction
Days of Purgatory

Websites
www.wantedman.org
www.danceswithcorn.com

chapter one

Bloody Murder

*"What hast thou done? the voice of thy brother's
blood crieth unto me from the ground."*

~GOD~

JACK GREER CLUTCHED AT his chest and gasped. He wasn't all that old but his skin had a sickly gray pallor and yellow showed in his eyes. His mouth twisted in an ugly grimace. He toppled over and was dead before he hit the dirt encrusted plank floor.

Liam, his eighteen year old son, crouched beside him. "She killed him."

The air was thick and heavy with cigar smoke. "Who'd he say killed him?" a slightly slurred voice asked from amongst the bystanders. The only answer forthcoming were murmurs that mutated into wisecracks, which jumped from person to person like a contagious cough.

Deacon Coburn stood and moved away from his corner table at the Alamo Saloon. He was hatless, his hair shaggy and loose on his broad shoulders. His gait was easy, his demeanor peaceful. As he was noticed, onlookers parted to make a way for him. Whispers were choked off as though he had demanded silence. He stopped and studied the man stretched out on the floor.

Liam Greer gave him a sideways look. "She killed him . . . she killed him." His teeth were clenched, his lips peeled back in a nasty snarl.

Coburn knelt beside him. He examined the body, his hands deftly searching for a wound. He gingerly patted and probed before finally resting a palm on the dead man's chest. "Unless there was poison involved, no one killed this man. His ticker stopped, is all."

"What do you know, mister?" Liam blinked away moisture and got to his feet. He jammed his hands into the back pockets of his trousers. "She killed him as sure as shooting him in the head."

"His heart gave out," Deacon said flatly. "There's no murder here."

"She killed him."

"Who?"

"She was the love of his life, his dream, as he used to tell me," Liam answered, baring his teeth again. He seemed to be on the verge of growling or screaming. The fierce expression didn't quite fit on his thin baby-face, but he kept it fixed and firm. "He never stopped loving her. Until today, I guess." He took a step back and let out a whoosh of air. "Her name's Delores, but she goes by Flora. I know where to find her."

"Holy moly! Everyone knows where to find her," someone said drunkenly.

Consensus of that opinion came in the form of rough laughter accompanied by a slew of crude remarks. Liam Greer lurched forward, hands fisted. It was obvious he had a boulder-sized chip on his shoulder which produced bravado—it was equally evident that beneath the false front he was a lost little boy seeking to make his way in a world that had done him wrong.

Deacon Coburn rose. He rested a restraining hand on the young man. At first there was a herky jerky spasm of resistance, but Coburn gave him a shake and held fast. His face wrinkled in a sympathetic expression saturated with understanding. It had a calming effect on Liam Greer. His posture relaxed as his hands opened against his thighs.

Coburn bore in on the hard-edged spectators. Droplets of sweat glistened on every face. Some were fanning themselves against the oppressive Kansas heat. He thumbed aside the corners of his walrus-like moustache as he leaned in close. His dark eyes narrowed. He surveyed the crowd so intensely that many decided it'd be a good time to check out what was happening elsewhere; eyes darted to the floor or off in the distance.

Deacon Coburn spoke in a low voice full of controlled passion. "We're all hewn from the crooked timber of humanity." Something intangible in his bearing commanded respect and attentive ears. "Ain't none of us straight or righteous, ain't none of us clean. We're all sinners of one kind or another so there's not much credibility in our judgment of others."

A salty apology was muttered. Others nodded agreement. Feet shuffled as the throng of gawkers began drifting back to their doings, stirring the stagnant air. Long wedges of late afternoon sunlight streamed through the open doors and milky window panes to cast ever shifting shadows across the barroom.

Liam Greer squatted to gather his father's belongings. There wasn't much to be retrieved. A small amount of cash, a jackknife, and an expensive sterling silver case. He found everything easily enough. He pocketed the money and blade, but clicked open the case. It contained a tintype of the woman he held responsible for much sorrow and strife.

He scrutinized the picture. In it she was young, vibrant and beautiful. Thick cascades of luxurious hair framed an oval face, highlighted by eyes alive with mischief. He was, not for the first or last time, intrigued by her. His mind drifted to a longstanding daydream that haunted him and kept him edgy. He imagined finding her, meeting her, talking with her.

Deacon Coburn interrupted him. "Here," he said, extending a shabby quilt. "Put this over him until the undertaker gets here. I sent word, so he'll be along shortly."

Liam shifted around on his heels to arrange the blanket. "Thanks."

"After you've said your goodbyes, stop by for a visit." Deacon gestured toward the back section of the room. "I'll help you if I can."

Liam Greer frowned as he nodded. He watched the tall man walk away, wondering what his racket was—what ploy was he working? He considered the idea and his lips tightened into a small grin. Almost automatically he began mulling over how he could turn the man's kind offer to his advantage. The possibilities needed to be split open and picked apart. He wiped his brow and glanced at the door, wishing for even a whisper of a breeze.

Outside, the streets of Abilene were bustling. In front of the Alamo a seasoned teamster was barking orders to a slow-moving team of mules. The crack of a whip was followed by squealing heehaws. A cuss-ridden protest came from someone on the boardwalk. Several patrons spilled onto the veranda to get a better view, but the commotion soon passed.

Greer slipped the sterling silver case to an inside pocket of his tattered vest. He hooked his thumbs in the waistband of his trousers. Slouch-eyed and stoop-shouldered, with a crop of downy peach-fuzz instead of whiskers, he cast an unfavorable first impression.

He lazed past poker games while checking out the paintings of naked women on the walls. His gaze lingered longest on the largest, which was a portrait of a hussy known as Lucy. She was made up to resemble Cleopatra with a huge peacock perched on either side of her.

He came alongside the table to which he'd been invited. After casual introductions, he took a seat and straightaway noted the Bible in front of the man across from him. It was open, with a shot glass of whiskey on one side and a half-empty cup of black coffee on the other.

"You a preacher or something?" Liam asked smartly.

Coburn was noncommittal. "Or something."

Greer flashed a crooked grin. "What can you do to help me?"

"I offer you friendship."

"That's all?"

Hearing the sarcasm in his tone, Coburn eyed him directly. "The world's a hard place and life's a long road with lots of gnarly turns. We all need each other. Friendship is the grease that eases our way. Choose your friends wisely."

"I didn't mean nothing, mister. I'm upset, don't you know?"

"All the more reason to accept my friendship."

Greer bobbed his head. "And I do."

"What are your plans?"

"We came here to sell a string of horses, you know." Liam slumped back in the chair. "Tomorrow I'll make arrangements for my father's burying and take care of the business deal. That'll get me a set of fresh clothes and a small grubstake for the future." He started drawing invisible circles on the table with a finger. "I need to be getting myself a gun too. In a few days I'll be riding out of here in style."

"To where?"

"Does it matter where?" Liam queried, cocking an eyebrow. "I just know I ain't going backwards. There's nothing but misery and sour luck behind me."

"You ever work cattle?"

"Nope, only horses. Pa fancied himself a first-rate horse trader."

Coburn leaned forward, elbows resting on the table. "If you're of a mind I could hook you up with Big Bull Wallace. He's got a sprawling ranch in East Texas. His crew brought a herd north a while ago. Some of the boys are still hanging around town."

"I'll chew on it a spell." Liam gave him a half-hearted shrug. "Thanks for the offer." He pushed the chair back and got to his feet. "Pa was going to stop in and see that woman. I guess the chore falls to me. I'll go say my piece and be done with it, be finished with her."

"Maybe you best leave it alone, son."

"I ain't your son. Friends is one thing, kinship another."

"Not really, Liam." Coburn's manner was stern and uncompromising. "It's best when those lines get interwoven. We all got the same blood, the same ancestry. Any differences between people are superficial and every one disappears when eternity comes knocking."

Greer frowned. "I wouldn't know anything about that stuff, but I'll take your opinion and weigh it for myself," he said, sounding sincere. "Can we talk again?"

Coburn smiled warmly. "We surely can."

Liam Greer offered a nod good-bye. He spun around and walked to the front door. When he stepped outside he immediately turned north toward an address on the far edge of town.

Deacon Coburn tossed off the shot of whiskey and held it at the back of his throat. He took a mouthful of cold coffee and swished it all around before swallowing. He assessed the activity in the room for a few moments before returning to his neverending Bible study.

Daniel Twosongs was exhausted, but would not be swayed or slowed. Desperation prodded him. A rescue mission had him motivated to push past the upper limits of endurance. No deprivation could prevent him from forcing himself to press on. A renegade vender of death was loose and had to be stopped before achieving his ultimate goal.

The heat was brutal, scorching Twosongs to the bone, but it was the humidity that was backbreaking and disheartening. The moisture-laden air was incessant and pervasive; no place to flee from it and no relief on any foreseeable horizon. His body felt like a sponge that had been twisted and thoroughly wrung out, yet perspiration still leaked from every pore with each step he took. He was on foot and had been for better than three days.

The sun was low, with a couple hours of daylight remaining. The sky was akin to a slab of streaky gray slate. In the distance, clusters of black-veined clouds were being formed into menacing mountains that occasionally produced flashes and sparks, as though gnomes were slamming pieces of flint together.

He was southwest of Abilene, tracking a killer who was fueled by revenge. He had gotten close to the rogue, but then was bushwhacked. The thug had lain in wait and dry-gulched him. It had been cunning and cowardly.

The first bullet missed him by a whisker. He heard the hiss of it pass. The second shot came almost instantaneously. It struck his horse. Blood and brains splattered over him as the mountain bred pony reared up in its death throes. He tumbled off, rifle in hand. Using his fallen mount as a shield, he returned fire though he never caught a glimpse of his target. That didn't matter. He had no doubt that the sniper was the man he was trailing.

After a cautious while of watching and waiting, he surmised the murderer had departed. The situation was grim but not hopeless. He had been in tough spots countless times before, and was fully confident of his stamina and survival skills. He said some kind words over his horse, then left it out in the open for the coyotes and carrion feeders. He found a hollow and cached his saddle and rig, camouflaging it with a thick covering of prairie grass.

All he took was his Winchester, a bedroll which was slung over his shoulder and a canteen with an ounce or so of water remaining. He had many miles to go before resting. As was his pattern he intended to walk until midnight to take advantage of the relative coolness of the evening. He would catch three or four hours of shuteye, then be up and on the move again.

He was wishing for a drop in temperature just now. Two turkey buzzards were circling languidly, high above him. The pair of scavengers saw Twosongs as a prospective feast, a lone dot moving across a boundless landscape of grassy vastness. He knew that the red-skulled birds would patiently follow him, waiting for him to collapse and die.

The vultures had nature for an ally. Time and weather circumstances were ticking against him. Dehydration had weakened him. He was dizzy and his head ached. His lungs were hurting. It seemed as though he was breathing through a rag saturated with water.

The irony did not elude him; his throat was parched, his tongue swollen and cracked, but the soggy air could not quench his thirst or relieve the discomfort that clawed at his joints and muscles. He ignored the pain and discounted his present misfortunes, merely accepting them as a momentary reality to be overcome.

To that end he maintained a steady pace, purposefully staying on task. Fear was in him, nagging and nipping at the corners of his mind. He might already be too late. His determined efforts to prevent a scoundrel from carrying out a vengeance murder could all be for naught. Odds were that his old companion would be dead before he could warn him.

Daniel Twosongs refused that possibility.

≈≈≈

When Abbey Langton exited the dining room she went directly to the front desk of Drovers Cottage. It was a three-story frame structure not far from the railroad depot. Her train had arrived early in the afternoon. She checked in and took a much needed nap. A grumble in her belly awakened her. She decided it was suppertime. She freshened up and came downstairs.

Now, clutching a fashionable purse in her right hand, she strolled across the lobby as though she owned the place. She carried herself with the sensibility, assurance and maturity of a middle-aged woman of means, though truth was, she was only eighteen years old.

The hotel clerk, a handsome enough gentleman who'd introduced himself as Sam Beadle, was occupied with another customer, so she paced impatiently, her irritation evident in the stony set of her face. When it was her turn she quickly stepped forward.

"Is there a problem with your accommodations, Miss Langton?" He noticed that she had changed from her dusty traveling clothes. She was now wearing a billowing yellow dress with a high collar, along with a stylish hat tilted at a rakish angle atop a loose knot of gold-tinted auburn hair. There could be no denying that she was pretty, tiptoeing exceptionally close to beautiful. Neither could he refute the fact that he was strongly attracted to her.

"No, not at all, Mr. Beadle. They are quite suitable."

"We do have an in-house laundry, for your convenience."

"That's good information to have. Thank you."

"How else can I be of service?"

She forthrightly asked, "Where could I find Deacon Coburn?"

"What business would you have with Deacon Coburn?"

"How is that any of your business?"

"I suppose it's not. I was just wondering, Miss Langton."

"Just wondering? Try just wondering something else, Mr. Beadle."

He straightened his posture, endeavoring to measure her. He was five foot ten. He figured she was three or four inches shorter. "If Deacon Coburn is in town and not taking care of selling longhorns for Big Bull Wallace he'll be at a corner table at the Alamo Saloon."

"The Alamo Saloon," Abbey said, awe in her voice. "It was outside the Alamo Saloon that Wild Bill Hickok gunned down Phil Coe and Mike Williams last October."

Beadle raised an eyebrow, impressed. He regarded her with frank admiration. "That's right," he said softly. "Among whatever other jobs come my way I'm a stringer for the *Abilene Chronicle*. My account of the shoot-out was picked up by some of the eastern papers."

Interest flared in her eyes, though she quickly hid it. A sudden scurry of movement took her attention elsewhere. A powerfully built cattle-dog trotted in from the broad veranda and curled up to one side of the door. Its coloring was distinct, blue-speckled with sable-rimmed black patches over both eyes, which were alert and expressive.

Abbey thought it strange that the man didn't step from behind the desk to chase it out. She gave him a wrinkly-eyed scowl. "Aren't you going to shoo that dog?"

"I could," Sam answered, "but it'd be a pointless exercise." He held his hands up in mock surrender. "That dog has an independent streak bigger than the whole wide west."

"To whom does it belong?"

"No one . . . everyone," he said, tilting his head to the side. "It came north on a drive in '69 and adopted the community. Old Blue's an amiable scamp so the populace reciprocated."

"Old Blue?"

"It answers to Old Blue when it's not being typically stubborn. It understands English just fine when it so desires," he explained, glancing at the animal. "The name Old Blue fits its look and personality, though I don't think the dog's all that old. Maybe six or seven years."

"Who sees to its care?"

He laughed and rolled his eyes. "Who doesn't would be a fairer question. Old Blue gets fed and treated like the heir apparent. It regularly makes the rounds from saloon to saloon, hotel to hotel to socialize, or to lounge contentedly in whatsoever place it pleases."

She had been watching Old Blue. Now she returned her gaze to Sam Beadle. She found herself somehow charmed by him and wanted to pick up the conversation where it had been diverted. "You're acquainted with Wild Bill Hickok?"

"You betcha," he replied, almost nonchalantly. "He was Marshall here for most of '71, but those wild days are over and done. Everything's changing here in Abilene."

"It still seems abundantly exciting to me."

"In comparison to the way it was, this town's now a church picnic," he told her, leaning his shoulders against the wall. "The railhead's moving south to Newton and Wichita, and westward to Ellsworth, Hays, and Dodge City." There was genuine sadness in the cast of his stance and glint in his eyes. "Abilene had a great run, but its days as a cowtown are numbered. Civilization is encroaching on us. The city fathers and good folks of Dickinson County have made it clear they want nothing more to do with the Texas cattle business."

"How'd they do that?"

He squinted at her. There was disgust in the expression. "In February a petition against the cattle trade was signed by eighty percent of the citizens. This spring's action was piddling. Next year's will be nothing." He shook his head, glum and cheerless. "Wheat's the next big thing, but it won't be anywhere near as thrilling as being a cowtown."

"You sound melancholy."

"There's nothing like a boom town, Miss Langton," he said, lips pursing into a mirthful smile. "A boom town is reckless, exhilarating, and full of itself. I came here with the Kansas Pacific in the spring of '67. It was a squalid camp made up of a dozen or so log huts with dirt for roofing. It became freewheeling and lawless, but the fun's all done now for sure."

Abbey responded with a shrug and swift shake of her head. "Too bad for me. I wanted to come and be a part of that hurly-burly tumult."

"The west isn't finished its growth spurts, Miss Langton. There'll be no end of rough and tumble happenings down the trail," he replied earnestly. "Before the end of the summer I intend to pack up and move on to Dodge City. When the fun's all done there I'll move on again."

She looked at him closely. He was sharply dressed and clean-shaven, with a tousle of brown hair. His eyes were deep-set and vividly blue. She caught herself before her imagination took off on a girly reverie. "You say I'll find Deacon Coburn at the Alamo Saloon."

"On Cedar Street," he answered, boldly studying her. He was convinced he detected a rosy blush showing on her cheeks, which captivated him. "A young lady of your quality ought not to go into the Alamo unattended by a gentleman, Miss Langton."

"If Deacon Coburn is there I'll not be unattended, will I, Mr. Beadle?"

"Unless he's busy elsewhere, he'll be there. That's where he holds his services."

"Services?"

"You really don't know him, do you?"

"I knew him long ago, Mr. Beadle." She spun around and strolled away.

Sam Beadle sidled after her for a couple steps. He judiciously appreciated the gentle sway and flow of her skirt. He grinned approvingly when Old Blue got up and followed her out.

~~~

Charley Jondreau had given in to his catlike curiosity, and now, he regretted it. There was turmoil here, which based solely on appearances, could put him in a bad spot. He was alone, but for how long? He needed to skedaddle, but instead, stayed put to investigate.

He had stabled his horse, a bridle-wise pinto with a sociable disposition, in a dusky stall at the back of the livery. While closing its gate, which creaked noisily, he'd spotted a tarp bunched up in the adjoining compartment. He was now on a knee and holding up a corner of the canvas. His eyes were narrowed into slits as he looked at the corpse of a man in the shady light.

He was naturally wary, but there was more to it than instinct. He had premonitions and insights that came over him by and by; a foreboding that he had no control over, which would enshroud him like a bleak cowl. The sixth sense had a physical manifestation—a tangible acidy odor would rise up out of nowhere and fill his nostrils, which he referred to as the smell of the skunk. Strong and disconcerting, that stench was on him as he appraised the body.

It was murder. Of that there was no doubt. The evidence was beyond obvious, but more than that he could *see* particulars. The killer knew his victim. It had been personal. This was not the end result of a dispute over water rights or a disagreement about ownership of property. It had been intentional and premeditated, having all the elements of a blood feud that had festered for years. The body had been dumped here to send a message to others.

Charley Jondreau *saw* all of this and more. Trouble was coming and he wanted nothing to do with it. He was a drifter and explorer. He tended to avoid getting involved in the affairs of others, preferring to stay on the periphery and make observations. He had ridden into town simply because he was desirous for whiskey. The possible entertainment of a poker game or a woman was also in the back of his mind.

He returned the canvas tarp to exactly how it'd been when he found it. He was meticulous in attending to details, making sure every crease and crinkle was as he had first seen it. He stood, taking in his surroundings. He was still by himself in the livery. He considered saddling his stallion and getting lost in a hurry, but he was tired and thirsty for something fiery and fine to wash down trail dust. He also knew the horse was spent and needed a good rest.

He took off his droopy-brimmed hat and removed a handkerchief lining its crown. He mopped sweat off his face and smooth-shaven head. He routinely took a razor to his scalp, but few ever knew that because he seldom removed his headgear in the company of others.

He went outside. Twilight was stretching its pinkish hues across the sky. He paused for a quick look at the colors, then was on the prowl, a solidly built man moving rapidly on agile feet. He wore a six-shooter holstered high on his right hip. A superbly balanced throwing knife was in a fringed leather sheaf hooked on the same belt on the left side. He was proficient with both weapons, but only in matters of honor.

He entered the Alamo Saloon just as two dark-suited gents were carrying a body out. He stepped aside to make room for them to pass. His teeth clenched as a chill chased up his spine and his guts cramped momentarily. He'd been in town for less than an hour and had already been in contact with death twice. Not a good omen.

The barroom was crowded and loud, full of smoke and chatter. He went to the bar and purchased a bottle of cheap whiskey. He took it and a shot glass to the only unoccupied table in the place. After snapping back a couple shots, he nursed the alcohol. He kept silent, his eyes roving the room without ever settling on or making contact with anyone.

As always in new encounters he was fully aware that others were checking him out. The brashness and lack of subtlety amazed him. There were gestures and whispers, but he paid no heed to them. On sheer principle he generally rejected the opinions offered by others. He had his own ambiguous yet hardnosed code of ethics and morality. He would never live for another's approval or acceptance. He was not about to apologize for his past or present.

His swarthy features were often passed off as being weather-beaten and tanned by the sun and wind, but there was another reason for his reddened complexion. He was of mixed heritage, born in a longhouse village in the Great Lakes region. The settlement had been nestled near the north shore of Lake Erie in an area known for its marshes and peat bogs. He was Scotch-Irish and French, along with a healthy amount of Indian blood in his veins. His paternal forebears were trappers for the Hudson Bay Company. His mother and grandmother were Iroquois.

He was a deeply conflicted man with an enormous amount of sorrow in his eyes. There was a constant tension wound up in him that he sought to keep under wraps, but it could unravel and explode without warning.

His fuse was long, but once lit, it burned at a furious speed. When that occurred, his fists would get a good workout.

Charley Jondreau sipped his whiskey, listening carefully. In doing so he picked up tads of minutiae and scuttlebutt to be filed away for future reference. He took note of a man hunched over his table concentrating on a book. When he turned a page, Jondreau's face flinched into a surprised scowl. Unless he was grossly mistaken the man was reading a Bible.

The rocking of the train kept Naomi Engle alert and awake. There were huge tears welled up in her eyes as she bit down hard on the inside of her bottom lip. All that she had ever known was gone. In a whirlwind of shocking decisions she had discarded her life in a desperate grab to find a new one. She was a tall and dark-haired beauty dressed in layers of somber gray clothes that were not at all flattering. She wore a bulky black bonnet that obscured her face.

Dusk was settling over the passing countryside, but she was too fidgety and out of sorts to doze off. She was just starting on a journey to put heartaches behind her. She had prayed and planned fervently, but life hadn't turned out according to her intentions.

In her thirtieth year, she should be raising a passel of children and being a helpmate to her partner, but that was not to be. Instead, she was a childless widow woman riding the westward rails alone. It had only been eight months since she buried her husband of over twelve years. It'd been a vibrant relationship, except for a lament that had blighted their life together. For reasons never made clear to her by God or midwives she had not conceived.

It was not for lack of trying. From the beginning of the marriage she was diligent in performing her wifely duties. Initially her enjoyment of the intimacy embarrassed her, but she got over that chagrin soon enough. The carryings-on in their bedchamber had been vigorous and often, but nature did not take its course.

Outwardly she had resigned herself to being barren. She fixed a smile in place and feigned happiness; never more so than as her sister and sisters-in-law all proved to be exceedingly fertile. At each birth of a new niece or nephew, Naomi had been gracious and overly generous. She was so convincing that no one ever suspected that inwardly a bitter kernel was sinking its roots deep into the soil of her heart.

She wasn't even aware of it. To her way of thinking she was making the best out of a great disappointment and doing all things possible to rise above it. She prayed continually. She beseeched the throne of heaven with an urgency that had no end. There was nothing else she could do but trust that grace would sustain her and be sufficient.

As she moved through the busyness of her days cheerful and upbeat, the acrimonious seed in her heart was doing nasty things. Degree by degree the tendrils were making significant inroads to twine around all those things she held dear and beloved. The weed was gaining toxic potency, but she remained oblivious to it. Her level of denial was so tremendous that she was abysmally ignorant of the dangerous growth sprouting within.

It was a hidden part of her that came gushing out when tragedy stuck its piercing sword through the core of her existence. The harmful substance blossomed and seeped out to discolor all her realities. The calamity happened on a perfect autumn afternoon when the community was gathered together to raise a barn for a young newlywed couple.

Adam Engle had been his old jovial self, working harder and faster than anyone else on the crew. All the while he labored he was smiling, laughing, or making wise cracks. He set the pace and it was up to others to keep up. Everyone enjoyed him. He had a way of turning ordinary assignments into fun-filled ventures.

The job was almost finished when a seemingly innocent stumble became a horrible accident. It had transpired in a speedy sequence that created gasps and shouts. Adam was at the peak of the roof gathering up a half-bundle of left-over shingles. He slipped, took two sideway stutter steps to find his balance, but his feet got entangled together.

For one frozen second it seemed as though he was going to get steadied, but then his face contorted with the knowledge he was going to tumble. The armload of cedar slates went flying. He grasped at air as he pitched backwards off the edge. He flailed and thrashed, wildly attempting to get his legs under him. It was futile exertion. He landed flat on his back, striking the ground with a horrific thud. His head bounced thrice and came to rest in a weird position.

Naomi had been closeby. She'd seen the entire dreadful mishap unfold. The expression that marred her husband's countenance as he precariously reeled would never be shaken; it embroidered itself on her memory. It was chaos as she knelt beside him. He was blacked out and paralyzed, his back broken and blood trickling from the corners of his mouth.

She sat at his bedside for a week. He never once flickered into consciousness. Night and day she remained dedicated and alert. No amount of coaxing or counsel from family and friends dissuaded her. She would not be deterred. Others took charge of his nursing while she monitored every aspect of his care. She cried and prayed; she prayed and cried. The tears and supplications blended together into a forsaken, frantic entity.

Seven days after the fall, Adam Engle took his final breath as dawn arrived bright and beautiful. She was alone with him. She shut their bedroom door and latched it. She lay down on the bed and wrapped her arms around him, her head on his chest. She held him fiercely. Her body quivered with emotion as she sobbed and cursed the darkness engulfing her.

The one-two punch of God, fate, fortune, or destiny was too much for Naomi Engle to submerge beneath layers of faith. To be childless was terrible enough, but at least she'd had an attentive husband to comfort and care for her; a loving man to help her sort through and submit to the abstract and seemingly hurtful vagaries of life.

He was gone. Loneliness crushed in all around her. She wept, and all the while bitterness surged in the crevices of her soul where questions directed to God were fashioned into lances to relentlessly jab at heaven. While she was holding him, as warmth was being snatched from his body, she resolved to find a fresh beginning.

Now, as she began to adjust to the back and forth rhythm of the train, she renewed that resolution. She did so intensely. She stared out the window and could distinguish enough of her reflection in the murky glass to see that her cheeks were shining with large teardrops. She palmed them away, released a low sigh, and unclamped her teeth from her bottom lip.

Jackson Scully was thoroughly played-out. He was scruffy and frayed, as wrinkled around the eyes as a sunbaked slice of fruit. He looked much older than his thirty-eight years. The miles and booze had not pampered him. There was an ample amount of white on parade in his hair and scraggly beard. He sat on the edge of the bed putting his socks and boots on.

The woman behind him was curled beneath a rumpled sheet. Her flaming red hair was a topsy-turvy mess on the pillow. Her eyes were wide, watching him. He had been with her since the middle of the night. She'd greeted him with a weary smile and a kiss on his cheek when he knocked on her door shortly after he'd skulked into Abilene.

"Will I see you again?" she asked softly.

He glanced at her. "I always ramble back to you."

"Maybe I want more than flings now and again."

"I ain't sure what that means."

"It's been years, Jackson."

"They do fade away like smoke, girly-girl."

She beamed on hearing him use a favorite term of endearment. "You've aged plenty. You weren't even beginning to gray the last time we were together."

He grunted. He had come to know her when he was stationed at Fort Smith. He habitually frequented her dance hall and brothel, a tightly run establishment catering to the lusts of soldiers, gamblers and cowboys. She was a mercenary businesswoman, recruiting and turning out ladies of easy virtue wafting along on the shifting social tide following the Civil War.

She reached over to rub his shoulders. "I want to change."

"What?" He scowled at her. "Change what?"

She rolled over and knelt behind him. In a burst of modesty she clutched the sheet around her and tucked it tightly. "I want to change us. I want to change my life."

Scully laughed derisively. "That hardly seems possible."

"Why?"

He ignored the question. His head wagged slowly as he remembered. He'd had more than his share of soiled doves, but she was special. She had bewitched him from their first transaction. It was a mutual allure. He became a constant visitor. Soon money stopped changing hands. The fervent emotions set loose made their relationship complex. Real affection developed between them, but those sentiments were complicated and never fully explored.

Cavalry duty took him elsewhere, while opportunities in commerce kept her on the move. Their paths had crossed from time to time as he deliberately kept tabs on her from afar. He tracked her whereabouts by pinning his ears back around campfires and in saloons.

In those places rumors and news was gathered and dispersed as effectively as telegraph wires. When liquored up and prompted to do so men bragged loudly about where to find the finest scarlet women and the escapades that made them memorable.

"Why?" she repeated insistently. "Why can't we make a new life?"

"We're a mite old for starting over, don't you think?"

She leaned against him, her hands tightening around his waist. "No, we're not," she answered, squeezing harder. "The risk is that we'll squander our years and the chance will pass us by. I've got money, bonds, plus timber and mining investments. We can go anywhere. I can escape the past and my reputation. We can do it together and build a respectable life."

He roughly pushed her away and stood. He took a couple limping steps, his left leg dragging almost as a dead weight. "What's wrong with you?" There was serious animosity in his voice. "We got a pleasant thing together. I have no intention of changing anything."

She scoffed. "A pleasant thing? Isn't that fitting and dandy? What kind of fool am I?" She slid off the bed and shed the sheet. She strolled to a closet and got a flower-decorated robe. As she slipped it on and adjusted it, she confronted him. "You waltz in any time you please and crawl back into my good graces, and for you it's all just a pleasant thing?" She knotted the frilly belt around her flat tummy. "I may be crazy but I want a much different life, Jackson."

"Wanting and doing is two different proposals, Flora," he said, giving her a flippant wave of a hand. "You're harping and crabbing, but I ain't figured on about what."

She shook her head, exasperated. "I can't walk the streets without getting snide looks and whispers. I sold all interests in the sporting house and got out of the whoring trade two years ago yet I still have cowboys pounding on my door at all hours."

"Your fame follows you," he said, chuckling. "Ain't much you can do about it because that's the price you pay for the life that chooses you."

"My fame can go to blazes."

"It could, but it won't."

Her mouth tensed, her eyes narrowed. "You're mistaken. I will relocate to someplace where my notoriety doesn't precede me and reinvent myself. Mark my words, Mr. Scully. I'll change my life. Are you interested in partnering with me?"

"I want no changes between us. Ain't anything wrong with my life."

"Really? You live looking over your shoulder worrying on what's behind you."

"The hell I do. I ain't bothered about nothing on my back trail."

"Why'd you sneak in here well after midnight?"

"I rode long and hard to get here, girly-girl," he replied quickly. "I was in a hurry to see you. It just so happened to be nighttime when I got to town."

"I know you, Jackson Scully." She tossed her hair back, finger combing it as she sat on the bed. She patted the mattress, inviting him to join her. He did so. She tilted her head to stare straight at him. "I know your mannerisms, I know your habits. Something's coming up on you, which is all the more reason to throw in with me and be done with the past."

"I don't know what bug's gotten into you," he said, "but I got an unfinished job that needs tended to before I can even entertain your highfalutin ideas. And I ain't saying I'm going anywhere with you, but at least I'll consider it."

"Don't waste your time thinking, mi amour," she said, smiling. Her lively eyes lit up. The elusive emerald hue in them flashed playfully. "My mind is set and I'm not waiting."

"You're a hard bargainer, I'll grant you that much."

She giggled, dropping a hand to his thigh. "Why fight me on this?"

"You don't need me to start fresh somewhere."

"You're correct, I don't."

"So why pressure me?"

"My heart. How am I supposed to explain my heart to me let alone you?" she asked, lips puckering sadly. "Do you know how many men I've been with, Jackson?"

"I don't think about it."

Her forehead creased. "Hundreds. Thousands, maybe."

"And I definitely don't want to talk about it."

"Don't be a prude. You've had lots of women."

He offered a feeble reply, "Only working girls."

"Have you ever felt for any of them the feelings you have for me?"

His expression froze. He held it on the floor and declined to look at her. His right hand went over his mouth for a moment before it raked its way through his bushy whiskers. There was silence between them that seemed to make the room smaller. He let out a whistle of air as he admitted aloud what was in his mind. "No. I always come back to you."

"Are you ever sorry when you do?"

"No. Never, Flora."

"Neither am I," she said adamantly. "You're the only man I've ever *wanted* to make a life with, but your boots never stay under my bed long enough to do so."

"Well, leave it with me." He draped an arm over her shoulders and gave her a gentle hug. "I've got some business to take care of here, but first, can you rustle me up some grub?"

She eyed him suspiciously. "Will I see you again?"

He gave her a slight nod. Her mouth pinched, indicating that she wasn't satisfied with his response. She stood and walked out of the bedroom. He heard cupboard doors being opened and slammed shut. He would not be drawn into the kitchen until she told him that the meal was served. He had too many other arrangements running rampant inside his head.

He was thinking about what had brought him to Abilene. He realized his gimpy get-along was too easy to identify so he was positive of two facts: He had to remain mounted whenever he was in public and the affair had to be concluded under the cover of darkness. Therefore, if all went according to plan, when he pulled the trigger later tonight he would be on horseback.

Abbey Langton stopped on the boardwalk not far from the Alamo Saloon. Her mouth was dry, her stomach tense. She tried moistening her lips, but couldn't produce enough saliva. She took a deep breath. She stooped over and grabbed Old Blue's neck. She petted the friendly animal. It responded by enthusiastically pawing her.

"Thanks for shepherding me, but for the sake of my mother's memory, I have to go the rest of the way myself," she said in a shaky voice. "You stay put. I'll be fine."

Old Blue cocked an ear at her. It whined as it plopped down on its buttocks. Dusk was turning to dark. Abbey dramatically inhaled another gulp of air. It was hot and gritty like sand scraping down her pipes. Her steps were measured, decisive.

There were a couple grizzled cowboys hanging around on the veranda chewing tobacco and chattering animatedly. They both eyed her as she approached. She attempted a brave smile, but it was unconvincing. They tipped the brim of their hats and inched out of her way.

Three double glass doors were propped open. Abbey entered the Alamo using the middle set. She froze in her footsteps. Her nerve and mettle were waning. The saloon was packed and hopping with hustling motion. She stood still as weakness flooded down her legs. She felt wobbly. The low noise of numerous conversations blended into a buzzing hum, which decreased in volume as more and more patrons spied her.

It was an elongated room, forty feet or so wide. Along the south side was an elaborate bar festooned by polished brass fixtures and rails. She gawked at the roughneck crowd, realizing she was completely out of her element. Her hands flexed tightly on her purse. She moved tentatively, catching a reflection of herself in the outsized mirror behind the bar.

The glimpse of her scared eyes startled her and steeled her determination. She stiffened her backbone and took sturdy steps. She sensed him before she saw him. His eyes were on her. A squeak peeped out as she stared at him, seeing him through the eyes of a nine year old child. In her memory he was unchanged. Their gaze connected and locked.

Recognition hit Deacon Coburn with force. He got to his feet so hastily that his chair tipped over. His mouth hung open; his eyes gaped into huge circles. Silence thickened in the barroom. All focus was on a private reunion happening, as it were, on a public stage.

Abbey's world became a spinning montage of images twirling through her mind. She recalled everything about him. He had shown up at their home wearing ratty Union Army blues, looking to exchange work for a meal. He stayed for half a year, always treating her with kindness. She had known him as Mr. Lawrence, a nice man who toiled hard repairing their ramshackle farmhouse, and in his gentleness, stirred hope and love in their hearts.

"My Lord!" he exclaimed in a raspy croak. "You're as beautiful as your mother."

"Thank you," Abbey said quietly. Without even being aware of it her legs had functioned properly and she was standing in front of his table. What came out of her voice box next was numb and not at all what she had rehearsed. "Your letter got there just short of too late. It blessed her in her final hours. She was holding it against her heart when she died."

The words slashed him like a fiery blade cutting painfully to the bone. His complexion paled as his jaw twitched. He faltered. He grabbed handfuls of air to find his equilibrium. Leaning crookedly, he set his chair aright and slumped down. "Angela is dead? When? How?" The questions were wrenching, like shards of glass on his tongue.

Abbey sat across from him. She wiped the tears flowing down her face. She reached into her purse and came out with a manila envelope. "I have a letter for you," she said slowly. "I'm sorry it has taken me so long to get this to you, but I thought it best to deliver it face to face. I had much growing up to do before I could make the trip."

Deacon's chin was trembling as she handed it to him. He gripped it urgently.

Abbey exhaled a shivery breath, as though a wintry wind had blown over her. "Mom wrote it, sealed it in the envelope, and made me promise to see that it got delivered to you. She passed a few hours later. That was almost exactly three years ago."

He turned it over in his hands, scowling at his name penned in a fragile scrawl. When written, he had been in New Mexico helping the Weitzels rebuild their homestead after an attack by a terrorist mob. Now realization stabbed at him—while immersed in working with his friends, the only woman he'd ever loved had been dying. That knowledge was almost too much for him to comprehend. He was lightheaded and queasy.

He squeezed his eyes shut. The barroom went far away. He could see her clearly. The loveliness of the sight was vivid in his mind. She moved unhurriedly in the pretty glow of candles, her jumble of auburn hair loose and bouncy on her shoulders. He groaned loudly. He clapped a hand over his mouth. His watery eyes were mere slits.

His hands had a jittery palsy. He fumbled with the envelope. In a display of heartfelt frustration he tore it apart. He shook out a single tri-folded sheet and opened it. His breathing was uneven and spasmodic as he read what was before him.

June, 1869
Xenia, Ohio
Dear Deacon: I'm glad to finally know your given name, but you will always be remembered as Lawrence to me. Thank you for your letter. I received it with a mixture of joy and remorse. Joy to learn that you are safe and well—remorse for the life we could have enjoyed.

You seek my forbearance and forgiveness. I freely grant all that you request. I do not regret the night we shared together. I treasure it, wishing there had been many more. Neither do I have any shame for the love I've nurtured in my heart for you. Know that my deep, abiding affection has never wavered.

I'm certain that sooner rather than later Abbey will make her way west. She is headstrong and full of dreams. If your paths ever cross in those western lands, please care for her as you would your own daughter. She harbors tender feelings for you.

Life has given me a bit of a kick. I'm not long for this world. Your sweetness has stayed with me all these years and sustains me in these difficult moments. If at all possible, I will wait for you just inside the Eastern Gate.
All My Love,
Angela

His cheeks were wet with tears. The rawness of emotion was impossible to hide. He rubbed his eyes with the heels of his hands and held onto his forehead for a long while.

"You loved each other," Abbey said, breaking into his solitude.

Sudden-like, he nodded. "More than either of us ever understood."

"I never saw it. I was just a child, too little to know."

"I reckon so." He motioned to the bartender. A moment later his unusual combination of coffee and whiskey was delivered. "Bring the lady a tall glass of soft cider."

When the drink was set in front of her, Deacon Coburn thoughtfully fingered his Bible. The black leather cover was soft and shiny because he often gave it a fussy oil rubdown, attending to it with profound devotion. Handling the letter gingerly, he placed it in the center of the Good Book and closed it, leaving his hands resting on it.

A tiny gasp swirled out of her as she sat bolt upright. "Oh, my!" she murmured breathlessly. A sprinkling of teardrops fell from her eyes. "I put your letter in her Bible and arranged it in the coffin. It's buried with her."

He took hold of her hands firmly. "You're a thoughtful and considerate, young lady. That was a precious thing to do," he said, exhibiting an encouraging smile. "If you're anywhere in close proximity when my time of dying comes please see to the same for me."

She pushed a sly grin past her tears. "I just got here, so you better not be planning your funeral any time soon, Mr. Lawrence . . ." Her eyebrows tented and she put a hand to her mouth to stifle a chirpy giggle. "Sorry. What should I call you?"

His eyes brightened. "Deacon. Everyone knows me as Deacon."

She sighed contentedly. He glanced around the room. The crowd was getting back to its conventional state of rowdiness. Most no longer had any interest in their concerns, but there was a lone exception. A dark-hued man in a droopy-brimmed hat was coyly watching them. Coburn gave him a brisk once-over before deciding he had more important matters on his plate.

Making amends and catching up with Abbey was top priority. He hemmed and hawed, attempting to ascertain a topic to get started. At first their dialog was a hesitant stammering and stuttering as they stumbled along remembering. The last time they'd seen each other had been on a bitter cold February night in 1864, while engaged in a tic-tac-toe tournament. In a short while they eased into a comfy conversation, picking their way through eight years.

~~~

Darkness was creeping across the sky. Liam Greer loitered behind a time-worn oak tree. Tension had a vicious grip on him. His hands were twitchy and restless as he mustered his courage. He was fifty or so yards from the house he had determined to be the place. It sat off by itself, a quaint clapboard bungalow painted white and trimmed in green.

The dancing glow of light flickered in several windows. A horse was saddled in the side yard, tethered to a post. He had been watching and waiting for what seemed to him to be hours, but actually was only thirty minutes.

He shuffled his feet and picked at a jutting splinter of bark. It broke off in his hands. He toyed with it, turning it over and over as he considered his options. He had his words all worked through his head. What he had to say to her had been replayed many times.

The front door opened. Liam body-hugged the tree and held his breath. He cautiously kept the scene in his line of sight. A man stepped out. He paused on the porch and looked around as though he expected there to be trouble. His hat was pulled low on his forehead. He gimped his way to the horse, his left leg plodding along awkwardly. He pulled a rifle out, and after checking the action and load, returned it to its saddle scabbard and mounted the animal. He gave the horse a kick. It whinnied and snorted, and headed toward the center of town at a canter.

Liam Greer remained motionless, straining to keep an eye on the man. He dawdled near the tree until horse and rider disappeared. Even then, he vacillated and scuffled around in a circle, seemingly unsure of what to do next. He gathered his nerve and abruptly proceeded to the house. He took the step onto the porch with a jump and pounded hard on the door.

He heard footfalls approaching from the other side. The sound of the lock jiggling was accompanied by a lilting voice. "Crimany, Jackson! What did you forget . . ." She stopped in mid-sentence as the door cracked open. She eyed her visitor, seeing a youngster who hadn't even started shaving yet. His manner agitated some strange feelings deep within her. He had a hurt and mournful look that prevented her from immediately shutting the door.

"Are you Flora?" he asked, scratchy-voiced.

"I'm not in that business anymore."

"Are you Flora, is what I asked?"

"Get out of here." She tried to slam the door. He stuck his foot out to stop it and gave her a colossal push backwards as he bulled his way into the house. She almost fell, but caught hold of a chesterfield to prevent herself from hitting the floor. She swore beneath her breath.

"I'm here for Jack Greer," Liam said bluntly.

The redhead exhaled a throaty laugh. She was wearing a silky maroon robe covered with roses and vines. Though it didn't need doing, she readjusted the belt around her waist, obviously making sure she was completely covered. "It'd be best if you leave right now."

"That's not going to happen until I get me some satisfaction," he said, taking a swaggering step toward her. "Why don't you sit down and be comfortable."

She laughed again; there was something barbed and bitter in the tone of it. "That's mighty bold talk for a brat kid." She got a hard backed chair and placed it near a low table with two radiant oil lamps on it. Several candles and other lamps were strategically situated around the compact living room. As she sat down she motioned for him to do the same.

Liam perched on an arm of the chesterfield. "Jack Greer is dead."

"Is that supposed to mean something to me?"

"I'm Liam Greer. Jack was my father."

"So you say."

"You were married to him. Back when your name was Delores."

She was stone-faced. She casually crossed her legs and fondled a strand of hair. "I needed him to get me out of St. Louis. That's all there was to the marriage."

"Not quite," Liam said thinly. He glared at her. "You made a baby together. I was born somewhere in the vicinity of Little Rock."

She studied him. "You're Jack Greer's boy? It still means nothing to me."

"You killed my father."

"Did I now?"

"He loved you always," he replied tersely. The words were somewhat garbled because his lips were curled back, his jaw clenched. "You gave his heart a fatal blow. He never recovered from the wound. It took some years but slow and sure you killed him."

"Please don't take me for a fool," she said, anger roiling in her eyes.

"Not a fool," he countered, "just a hard-hearted whore."

"You can go to hell and burn, you miserable whelp. Why did you come here?"

Liam glowered at her. "You destroyed a good man. You need to take that to *your* grave."

"I'll take much more than that to my grave," she said, tilting her head and pursing her lips in an adamant expression. "All of which is none of your business."

"What's the big secret? You're a whore. Everyone knows your business."

"It could be a bit more complicated than you can grasp."

"Complicated or not; famous or not, a whore is just a whore," he shot back, sneering. "Are you going to tell me that you're not Sweet Flora, whore extraordinaire?"

Her expression became brittle. "Am I supposed to be impressed because you've been privy to a bunch of lies and some farfetched flights of fancy?"

"I ain't here to impress a whore."

"You keep calling me a whore. Did you only recently learn that word?" She shifted forward on the chair. "Let me tell you something, you lily-livered punk. Nothing you say or do to me can be worse than where I've already been."

"I've spilled my guts. I got nothing left to say."

"Poor baby. You plan on being a man anytime soon?" She blasted an icy stare at him. "You know nothing of my life. Nothing!" she said, her voice raising a couple decibels. "I was scarcely eighteen years old when I ran off with Jack Greer. I squeezed a scrawny runt out less than nine months later and was gone shortly thereafter. I haven't laid eyes on him since then."

"He put eyes on you every day." He reached into his vest and pulled out the sterling silver case. He clicked it open to once again examine the photograph.

She flinched. She instantly identified the case as a prized possession that had been mislaid in the hasty and careless escape from her marriage of convenience; it had been missing and lost for half her life, but she'd never forgotten it. "That belongs to me."

"Nope. It's mine, all mine now."

The callous crust of her exterior was beginning to develop signs of strain. She visibly softened. "I remember the day I sat for that portrait to be taken. A few weeks later I was the beneficiary of devastating news." There was honesty and vulnerability in her tone. "Shortly after that, I met Jack Greer. I used him to make my getaway."

Liam grouched a spiteful chuckle. He kept the tintype in front of him, his eyes flitting back and forth from it to the woman across the room from him. She was still beautiful, with chiseled cheekbones accentuating a perfectly formed oval face, but age was an identifiable presence. Webs of wrinkles were taking shape at the corners of her eyes, which remained bright and impish, but it was also evident that a bleak and weary shade had been cast.

"It belongs to me. May I have it please?"

"Nope," he snapped, rising to his feet. "I no longer care for it, but you ain't getting it. I'll keep it and barter a fair deal down the trail a ways."

"I'll pay cash for it here and now. Name your price."

"Nope."

She stood and flipped her hair back. It was full and elegant; falling across her shoulders like eddies of flaming waves. "Put the case on the table there," she ordered humorlessly. "Then peel those britches off. I'll make a man out of you and be done with it."

"You're sick."

"Not at all." Her hands went deliberately to her neck and lingered for an enticing moment. Then in a precise way she widened the gap in the robe far enough to grant him a generous glimpse of cleavage and the al-luring swell of her bosom. "I'm just a hard-hearted whore looking to turn a trick and possibly bag a virgin if I'm lucky. All in exchange for property that already belongs to me. Give me the tintype and I'll do you like you've never been done."

His eyes were fixated on the alabaster valley leading to her bellybut-ton and below. He felt hot blood increasing in him; usually an enjoyable sensation, but in this circumstance, the physical response repulsed him. He clicked the case closed and returned it to its pocket. His narrow face was the color of blood, his hands knotted up and tapping against his thighs. "You can kiss off and die," he shouted venomously. He spun and stomped away.

"I will soon enough." Her words were unheard. The cavernous force of the slamming door swallowed them whole. It was such a jarring swoosh that candles sputtered and windows clattered, sounding as though some glass had actually been broken.

Outside, Liam Greer bolted. He ran as fast as he could, his knees pumping up and down almost out of control. Angry tears blurred his vi-sion and streaked his cheeks. He didn't stop running until he came close to Ed Gaylord's Twin Livery. He ducked in behind the stables and sat in the darkness, with his back against the wall. He pulled his knees up, arms locking around them like a vise. He silently seethed and spat curses at the star-speckled sky.

His body shook with tremors as he wept and stuffed filthy emotions down.

Pete Axler was making his rounds, a part-time lawman being vigilant. Tall and lean, he carried a lantern, its yellowy beams providing a slant of pale light as he covered the same footsteps he did every night. Longhorns were mooing and rumbling from the Great Western Stockyards to the east, and the palpable stench of manure perfumed the humid air.

He moseyed along in a laidback and unruffled manner, eyes active and ears filtering out the natural noise of a cowtown. He was grateful for the job; not thrilled with it, but surely appreciative. He had it due to the deluge of lawless flotsam drifting in on the currents of cattle drives, but that ebb and flow was all in transition now. Every shipping season Abilene employed extra officers, but with the systematic phasing out of the Texas cattle trade in full swing, that tradition was undergoing review. Fewer men were hired this year than last and next year the decrease would be significantly greater.

A gurgle came floating out of the darkness. Pete Axler tarried in mid-step near the entrance of the livery. He was a plodding, methodical thinker. What touched his ears conjured up images of a beast in severe distress, mournful and pain-racked. It was weak and muffled sobs; wet and thick, as though it arose from lungs full of fluid.

He lifted the lantern high and peered into the Twin Livery. He listened intently. There was no gurgle or sob that he could detect. All appeared to be quiet and normal. He vaguely wondered if the night was playing tricks on him.

An assessment told him that the horses stabled were all peaceful and still. He knew horses as well or better than anyone, having a way with them that was uncanny. He had bred and raised them in the past, and wanted to get back to doing so again, but that was an iffy proposition. He was squirrelling away a nest-egg with plans to return to ranching, but was worried that likelihood was destined to die on the vine of his good intentions.

The blubbering cut through the air again, short and sporadic. He froze. He definitely heard it. A goosepimply creeper slid down his spine. He ignored it. He was confused. It wasn't an animal in misery. The strange sound was human. He was convinced that it emanated from deep within the substantial building. Someone was hurt bad and crying.

He entered and moved along the main corridor. Darkness encroached all around him. He poked the light into nooks and crannies, laboring to see anything irregular or troublesome. At the far end of the passageway, he pushed back the gate of an empty stall and the hinges creaked loud and eerily, making him jump a bit. In that startled moment he was sure that he heard the rush of movement outside. He held his breath and strained his ears to listen.

He blocked out all the customary clamor of a stable. Horses swishing tails or blowing were disregarded. What remained was silence. There was no doubt in his mind; the noise that had drawn him into the livery was no more. It had been outside, not inside. Unbeknownst to him, on the other side of the back wall, a stress filled young man had rapidly slipped away.

Axler started to leave to reconnoiter the outer walls of the building, but a nearby piebald pinto neighed and stomped a hoof, catching his consideration. Its black and white coat shimmered in the lamplight. He admired its lines and spoke gently to it. He stroked its mane. The gregarious horse responded by nuzzling his shoulder.

He lifted the lantern higher to get a better look at the steed's hindquarters. When he did so, the beams splashed into the adjacent box stall. He saw a loosely pleated tarp that appeared completely out of place. He went to it and settled on his haunches to lift an edge of the bundled up canvas. A pair of dead eyes stared at him like perverse marbles.

Pete Axler had seen death up close more than once in his time as a peace officer. The corpse was a big-boned fortyish male, round-faced and a bit chunky, with an unkempt wisp of chin-whiskers. He removed the canvas tarp and hung it over the top railing. He knelt and turned the body over to study it and learn what it could tell him.

It was a clear-cut case of murder. The killer had waylaid him from behind, likely hidden in a sniper's roost at a safe distance. There was no exit wound. After a large caliber bullet to the base of the skull had done the deed, the body had been brutalized. The victim's throat was jaggedly slit and he'd been bled out elsewhere before being dumped, stashed here.

Axler stood. He angled the kerosene lamp at the dirt floor. Amongst numerous nondescript footprints there were a couple foot-long grooves that riveted him. He took a knee again and fingered the scores. He shone the light out of the stall and followed the distinctive marks for ten yards or so before the gouges ended. They were spaced apart at consistent intervals, creating a pattern that fascinated him. He wondered about the meaning of them.

He went to have another look at the body. He hung the lantern on a peg in the stall and fiddled with the wick until it burned a bit brighter. He pushed his hat up his forehead and wiped away a sticky sheen of perspiration.

Getting involved in a murder investigation hadn't been on his list of things to do tonight, but that was the unpleasantry before him. He wanted to keep things quiet, but realized that would be wasted energy. He knew that the grapevine in town would be humming with hearsay in no time at all. He thought through the next steps and went into action to implement them.

Sam Beadle was a collector and purveyor of facts. He had been blessed or perhaps cursed with an insatiable nosiness that kept him alert and on edge, continuously probing and searching. There was always one more question to ask before satisfaction set in. He was a jack of all trades writer and networker who'd learned his lessons well in Souderton, Pennsylvania.

Born and raised in the east he had become a true man of the west. A sense of history motivated his thinking and mobilized his choices. The sweeping tide of the past rushing buck-wild into the future was beyond his capacity to control or even regulate, but he was doing more than just hanging on. He carried himself with a mix of humility and daring, some-time participant oft-time reporter of events; creating a written record of goings-on was essential to him.

He was out and about, snooping around along Texas Street on his way to the Alamo Saloon. He spotted Pete Axler ahead of him, hurrying at a jackrabbit pace, which spiked his interest. When all was well Pete had the gumption God gave snails; he mostly got to wherever he happened to be going, but seldom on schedule and always unaware of his tardiness. The fact that he was walking faster than his usual slow drag meant that something was amiss.

"Pete," Sam called, scurrying after him. "Hey, Pete! Where's the fire?"

Axler stopped, turning to him. "Fire? What fire?"

Beadle flanked him. "Where you heading?"

"I got some dealings now," Pete answered, rubbing his jaw. "What fire?"

"There's no fire . . ." Sam was grinning. It was easy to forget that his rangy bone-rack of a friend was devoid of a funny bone. It wasn't that he was dull or dimwitted; it was simply that for reasons unknown humor fluttered past him without ever tickling him.

Axler had a bewildered frown, which more or less was permanently drawn on his face. The lines lessened and deepened on occasion, but were never completely erased. "Why'd you ask about a fire if there ain't one?"

"Why are you in an almighty hustle?"

Axler puckered his mouth. "I need to attend to some dealings."

Beadle's inquisitiveness was automatic. He glanced around. The streets were relatively quiet. He leaned in close and spoke lowly. "Exactly what dealings, Pete?"

"Leave me to it, Sam."

Beadle pressed him. "Something put a burr under your butt, Pete."

Axler scratched his bristled chin. He had a perpetual two-day stubble. His brain was working as Beadle waited patiently. Contrary to assumptions because of his dilly-dallying ways, Pete was actually one of the sharpest observers Sam had ever known. Given the opportunity, when he wasn't being bulldogged by brash talkers, Pete conveyed reliable insights and wisdom that others often missed. He had a proclivity for solving problems by sitting and whittling, processing tipoffs and ruminating on clues much like a cow chewing its cud.

"You got something to tell me, Pete. You know you do."

"I ain't got time to spar with you, Sam."

Beadle smiled at the choice of words. In his quest for knowledge and experience he had taken boxing training from a professional at a club in Pittsburgh. When necessity demanded it, he was quite efficient with his dukes. "I'm just looking to help, like always, Pete."

Axler still had his hand posed at his chin. "I tell you and the town will know."

"Tell me or don't tell me and it matters not," Sam said slyly. "There's not a chance in a million that I won't tag along with you until I get all the answers I need."

"And you call yourself a friend of mine?"

Beadle chuckled. "Come on, Pete. I am who and what I am. I could no more ignore a bit of mystery than you could pass by fine horseflesh without checking it over." He gave him an expressive shrug. "And like it or not, you racing around as if you got a bad case of the back-door trots to the outhouse is about as mysterious as it gets," he added, eyes full of laughter.

"I suppose," Pete allowed, adjusting his gunbelt. In his cautious and deliberate manner he sketched out the no-frills news he had regarding the body in the livery. Predictably true to his peculiar practice, Sam whipped out a flip-top tablet and pencil to take notes.

A few minutes later the men separated, going in opposite directions.

Jackson Scully had guardedly watched the entire exchange between the two men. He wasn't close enough to hear a single word spoken, but certainly had suspicions as to the topic of their conversation. His horse, an even-tempered black gelding, stood as still as a statue. He sat in the saddle, easy and comfortable, ensconced in the darkness of an alley off Texas Street; he had an unencumbered view of where it intersected with Cedar Street.

Which, if all progressed as he presumed, was where his target would cross and he'd have a clean shot. There was no margin for error. He had one chance to put a bullet in the head of the man who was the object of his personal vendetta. It would be dicey, but he was confident that he could do so and escape into the countryside. If he accomplished his goal, any possibility of returning soon to the red-haired woman who had enchanted him years ago would vanish.

The heat of the night was getting more pronounced rather than decreasing. Sweat beaded on his face and trickled down his neck, back and front. It surely distracted him, but wasn't the utmost rift in his focus. Instead of concentrating on the killing ahead, he was replaying the discourse with Flora. She had gotten inside his head and planted seeds of dissatisfaction.

Until a short while ago, he thought he was content. He was never going to be mistaken for mister happy go lucky, but he'd come to reasonable terms with fate. His life wasn't the one of military pageantry and theater of war glory he had envisioned in the upstate New York of his childhood, but he'd had more than his share of exploits and adventures.

He had been an outstanding soldier, but his career path was irrevocably altered by the explosion of a cannon ball at Bull Run. Shrapnel tore apart his left thigh on the first battlefield of the Civil War, leaving him an empty husk of his former self, brooding and resentful. He hobbled his way across the miles and years suffering with chronic pain and misery.

The wound bent him in unimaginable ways. He had done the best he could with the physical and emotional resources available to him, but he knew that he wasn't a good man. There was rancid rottenness at his core that spilled out all over the place. Some god-awful deeds achieved because of a misbegotten sense of honor and loyalty preoccupied him every so often, but never enough to sway him from the path of retribution he was on. He felt like a shriveled up old geezer grasping at straws of revenge playing out a script that compelled, obsessed him.

With his Henry rifle across his lap, Flora's grandiose chatter was droning in his brain like the steel on steel churning of a steam engine. He kept mulling it over and over. The notion of reinvention and starting fresh was abstract and weird to him, but somehow it had made inroads and he was seriously contemplating it, imagining what it might look like.

Presumably it would be a legitimate enterprise. She had spoken of timber and mining interests. There were fortunes to be made in those speculations. He pictured himself with a neatly trimmed beard and decked out in the fancy attire of a banker or tycoon, complete with a classy vest and gold chain attached to an engraved pocket watch. He'd be leaning on an intricately carved cane with a heavy silver knob. The imagery made his lips curl in a smug smile.

Externally he could clean himself up to give all the appearances of respectability, while inwardly remain devious and manipulative; those traits would never cease to serve him well in the high stakes realm of industry and boardrooms. Flora, with her stunning combination of beauty and magnetism, could be the soft and seductive face of their partnership while he operated in the cutthroat zone of blackmail and intimidation.

The brainstorm was gaining traction, but then a wisp of movement on the street pulled him back to his focal point. He marshaled his attention as a muscular cattle-dog loped through his field of vision. He gritted his teeth and breathed the Lord's name in vain. He put all the ridiculous and frivolous thoughts about new beginnings out of his mind.

He spat and soundlessly cussed again. He concentrated on why he was in Abilene. His undertaking required unmitigated vigilance. He figured he had tonight or perhaps, if luck chose to be bighearted, another twenty-four hours to put a bullet in Deacon Coburn's skull. If the preacher was still alive then, Jackson Scully would be forced to recalibrate his vengeance.

Liam Greer had bloodshot eyes and was still breathing shallowly. He slumped along in a shaky shuffle, head down and shoulders sagging. He had been walking in circles ever since he vamoosed from the backside of the livery. His thinker was a mess. He couldn't latch onto any of the scattered pieces of homicidal thoughts agitating his brain.

Inside the aching pain, he hazily plotted to kill his mother. He didn't know if he was frightened or angered by the possibility of murder. A red-hot liquid bitterness was hardening over his heart like the hammered metal of a horseshoe. The inner turmoil had sunk its prongs in him. Its hurt was grinding, twisting, gouging. He didn't care. He intended to use it.

The moon was pasty white and low in the sky. He stopped to stare at it. He steadied his lungs and tamped down his emotions. When he was sure he had all under control, he continued on his way. He came to the boardwalk veranda of the Alamo Saloon and stepped onto it. He was greeted by a blue-ticked dog stretched out near one of the doors. Old Blue never flinched or moved, but growled low and menacing, its eyes narrowed on him.

Liam regarded it with fierce contempt. He considered giving it a walloping kick, but its size and aggressive manner caused good sense to prevail. He eased past it and entered, determined to be busy bending an elbow for a long spell. He walked straight to the bar and ordered a beer. When it arrived, he swallowed a foamy mouthful and had a look around.

He nodded to Deacon Coburn. He was sitting with a woman in a frilly dress the color of sunflower petals. When Coburn responded with a tip of his head, she glanced over her shoulder in the direction of the bar. Liam caught a glimpse of her face. His expression bucked up. He boldly sauntered to their table, the smattering of a swagger working its way into his steps.

"I beg your pardon for interrupting," he said, placing his mug on the table. "May I join you, if only for a few moments?"

Coburn made a magnanimous gesture. "Liam Greer, this is my daughter, Abbey."

Her eyes flickered, seemingly in surprise. Liam offered his right hand, which she accepted with a firm shake. "Pleased to make your acquaintance," she said tonelessly. Tension promptly materialized between them; it came off her in ripples.

He gave her a squinty-eyed scowl that conveyed confused skepticism. "Likewise, I guess." He swung a chair around and straddled it. "You live here in Abilene?"

Abbey was distrustful. "Why do you ask?"

"No reason. Just trying to be friendly."

"We're not friends yet, Mr. Greer."

Anger flared in him. "Good golly, you don't have to be an old biddy about it."

She sparked a smile, disarming him. "Do I look like an old biddy to you?"

He raised his eyebrows and shrugged apologetically. "I ain't blind. I surely didn't mean nothing like that, Miss Abbey. Sometimes I get a dose of that foot in mouth disease."

Coburn had an inflexible smile. "You may want to cut him a wee-bit of slack, Abbey. He's had a powerfully bad day." He measured the young man's mood. "How'd it go?"

Greer shook his head, discouraged and embittered. "I should've listened to you. That woman has nothing I want or need. I'm done with it."

"Likely best you found that out for yourself," Deacon said, "though you ought not to be too brittle in passing a verdict on her. Unless you're a paragon of virtue who never has nor ever will stray from the straight and narrow, you should reserve some mercy for her."

Greer took a sip of beer. "I ain't rightly sure what mercy is, sir. I only ever learned how to scratch, claw and survive, to get and do and fend for me and mine."

"That's a wretched outlook doomed to a desolate end, young man."

"It's all I know," Liam answered, hands held at half-mast. "Pa had tenderness and mercy. Look what it got him. A heart busted up so bad he could never really live." He leaned forward, chin on the back of the chair. "Could I ask you a big whoop of a favor?"

"I told you before, if I can help, I will."

"Tomorrow will you come with me to arrange for my father's burial?"

Coburn tilted his head in assent. "Certainly."

"Can you also say some Bible words over the grave?"

"If that'd comfort you, yes."

"It ain't about comforting me. It doesn't mean anything at all, but Pa read Scripture off and on," Liam said, sounding wistful. "He could even quote it once in a blue moon."

"Did he have a favorite passage?" Deacon asked intently.

Greer pulled on his cheeks, thinking. "The one I heard him say more often than not had to do with iniquity and all us sheep going astray or something. Do you know that one?"

Coburn recalled the familiar phrases of Isaiah. "*All we like sheep have gone astray; we have turned every one to his own way; and the Lord hath laid on him the iniquity of us all.*"

"That's the one," Liam said, eyes widening. "Does it mean anything?"

"It's the story of my life," Deacon responded sternly. "And your story too. It's the story of every man and woman who ever breathed air in this wearisome world of adversity."

Greer's face became bewilderment personified. His mouth dropped open and he raked a hand through his hair. "I ain't smart enough to take in what you're telling me."

"It ain't about what's inside your head," Deacon said, smiling broadly. "Examine your heart, Liam. All you need is right there, written by the finger of God."

Greer guffawed. "That's impossible ballyhoo!"

"Not ballyhoo," Deacon replied gently. "Unless my understandings of Scripture have all gone to rot, not only is it possible, it's simple and far-reaching reality. It takes a journey of humble searching, but the way, truth, and life can be found and experienced."

"Sounds like a riddle," Liam said, head wagging.

"Sometimes it is," Deacon admitted straightforwardly. "A cosmic conundrum wrapped in the riddle of the cross, but grasping the answer makes all the difference."

"You're gospel sharp, sir. I ain't."

Abbey cleared her throat. She had been listening carefully, learning much. Her eyes were soft and sensitive as she addressed him. "I'm sorry for your loss, Liam."

The sound of his name on her tongue gave him a warm jolt. He resisted it. He toughened his resolve and brushed her off with a dismissive wave. "It doesn't matter. I just gotta put him in the ground. That might be difficult, but then I'm moving on." He craned his neck and jacked a thumb toward the bar. "He died right over there just a few hours ago."

Abbey saw through the false bluster and had empathy for him. She hesitantly reached out and touched his shoulder. "There's really nothing that'll take away the emptiness."

Greer was moved by the sympathy shining on her face. He looked her over with sad eyes, enjoying her sheer prettiness. "I ain't empty, Miss Abbey. I'll be bang-up fine and he's better off now. His body died this evening, but inside he'd been dead for years."

Abbey acted with reluctance, seeming as though she wanted to dig deeper but unwilling to do so. There was moisture showing in her eyes when she finally spoke. "I know something about grief. You have to find your own way through it. If you don't take steps to do so the heartaches of loss can make an overwhelming mess of your perception and attitude."

Greer was persuaded by her transparent gentleness, but before he could respond there was a shout and hullabaloo that captured the tavern's nerves. Abbey turned in her chair to see Sam Beadle standing in the doorway. He was sweating and breathing hard, as though he'd been running around. His chest was rising and falling, his hands on his hips.

"Get a wiggle on, Sam," someone yelled with a grunt. "Your lip ain't hobbled, is it?"

Beadle stifled a laugh. "If anyone's interested there's a dead body at the livery," he reported, his voice ringing loudly. "Pete says it looks like a murder."

Hoots and hollers of excitement scorched the already blistery air. Chairs scraped on the floor and some toppled over in the sudden rush of movement toward the front door. Beadle hurriedly stepped aside just in time to avoid being trampled. More than half the patrons poured onto the street, some reeling drunkenly.

Deacon Coburn stood. He removed his hat from the back of the chair and put it on. "I should go have a look-see. I may be able to be of some assistance."

"I'll stay with the lady," Liam said, "and I'll be a perfect gentleman."

Abbey harrumphed and leaned forward to blast him with the hardest, coldest look he'd ever seen. "You better believe you will, mister. I do not tolerate any shenanigans."

Coburn was grinning as he sauntered away. She was definitely her mother's daughter.

Charley Jondreau wasn't going anywhere; he would not be following the gawkers to the livery. The heat had done him in. It was as hot as a whorehouse on nickel night. Besides he was having a grand time. He surreptitiously kept up his surveillance. Sitting alone with his whiskey he found the entertainment to be more than satisfactory. He had zeroed in on the shaggy-haired Bible reader and the activity at his table. The yammering din of a packed barroom hadn't allowed him to piece together any specifics, but now, with the crowd thinned out he might have an opportunity to hear enough of the young couple's conversation to do so.

Deacon Coburn didn't even get outside before he was sidetracked.

Sam Beadle caught hold of his arm. "Can I have a word? Just a word, Deacon?"

The men eased onto the veranda. They sat side by side on a battered old bench. The moon was taking on yellowish hues as it made its ascent to the top of the sky. Old Blue barked once and came up to nuzzle and lick them. It received their affable petting with its tail wagging its body, then dropped onto its belly and coiled up halfway under their legs.

"Is this about the killing at the livery?"

"No," Sam replied tersely. "It's about Miss Langton."

Coburn eyed him, somewhat thrown off by his tone. "What about her?"

"What's her story?"

"You can tire a body out, you know that, Sam."

"What?"

"Not everyone's story is your business."

"It's different this time, Deacon."

"Different how?"

"People said you were crying. I heard it from more than one."

"People would be right. What of it?"

Beadle shifted his bottom and crossed a leg. "Trust me, I'm not looking for a byline, I swear. My reasons for asking about her are personal not professional."

"Personal?" Deacon's hackles were up. "Then maybe you best spill the beans."

Beadle leaned back and gave him a scowl. "What's the problem here?"

"She's my daughter."

Beadle wheezed a gasp as his eyes popped open. "Balderdash!"

"Balderdash?" Deacon remained edgy. "Are you calling me a liar?"

"No," Sam said with firmness. "I'm shocked, is all."

"We all got something chasing us, Sam."

"I guess we do."

"Her mother died three years ago. Abbey brought me a missive from her." Deacon's tone was sad and croaky. "It's a private matter, Sam. I tell you as a friend."

"It's as a friend I heard it."

"You spoke of it being personal. Do we need to have a conversation?"

Beadle gave him a weak smile. His cheeks blushed. "Don't bust my chops, Deacon. She's a beautiful young woman. Every eligible bachelor in town will be lining up to make a run at her. And some of those won't be at all honorable about it."

"Well, you let it be known, Sam," Deacon said in a voice flattened out by an uncharacteristic meanness. His dark eyes were flinty. "Any man, eligible bachelor or otherwise, who treats Abbey Langton unkindly or without the utmost respect, will answer to me. And make no mistakes; the milk of human kindness will curdle in me as quick as a lick."

Beadle swallowed dryly. "I've never seen this curly wolf side of you."

Coburn's expression loosened up some. The air was still and stifling. He filled his lungs and exhaled wearily as he fixed his gaze straight on him. "Don't be conned by my elbow grease stabs at goodness, Sam. The beast in me is alive and well. I fight it every day."

"Unfortunately I am well acquainted with that struggle."

"Fortunately, you mean," Deacon said, pushing his hat up. "Knowing and recognizing the beast that resides within is our only chance to temper it and keep it caged."

"You'd know more about that sort of thing than me."

"Knowing is only half the battle." Coburn locked his hands around a knee. His movement disturbed Old Blue. The dog got up and stretched. It gave the men a cursory look, then roamed onto the street and sat like a sentinel, ever watchful.

Beadle chuckled. "Old Blue has already adopted Miss Langton."

"It appears to me that Old Blue isn't the only dog digging around and taking an interest in her," Deacon said, dour and serious. "Tell me, Sam. Do we need to have a conversation?"

"As her father, yes we do," Sam replied directly. "I won't make any bones about it. If the lady is agreeable I'll be seeking to keep company with her."

"Are you asking for my permission?"

"I suppose I am. Or your blessing."

"You're a full grown man, Sam," Deacon said, abruptly turning to face him straight on. "You've been through the mill, which gives you some wisdom regarding the consequences. You can make your choices as you so decide. That young lady appears ripe, but she's green."

"Are you telling me not to pursue her?"

"No. Don't trifle with her heart, is what I'm telling you."

"Not my intention at all. I'm looking at the future."

"Just remember that I bear responsibility for her well-being," Deacon told him, wagging a finger. "And be assured, Sam. Friend or no friend, if you ever make that girl cry anything but happy tears you'll be one sorry individual. You'll be walking funny for a stretch of time because I'll see to it that you lose a couple items of anatomy that you value."

"I intend to keep those hanging, thank you very much."

"Then I reckon we have an understanding."

Just then, acting as though it had been shrewdly eavesdropping, Old Blue jumped up and rushed back to them. It had a sloppy grin, its eyes glinting approval in the moonlight.

From the moment Deacon Coburn walked away from his table, Liam Greer and Abbey Langton engaged in back and forth banter centered on their lives and feelings. It was not at all timid or tentative, but instead, it had all the jabs and parries of verbal fencing. The jousting began with Greer probing for the lowdown on the man who'd introduced them.

"What's your father's scam?"

"If you think he has a scam why not ask him?"

"Because I'm asking you."

"I have nothing to tell you on that topic."

"Are you in cahoots with him?"

"I'm in the Alamo Saloon with you."

"Are you protecting him?"

She laughed airily. "Does Deacon Coburn appear to need protecting?"

"A pretty woman is good cover for a confidence game."

"Are you accusing me of being a criminal?"

"Your old man's a religious sort, which is the same as a swindler."

"Your opinion is misguided and malicious."

"Bible thumpers like him are straight-out flimflammers."

She skewered him with a withering gaze. "If you truly believe that in your heart, why'd you ask him to read Scripture at your father's graveside? If anyone here is a fraud, it's you."

"The Scripture ain't for me, at all. Not at all. It's for Pa," Liam said adamantly. "The only time a man needs religion is when he's gone up the flume."

"You *doth protest too much, methinks.*"

"What? Is that Bible?"

"Land sakes, no. Queen Gertrude made that remark in Hamlet."

"Hamlet? Where's that? What happened there?"

She stared at him, incredulous. "Where's that? What happened there? Are you giving my donkey's tail a yank?" she sputtered sarcastically. "Hamlet is my favorite Shakespearean play."

"Shakespearean play?"

"William Shakespeare, a poet and playwright of the Elizabethan era," she answered, eyes cutting and astonished by his ignorance. "Hamlet is one of his most famous plays."

"You're talking book learning. I ain't ever had any schooling."

"That's a tragedy."

"It ain't ever harmed me none," he fired back, almost snarling. "I can cipher enough to get a fair price buying and selling horses. I won't be gypped in any trade." He was in her face, leaning forward over the back of the chair. "I can tie every kind of knot there is and use rope better than anyone. I know the trail, what plants can be eaten and which ones are poisonous. I can find water in the driest country. Could your Shakespeare goober do any of that?"

She was staunchly unshaken. "Not likely."

"I got the only education that matters here in the west."

"Which is just fine," she said, "but you're missing out on so much. Imagine how rich your life would be with all your expertise and also being fluent in Shakespeare."

"Rich?" His voice was shrill as he came up off the seat as though he had been prodded by a hot poker. He was nearly standing, bent over like a half-open pocketknife. "I'll be rich someday soon. You can bet on it. Rich and famous." He inched closer to get eyeball to eyeball with her. "People will be talking aplenty about me. My name will be in all the papers. When I stroll down the street parents will step aside and point me out to their children."

"How will all this be accomplished?"

"That ain't your concern. We ain't friends yet, Miss Abbey."

She rolled her eyes and pressed a smarmy smile, not flinching away from him at all. "If you ever want a friendship to develop between us you'd do well to back off."

He relaxed. His droopy eyelids flickered and he suddenly gave the impression of a rascal caught in the middle of misbehavior. He forced a lopsided grin at her as he whirled the chair around to sit on it properly. He lounged lazily backwards. "You live here in Abilene?"

She was annoyed by his demeanor. The revisiting of his opening question to her increased her agitation. She replied as she had previously. "Why do you ask?"

"Why not? I don't know how else to make friendly."

She held her eyes on him. There was no hint of faith in him showing on her face, but she sighed and said, "I do now, as of this afternoon. I took a room at Drovers Cottage. I'll be looking for a boarding house or other suitable long-term accommodations within the week."

"Ain't you gonna live with your father?"

"I don't expect I will. He's a rambler."

"So am I."

She frowned, not knowing what to make of him. She turned in her chair and as she did so, was at once disconcerted by a darkish man in a floppy-brimmed hat staring at her. His eyes were piercing, menacing. She tried to glance away, but was compelled to stay locked in on him. He never acknowledged that he was even looking at her. His face was an unreadable slate of granite, impassive and secretive. Her skin crawled. She shuddered and pursed her lips tautly.

Greer became aware of her response. He followed her gaze.

She shifted uncomfortably and whispered, "That's a creepy looking man."

Greer puffed out his chest and thrust his sloping shoulders forward. "He ain't so creepy or tough, Miss Abbey," he said loudly. "I could take him, no problem."

"Shush yourself."

"Why would I? I ain't afeared. I can protect you from the likes of him."

She grabbed his shirt sleeve. "Don't start any fight on my behalf."

"It'd be a brief lambasting. I'd have him hogtied in a flash."

Her hands dropped to the handbag on her lap. "Let's just ignore him, Liam."

"If you insist, Abbey."

Amusement danced in her eyes. She was no longer Miss Abbey to him. "I do insist."

He took a short pull on his beer. His baby-face puckered up as if he had taken a swig of vinegar. "It's warm and gunky," he grouched, then finished it off with a grimace. He went to the bar to purchase a fresh refill. While he was returning to the table, he was joined by Coburn coming in from outside. He removed his hat and placed it on the back of his chair.

"Everything fine here?" Deacon asked, taking his seat.

"As swell as swell can be," Liam replied, enthused. "Me and Abbey are getting along so well that I think maybe we're almost friends now, isn't that right?"

She moistened her lips. "If you say so, Liam."

Liam Greer let loose a whoop and whistle, hooting gleefully. Abbey Langton had her eyes lowered, her concentration fastened on her hands, which were clasped white-knuckled around her purse. By the way a sizable bulge formed in his brow it was unmistakable that Deacon Coburn easily discerned the muddled currents between them.

Not too long afterwards, Pete Axler arrived at the Alamo on the heels of the throng of hangers-on who had paid a visit to Ed Gaylord's Twin Livery. It was a higgledy-piggledy of mania, with every tongue flapping about the dead body. A killing that resulted from a fair fight was acceptable, but this here was homicide. The suspicions and collective intelligence of the mob was that the murderer was even now in their midst.

"Any new arrivals in town?" someone asked, sounding naïve.

The answer came from a broken-toothed old-timer. His eyes were bulgy, his chin tobacco stained. "It may not be for much longer, but we're still a cowtown." He slammed a palm down on the bar and uttered a curse-ridden oath. "There are always interlopers on these streets."

With that, lots of interest in the room bent in Charley Jondreau's direction. He appeared to pay no heed to any of it. Some pointed fingers, others muttered to each other while having a good gander at him. Pete Axler didn't miss any of the actions. He filed his observations away as he made headway from table to table investigating in his usual lackadaisical manner.

The barroom took on a muted atmosphere. Voices hushed as patrons clustered together to run their commentary in close quarters. It became as quiet and eerie as a bone orchard, with an expectation that all hell was about to break loose. Liquor kept being poured; the clink of glass on glass frequently punctuated the mutters and heavy breathing.

When Axler came to Coburn's table, he glanced at the stoop-shouldered man and took in details, then touched the brim of his hat to the lady. He pulled up a chair and sat, purposefully keeping his back to the red-skinned drifter. "Have you seen Sam?"

Coburn nodded. "He was here earlier. We yakked some."

Axler considered that for a bit before saying, "I'll scare him up later. I figure with his sniffer he might already be ahead of me."

"I wouldn't count on Sam for any insights on this one, Pete," Deacon counseled, hands folded on top of his Bible. "His sniffer is preoccupied elsewhere."

Axler rubbed his whiskers. He crouched in close to Coburn and spoke in a barely audible tone. "Can you tell me anything about that Injun over there?"

"He came in a few hours ago," Deacon replied, matching the low pitch. "He makes a pretense of minding his own business, but he's had his snout pushed out toward this table."

"Ever seen him before?"

"Not that I recall," Deacon said, eyes narrow and wary. "Be careful, Pete. He's wearing a gun high on the right side. I'll back your play as best I can."

Axler stood with unexpected fleetness. Without delay he went to the confrontation and stopped in front of the stranger's table. "Is that your piebald pinto stabled at the livery?"

Jondreau shrugged. "The pony ain't for sale, at any price," he said nonchalantly. "I don't chit and I don't chat, buddy-boy. If you got something to say spit it out."

"Alright. Come over to the jailhouse with me for a conversation."

"The jailhouse?" Charley quipped, eyes fiery. "What would be the topic?"

"The body in the stall beside the pinto, for starters."

Jondreau's lips bent downward into an expression reminiscent of a bulldog. "For starters? It seems like you got an agenda to work over. What other crimes you want to pin on me?"

"The conversation at the jailhouse wasn't an invitation."

"You might want to pull your horns in, hoss," Charley said caustically.

"My horns ain't out, mister. It's too danged hot to kick up a row," Pete replied, even and low-keyed. "I'm just looking for a private one on one sit-down with you."

Jondreau wasn't budging. "Friend to friend, eh?"

"That'd be my approach to be sure."

"Too bad I'm not having any part of it," Charley said, fingers of both hands tapping out a tattoo on the table. "I ain't leaving this joint until I'm good and ready. If you're of a mind to take a dirt bath, then try forcing the issue. I'll be the one standing over you."

Axler reached for his pistol. What happened next would become legendary. There were gasps and hisses at the swiftness of it. Exaggerated anecdotes and inflated yarns would spread like wildfire about the showdown between Pete Axler and Charley Jondreau. The talk would always center on the rapid draw of the man who remained seated throughout the encounter, though the six-shooter's appearance was so lickety-split that no one actually followed it.

One moment Jondreau's right hand was drumming; a sliver of a second later his gun was above the table and aimed at the lawman's belly. Axler's pistol hadn't even cleared leather; it was still in its holster and he held his hands shoulder high and open. Silence consumed every fragment of sound in the saloon. Time took on a mind of its own, ticking at an excruciatingly slow pace. Tension was a nest of coiled copperheads slithering between them.

"I don't know you well enough to miss you when you're dead," Charley said, calm and in total control. "This is the way it's going to be. You give me a fair listen and no one dies here."

Axler was rigid, motionless. "Let's make a try for that outcome."

Jondreau never lowered his weapon. "I don't know nothing about the body in the livery. I'm innocent of any wrongdoing. I stopped in this town to give my horse a rest and a good feed of oats, and to drink some whiskey. Leave me be and I'll be gone at first light."

"Can't do it, mister."

"Then say your prayers, buddy-boy."

"Go easy!" Coburn leapt to his feet, shattering the prickly stillness. He raced to insert himself into the thorny situation in an effort to defuse it. "Mister, you don't strike me as stupid enough to be a walking dead man," he said, hands up in surrender as he approached the gunman. "You ain't going to shoot an Abilene peace officer in a barroom full of witnesses. You wouldn't make it to your horse alive. You might not even make it out of here."

Jondreau gave him a bulldog glare. "I could surprise you, preacher-man."

Coburn exhaled a distinct whistle of air. "That's a lot of slaughter, my friend."

"It won't be the first bloodletting for me."

"Me neither."

Jondreau eyed him doubtfully. "What are you telling me?"

"I was knee-deep in it at Fredericksburg, Chancellorsville, Gettysburg," Deacon answered, edging a step closer to him. "By pulling the trigger I dispatched hundreds to meet their Maker. Oft-times at night I hear the screams and see the faces of those I killed, and for what? I've had a bellyful of bloodshed. It must be avoided at all costs."

"Then tell buddy-boy lawman to let me ride away."

"We may be able to make that happen, but not just now," Deacon said, eyebrows rising hopefully. "You claim you're innocent. I believe you. I take you at your word and will be on your side unless evidence proves your big bazoo is full of lies." His voice was strong and authoritative, yet had a soothing, pacifying timbre. "If you got nothing to hide then go along to the jailhouse for a conversation and all will be well. I swear."

Jondreau balked, letting out a deadpan chuckle. "That ain't the usual payoff for me. I've been slammed behind stone walls before when I was guilty of nothing."

"I can't fix, change, or do anything about the past," Deacon countered, "but I do have some juice around here. You've been spying on me awful close. What have you learned?"

Jondreau's neck muscles visibly twitched. His eyes went dead and vacant. Then for a transitory flicker nothing could be seen except the whites. His eyelids momentarily quivered. It was freaky, but then his eyes were normal; steely and keen. "I trust you, preacher-man."

Coburn dropped his hands to his beltline. "I give you my word, my friend."

Jondreau spun the gun over in his hand. He offered the butt to Axler.

In the afterclaps of the brouhaha, Liam Greer walked Abbey Langton back to Drovers Cottage. She wanted to be alone and despite her protests he had persisted in accompanying her. The moon was high and bright. Stars were an array of lights spread across the sky like millions of candles. They strolled side by side with Old Blue positioned between them.

The dog had growled at Liam again, but he dismissed it with a smart-alecky comment. He was displeased that it was tagging along to intrude on them, but took note of her affection for the animal. She was disconcerted by how it had belligerently greeted him and said so. He assumed that he'd convinced her that the dog's hostility toward him meant nothing.

However, despite her surface agreement, she felt in her gut that Old Blue could be relied upon. She had already given the outgoing canine a piece of her heart. Its instinctive wariness of her escort kept her alert and apprehensive. Coupled with her own intuitive discernment the animal's impulse served to increase her dislike of Liam Greer.

She remained civil. She felt sorry for him, losing his father and such, but even so, she wanted to be rid of him. He did not strike her as being nice or courteous. He was a blowhard; a blabbing chatterbox so full of blarney it was difficult for her to take him serious. Just now he was going on and on, all aroused and boasting in a way that was getting under her skin.

"Did you see it? I still can't believe that quick draw," he said, hands waving expressively.

"Ain't no one alive could be any faster. I'm going to get me a pistol rig and learn how to use it. I'll practice and practice and practice. You mark my words, Abbey. I'm going to be a known man with a gun. No one will dare to challenge me."

"Really?" There was mockery in her voice. "When you first saw that ruffian you told me that you could beat and hogtie him. Now he's your hero, so what of it?"

He scoffed. "I was talking about a fistfight. It'd be easy to take him in a bare knuckles knockdown." He stopped and took a boxer's stance. "I'd fake him out and duck underneath before giving him a right-left combination." He grunted and threw a rapid flurry of punches.

Both Abbey and Old Blue ignored him and kept walking. The glow from the first floor windows of Drovers Cottage beckoned her. She could hardly wait to be free of him. They were ten yards beyond him before he realized he didn't have an audience.

"Hey, wait up!" he shouted, bolting toward them.

"Goodnight, sir. I can make it the rest of the way on my own."

He tried to get on the opposite side of the dog, but Old Blue criss-crossed quickly to thwart him. "I'm delivering you straight to your door. No reason not to do otherwise."

Her shoulders sagged in resignation. "Fine. Let's just make it quick."

They went the rest of the way wordlessly. The lobby was quiet. Sam Beadle was behind the desk doing paperwork of some kind. He glanced up from it and watched them. A crease plowed a furrow in the middle of his forehead. Old Blue took up residence just inside the door, stretching out with its head on its paws. She stopped at the bottom of the stairs for a moment. Her room was at the end of the hall on the second floor.

She held the railing as she climbed the steps as hastily as she could without running. Liam scooted along beside her. The lamps on the walls were all turned down low so the light was gray and gloomy. She hurried down the dim hallway trying to stay ahead of him. She went straight to her room and turned to face him. Her purse was folded under her left arm.

"Thank you for seeing me safely home," she said, forcing pleasantness. She stared full in his face, her back against the door. "I'd appreciate it if you'd be a gentleman and leave now."

"Nope, not quite yet, Abbey." His tongue circled his lips. "I'm getting me some." He was breathing in hitches as he squeezed his eyes shut and insistently pushed himself against her. He leaned in for a kiss as his right hand clumsily made a grabbing dart toward her bustline. His pitiful going for it had all the genteel tenderness of a two-by-four upside the head.

She was having none of it. Her heart and mind were fused together with a resolve that had been nurtured in her as a child. Before his lips brushed against her flesh or his hand found its objective she reacted with decisive haste. She swished her skirt aside as her right leg came off the floor. She heaved it with robust exuberance, driving her knee into his crotch.

It struck squarely. His body convulsed. He gasped wetly. A splattering spray of spittle misted her cheeks. He squealed. He quavered backwards, teetering and off-balance. He grabbed himself. He swore at her. He bent over and did a funny little hopping dance with his hands cupping and clutching at his inflamed testicles. When he attained a reasonable stability, he was face to face with the beady muzzle of a derringer.

Abbey held the short-barreled pistol mere inches from his head. "You're nothing but a sick pup that needs to learn common courtesy," she said, voice stoic and unwavering. "You ever come near me again and I will not hesitate putting you out of your misery."

He spat the foulest of obscenities at her in a top of the lungs screech.

She never even blinked. "Repeat it and see if I don't squeeze this trigger."

There was a flurry of footfalls on the stairs. The violence of his cuss-words brought Sam Beadle running. He halted to evaluate the scene. What he saw caused him to suppress a grin that yanked hard on his lips. "Is there a problem here?" he asked, approaching them.

"Not anymore, Mr. Beadle," Abbey replied, eyes widening as she kept the pocket pistol leveled at her would-be assailant. "I've given Mr. Greer a lesson in manners."

"I see," Sam said, turning to face him. "Do you need any assistance?"

"It ain't nothing to nobody so choke on it," Liam answered, red-faced and spitting mad. He leered angrily at her, his mouth working as though he was going to blaspheme or name-call her again. She waggled the weapon, daring him. He muttered something unintelligible. He bared his teeth and stomped away. He pounded down the stairs. Old Blue started barking and snarling, but then grew quiet when the front door was slammed.

Beadle took a wary step toward her. "Do you require anything, Miss Langton?"

"No, thank you, Mr. Beadle," she said assertively. She knelt and returned the derringer to the ankle holster strapped on the outside of her right boot.

"You're breaking the law," Sam told her, eyes laughing.

"Am I?"

"There's an ordinance against carrying firearms in city limits."

Abbey stood and flashed him a wickedly brilliant smile. "Is that so? I can keep a secret, can you, Mr. Beadle?" she asked merrily. "You wouldn't want a lady to be defenseless?"

He let loose a rolling chuckle and spoke around it. "You may be many things, Miss Langton, but it appears to me that you would never qualify as being defenseless."

"Well, it is the wild west, isn't it? Goodnight, Mr. Beadle." She entered and closed the door. She pressed her backside against it and took several deep, soothing breaths. Her body was tense. She could feel the muscles bunched up across her shoulders, along her spine, and down the back of her thighs. There was also an ugly tightness popping in the pit of her stomach.

She wiped the dried remnants of Liam Greer's saliva off her cheeks. She undressed in the dark, with only sallow moonlight coming through the window to guide her. She removed the pins from her hair and placed them in the fancy hat, then set it on the top shelf of the armoire. She put the boots beside the door, the derringer on a bedside table. She folded her outer garments and layered slip over the arms of a wing-back chair.

She went to a chest of drawers washstand that had a tall oval mirror above it. She poured a splash from the blue patterned porcelain pitcher into its matching basin. She rinsed her hands and scrubbed her face in the lukewarm water. She shook the thick mane of her golden-brown hair free and gave it a slam-bang brushing. She drew the curtains shut, then lit an oil lamp.

Despite the emotional fullness of the day there was something prickling her imagination, having to do with a childhood hobby that had become increasingly obsessive over the years. At her home in Ohio she'd collected newspaper clippings about happenings in the west, gathering them into a thick stack of scrapbooks. An idea had been lurking at the edge of her mind since shortly after suppertime, and now, she seriously wondered if it was even conceivable.

All she owned had made the railroad trip with her. Clothes and personal care items in an unwieldy carpetbag and everything else secured in two good-sized trunks; wooden with brass and leather bindings. Excitement had her almost giddy.

What was on her mind had to be impossible. In her bloomers and with the oil lamp in hand, she unlocked one of the brass-cornered crates. She lifted the lid to see all was as she had packed it. There were a dozen scrapbooks on top. She rummaged through the pile, selected the one she wanted, and went to sit on the edge of the bed.

She adjusted the wick to make the flame brighter before placing the lamp beside the derringer. She lovingly flipped through page after page of items. She knew exactly what she was looking for and where to find it. It was an article about Wild Bill Hickok's shooting of Phil Coe and Mike Williams outside the Alamo Saloon in October 1871.

When she came to it she did something out of the ordinary; she focused on the byline, something that had never been important to her. Unbelief made her bug-eyed and breathless. She was shocked, fretful, eager, thrilled, worried. She didn't know what to do with the crazy feelings bubbling inside her. She collapsed back on the bed and embraced the scrapbook to her bosom. A shrill sound escaped her lips; it was the blissful giggle of a school girl.

The news report was penned by one Samuel H. Beadle of Abilene.

Sally Twosongs had frigid sludge flowing in her veins. She was frightened; terrified, even. She had been here before; she knew that she would see it all unfold again. There was nothing that she could do no matter how fiercely she tried. Powerlessness was real and unrelenting. All that remained was for her to stay faithful to the second sight.

Two men were already dead—an old one who had survived atrocious travails, but still managed to be in awe of the wonders of creation and pass along ancient wisdom. The second man had crossed lines to aid her and now he awaited a gravedigger. She had seen it all happen, but had been unable to prevent any of it. Others were still in danger.

Fear was a vile creepy-crawler gnawing on her adrenals, yet she stood strong and defiant. Her eyes were being assaulted by disordered scenes scattered across an ever-changing panoramic landscape. She watched it all transpire from a far horizon through a vaporous haze. The sky had a luminescent quality, shimmering grays and greens with pillars of odd colors mixed in.

The noise was throbbing; the chaotic mix of a lunatic whirlwind filled her head. Voices shouted curses, horses snorted, and hearts were a broken drumbeat pounding out of sync. Somewhere on the outskirts, judging by the increasing clamorous racket, a flock of crows were gathering strength in numbers, cawing erratically.

A beastly monster chased over the countryside. It was disheveled and peg-legged, with furry jowls and jaundiced eyes, the lids thickly bloated. Huntsmen had come alongside it, but in the caverns of its heart it was a singularly lone predator. Gluttonous hunger growled in its belly. It had already feasted on many kills, but its appetite for blood could never be satisfied.

Sally Twosongs kept her vigil. She looked and saw a mystery; something that she couldn't identify. It was shiny and inviting, and many hands were stretched forth to grasp hold of it. Was it a coin, a packet, a trinket, a treasure, or a talisman? She had no answer.

It was beautiful, powerful, hypnotic. The mesmerizing effect over those souls reaching for it was obvious. The beastly monster clutched and grabbed for it, but it spun just out of its reach. Lust was moldering in its yellowed eyes. The choir of crows was becoming louder and more agitated; the discordant shrieks were bloodcurdling.

A fair maiden stood off to the side, her hair being tossed about by swirling updrafts. Sadness engulfed her. She was weeping, eyes obsessed by the gleaming object. The deep shade of a towering tree obscured her. The shadows swaddling the woman had a definite shape that pricked Sally Twosongs, but no amount of concentration provided any comprehension as to why; the outline was indistinctly cast and she was unable to see it fully.

The air grew hotter and hotter. The wind became thunderous, accentuated by hundreds of crows in a frenzy of flapping wings. The peculiar colors in the sky were rising and falling, jumping around and sparking like the unbolted machinery of a runaway locomotive. A booming sphere of lightning crashed across the scene, shocking and horrifying in its fireball fury. Chaos exploded. The wind was saturated by the odor of charred earth. A single gunshot rang out.

Inside a tranquil instant of perfect stillness, Sally Twosongs was appalled by an abominable sight. She recoiled in her footsteps. She saw a dead body, spread-eagled and face down in the dirt, bleeding from a gory hole in the dead-center middle of the back. She wanted to run to it, but was refrained. She was merely an observer.

A massive horde of crows flew at her, beating against her eardrums, beaks spitting and snapping, wings hammering, lungs squawking and screeching. She came awake, sweating and gasping for breath. The terror that had tormented her in the nightmare dissipated as rapidly as threads of smoke banished by a stiff summer breeze.

A glow of moonbeams slipped through the window to brighten the darkness of her room. The sheet covering her was damp with perspiration. She flung it off and sat on the edge of the bed. She was puzzled and antsy, but only momentarily. Calmness came over her, warm and comforting. She innately understood that the recurring thought-dreams were the by-product of the spiritual breaking through to invade the physical realm.

She was Navajo, fifteen years old and becoming a devout, mystical young woman. She had survived and overcome being kidnapped and molested by a madman. In the healing aftermath of the ordeal, she had a vision of the risen Jesus scarred by his death on the cross. He had placed a hand upon her heart and promised that they would walk her path together. In that otherworldly encounter she received a special empathy and psychic gift. She came to regard the visitations, which by and large occurred whilst she slept, as sacred.

She stood brusquely. A likeness of her father Daniel bounded to her mind. She worried on him. She had an urgent prompting to pray. She didn't want to disturb her mother Consuelo, who was sleeping in the next room. It was past midnight.

She yawned and rubbed her eyes. She was wearing an ankle-length cottony nightgown. Her skin was crinkly and clammy from dried sweat. She scooped up a knitted shawl and put it around her shoulders, then slipped on a pair of soft-soled elk-hide moccasins.

The floorboards squeaked ever so slightly as she padded around. She stood still in the moonlight and enjoyed its gentle solace. In the chambers of her heart she knew that everything happened for a reason, but presently, doubts were stringing her along. She theorized as to where she fit or what she could do. She innately understood the need to trust, to walk in faith.

She was alone, but not lonely. She touched an envelope on her dresser. It was a week-old letter from her longtime friend Caleb Weitzel. She had read it dozens of times. He would be traveling through and stopping in for a visit. She had an eagerness to see him, to share all her thoughts and aspirations with him. She briefly deliberated on when he would arrive.

She picked up her favorite wooden flute. It was aromatic cedar, intricately inlaid with chips of turquoise between the holes. Her name was burned in sweeping script along each side. It was almost an exact replica of her first flute. The original, a Christmas gift from her father, had been destroyed in an awful fire. The two of them had worked together on the replacement.

She went outside, quietly closing the door tight behind her. The air was cool and refreshing. She looked at the moon, which had golden hues. She spoke a blessing in her native language. Her words came rushing out in a forceful whisper; strong, guttural, persistent.

Satisfied and serene, she leapt into a graceful sprint toward the woods that fringed their home on a secluded hillside. Her footfalls were silent. She found her special spot in a grove of aspens. She sat cross-legged and bowed her head low to listen to the music in her soul. After a moment, she began softly playing her prayers, the evocative melody rising to the Creator.

Hundreds of miles to the northeast, Daniel Twosongs was camped on the open prairie. Dog-tired and dusty dry, he had munched on roasted rabbit, which kept his hunger at bay. He washed it down with the final mouthful in his canteen. Finding a source of water would be top priority when he set out at first light. If he had his bearings correct he estimated he had two hours of walking at dawn before he came to the Smoky Hill River.

The evening hadn't cooled off much. His body ached, muscles knotted up and cramping. The continuous muggy heatwave had an enervating effect, zapping his strength and demoralizing him. He had just finished saying prayers for his wife and daughter in Taos. There was so much more roiling around inside to disturb him. His heart was burdened, his mind active.

Heat lightning flickered all along the eastern skyline. In the distance a trio of wolves was yap, yap, yapping a point counterpoint refrain that carried and echoed almost in harmony. A smile creased his lips as he listened. The notes rose and fell in rhythm. Somehow the song of the wild provided a measure of comfort to him.

He was bedded down far removed from the tiny campfire. Sleep evaded him. A murderer was loose and on a rampage. He closed his eyes, but desperation nipped at him. Time, distance and exhaustion had his brain on edge and downcast. Worry, usually far removed from him, was making its presence known. The feelings were foreign, but so real and disquieting.

He took a long breath and gave a huge mental heave-ho. It took a half-dozen of those meditative exercises before relaxation began to massage away all the unsettling clutter distracting him. He single-mindedly centered himself.

There was no usefulness in borrowing trouble. Until he learned otherwise he had to proceed with the firm belief that Deacon Coburn was safe, so after a few hours of slumber he intended to press on. He figured he had to put in one more day of heavy-duty hiking. If there were no detours, then by shortly after nightfall tomorrow he expected to be in Abilene.

 He stared at the canopy of stars. The night lights were glorious, reflecting the One who had hung them in place. There was no end to the language written in plain script above him. The handiwork of God as publicized in the heavens spoke volumes to his soul. He studied the beauty, connecting the sparkles together into words of faith that strengthened him. He considered the wondrous majesty enshrouding the Creator of the universe.

In a heartbeat a longstanding realization overwhelmed him. He was once more reminded of who he was and who God is; as always he was in awe of his smallness. God *is* the great *I AM*, the Alpha and Omega, the beginning and the end, the first and last, which is, and which was, and which is to come, the Almighty; marvelous redeemer, longsuffering savior, true friend.

Daniel Twosongs had freely received the unmerited favor God lavished upon him, yet he remained cognizant of the wretched poverty of his piety and virtue. He had no delusions about his condition or who he was; he was a beggar in rags, or more accurately, a naked blind man groping his way through a fallen world cursed by a slinking darkness that long ago took root.

The tangled vine of sin twined its branches around every human endeavor. He had experiential proof that he wasn't immune to its influence or choking consequences. With his hands behind his head he humbly recalled his constant need for the Master's grace.

He exhaled a husky sound. "Jesus Christ, son of God, have mercy on me, a sinner," he said, voice coarse and whispery. He repeated the supplication several times. The wolves yelped a threefold amen. He grinned. The animals had moved in closer. He had no fear. The noble beasts were God's creatures, perhaps sent as messengers or simply to keep him company.

Peace blanketed him. Moments later he was fast asleep.

~~~

Sam Beadle was smitten. He sat at his desk in his cubbyhole room on the backside of the first floor of Drovers Cottage, fidgeting and fussing with a pencil. A rocklike lump had set up housekeeping in his throat. He was out of his depth and had no difficulty accepting that fact. A matter of the heart had him extremely undone. He had experienced infatuation once or twice, but in those instances his emotions had never been so thoroughly engaged.

There would be little rest for him this night. A lamp was turned up to its peak in front of him. He was supposed to be writing in his journal and making notes for a novel he intermittently labored on, but being as distracted as he was, the plotline was being uncooperative. Over and over again he tried to concentrate on it, but without any success.

All he could see in his mind's eye was the form and face of Abbey Langton. He had fallen hard for her. Nothing in his past had prepared him for the gravity of the sensation dropping through him like a cast-iron anchor; it tugged heavily at his heart. He was in his thirtieth year. He assumed her to be twenty-five or so, which seemed to be the ideal age difference to him.

He began to intentionally make a step by step plan to pursue her. He jiggled the pencil, but then dropped it and gasped as questions galloped through his mind. If she was Deacon Coburn's daughter, why did she sign the register as Abbey Langton? Was she already married? Did she have a husband and children in the Old States? Had she been widowed? If she was married or widowed why had she never corrected him when he addressed her as Miss Langton?

He was more than a little confused. He got up and went to the open window. He stuck his head outside and filled his lungs. There was no reprieve from the humidity or any freshness in the air, but nonetheless, looking into the darkness was conducive to uncluttering his mind. He rested his elbows on the windowsill.

He turned the queries over and over, giving each one the same kind of analytical probing he would any journalistic initiative. Progress came in a hodgepodge of random pieces as he reran every interaction he had with, or about her. His smile was growing enormous and cresting in his eyes, but it faded away as he contemplated Coburn's reaction to his query; something in the man's forthright manner spurred him.

He stood with a jerk and banged his head against the sash of the window. He muttered a trivial expletive and rubbed the stinging bump. He delved into the totality of their conversation, pacing very slowly around the room.

Deacon had been prickly and direct, but there was never a hint or suggestion that Abbey Langton wasn't a footloose and fancy free bachelorette. His aggressiveness was about sheltering her from dubious suitors and silver-tongued charlatans, which was understandable. He had an obligation as her father to protect her as best he could.

Sam Beadle respected the lay of the land around him. He heaved a loud sigh of relief. Most of the questions that had startled him and caused concerns had been shot down. One particular line spoken by Coburn remained to taunt him: *That young lady appears ripe, but she's green.* The corners of his lips slyly turned upward. There was still cryptic ambiguity surrounding the lady, but unraveling the unknown would be the thrill of the chase.

Tiredness eased its way through him. His clothes were sticky and stiff, having been sweated and dried several times over the course of the day. He snuffed the oil lamp's flame. He stripped down to his underwear as he continued thinking it all through, searching for some logical advance to begin his purposeful pursuit of her.

He stretched onto his cot-like bed, yawning. Her smile and appealing eyes were plastered on the walls of his mind. His imagination was alive and kicking. A single sentence repeatedly had him wondering about its ramifications: *That young lady appears ripe, but she's green.*

Now he *had* to know her story. He lay awake dreaming for several hours.

Flora was distraught. Shame and regret had broken down hardened walls erected over many years. Her distress shattered the silence of the night. Sequestered in darkness, she sat on the chesterfield in her living room. A cigarette was perched in the fingers of her right hand. It was the third one in a row she had rolled and lit. She hadn't smoked any of them. Instead, she was merely contemplating the red ember. When it burned close to her fingertips she flicked the smoldering butt into an ashtray and got the fixings out to make another.

A guilt-ridden trip down memory lane had her on a crying jag. Her breathing was fitful and irregular. She was inside musings that were vivid and real, which both soothed and shattered her. In the recollections it was before her life had been radically altered by self-destruction and self-loathing. She was eight years old and with her mother.

It was Sunday noontime. The sun was a glimmering jewel set in an unforgettable blue. Dressed in finery, complete with tight white gloves, they were walking home from church, hand in hand alongside a park lined by picturesque shade trees. As was prevailing custom, they were conversing about the priest's homily, which had been pertaining to Barnabas. Her mother always wanted to make sure that the practical application truths were not lost on her child.

"Father Martin's message was quite inspiring," her mother said, gesturing to an empty bench that often was a place for them to sit and enjoy the warm sunshine. "When he reads Scripture and tells a story he makes the Bible come alive."

"He made me wish Barnabas could be my friend, Mama."

They sat side by side. "Oh, yes. He would have been a wonderful friend. How special must it have been to have known Barnabas? His name means *son of encouragement.*"

"Encouragement is important, isn't it?"

"It's vital, Delores. From time to time we all need to be encouraged." She sighed sadly, her eyes drifting to someplace faraway. "If we want to receive encouragement, then whenever we can we must encourage others. Life has many upsets and disappointments. No one can make it through all the difficulties alone. It's too bad your Daddy didn't hear what Father Martin had to say this morning. He always needs lots of encouragement."

"I'll try harder to encourage him, Mama."

"That's not your responsibility, child."

"You told me that we all bear responsibility to each other."

"That's true, Delores," she replied, giving another unhappy sounding sigh. "It's not an easy balance. You cannot fix the results of the bad choices others have made. All you can do is point them in the right direction by telling them all about Jesus and second chances."

"Daddy doesn't know about Jesus," she said, in a way that was more of a confused statement than a question. "Then it's up to you to tell him, Mama."

"I've tried and will keep at it."

"Why doesn't Daddy come to church with us?"

"He's got some funny ideas about church, Delores. He's wrong."

"What can we do to help him be right?"

"We can see to it that he smiles. When he smiles he's a wonderful man."

"I make him smile most days. That's encouragement, isn't it?"

"I suppose it is. You cause everyone to smile just by being you." She took hold of her daughter's chin to look at her directly. "You're a special blessing. There's only one of you in the whole world and don't ever forget that, Delores. You are unique. There's no one like you anywhere. From the day you were born you've been my cherished gift from God."

"Tell me about my name again, Mama."

"How many times must you be told?" She laughed in a familiar, playful manner. "As you already know, Delores is short for *La Virgen María de los Dolores*. In English that means *Virgin Mary of Sorrows*. It comes from your Spanish grandmother. She was a great lady of faith. She taught me to find a way to thank God for every circumstance, and search for hope in my trials.

"I wasn't much older than you when she sat me down and instructed me to memorize these Proverbs of Solomon: *Trust in the Lord with all thine heart; and lean not unto thine own understanding. In all thy ways acknowledge him, and he shall direct thy paths.*" She gave the little girl's hand a gentle but firm squeeze. "Never forget that God allows situations for purposes we may never comprehend here on earth, which is why we must stand strong on his promises."

Suddenly Flora jerked back to the present when the cigarette singed her fingers. She was snuffling and gasping air. The noise of her emotional disarray filled the night. With a contraction of her wrist the burning weed joined the other discarded ashes. She instantly got busy building another. Her fingers were shaking. She fumbled around.

Her mother's voice rang in her ears. "*Lean not unto thine own understanding,*" she spat the words out between sobs. When the rollup was finally ready, she put a match to it and inhaled the first drag deep to the bottom of her lungs. She held it in for more than thirty seconds before releasing it in a thin stream. Smoke wreathed her head. She coughed and hacked, but that didn't prevent her from taking another hefty pull on the cigarette. She smoked it down to its nub and deposited it into the ashtray.

"Direct my paths," she said, guffawing bitterly. She stood and moved through the darkness to her bedroom. She was still wearing the silky maroon robe bedecked with delicate looking flowers. She flopped onto the bed and crooked her body into a near fetal position. She rested her head on a pillow and got a semblance of control over her breathing. She licked the inside of her right index finger where it was developing a blister from the cigarette burn.

There were frenzied images tripping through her mind. She tried piecing them together. She was truly aghast. What were the twists and turns that had derailed her? She had been a cheerful and dutiful child full of dreams. At what crossroads had that little girl named Delores become a well-known prostitute and consummate brothel operator known as Sweet Flora?

The thoughts sickened her. She had begun billing herself as Flora for two reasons. Her maiden name was Lafleur and then, the first man who ever paid for her services gave her a gigantic cash bonus because he proclaimed her to be a rare flower. She no longer had any desire to be Flora; she sought to bury her in the deepest possible grave.

Her soul ached to be Delores again. The agony was uninterrupted; when she slept the anguish goaded her and she began each day attempting to smother it. She wondered if she'd ever be able to shed the infamy Flora had created so that she could be Delores once more.

The surname didn't matter; she could pluck one out of thin air to fit her. She earnestly wanted to be Delores; to remember and experience even a tiny portion of who she could have been before rottenness and her reaction to it had transformed her life into an epic tragedy.

"Direct my paths, Jesus," she prayed unpretentiously. There was no snickering or mockery in her voice; no acrimony or cynicism. Her heart was laid bare as she helplessly made a desperate lunge at faith. She reached for her childhood belief the way a brutally emaciated woman would clutch and grab for a crust of bread.

In response to her extreme turmoil, the slouch-eyed face of Liam Greer popped into her mind like a zealous joker determined to destroy her. A mournful wail, originating in some bottomless abyss of remorse, ripped out of her. She tucked even tighter, her knees drawn up against her chest, her arms knotted around them. Her entire body heaved with grief as guilt rose up and ruthlessly slammed against her.

She had given birth and immediately discarded him. In actuality, she had deserted and abandoned him long before she had ever felt him move in her womb. From the first signs of the pregnancy she had denied he existed. She had done everything to forget him. Now he was here in Abilene and he had custody of her sterling silver case. She'd lost it and given up on ever finding it, but in all her prodigal ways it had never been far from her mind. She was frantic to get it back. She sobbed over and over again, gulping air and shivering.

The sterling silver case was a family heirloom from her maternal grandmother. It had been entrusted to her by her mother when she was only ten years old. The photograph had been taken on her eighteenth birthday. For those reasons it was a priceless treasure, but her longing to hold the case and see the tintype again had nothing to do with what could be easily perceived.

What really motivated her to obtain it was concealed. It was the unseen which was more valuable to her than all her material possessions. What she had painstakingly hidden behind the portrait was what she truly coveted. Her sin-stained compromises had blinded her and eroded its exact significance, but she reflexively understood it to be a touchstone for her heart.

Her subconscious was a pock-marked battlefield. She was straining to be free of disgrace and humiliation. Doubts and fears were in hand to hand combat against a fragile but compulsive stick-figure of hope yearning to make a new beginning. In the midst of the sniffing and weeping she began speculating how she could retrieve the sterling silver case. She tossed and turned back and forth, unable to reconcile the convulsive and confused conflict fuming inside her.

When she fell asleep, the pillowcase was soaked by tears.

chapter two

Reckless Choices

"Can a man take fire in his bosom, and his clothes not be burned?
Can one go upon hot coals, and his feet not be burned?"

~SOLOMON~

AT DAWN THE NEXT day, Deacon Coburn was moving around behind the
boardinghouse where he had kept a room since coming to Abilene in the
summer of 1870. The sun was a red line in the east, casting shades of gray
across the yard.

He stretched and filled his lungs, grateful for the new morning. He
had his Bible in one hand and a dry hambone in the other. He set both on
a stool-high stump of a tree before heading to the water trough beside a
vegetable garden.

He needed a shave, but chose to forego that chore; he would visit
the barbershop later. He took advantage of that particular luxury once or
twice a week. He could certainly handle the task without much effort, but
in candor, he purely appreciated hanging out with Whitey Fitzgerald, an
excellent barber and a dabbler in the practice of dentistry.

Whitey Fitzgerald had a colorful history and fly-by-night credentials.
He was a former slave from Alabama who'd learned his craft without fanfare or documentation. An unrepentant gossip and teller of tall tales, he
jabbered a high-speed commentary while the scissors clipped, the razor
scraped, or the pliers extracted a tooth or two. Each paragraph was punctuated by a habitual noise; a snappy click-click made between his cheek
and gum.

Thinking of him made Coburn chuckle. He removed his shirt and
laid it aside. Beneath a mat of body hair was evidence of his years-ago
run-in with a renegade band of Utes in the Angel Peak badlands of New

Mexico. His torso was crisscrossed with scar tissue. Sometimes, in joyless dreams, he would still see the milky left eye of the merciless leader who tortured him.

He worked the handle of the pump, dunking his head beneath the stream and splashing water on his upper body. He shook his head hard and finger combed his hair with both hands. He did a dozen deep knee bends and the same number of jumping jacks to get his blood circulating. He stretched again, arching his back and jiggling his arms. He waited for the moisture on his skin to become a relatively dry stickiness, then picked up his shirt and put it on.

The sun was merely peeking above the horizon but the air was already hot and muggy; it was going to be another scorcher. He glanced around distractedly, as though he was looking for someone or expecting company. There was much on his mind. He had it compartmentalized and now, was ready to begin systematically taking it all apart. He sat on the stump, Bible in hand and hambone balanced on his lap.

He slid Angela's letter out. As he read it over and over he pictured her as he had known her. The words penetrated his psyche, stirring up a sense of loss and loneliness. A bittersweet smile pinched at his mouth. Despite her forgiveness and forbearance, guilt remained; a skeleton that refused to be buried. Though it had subtlety, he was seldom unaware of its presence.

Rather than dismissing or choking it off he accepted all the conscience battering feelings set loose in him. Bloody thoughts no longer dominated him, but lingered to arise and haunt him on intermittent occasions. He had extensive self-knowledge; he was mindful and sensitive to his many failings and shortcomings, but he held himself to a higher standard than others.

There was a glaring blind spot within, that hung around as an unstoppable force. It was an unassuming paradox; the grace and acceptance he offered others he was seldom capable of providing for his inner man. A multitude of regrets were layered remnants in his soul.

Though his heart and mind knew better, he sensed he would never be entirely cleansed. Fetid bits of muck from the past clung to him; he was unable to unconditionally forgive himself, which given the unadorned stoicism of his religious upbringing amongst the River Brethren of Conoy Creek, seemed natural to him. The pigheaded judgment was a complicated web that had been easily woven into the convoluted tapestry of his character.

He had wronged a good woman, but on this day, he was realizing more and more that he had a rare opportunity to redeem that piece of his past—a second chance to do right. He intended to exert all efforts necessary to atone for his pitiful behavior with Angela Langton by honoring her final request and caring for Abbey as his own daughter.

That idea was serious weight on him. He wondered about his ability to shoulder it. He felt inadequate and thoroughly unprepared for the responsibility. Just then, a blue-ticked blur raced around a back corner of the two-story house. His face became a wide smile. "You're late, Old Blue. I was about ready to start gnawing on this bone."

The dog tilted its head as it sat down in front of him and immediately offered its right paw. Deacon shook it heartily. It uttered a muted whine of contentment when he handed over the hambone. Old Blue chomped hold of it and turned around in a circle before settling on its belly, its eyes fixed on the man as it chewed on its first meal of the day.

Coburn returned the letter to its resting place. "I understand you've made friends with a young lady named Abbey," he said, speaking directly to the cattle-dog. He began to slowly thumb his way toward the back of the Good Book. "You'd be doing me a special kindness if you stick close to her, Old Blue. I'm mighty concerned about her."

The dog responded by pausing in mid-chew, ears perking up attentively.

"There's a fella named Liam sniffing around her."

Old Blue growled. It was low and angry.

Coburn eyed the dog suspiciously. "You know something I don't, Old Blue?"

The dog stood and barked twice, then flopped down and returned to its breakfast.

"The boy's father died," Deacon said quietly. He leaned forward, arms resting on his knees. "He's had a rough go of it, but just the same, I sense he's slightly off-kilter. I don't know if I can help him or not, but I'll try." He lowered his eyes and dug into his Scripture reading.

His study was never superficial or haphazard. The daily devotional habit had been well established in early childhood; it had waned for a shell-shocked season after the battle of Gettysburg, but as the years and miles faded into the past he had become increasingly devoted to his methodology. He plodded along from cover to cover; when he came to the end of Revelation, he spontaneously returned his bookmark to the first chapter of Genesis.

He had wholehearted regard for God's written exposé to mankind. It didn't remedy all his uncertainties; neither did it always deliver comfort or alleviate self-reproach, but its grimly realistic account of human nature amazed him. It did not sanitize humanity's messy frailty and defects, which gave him immeasurable hope. And since doubt coexisted with faith in him, hope was the essential ingredient that fueled his knack for shedding crud to keep pressing on.

He found much of the Bible's substance to be violent and graphic. Rapes, murders, a tent peg driven through a head; castrations, beheadings; mutilations; whole cities wiped out and utterly destroyed; entire nations carted off into slavery and refugee status. Plus there was always plenty of sexual content; dancing, debauchery, and drunkenness fleshed out in poetic fashion. Mix in all those pesky plagues and pestilence, and the unfolding of history was compelling.

From the context of his experience, Deacon Coburn had determined that at its core the Bible was a love story about God's unremitting courtship of the human race. Jilted again and again by pride and idolatry, God's longsuffering love was endless. In spite of the darkest levels of depravity, the forever and depthless attributes of God's love refused to be rebuffed.

He leaned back and lifted the Bible up close to his face. He was in the New Testament, mining gems from the epistle of James. "Look here, Old Blue. These two truths need to be connected in my life, especially now." He placed a finger on a passage in the first chapter. "*If any of you lack wisdom, let him ask of God, that giveth to all men liberally, and upbraideth not; and it shall be given him.*" He turned over a page and read another verse. "*But the wisdom that is from above is first pure, then peaceable, gentle, and easy to be intreated, full of mercy and good fruits, without partiality, and without hypocrisy.*"

The dog thumped its tail in agreement. It dropped the hambone and leapt to its feet to come close and rub up against him. Coburn grinned. He clapped the book shut, then carried on and exuberantly petted Old Blue. He stood and turned toward the brightness of the rising sun. He tilted his head skyward and closed his eyes to pray while enjoying the sunshine.

Daniel Twosongs had been walking briskly for three hours by the time the sun rose above the eastern horizon. He had miscalculated; there was still no sign of the Smoky Hill River in sight, but he guessed it had to be close. He was on a sloping incline. In his mind he imagined at its crest he would see the glint of the sun skipping on the ripples of a stream.

His flat-brimmed gray hat was pulled low on his forehead. Even so, his eyes were squinted against the brilliant rays. He was dehydrated and achy all over; his joints felt as though they were all grinding bone on bone. His muscles were twitchy and jumping, threatening to constrict into spasms.

He kept moving because of necessity. Water wasn't going to come to him. The one step in front of the other sameness had to be maintained at all costs. A raw form of determination had become a burning mass in the pit of his stomach. He refused to be defeated.

He was not alone and was grateful for the company. The three wolves had stayed with him all night. He greeted them aloud as he broke camp in darkness, then set out. The animals were quiet and ghostlike as he'd begun on his north-easterly course, but he had been alert. The closeness of the wild canines gave him much encouragement.

Now, in the fullness of daylight he read behavior patterns, and understood that he was being actively herded. The animals were each fifty or so yards away forming a loose triangle that had him in the center. He drew strength from the wolves, but it wasn't enough. He could feel his body flagging. He pushed and pushed against the barrier.

Fatigue finally slashed through the sinewy ligaments of resolve. His willpower and energy gushed out of him with the forceful pop of a pin-pricked balloon. He stumbled. He lost his balance. He tried to catch it without any success. His Winchester went flying. He fell forward for several yards before hitting the ground hard.

He gathered his senses and picked himself up. He took a wobbly step that preceded a nosedive into the grass. Powdery dust filled his mouth. He tried standing again, with the same result. His thirst hurt; his throat was swollen almost shut. Weakness swarmed over him. He could feel consciousness ebbing away. He breathed slowly, drifting along. He passed out.

There was no counter to keep tally of how long he remained unconscious. Inside his mind he was drowning in a sea of sand; waves of it crashed over him. He thrashed and flailed his arms to gain the surface, but kept sinking, sinking, sinking. An urge to give up and die gripped him as blackness trounced and beckoned him. He fought against it.

Heat touched his face; a hotness that was thick and sticky. He kicked and struggled to be free of the darkness. He gagged. Gooey salt was slimy on his tongue. The bitter flavor of it choked him; it had the putrid stench of spoiled meat. He retched and heaved against it. He swam up and up. He came awake feeling an abrasive wetness on his cheeks.

His eyes opened and focused on a wolf straddling him. The beast was licking his mouth. He didn't recoil because he felt peace and assurance. He touched its neck, stroking gently. He had perfect clarity as he stared into the yellow-encircled orbs of its dark eyes. In the face of the wolf, for the briefest of moments, he *saw* Sally Twosongs; he *heard* her prayers for him.

The animal backed away hesitantly. It growled. He didn't move. The wolf became insistent, yapping and woofing as if it was demanding that he get up. He stood. He quivered and took shaky steps, weaving sideways. He righted himself. He bent over, hands on his knees as he took dozens of deep breaths. He got oriented and scanned the surroundings.

The wolf remained closeby, watching him. He noted that its two partners were padding back and forth along the topknot of the small hill he had been climbing. He had to be deliberate to make his legs work. He picked up his rifle. He returned to his course, tentatively at first, but then he gained confidence and some speed. The four-legged angel of mercy gave a robust yowl of a cheer and fell in behind to follow.

His nostrils flared. There was a faint whiff in the air that grabbed hold and wouldn't let go. He sniffed and tested it over and over before he was satisfied. His sore and split lips produced a puny smile. He smelled water. It thrilled him; excitement roiled through his veins and gave him a surge of energy. He sped up. His strides became lengthy and buoyant.

When he was within a stone's throw from the hilltop a crow cawed loudly. Its shadow passed over him and he craned his neck to see it. The crow was humongous; the size of a golden eagle, arcing and biding its time high above. Its head was misshapen and grotesque, its wingspan immense. It dipped low and squawked angrily at him. He saw its crazy eyes, dull and unreflective. A tremble chilled down his spine. He recognized the bird as an old foe that had harassed him and prevented him from stopping a murder.

The trio of wolves began snarling and prancing around skittishly. Twosongs stopped stockstill at the summit. His eyes widened. Less than a hundred yards of rolling grassland separated him from a lazy moving river, its water dark and winding like a ribbon around clusters of trees. He began his descent. The crow screeched, the wolves howled.

Daniel Twosongs hustled, legs rising and falling with renewed vigor. The black wraith of a crow streaked across the sky cawing aggressively as it soared. It suddenly plummeted and swooped at him, blasting a high-pitched shriek. He ducked and raised a forearm, but not before its talons struck his hat off his head. He dropped to a knee to catch hold of it.

The wolves enfolded him in a defensive wedge as the enraged bird ascended to make ready for another attack. It folded its wings back and plunged at him. He dove and somersaulted out of the way. A wolf, the one that had roused him, launched itself at the crow. The furious collision occurred five feet off the ground, causing the crow to tumble crazily. Two wolves pounced on it, as the other took a guarding position in front of the man.

He watched as good and evil clashed. The battle was vicious; a biting, clawing, snapping, hissing, spitting flurry of fur and feathers. He knelt with his Winchester gripped tight, seeking an opening to take a clear shot. Bullets had proven to be useless in his previous meeting with the bird, but nevertheless, the firearm was shouldered and aimed.

The crow fought valiantly, but was outmatched by the tag-team action. An eye was gouged out, yet it continued to be a screaming whirlwind of pecking and scratching. The wolves were ferocious, thrashing and mauling it until all it could do was back off and leap into the air, flapping its wings with concerted effort. It momentarily hovered, cackling hideous laughter. Its remaining eye cast hatred at the man before it escaped, bleeding and wounded.

Twosongs never pulled the trigger, but kept the gun lined up on the crow until it was a mere speck in the blue sky. Then he breathed deeply and got to his feet. His protectors were nursing and caring for each other. He expressed his thanks to the wolves in Navajo and called upon the Creator to safeguard them. The animals yapped joyously in reply.

He made his way downhill toward the stream and its promising refreshment. His companions stayed with him step by step, then approached the water first. Each one drank voraciously. He removed his hat, observing and wondering about the animals. He took his bedroll and canteen off his shoulder. He set his gear in the shade of a willow tree.

He crawled to the water's edge and buried his head in a cool pool. He never allowed himself to have a drink or even a taste; he had no desire to shock his innards into cramps. Instead he held his breath for a full minute and made a huge blubbering noise as he got on his hands and knees to shake his head. He felt lonesome. He looked around.

The wolves were gone. He gasped and clambered to his feet. He turned around and around, his head rotating so rapidly that it appeared to be on a swivel. He shaded his eyes with both hands and studiously examined the terrain in all four directions. There was no evidence or hint of the magnificent beasts anywhere on the prairie.

Twosongs shivered and bowed his head. "Thank you, Lord," he prayed, thin and hushed. He was astounded by what he had just witnessed and experienced. Humility broke over him; it mixed in with reverence, which became a vital sense of purpose.

He knelt to cup a handful of water to his mouth. He sipped just enough to moisten his lips and tongue. He swallowed and almost vomited. His throat burned. He tried again. The trickle of wetness went down easier. He took half a mouthful without any problems. Little by little he filled his belly, pacing the intake to allow his body to receive fluids without jolting it too much. The water was akin to a soothing elixir delivering a flow of potency into his muscles.

An hour later he was sufficiently recovered to continue his journey.

Charley Jondreau was familiar with jail cells. He had seen the inside of many of them, mostly for bogus reasons, but occasionally for rowdy fisticuffs. He had a lifelong penchant for being in the wrong place at the wrong time. He would inevitably yield to a latent benevolence or to his unquenchable curiosity; one or the other was always the culprit. His last incarceration had been five years ago in Welland County.

Those lodgings had been provided because a magistrate wasn't amused by how Jondreau had arbitrated a difference of opinion over payment for a bale of pelts. The skins in question had been the product of a season's worth of trapping; hard work that Jondreau had put in.

He bartered with Jonesy Smith, a local merchant with political connections and a sometimes maligned reputation for fairness. The haggling got intense. Offers were made and rejected. Tempers flared. Oaths were spoken before a bargain was struck. On the strength of a handshake Jondreau swapped the hides for a yearling colt and a winter's supply of dry goods.

He was pleased. He already had a dapple gray with trail sense, but it was slowing down and getting along in age, and he wanted to raise and train its replacement. The foodstuffs would be parceled out fairly to those needy ones in his extended clan. It was his intention to do as much good for them as viable before he gave in to his desire to satisfy the inquisitive seeker within.

The colt, a piebald pinto, was delivered on schedule; the dry goods lagged behind. When pressured, Jonesy Smith provided elaborate explanations as to reasons for the delay. Jondreau made a pretense of patience, but his long fuse was smoldering. He visited the trader several times but was always diverted or given excuses. Smith was oily smooth and strung him along with tales of the severe straits of his own economic troubles.

At first snow Jondreau concluded that the arrangement was broken. The dry goods would not materialize; he had been cheated, swindled. Never one to look to others for help he calmly took matters into his own hands. In a pinkish twilight haze Jondreau squatted on his heels in the woods near the Smith homestead and waited.

When Jonesy Smith made an early evening trip to the outhouse he was greeted by Charley Jondreau. Smith feigned regret and unhappiness for what he called a misunderstanding and attempted to wag his tongue and spin a believable fix. He promised to immediately abide by the original agreement and also, he would include an extra two months more of supplies, but chattering time was over. Jondreau's honor had been violated.

The fight, which given the comparable age and equal physical size of the combatants should have been an entertaining tussle, was such a one-sided affair it could hardly even be called a fight. Smith never landed a blow. Jondreau ruthlessly beat the man to a bloody pulp.

By the end of the affair Smith required the services of a doctor. He had a dislocated shoulder, along with several broken ribs and a nose mashed into a flattened mess. He was wheezing in and out of consciousness. Jondreau wasn't even breathing hard. The only marks on him were self-inflicted; the knuckles of both hands were scraped raw and bruised.

Rather than run, he saw to the care of his horses and put all other matters in order. In the cold, gray dawn he strolled to the local constabulary and told his story. He was promptly tossed into the hoosegow, pending an investigation. There was no paperwork to confirm his version of the trade. The extent of the injuries suffered by Jonesy Smith demanded a stiff sentence.

Jondreau didn't much care. He was fed and sheltered as lake effect winter storms and blizzards lashed the countryside. He had no woman or children to entangle him, so he settled in to outlast the bitter weather. When a mid-January thaw came and lingered he made a decision. In his mind, he had served enough of a penalty for the supposed offense of securing a measure of justice—his account was paid in full. The verdict was in, which put him into action.

On a moonlit night he broke out of jail with an extraordinary ease; fact was he could've done so at any time of his choosing. He moved rapidly. He got his dapple gray and yearling pinto. He gathered a handful of possessions and said a few goodbyes. He skedaddled to a safe-haven along the Grand River; a hideout he'd taken advantage of on other occasions.

When spring blossomed he began heading west and south, following a trail that soon led him far from the Great Lakes. There was no final destination in his thinking. He was a lone pathfinder, wandering along from place to place. He enjoyed the currents of whim or chance and savored the adventures, stopping at random locations to explore and learn.

Now, here he was lying on his back on a cot in another jail cell; a ten by ten red-brick and bars box. He had been in worse places. There was one fine-sized window with a thick steel grate over it that allowed a bit of air in. He was being amused by charting dancing dust mites in the tiny squares of morning light reflecting on the wall above him.

He was relaxed, with his hands locked behind his head. His droopy-brimmed hat was pulled low on his forehead. He had no reason to grumble, sulk, or plan a jailbreak; he would let circumstances play out. If things took a nasty turn toward haywire he was confident in his savvy and ingenuity to make a midnight run and be gone.

The door to the outer office opened. The lanky lawman came down the passageway.

"It's about time, buddy-boy."

"The name's Axler. Pete Axler."

Jondreau muttered a snide chuckle. "Until this shakes out in my favor, buddy-boy is the best you'll get from me."

"Fair enough." Pete inserted a key and jiggled it a bit before the cell door opened. "You want to tell me your story one more time just to make sure we both got it straight?"

Jondreau remained in his resting position. He pushed his jaw forward as he spoke. "I spotted the tarp when I stabled my horse. It was out of place so I had a closer look. When I saw all I needed of the body I covered it exactly how I found it."

Axler scratched at his whiskers. "Was there any other evidence?"

"I saw plenty."

Axler squinted. The seemingly permanent frown deepened. "What?"

"It was a bad blood murder, a personal grudge or vendetta."

"I figured that too."

"The killer planned it out," Charley said flatly. "The body could have been buried or left anywhere, but it was dumped at the livery to send a message. The question is who's supposed to get that message? You answer that and you'll know why the man was murdered."

"And the why will lead to who pulled the trigger," Pete said, stepping back. "Give me the day. If your version checks out, you'll be released bright and early tomorrow."

"My story will check out, buddy-boy. You got no reason to hold me."

Axler closed the heavy door with a slam; the lock clicked loudly. "For the record, you ain't being held on suspicion of murder. You're behind bars for flouting a city ordinance against firearms and pulling one on a law officer."

"Ain't much of a crime carrying a gun, eh? Besides I knew nothing about that order."

"It's posted at various points in and around town," Pete replied, smiling.

Jondreau gave a dismissive shrug. "Tell preacher-man I want to talk to him."

"His name's Coburn. Deacon Coburn."

Jondreau grinned, all smug. "Tell Deacon Coburn I want to talk to him."

Axler nodded agreeably. He carefully double-checked the lock. He turned and departed.

Charley Jondreau removed his hands from behind his head and sat up. He swung his legs to the floor and perched on the edge of the cot. He took his hat off and rubbed a hand over a crop of stubble. It would be a few more days of growth before his scalp got itchy. When a break came for him to take a blade to it he expected to have this predicament put far behind him.

The sun was low in the east, an orange-whitish ball balanced atop a ridge of the Flint Hills. Jackson Scully had no inclination to pause and take note let alone appreciate such beauteous wonder. He was shambling around a campsite south of Abilene. It was in a woodlot at an elbow on Mud Creek north of where it emptied into the Smoky Hill River.

His boogered up left leg was torturing him. Mornings were always the worst. Getting up and about was more and more becoming a distasteful chore. He moved with all the dignity of a sideshow freak, having to clutch and hoist his leg to drag it along. The aching sting was knifelike and constant; it sliced from his hip down his leg, all the way up his spine and across his back.

In an effort to relieve the chronic annoyance he had been self-medi-cating for years, using a mixture of whiskey and laudanum. The side effects were a buzzing numbness in his head along with a perpetual queasy sick-ness. He seldom had much of an appetite, but often forced himself to eat and pretended to enjoy it.

He urinated against the trunk of a live oak. He tucked in and but-toned up. He yawned as he hitch-hopped his way back to the reddish-gray ashes of the campfire. He wanted fresh coffee, needed it. He bent over to pick up some dry sticks. Groans issued from his throat; low murmurs of discomfort common to him though he wasn't even aware he made them. He squatted with much straining effort to stir the coals.

His saddle and gear were on the ground not far from his bedroll. The black gelding grazed nearby on a long picket line. He got the fire restarted and fed it fuel. The coffee smelled good as he fixed it in a pot that obviously required a thorough cleaning. He set it on a flat rock at the fire's edge. He liberated a bottle from his saddlebags and took a swig of the laudanum laced whiskey before pouring a splash in his tin cup.

When the coffee boiled he put the pot and bottle within reach, and settled on his butt, his back resting against a tree. His left leg was stretched out, his right one bent up. He filled his cup with coffee. The aroma flared his nostrils. His lips puckered in anticipation. The first sip was too hot. He waited a few moments then tried again. It burned down his throat. He grimaced.

He began trying to sort out what he would do next. His head was a clouded quagmire of conflict. He wanted nothing more than to finish the job on Coburn and get away. The chance to murder him hadn't presented itself last night; half the town's population seemed to scramble through the targeted intersection, but the preacher never came into his line of sight.

Jackson Scully was bent on accomplishing vengeance but, just now, he couldn't concentrate on it. He was distracted. Flora had gotten inside his head. Her aspiration for change and a new beginning had his brain under a beguiling abracadabra, opening doors to possibilities of which, until last night, he had never imagined.

He finished the cup of juiced up caffeine, reached for the bottle and fixed a second one. The coffee was gummy and grainy, but it blended in smoothly. He gulped a mouthful and swallowed it a dribble at a time. He shifted around, wincing as a stiletto of pain hacked at his left thigh. He moaned loudly as his body stiffened. His face hardened into a teeth-clenched scowl. When the agony passed, he slumped against the tree, swearing sullenly.

He steadied his breathing. He uttered a plea for relief that was fortified with profanities. His skin was covered in a slick layer of perspiration, partly due to the cruel pangs of affliction, but mostly because of the persistent heat and humidity. He cussed again. He emptied the contents of the cup onto a tuft of brown grass. The parched soil lapped it up.

He began wondering if sleeping in a proper bed and sitting on cushioned chairs would be helpful in reducing his suffering. In a profound moment of flawless sobriety he concluded that anything would be better than the outdoors lifestyle that found him mostly squatting or hunkering down in a bedroll on the hard ground.

He seriously thought about Flora. Her passion and pleasure enthralled him. He didn't know much about love and doubted his capacity to express his feelings for her in those terms, but realized she had a special tenderness and affection in her heart reserved just for him. Perhaps in her plans for a fresh start somewhere she had latched onto a feasible idea.

Jackson Scully exhaled a grunting moan. He determined that he was indeed interested in partnering with her. The prospect to do so was forthwith. A discordant struggle still raged in him; a fury that demanded retribution. He couldn't lock down any details but knew for sure that by hook or crook, before hightailing with her, Deacon Coburn would be a dead man.

Naomi Engle fluttered awake to an unpleasant memory. The vividness of it startled her. She didn't like it at all; she wanted it to fade into oblivion, but it kept returning to take up space in her head. She rubbed her eyes and wiped drool off her chin. She opened the drawstring handbag on her lap and found a peppermint. She popped the candy in her mouth and swirled it from cheek to cheek. Its sweetness tasted good on her tongue.

Naomi stretched and leaned forward to look out the window. The train was chugging past mile after mile of green scenery. She enjoyed watching it rush by, listening to the steel harmony of the rails. Her eyes bent skyward. Big white clouds were taking on the shape of a medieval castle surrounded by a bright blue moat. She smiled at the sight.

She shifted around some. Her derrière was numb, her legs stiff and achy. The soreness was a nagging nuisance that she was certain she could outlast because there would be plenty of opportunities for walking soon enough. She sighed sadly; it snuck out, overpoweringly mournful. She put a hand over her lips and settled back in her seat.

She couldn't shake loose of the reminiscence that had invaded her sleep. The finality of the episode kept forcing itself on her consciousness. It was her last encounter with her only sister, who was three years older, but acted like an elderly matriarch. It commenced as kindness, but that masquerade was rapidly stripped bare as it deteriorated into an upbraiding confrontation. Instead of fighting it, she closed her eyes and allowed it to replay.

It was a mere week ago when a mid-morning knock on the door startled Naomi. It was firm and authoritative. Naomi wasn't expecting company. She really didn't want to be disturbed or bothered; she was far too busy taking care of all the necessary details to put the past behind her. The rapping on the door came again, louder and more insistent. She answered it and was surprised to see Martha. She was hugely pregnant, due to go into labor at any moment.

"Good morning," her sister said cheerfully. Her cheeks were rosy and beaming. "I've brought you a fresh baked blueberry pie." She pushed past Naomi and bustled into the house. She placed her offering on the kitchen table and busied herself getting plates. "Would you be a dear and put the water on to boil? I thought we could have sassafras tea with our pie."

Naomi eyed her suspiciously. She set the kettle on the cook-stove. She opened the firebox and placed a split log on top of a bed of hot coals that endured from preparing her breakfast of bacon and eggs. The wood was soon crackling, its maple aroma filling the air.

Silence settled between them. Naomi kept a wary eye on her. Growing up they had been as tightly connected as possible, though latent sibling rivalry was periodically manifested in their actions and attitudes. As a child Martha had been playful and mischievous; her carefree bearing and friendship gave no forewarning that she would become a rigid and prudish woman.

That transformation was activated in adolescence and enflamed when she married into the prominent and influential Hochstetler family. The clan's high-ranking and widespread dominance in the community gave rise to a legalistic pride within Martha; the position and prestige had emancipated a holier-than-thou Pharisee full of zeal and criticism.

The pie was sliced and served; the tea steeped and poured into utilitarian stoneware mugs before there was any indication of a conversation between them. They sat across from each other on beautifully ornate oak chairs at a matching table; the sturdy set had been designed and built by Adam Engle. He had been an exceptional craftsman.

"We are all concerned for you, dear," Martha began as she took a sip of tea. "I know much has already been asked and answered, but the Lord's impressed on me to try once more."

"Try what, pray tell?"

"To understand your decisions," Martha replied, taking a small bite of pie. She put the fork down and pushed the plate aside. "To help you see your folly."

"My folly? Please explain."

Martha folded her hands together. "Why must I do so? Are you obtuse?" Her tone was soft and malleable, belying the inflexible glint showing in her eyes. "You have auctioned off everything. It's difficult to grasp that this house and all the furniture now belong to another family who'll take possession upon your departure. I am aghast, and many brothers and sisters are also in an uproar, prattling about you being daft. Are you touched in the head?"

Naomi slipped a sliver of her bottom lip between her teeth. She held it, ready to bite down hard if that was required for her to keep a civil tongue. She eyed a spot in the middle distance and remained quiet. She was doggedly determined to follow-through on the Biblical exhortation to *live peaceably with all men, if it be possible, as much as lieth in you.*

"You're not the first woman to bury a husband."

Naomi's teeth tightened slightly. She stared at her sister, coldly furious.

"In time your heart will heal," Martha counseled, sounding clinical and dispassionate. Her head was held at a slight upward angle. "It hasn't even been a year since Adam's death. There are appropriate men amongst the brethren who would be happy to take you as their wife. After a proper interlude of mourning it could all be arranged without any fuss."

"Husbands are interchangeable pieces, then?"

"Don't be foolish, child," Martha said tersely. "All I am saying is that there are options here for you to explore. This is home and where you belong."

"Martha, I have no children for which to be responsible," Naomi explained, demonstrating patience and restraint. "I am not fastened to the land. My feet do not have roots in this soil. There is life and beauty and newness to be discovered beyond here."

"You are gravely mistaken, addled by worldly desires."

"Worldly desires?" Naomi queried, stifling a snicker. Her mouth tensed up. "Why am I made to be a bugbear, and shunned and treated as though I have the plague?"

"You're breaking Mother's heart," Martha answered matter-of-factly. "Instead of being flighty and running away you ought to move in with her. She is beside herself with grief."

Naomi released her grip on the inside of her lip. Her posture visibly stiffened. "You are incorrect, Martha. Or you are a liar," she said, without qualms. "I was with Mother yesterday afternoon and evening. We prayed and cried together, and talked through all these matters. She shared wisdom and grace that you would do well to embrace. She gave me her blessing, which I gratefully received." She paused as a teasing smile turned her lips upward. "Mother also gave me something personal and special to pass along if I am fortunate enough to find someone."

Martha became agitated. She evidently inferred something from her sister's last sentence that stirred an angry response. Her eyes widened as her hands flexed fitfully. "So you *do* intend to fetch a man out west and try again to have a child?"

"I have no such intention, dear sister."

Martha's ire was stoked and rising fast. The veneer of concern and all pretensions of caring were gone. Her jaw and lips were quivering. "What keepsake did Mother give to bestow on any possible issue of yours? It better not be one I have marked for my children."

"Oh, Martha, your pettiness is so unbecoming." Naomi's voice was calm. "My ticket is purchased and all my affairs are in order. My only plan is to get on a train in two days."

Martha stood. "Then I no longer have a sister." She slammed the door strongly.

Naomi shuddered. Her eyes opened as the recollection of the incident floated into the background. That exchange had been seven short days ago. By now Martha had likely delivered a newborn to join her brood of four. The baby, boy or girl, would probably only ever learn about his or her Aunt Naomi in some accidental manner.

The train's whistle blew. She realized there was wetness on her cheeks. She chastised herself with the knowledge that to make a go of it in the west, she had to toughen up. The past was the past; she was stretching forward to take hold of the future.

There would be no shirking or turning back. All of her belongings were in a handcrafted cowhide suitcase, which had been a gift from her husband Adam; it was the only memento she had from her previous life. All those yesterdays would be put behind her.

She considered the positives of her situation. She had willpower and an undisguised belief in the green pastures of tomorrow. Along with her strength of character, the proceeds from the sale of property provided the financial resources to make a good start. No one could ever guess that a considerable sum of money was belted around her waist beneath her corset.

So far her journey had been uneventful. Days and nights blended in and got all mixed up as the train rocked its way across the country. She took advantage of every stop to get out, walk around and make idle talk with local folks. St. Louis was the next milestone ahead. She expected to linger there for a week or more to sightsee before continuing her trek to Abilene.

"Hey, don't be such a crybaby, Dogface!"

Liam Greer cringed. Tears were burning his eyes, blurring his vision. He was twelve years old and racing as fast as his legs could carry him. Benny Slaton, a loudmouth bully with a sadistic streak, was hot on his heels.

Liam was scared. He had already taken a roughhouse beating. He could taste blood on his lips and felt it trickling from his nose. His sides and stomach hurt. He was sure bruises were already forming. Making the walloping more ghastly was the fact that while being stomped on his bladder had evacuated its contents. He was mortified and humiliated—a blotchy stain could be clearly seen across the crotch and legs of his trousers.

Benny Slaton was getting closer. He was bulgy-eyed, his face cracked wide by a slobbering grin. Liam Greer wanted to spin around and make a stand; to ball up his fists and give better than he had taken. Even as that thought flashed through his head he knew it was not at all in the realm of possibility. Benny was bigger, stronger, meaner.

Liam's only hope was to run faster. He tried harder and harder. He darted down an alley. He gasped and skidded to a stop. Fear and outrage mushroomed in him. His throat constricted. His escape route was a dead-end, blocked by a tall wooden fence. He jitterbugged around just as his antagonist slammed into him. Liam went sprawling on his back in the dirt. He cowered and squirmed, frantically striving to cover the wetness.

Benny towered over him, immediately seeing the telltale dark spot. His mouth dropped open, his eyes twinkled. "Looky here, looky here," Benny sang, "Dogface Greer is a pussified piss-pot." He repeated it over and over, laughing and dancing a little jig around him.

The catchy refrain echoed across the years. Shame still blanketed Liam Greer; he often crawled inside of it and attempted to hide. He had much practice in doing just that, without any relief. Even now, the rottenness of Benny Slaton's abuse resurfaced to taunt him. He shivered and glared at nothing as he took hold of the residual imagery and strangled it.

Liam Greer had never been a stranger to mockery and ridicule. No matter where he went he seemed to incite or embolden disparaging behavior from others; being bullied or picked on was a common theme of his childhood. Benny Slaton had a longstanding claim on being king of the hill, but he was not the first, nor the last browbeater to beleaguer him; Benny just happened to be especially efficient and the most vindictive.

Liam Greer didn't care and none of it mattered anymore. That's what he told himself while sitting on the sun-drenched steps of the Merchants Hotel. The truth had some complexity and was lurking beneath layers of carefully constructed denial: Benny Slaton had staked out a chunk of territory in Liam Greer's subconscious. Disgrace and worthlessness had climbed up inside an inner lair and insidiously sank creepers that fed on him.

Greer shook his head rigorously. He wanted to be free of all the ugliness; the reeking garbage had power over him which he loathed with a visceral revulsion. Benny Slaton was nowhere to be found. If their paths ever crossed again he was sure that Benny Slaton would be the sorriest individual to ever draw breath; Liam intended to kill him dead. To that end he needed to get busy with his plans to carve a swath of notorious celebrity.

He had a small fortune of cash in his pocket from selling the horses that he and his father had brought to Abilene. The deal had been finalized an hour ago. A high-spirited palomino stallion was kept back; he intended to name it Hero and make it his own. The mule that had performed well as his mount would be relegated to pack-animal status.

Liam slipped off the steps. He filled his lungs and exhaled a giddy laugh. He clapped his hands and took a couple skipping steps before settling into his natural slouchy gait. He still had a full day ahead of him. A shopping spree of sorts was on the agenda; a set of clothes, a top of the line pistol rig, supplies for the trail, including a few plugs of chewing tobacco and a suitable stash of hard candy. Abbey Langton would also be called upon for a visit.

First, however, there was a funeral that he was obliged to attend.

Abbey Langton had just finished a brunch of pancakes and sausage. She dabbed a napkin at the corners of her mouth and looked around. The dining room of Drovers Cottage had a sparse crowd. She set her plate aside and almost instantly a waitress was there to clear the table. Abbey gave a nod of thanks as she snapped open the latest edition of the *Abilene Chronicle*.

She perused the newspaper, taking delight in the local flavor. There was a bold half-page advert proclaiming a large-scale sale at McInerny's Boot & Saddle Shop on Texas Street. A couple side-by-side social announcements kept her interest for a brief interval, but then she read a featured article lamenting that Ellsworth was flourishing and had succeeded Abilene as the northern stopping point for the cattle trade. Her mind jumped. She made a cause and effect connection between the news item and the advertisement.

"I deduced I'd find you here, Miss Langton."

She looked up. "Why would you say that, Mr. Beadle?"

"I make observations," Sam answered, matching her expression. "It's the wrong time of day for Old Blue to be holding vigil in the lobby. Drovers Cottage tends to be on its afternoon route. I presume it's waiting for you. It seems that you have stolen that poor dog's heart."

Abbey crinkled her eyes at him. "I suppose I could do worse."

"Indeed." Sam appeared to be flustered. His cheeks became crimson. He was a man equipped with many a witty comeback, but none were readily on his tongue, which apparently was tied about as tight as possible. He transferred a flip-top notepad from hand to hand.

"Would you be kind enough to join me, Mr. Beadle?" Abbey asked, making a grand gesture toward the vacant chair at the table. "I would be grateful for the company."

Beadle untangled the knot in his tongue. "I'm glad to do so." He swung the chair out and sat. "I was hoping you would have some time for me this morning."

She folded the paper and set it aside. "For what reason, Mr. Beadle?"

"I have an idea," he said candidly. He flicked the notepad open and placed it on the table. He eagerly dug around an inside pocket of his vest until he retrieved a pencil. "I would like to interview you for a human interest story."

"You require my time for professional purposes, then. Not personal?"

Beadle was caught off-guard. His cheeks took on scarlet hues as he shifted tensely in his seat. "To be honest I was using the professional approach to get to the personal."

"Is that so?" Abbey gave him an exaggerated scowl of disapproval. She held it for a short-lived instant; it melted into a wide-eyed grin. Her eyebrows shot up as she told him, "Your forthrightness has rescued you, Mr. Beadle. Give me your best professional spiel. I will then decide if the personal is worth the value of my time."

He bobbed his head approvingly. "I find your arrival here to be fascinating," he said, rolling the pencil between his thumb and index finger. "Readers will gobble up your story. A young lady travels west to deliver a letter from her deceased mother . . ."

Abbey cut in, "Who was the source for your information?"

"I spoke to your father last night."

"Did you?"

"Deacon Coburn is your father, is he not?"

"Is that what he told you, Mr. Beadle?"

"Yes, Miss Langton."

Her eyes flared. "Did Deacon give you permission for this inquiry?"

He hung his head. "Not exactly."

"I thought not." Her eyes shrank into severe slits. She pierced him with a stink-eyed glare dusted off from childhood. She held it, refusing to give an inch, as though she had the ability to make him feel her anger. There was iciness in her that dropped the temperature between them.

He was restless in his seat. "Shall I leave?"

"That's not necessary just yet, Mr. Beadle."

He brightened. "May I proceed?"

"You are free to do anything you so desire," she said with a sharp edge. "But if you want me to remain good-humored you will put your pencil and tablet away. I am not a journalistic project, nor am I a human interest story. I repudiate the entire notion."

"Of course, you are correct. I apologize, Miss Langton. I meant no harm."

Her lips pursed into a harsh and unflattering straight line as she weighed his words. She took a deep breath. Her countenance softened. "Apology accepted, Mr. Beadle."

"Thank you. I will put myself in a better light, Miss Langton."

"You will if you have any expectation of friendship with me."

Sam tried on a smile, but it quickly slid off. Full-blown silence began to take hold, but before it could become vast and insurmountable, he said, "That was some excitement you had to end your first day in Abilene. Do you anticipate any further problems from Mr. Greer?"

Abbey suddenly gave him a burst of self-assurance. "I think not. He's nothing more than a half-grown braggart, between hay and grass. He'll not soon forget what I taught him."

"What if he persists in bothering you?"

"Mr. Beadle, I have no intention of ever seeing Liam Greer again."

"He surely has other plans, Miss Langton."

"I cannot tell you how little I care for whatever is in his head," she replied, somewhat haughtily. She leaned against the table. "What of you, Mr. Beadle? Since your editorial gambit has been euchered, do you have another tactic to take with me?"

"I won't beat the devil around the stump, Miss Langton," he said easily. "Would you be kind enough to accompany me on a buggy-ride tomorrow morning?"

Her eyelids fluttered. "Why, Mr. Beadle, you're as game as a banty rooster."

"Would you please call me Sam?"

"That would be crossing the line from professional to personal, Mr. Beadle." she said, tilting her head. "I am not yet prepared for that familiarity. Perhaps after our morning buggy-ride I will feel different, but you better not start counting your chickens."

"Until tomorrow." He stood, smiling broadly. She was careful to only cast a fleeting glance in his direction. He walked out with a spring in his step. She hesitated for a few minutes, consciously attempting to keep her facial expression impassive. She picked up her purse and newspaper, and on a whim, decided to embark on a strolling tour of the streets of Abilene.

Old Blue met her at the door. She was gratified when it tagged along beside her.

The sun blazed at high noon in a blue sky that went on forever. The town was noisy and boisterous. Hoofbeats of horses and longhorns created a muffled pulsation, filling the hot air with puffy swirls of grainy grime. Cattle were being herded to boxcars, bawling continuously. Cowhands shouted and hooted shrill commands peppered with cusswords.

Flora stood near the graveyard, waiting and watching. She was tense. Her eyes were puffy from crying and erratic sleep. Her heart was turbulent. She wore a dull-colored dress with a high collar and long sleeves, along with a matching wide-brimmed sunbonnet. She wondered what words the broad-shouldered man could be saying about Jack Greer. The internment service had to be coming to its conclusion.

Pete Axler was dawdling off to the side, not far from her. He had arrived just a minute or two after her. They had exchanged stiffly muttered pleasantries. If the situation had been a social occasion she likely would have had some fun at his expense; Pete was an incorrigible bachelor who was painfully shy around women and it was so easy to fluster him.

When Deacon Coburn closed his Bible and sidled away from the grave, she gave a feeble wave in his direction. He acknowledged it with a slight motion. He knelt and spoke to the young man who had plopped down on the ground, his head hanging. The conversation was one-sided and brief. Coburn rose and ambled toward her. As he came near, they eased off by themselves.

"How are you, Flora?" His tone was reassuring. He had visited the barbershop; his chin and cheeks were smooth and his bushy moustache had been trimmed even with his upper lip. Whitey Fitzgerald had been a chatty bundle of information—Coburn now possessed some speculations and rumors regarding the body that had been uncovered at the livery.

"I don't know how to ask this." Her reddened eyes were flitting to and fro. Pete Axler was shuffling back and forth, making little ruts with the toes of his boots. A few nosy bystanders were gaggled together close to him making no bones about eyeballing them and nattering.

"Ignore the chirpy gawkers. They can't hear us, so just ask."

"It won't help. I shouldn't even be here."

"Does this have to do with Liam Greer visiting you last night?"

Flora reacted with surprise. Her mouth widened but no words emerged. Her complexion blanched. She regarded him narrowly and spoke with hushed astonishment. "Are you privy to all the secrets? Does nothing ever flee from your watchful ways?"

Coburn cracked a comforting smile. "I do what I do, Flora. I do the best I can."

"You always have, ever since we first met in Texas. Do you remember?"

His lips broadened, eyes glinting roguishly. "I came to your place of business to reclaim Big Bull Wallace. He was on one of his irregular benders."

She laughed; it sounded thin and tinny. "I modeled that joint after my Fort Smith operation. Big Bull fronted me a loan and was a sometime partner in the business. He spilled off the wagon about once a year. That was the only time he was a good customer." She made eye contact and held it steady. "You, on the other hand, were the straight-laced cowboy assigned to rescue the boss from my clutches. Several of my girls had their hearts all a-flutter for you."

"As I recall *you* flirted with me on more than one occasion."

"It's what I did at the time, sir," she said, attempting frivolity. She wiggled a shaky finger at him. "As *I recall* you diverted me with some strong-minded expertise. It wasn't until you came to Abilene that I learned of your tendency to be religious."

"It better be more than being religious, Flora," he replied categorically. "I mostly miss the mark, but I aspire to live a practically applied faith in the Lord Almighty." He placed his Bible under his left arm. "Otherwise none of life matters and nothing makes any sense."

Her eyes darted around, nervous-like. "I shouldn't even be here."

"So you already told me. What can a friend do for you?"

She beheld him, eyes as anxious and jittery as a frightened cat. She redirected her gaze and kept it fixed on the ground. "I'm in a fog," she blurted, with much emphasis. "There's evil in me, I know, but underneath all that evil, there's good, I think. The ledger is balanced against me, but I desperately want the good to be freed. I can no longer lean on my own understanding. I want to be a different person." She swallowed a sob. "Pray for me, Deacon. Please."

Coburn shook his head. "No, I can't do that," he replied, reaching for her hands. He gently took hold of them. "But I will gladly pray with you."

Her lips were quivering. Her breathing was labored and shallow.

He gave her hands a squeeze. "You be firm and agree in your heart with all I pray."

She stifled another sob and gave a nearly imperceptible nod.

His eyes squinted shut, which wrinkled his whole face. "Our Father and our God, giver of every good gift, thou art truly our stronghold and our only hope. I thank thee for Flora. We stand together and in the name of Jesus we beseech thee. Thou art the One who is intimately familiar with all her ways. She humbles herself before thee. She cries out to thee. Make open thy pathway to the desires of her heart. Pour into her what she is in need of in these moments of travail in her soul. Grant her discernment and wisdom and courage. Be thou her refuge; be thou the rock of her salvation. Hear her groaning, hear our prayer, Lord. Amen."

"Amen," she whispered, head still lowered.

He placed a finger on her chin to lift her face to him. Tears of sorrow were shining in her eyes. Beneath the glistening waterworks he saw buds of faith and hope. "Be at peace, Flora. Be encouraged by God's grace and mercy."

"I will try." Her voice was subdued, broken.

"Accept what God offers, Flora."

"That's easy to say, hard to do."

"It's in the hard doings that our character is processed and refined," he said forcefully. His demeanor became stubbornly adamant. "Now you listen to me, ma'am. Be encouraged by God's grace and mercy. And don't you duck your head to anyone. Walk these streets with your head held high and your heart bowed low in humility."

"Thank you, Deacon." She took a shivery breath, turned and stepped briskly away. She went swiftly past the gathered busybodies, shoulders straight and carriage upright. Her gait reflected gutsy determination. He kept still, focused on her until she went around a corner.

Axler came alongside him. "What was that all about?"

"I was just visiting with an old friend."

"It looked like a gospel mill meeting."

"I suppose there was some of that to it. What's going on, Pete?"

Axler pushed his hat up his forehead. "I want you to have a look at the dead man at the undertaker's. There ain't too many clues. I need someone reliable to test my thinking."

"Has he been identified by anyone?"

"No one has put a claim on him."

"Were there any papers or documents?"

"Nothing," Pete reported, giving a bewildered shrug. "Someone, most probably the killer, picked his pockets clean. It's like he dropped into the livery from nowhere."

"Let's go have a look-see."

"Afterwards, that Jondreau fella wants to see you at the jail."

Coburn nodded. The men walked side by side in silence.

It was midday. Liam Greer was all alone in plain sight. All alone that is except for a disconcerting memory rattling along the corridors of his brain. He sat on the ground at his father's graveside as two men filled the hole with dirt. The images were blurry and racing; a pivotal occurrence in his young life that ran over and over, shaping and defining him.

He shook his head fiercely to be free of it. He considered the present circumstances. He was grateful that Deacon Coburn had assisted in making all of the arrangements. He even valued what Coburn had said; none of the Bible words about redemption and eternity had anything to do with him, but he appreciated them just the same.

He was fixated on the shovels heaving dirt into the grave. The heavy thud-thud of the clods striking the pine box had a spellbinding effect on him. It was sickeningly seductive. He surrendered to the clatter inside his head, drifting backwards to a revelation that stunned him when he was fourteen years old; an eye-opener that came courtesy of Benny Slaton.

"That's hogwash!" Liam spouted, slumping as though he'd taken a wallop.

"No guff, Dogface," Benny answered proudly. He was sitting on an empty barrel and chewing tobacco while the other boy loaded a flatbed wagon with boxes of dry goods. "My ole man says your mother's a whore named Flora."

"Nope. My mother died when I was born. She's buried in Arkansas."

"Your boozed up father gave you a load of bull," Benny said, grinning maliciously. He spat a streamer of sticky juice and had to wipe gobs of it off his chin. "She's a strumpet, a Jezebel, a harlot, a whore. You do know what a whore is, don't you, Dogface?"

Liam squatted on his heels. He scooped up a handful of dirt and rubbed it between his palms. "Why are you telling me this garbage?"

"Someone has to wise you up," Benny answered, chuckling. "Your drunken sot father ain't got the crackers upstairs to do it, so it falls to me." His face was creased in glee. Sparkles were spinning in his eyes. "Your mother's a whore named Flora. She spreads her legs for money and she ain't cheap. My ole man's been with her more than once and he says she's well worth the ten dollars. That's the way of it, so you might as well just accept it, Dogface."

All the color had drained out of Liam. His hollow cheeks were white and pasty. He was dizzy, but got to his feet and took off running. Benny's raucous belly laughter rang in his ears. He made his legs go faster than ever before, on his way to confront his father. He pumped his arms and lifted his knees high. He took the backstairs to their apartment above a saloon three at a time and crashed through the door. It slammed against the wall.

"What the blue blazes!" Jack exclaimed excitedly. He sat on a chair in front of the open window overlooking the street, a bottle of gut-rot liquor in one hand, the tintype of the woman he had married in the other. "What's got you in such a helter-skelter?"

"Are you a liar or just a plain chucklehead?"

"You got the wrong pig by the tail, lad."

"Do I, Pa?"

"You got too much mustard in you, lad." He took a long pull on the bottle of tarantula juice and nearly squeezed his eyes shut as he swallowed. "You ain't too big in the britches for me to handle. I'll take you down a peg or two if you sass back again."

"Is my mother a whore named Flora?"

Jack Greer gasped and jerked as if someone had taken a corkscrew to his heart. His eyes were wide and wet with a swell of tears. "There 'taint no accuracy in that, Liam," he said, but there was no vigor or certainty in his voice. All the fire and combativeness disappeared. "Don't gainsay me. Her name was Delores. I buried her on a hillside outside of Little Rock."

"Your saddle-tramp cohort said different. Benny was ragging me about it."

Jack wilted. His mouth worked soundlessly for more than a minute. He sank deeper and deeper, seemingly shrinking into himself. "Oh, dear God, no . . . no." His breathing was huffs and sputters as he stared obsessively at the photograph. A mournful cry wrenched out of him. He placed the sterling silver case against his chest and sobbed loudly.

"You lied?" Liam staggered. "My mother's a whore named Flora . . ."

"Slaton should've kept his trap shut," Jack mumbled, glassy-eyed.

"You lied." The unvarnished truth impaled him. "All these years you've lied to me."

Jack Greer was a defeated wreck. His mouth opened and closed helplessly.

The years fled. Liam grabbed a fistful of dirt and tossed it into the grave. He uttered a grunt and hissed a surly curse, lips pulled back and teeth bared like a rabid wildcat. It was so vehement that the men stopped shoveling and eyed him. He ignored them and regained his feet. He kicked a clump of dirt into the hole. His shoulders were scrunched as he lazed away.

Deacon Coburn was shocked. The past came rushing against him as he examined the body positioned on a long table in a backroom at the undertaker's. "Whitey was wrong," he said quietly. His mouth was dry, his eyes misty. "He told me not to worry because the dead man was some boot-licker politician who got what was coming to him."

Axler was looking over his shoulder. "And you're sure he ain't?"

Coburn set his Bible down. "You ever listen to Whitey, Pete?"

Axler scowled. "I ain't got much choice when I'm in his chair."

"Whitey supposes every politician ought to be shot or hung."

The lines deepened around Axler's eyes. "One can't argue with sound reasoning."

"True enough as far it goes," Deacon said abstractly. "Neither can one ever truly escape the shadows of yesteryear. We accumulate a history that follows us." He had his right hand cupped on his chin, half covering his mouth. He turned askance. "You tossed an innocent man in jail, Pete. I never seen hide or hair of Jondreau before he popped into the Alamo last evening, but I can vouch for him. He didn't do this killing."

"How on earth can you be so sure?"

"The dead man's name is Yance Rawlins. He used to be muscle for a corrupt judge in Santa Fe," Deacon explained, sadness scratching at his voice. "I don't know if he had any family or not." He remembered some of the last words Rawlins had ever spoken to him: *Scully will be coming after me with bloody vengeance in mind.* He puckered his mouth. "The killer has a big hitch in his giddy-up. A rough old horse-soldier with rusty guts named Jackson Scully."

"Walks with a limp? On his left side?"

"Yeah," Deacon answered, exhaling a long whistle of air. "The leg functions as if it was attached by some sawbones who skipped anatomy class."

"That accounts for the pattern in the dirt leading away from the stall," Pete said, removing his hat. He pushed back strands of wispy blond hair that were sticking on his forehead. "Would you be kind enough to tell me how you come equipped with all this knowledge?"

Coburn forced a chuckle that was ambiguous; puzzling, even. "A few years back Rawlins did right and crossed a line to help me and some friends in New Mexico. It put him against his boss and at odds with Scully. Undoubtedly that gallant act has now cost him his life."

"This was revenge?"

"Pure and simple revenge, Pete. You can bet on it."

"Why here? Why now?"

"Rawlins could have been coming to see me . . . to warn me."

Axler tilted his head, eyes narrowing. "Warn you of what?"

Coburn stared at him. "The killing ain't over, Pete. I'm a walking dead man."

"What in tarnation are you saying?"

"Scully is still here somewhere and I'm next in his sights," Deacon replied, cool and offhandedly. "The sovereign hand of God intervened on my behalf, but the clock is ticking."

"What do you mean about the sovereign hand of God?" Pete asked, skeptical.

Coburn's jaw clenched momentarily. When he spoke his voice had an unbending quality that was raw and icily intense. "Rawlins got dumped and concealed in a public place because Scully figured that when the body was discovered a crowd would gather. He counted on me being amongst those who'd run to see it. My guess is that Sam saved my life last night. Scully was surely hidden in a getaway spot ready to pull the trigger on me, but missed his chance because I didn't go to the livery. Sam stopped me. He wanted to talk."

"Why ain't that just a piece of luck, Deacon? Why bring God into it?"

Coburn grinned. "One has to believe in luck to benefit from it. I don't. Like the Psalmist David, I choose to throw all the faith I can on the Almighty's sovereignty."

Axler put his hat on. "I can't swim in that water. It's way too deep for me."

"My days are numbered. As are yours, Pete."

"I ain't the one who's got a bushwhacker after him."

Coburn picked up his Bible and stuck it under an arm. "I got living to do, Pete. I won't be looking over a shoulder any time soon. When death comes to me, I'll be ready." He took a few steps toward the door, then stopped and turned. "I'll take care of the coffin and set the burial for tomorrow. I owe Yance Rawlins that much and more." He exited in his usual steady gait.

On the thoroughfare, Deacon Coburn squashed tears as he walked to the jailhouse.

Whitey Fitzgerald had been busy since sunup. He was a tightly wound bundle of kinetic energy who was ever-ready to leap into the middle of whatever was happening. He always had to get the lowdown regarding the whys and wherefores of life in Abilene. His mouth never seemed to stop flapping. He was opinionated and could jawbone with all comers on any topic. When no one was around he would frequently carry on a two-way conversation with the four walls.

He was smallish in stature but large in charm and personality. He had a quick wit and an easy laugh that could defuse bigotry whenever it came calling. There was no subservience or grovel in him; he had carved out a niche in the white man's world without kowtowing. His complexion was high-yellow, his nappy hair snow-white, as were his eyebrows.

One client after another had been in, but just now, his chair was empty. His shop was never less than spic and span because at every lull in business he would get to it. He'd clean up spotless areas again and again, all the while yakking or making his click-click noise. It sounded like he was clucking at a horse to get it to hurry.

He had finished polishing the big mirror and was sweeping the floor when he heard footsteps on the boardwalk. He spun around, smiling cheerily. "Good afternoon, Samuel. Come in and sit a spell so as I can spice you up all dapper and distinguished." Among a host of other eccentricities, Whitey Fitzgerald *never* shortened a person's formal name.

Beadle took a seat in the barber's chair. "Shave me as slick and smooth as a baby's bottom, Whitey. I've got a buggy-ride with a lady in the morning."

Fitzgerald readied a hot towel. "You expect to do some smooching?"

"Not tomorrow. I'll be happy if she doesn't cut out my gizzard."

"Feisty, is she?"

Beadle nearly sparkled. "That she is, Whitey. She's the marrying kind."

Fitzgerald stopped in mid-action. He had been rapidly sliding a straight-razor against the thick leather strop. "Well, glory be! You best tell me more, Samuel."

"She came to town yesterday. She's Deacon's daughter."

"What you say?" Whitey exclaimed, eyes popping open. "The man was in here not more than two hours ago. He never said word one about a daughter." His face screwed into a wrinkly mask that appeared to instantly age him a decade or more. "I declare Deacon is an enigma. He's the best man I've ever known, but he doesn't let anybody get too close, does he?"

"A fairer assessment has never been made, but maybe that's a good thing. It might be dangerous to be too closely acquainted with him," Sam said dryly. "I saw Pete on the way over. Deacon identified the body." He filled Whitey in without embellishing the facts too much.

"Are you telling me the dead man was a friend of Deacon Coburn?"

"That I am. And the murderer is gunning for Coburn."

Fitzgerald was working swiftly, his hands deft and sure. "I won't be backing away from Deacon. I don't care how many desperado bandits line up against him. Gunslingers, pirates, or highwaymen best come loaded for bear. I'd stand beside him at the gates of hell."

"Me, too."

"I ain't saying he's a saint, but he doesn't make a pretense about it," Whitey went on, using the razor with a theatrical flourish. "He be walking the talk and he knows in his bones that he comes up short. He never passes judgment or makes one feel that hellfire's coming upon them. He's got time for everybody, no matter who they be." He gave an emphatic click-click.

He finished the job by liberally splashing bayberry-scented lotion on. "And the way he packs the Good Book into his head, the Lord Jesus loves him for sure." He stepped back holding up a hand mirror. "That lady best shine on you 'cause you look dandy."

Beadle got up. He pulled a cigar out of an inside pocket of his vest and handed it over as payment, which was the typical transaction between them. "There you go, my good man."

"Thank you kindly," Whitey said, setting the cigar on a shelf. "That'll be my sundown treat sitting out front on my porch. Then I'll do my necessaries and hit the sack in back. I sure do sleep fine after a good smoke and a productive squat. My bowels be as regular as sunshine."

Beadle was chuckling heartily as he departed. Fitzgerald followed him to the doorway and stood still for just a moment to enjoy the brightness of the day. He then went about cleaning the straight-razor, treating the instrument with care. When it was put away, he started sweeping.

In a short bit of time, a loud and angry epithet would seize his attention.

Sam Beadle was moving along with a bounce in his step and a song on his lips. He was humming softly, as pleased as pleased could be. He was less than a half-block from the barbershop when he saw Liam Greer heading in his direction. Sam pondered his options; he could ignore or confront him. He processed the consequence of his choice and proceeded.

He adjusted his angle and came face to face with him in the middle of the street. The to and fro of commercial pursuits never slowed or acknowledged them; pedestrians ignored their presence and riders trotted past. A creaky buckboard loaded with burlap sacks of seeds was parked closeby. The pair of oxen suffered the heat and flies as the teamster snoozed.

"Mr. Greer," Sam said, somewhat sternly. He looked directly in his eyes. "I'm glad I bumped in to you. I've got something you need to hear."

Greer gave him a smirking once-over. "Don't you smell fruity. I'm heading where you just came from because I've got a date with a lady. She awaits, so let me pass."

Beadle leaned in tighter. "Abbey Langton is off-limits to you."

"I don't know you and I don't care to," Liam replied hotly. "You better step aside or you'll be sorry you got out of bed this morning. I'll pound the living snot out of you."

"Not likely." Sam smiled thinly. "I'm merely giving you a friendly warning. This doesn't have to come to blows. No one has to get bloodied here. Stay clear of Abbey Langton."

Greer backed up a step. "Who made you the high and mighty master? Abbey and I had a connection last night. She's expecting me, so get outta my way."

"Surely you jest. I saw the tail-end of the connection you made with her."

Greer sneered and spat a ball of saliva that struck the dust with a *plop*. He bull-rushed, but missed him completely because Beadle nimbly sidestepped. Greer stumbled. He caught his balance, spun around with his fists thrust forward. He began bobbing his head and shoulders. He gave the appearance that he knew what he was doing.

Beadle put his left foot ahead of his right, toes turned slightly inward. He subtlety shifted his weight by coming up on the balls of his feet. His arms were loose at his sides, hands open. Greer tossed a quick right that caught nothing but air, followed by a careless left hook which sailed harmlessly over Beadle's head. Greer tried the combination again with the same result.

Beadle's patience, foot work, instincts, and experience were far too much for his opponent's aggressive style. It was obvious that he was toying with the younger man, using his skills and training to avoid having to buffet him. "I don't want to hurt you, Mr. Greer."

"Hurt me? Huh! Put up your mitts and fight."

"Or embarrass you."

"Fight and we'll see who gets embarrassed," Liam said excitedly. He danced and weaved close to him. "You lousy *bastard*!" he screamed, his voice rising to a shrill level.

He attacked in a tantrum, shouting and slobbering, deranged and manic. He unleashed a looping overhand right that a schoolboy could have avoided; Beadle did so by ducking and fading back. The punch had been thrown in such unfettered wildness that the follow-through took Greer careening into the hindquarters of an ox.

The animal was not impressed; neither was its yoked partner. Both beasts roared snorts and heaved sideways. The driver awakened and promptly began bellowing and yanking on the reins to pacify and control the team. Greer skidded to the ground, arms outstretched in an effort to stop his momentum. He came to rest face-first in a steaming patty of horse manure that had only recently been deposited on the avenue by a gray mare.

Beadle loomed over him. "Abbey Langton is off-limits. Make that a priority."

Greer cursed and sputtered. He jumped and ran off in the direction he had come. Jeers and laughter came from an assembly of onlookers on the boardwalk. The teamster had the oxen placated, and now, put the bovines to task; the wagon wheels squeaked complaints.

Sam Beadle wiped sweat off his brow. He spotted Whitey Fitzgerald on the stoop of his shop, his hands held up in a questioning gesture. Beadle responded with an animated expression. He was no longer as pleased as pleased could be. Regret and angst had him in its grip.

He guiltily lowered his eyes and walked sluggishly toward Drovers Cottage.

Charley Jondreau was sitting on the edge of the cot twiddling his thumbs. The box was poorly ventilated. He was breathing shallowly. His cell was on the eastern side of the lockup; the afternoon daylight coming through the grated window was somber and dwindling. When Deacon Coburn entered from the outer office there was a trifling influx of air.

Jondreau pointed at the book under his arm. "Are you planning on doing some Bible reading to me, preacher-man? I understand many of those words, eh."

Coburn fingered his moustache and smiled. "Then perhaps you can explain a selection of difficult passages to me. I'm always open to deeper enlightenment."

"I doubt I could help a scholar like you," Charley said, tongue-in-cheek. "I only attended Reverend Winger's school for a few years. I learned reading, writing, 'rithmetic, and religion. He was a meticulous taskmaster, but he had a good heart and gentle soul."

"That's a likeable combination in a man."

"You own those same qualities, preacher-man."

"I appreciate your kindness."

"It ain't kindness," Charley rejoined sincerely. "I see what I see."

Coburn frowned hard. Deep lines dipped low on his forehead. He rubbed his cheeks, wondering if he was mistaken. He thought long and hard before finally speaking. "Do we have some common history? Have we had past dealings that I'm not remembering?"

"No. I see what I see."

Coburn rested a hand on the bars. "Tell me more."

"That Greer kid is a bad seed."

"What makes you say that?"

"I know. I have *seen* him."

Something in the man's precise cadence startled Coburn. "What?"

"I've *seen* him." Jondreau pushed his hat back and tapped his temple three times. "Hear me for I have *seen* what grows in his heart, Coburn. He plans to bed your daughter. He likely made a play for it last night, though she isn't really your daughter, is she?"

Coburn's eyes blinked uncomfortably. "Who are you?"

"Charley Jondreau." He stood and stepped close to him. He pressed his face between the bars. "Iroquois blood flows in my veins, as ancient as the stones. I have been where you have not been. I have seen what you have not seen. An eagle screamed on the day of my birth. It soared above the village and set watch over it many days. The Great Spirit poured a miracle into me." He returned to the cot and sat. "Abbey Langton is not from your loins. No chance."

"She's the only daughter I'll ever have." Deacon was uncompromising. "I'm obligated to all that is righteous to treat and care for her as though she was my offspring."

"You will do so, Deacon Coburn. She will be by your side when you die."

"I trust those words. They are straight and narrow."

Jondreau raised a hand. "Liam Greer has evil in him."

"As do we all."

"You cut capers and make merry with me, eh?"

"When conversing about good and evil I do not make merry," Deacon answered tersely. "The sin nature is in us. No one is without its imprint and effect. Some are overcome by it, while others, by God's grace, have a measure of success keeping it at bay."

"Ah, the two wolves within, good and evil," Charley said, hands coming together. He began twiddling his thumbs again, slow and methodically. "Liam Greer only feeds the evil one for he feels its strength and power.

There will be great sorrow wherever his trail leads. Many hearts will be pierced. I see much more. He *wants* to be evil."

"Then we must intervene," Deacon replied, leaning forward. His face was tense, his shoulders ramrod stiff. "We must come alongside him to bring healing or reform."

"Greer's not capable of being healed or reformed. He's unredeemable."

Coburn drew back. "No one's unredeemable."

"Bullspit."

"No one's unredeemable," Deacon repeated adamantly. The rigidity of his comportment revealed unwavering conviction. "No one is beyond the reach of God's love."

"That one is unredeemable. He's a mass of twisted evil."

Coburn wagged his head vigorously. He took a few steps back. He removed the Bible from under his arm and held it against his right thigh. His dark eyes showed calmness and a grin appeared to relax him. "Where will you go when Pete cuts you loose?"

Jondreau shrugged. "Wherever the hawk flies, I will follow."

"And if there is no hawk?"

"There's always a hawk. Perchance I must wait for it."

"You will wait this time," Deacon stated pointblank. "You are here for a purpose."

Jondreau studied him. He fixed his jaw in its bulldog position. "Edify me."

"You *see* what you see," Deacon said, snappish and testily. "You *see* a runny-nosed mutt whose heart is twisted by evil. I say untwist him. Rescue him from the path that leads to destruction. Mayhap like Esther of old, you have come to Abilene *for such a time as this*."

"You seek to push me with the Old Testament?"

"For what reason did the Great Spirit pour a miracle into you?" Deacon volleyed back with a curt and demanding intensity. "What compelled you to tell me about it?"

The inference rapped on Jondreau's conscience, but he remained passive. He chafed his hands together as he contemplated the challenge, neither accepting nor rejecting it. "Thanks for the visit, preacher-man," he said, lying down on the cot. "I must nap now."

Coburn tipped him a nod and departed. When the door clanked shut, Jondreau got to his feet and began pacing, slowly at first, but the tempo soon quickened. His heartbeat was calm and regular, but the velvety hair on the nape of his neck was goosed up.

Alone, his mind came alive with pro and con arguments, which he attempted to rationally analyze. Commonsense said that as soon as possible he should get saddled up and be gone for he had nothing at stake here. There was no upshot for him, yet he couldn't easily circumnavigate the virtue and inflexibility of his code. His arms were knotted tightly across his chest.

Round and round he went in the ten-by-ten cubicle, a man at odds with himself.

"The answer is still no, Jackson. Quit haranguing me."

At sundown, Jackson Scully had snuck into town. He had done so for two reasons. First he wanted to have a lusty bedroom romp with Flora; then when fully sated he intended to secure a hidey-hole near the Alamo Saloon and lie in wait to satisfy his vengeance.

It was now full dark. He should be on the move, but instead he sat at Flora's table picking over the remains on his plate. Pale, flickering light came from a dozen aromatic candles arranged around the room. She had prepared him a splendid meal, but there had been no hanky-panky.

She had rebuffed him, and done so with authority. All the while he ate he made innuendo laced comments, but she was pokerfaced. Her refusal confused him, but his blood was up and he had no inkling to be denied without forcing the issue.

"Let's have at it, girly-girl," he said, gruffly tender. "Your know-how in the kitchen matches your skills in the bedroom. The chicken and dumplings were tasty, but I'm here to beat the sheets with you. If you ever expect me to run off with you and start a new life, you're going to have to deliver the goods whenever I come a-calling."

Flora laughed. "Is that an ultimatum? You obviously do not get it, Jackson."

"Get what?" he asked angrily.

"Perhaps I need to be more specific about particulars. I am changing my life, with or without you, Jackson. Either way the changes have already begun," she replied, tossing her hair back. She still wore the high-collared, dull-colored dress that she'd put on early in the day. "If it's without you, from this moment on we are friends and nothing more."

"Friends? Are you serious?"

"I've never been more serious, Jackson," she answered, incisive and final. She held her eyes on him as she shifted forward on the hard-backed chair. "If, however, you want to make a future with me, then my bedroom and all those affairs are forbidden until we are married."

"Forbidden? Married? What the hell!"

"Those are nonnegotiable terms."

His mood blackened. "You never said anything about marriage yesterday."

"Yesterday was yesterday. I made my decision today."

"Well, you can unmake it now," he said, a reservoir of ugly in his glare. His mouth was a teeth-clenched gash in a setting of gray whiskers; it was a bilious and ill-tempered look. He started striking an index finger against the table top. "Strip out of that idiotic school-marm outfit and quit jerking me around. I came here to do you and do you good. Let's get to it."

"No. I am going to be a different person, Jackson."

His hands fisted. "Did you get religion?"

She stared at him, firm and unmoved. "I had religion once. I had faith long ago and far away, but lost it. I'm looking and have been praying to find it again."

"I've got me a holy whore."

"Don't mock me, Jackson. It's not at all funny."

He gave her a crazy-eyed grin. "You're a whore, Flora."

"Not anymore. Not in any way will I trade my body," she said insistently. "I won't do it for money, friendship, or nothing ever again. I am going to be a different person."

"I ain't asking you to trade your body for anything," he replied, slouching forward. "I always ramble back to you. I thought we had something special."

"You mean our pleasant thing?" she queried sarcastically. "Flings in the sack whenever you so please? You just called me a whore, Jackson. That doesn't sound *special* to me."

"Get off your high frigging horse, woman!" he shouted, slamming a fist against the table. "You're a whore and I'm a damn circus buffoon pretending to be a man." He stood and limped over to her. He knelt, his left leg angled awkwardly. He exhaled a weary sigh and softened his expression. "What we got is what it is, Flora. Don't piss on it or throw it away."

"It can be better. We can be better."

"No we can't. We are what we are, Flora. Our nature can't be changed."

She peered deep into his red-rimmed eyes. "That's too dreary an outlook for me. I will not accept it as a possibility any longer. I know better." She put a hand on his shoulder. "Deep inside me I know better. I wasn't raised to be a whore. I believed lies and have been lying to myself all these years." Her lips quivered slightly. She took a frail breath. "I was betrayed and misled. I deceived myself, but the lying and deception has reached its end."

"You're one nutty fruitcake, woman." He used her knees and the table for leverage to get to his feet. He shambled over and slumped onto his chair. "I ain't presently ready to give you a decision. That marrying talk screwed my thinking to a standstill."

"I won't back away from it, Jackson."

"I have unfinished business to attend to here."

She folded her hands in her lap. "I'm done waiting. I'm making my plans and will not be delayed any longer. The proposal is simple enough. Will you marry me so we can make a new life together? Or am I to plow into the future all by myself?"

"Ain't you a hard one," he said contemptuously. "I told you that I'd think on all this after I finished doing a job. You may have been stewing on this for a long while, but the idea was just sprung on me twenty-four hours ago. And the marrying part of the deal is fresh. What other surprises might there be? I need time to figure and decipher details."

"What can be more important than a new beginning?"

"There's a preacher needs killing first."

She sat up straight, wary. "A preacher?"

He scowled at her, presumably unsure of what he heard in her voice. "I don't know for certain if he's a preacher or not. He's a Bible reading troublemaker named Coburn."

Her reaction was panicky. "No!" She sprang to her feet, eyes large and worried.

"What? You know him?"

She bore in on him. "How could he have ever conceivably wronged you?"

"Coburn put the kibosh on the sweetest deal I ever had."

She stood over him. "I don't care, Jackson. I forbid you to harm Deacon Coburn."

"You forbid me?" He roared laughter. Spittle sprayed the air.

She waited. The green in her eyes was fiery. "He's a friend of mine."

He chuckled scornfully. "A former customer, was he?"

"Never once," she said, strong and terse. "Not that I didn't give it a try."

He tugged on his beard. "We have us an impasse here."

"No, we don't," she replied coolly. "You will not kill Deacon Coburn."

"The hell you say?" His right hand knotted and he shook it at her. "No woman commands me, so pound salt up your arse. I'll do what I damn well please."

"Listen to me, Jackson Scully," she said, without flinching or hesitating. The lines of her face were drawn taut and frigid. "You will cease pursuing Deacon Coburn. If you do not, I will go to the law. Your name will be known, along with a detailed description."

"Son of a pig!" His eyes were swollen. A vinegary odor came off him; bitter rage seemed to be seeping from his sweat glands. "Is that a bluff, or do you mean it for a real play?"

She cautiously inched closer to him. "I swear it's a real play, Jackson. And I won't back down. As long as I'm alive if anything untoward happens to Deacon Coburn—if a boulder drops on him from a blue sky—I'll be pointing whatever law I can in your direction."

His face was disfigured by a menacing grimace. His eyes roamed over her body, longing and disgust in them. "I ought to slit open your belly and let you bleed out on the floor."

She showed defiance. "If that's your pleasure, make it quick."

He glowered and quaked. He exploded, repeatedly pounding both fists against the table as a rasping noise tore from his throat. A tall candle in the decorative centerpiece tipped over; liquid wax spread across the linen tablecloth, followed by creeping flames.

"Stop it!" she yelled, grabbing hold of his sleeve.

He shook her off and cursed her to damnation. With a vicious sweep of an arm, the plate and utensils in front of him went flying across the room. He hopped up and chucked the table over. It crashed and glassware shattered. He hooted a chilling scream of a laugh. He shoved her out of the way as he stormed past. She shivered when the backdoor thudded shut.

She busily snuffed out the fire. Crouching in the midst of the mess, with stinking smoke tickling her nostrils, she stifled a cry. Hot, angry tears filled her eyes, but no murmur came from her lips. She heard him abuse his horse. It whinnied loudly. She felt sorry for the animal.

When Daniel Twosongs arrived in Abilene, the boney white and pockmarked moon was high in a starry sky. He had spoken to the first person he came upon and received directions. Now he was walking along Cedar Street on his way to the Alamo Saloon. Thumping hoofbeats were coming up behind him. A heckle and holler caused him to spin around, stepping aside to allow a cowboy on a black horse to gallop past.

The man was hunkered low in the saddle, his face pressed against the animal's neck. His right hand was continuously whipping the horse's sweat-lathered rump. A bewailing outcry and plumes of dust trailed him. Twosongs only had a fleeting glimpse. Despite the insufferable heat, he felt a frosty sliver of goosepimples form along his spine.

His belly cramped. He hadn't seen the face, but discerned it was no run of the mill cowhand. The rider's bearing and conduct was familiar; in his guts he knew that the man on horseback was the one who'd put him on the mission that brought him here. He winced. He adjusted his bedroll on his shoulder. The peddler of death had vanished into the darkness.

Twosongs strode directly to his destination. He moved in a rapid bandy-legged gait that conveyed confidence and a can-do attitude. He waltzed into the barroom without an ounce of tentativeness. A haze of bluish smoke clouded the air. The place had a fair-sized crowd, but it was a quiet night, uninterrupted by rowdies. He spotted his friend exactly where he'd been told to find him; alone at a back corner table reading by the light of an oil lamp.

He approached him on cat's feet. "Good to see you above snakes, preacher."

Coburn's head jolted up. His eyes flooded with emotion. A smile encompassed his face in cheerful wrinkles. "Ain't time for me to be a croaker just yet. I've been waiting to die all my life," he said wryly. "I would suppose that I got some more waiting to do."

Twosongs removed his flat-brimmed hat and put it on the back of a chair. "The wise man lives with death every day, while the fool chases the transient pleasures of this world."

Coburn stood. The men clasped hands and peered into each other's eyes, respect and affection passing wordlessly between them. When the handshake ended, Twosongs stretched by bending low to place his belongings on the floor. He arched his back before taking a seat.

"Jackson Scully is on a killing spree," Daniel stated flat-out. "He gut-shot Gray Eyes from a distance and left him to die in the desert. He's tracking Yance Rawlins . . ."

"He got Rawlins," Deacon cut in, head wagging in sadness. "The gravediggers will be working at dawn. We'll plant him under the sod mid-morning or so."

Twosongs pushed both hands through his shoulder-length black hair and twined his fingers together behind his head. "I'd like the opportunity to say a few words."

"Surely," Deacon replied, nodding. "Why kill Gray Eyes? He was a gentle old man with a wise and seasoned soul. Why would he murder Gray Eyes?"

"He's Jackson Scully and he enjoys killing." Twosongs dropped his hands to his lap. "He is an instrument of the prince of darkness and debauched by revenge."

Coburn had his elbows on the table. "I reckon that's accurate."

"He has you targeted. He even took a couple potshots at me," Daniel reported, giving an easy shrug. "Scully has a sickness that eats away at him. He feeds it with hate. It grows stronger each day, intoxicating venom in his bloodstream infecting all he does. There is darkness and light in the world. Revenge is a disease of the darkness; it kicks and rages against the light."

"True enough, but why murder Gray Eyes?" Deacon asked urgently. "I understand the vengeance enacted on Rawlins. I even accept Scully wanting me dead, but Gray Eyes?"

"I knew Gray Eyes many years. He taught me unchangeable truth older than the fossils. He despised evil and always stood against it. He had pride. He had compassion. He gave away all that the Creator poured out to him," Daniel said, much fondness in his voice. "Evil cannot ever tolerate good. Scully killing Gray Eyes was evil momentarily triumphing over good." He exhaled a sigh. "Sally Twosongs saw it in a dream before it happened."

Coburn bent forward. "Tell me of Sally Twosongs. She is well?"

"She is a princess," Daniel replied, pride flashing in his coal-colored eyes. "Her beauty can make me weep in wonder. She is a gifted learner of bygone years. There is awesome light and good in her. She stands strong. Her heart overflows with empathy and passion. Consuelo is convinced Sally Twosongs is a prophetess. I do not disagree."

Coburn was listening attentively. He motioned for his friend to continue.

"Her prayers have power. Her dreams come from beyond the chasm between time and eternity," Daniel said earnestly. "Sally Twosongs saw Gray Eyes bleeding to death amongst the sagebrush before a bullet was even put in him. She sent me to intercede, but I was prevented from getting there in time. Evil intervened to stop me." He spoke with an ordinary sincerity that was gripping and forceful. "A skinwalker in the form of an oversized crow attacked me. It was savage. I filled it with lead from my Winchester, but it kept coming at me. I had another encounter with that brutish skinwalker after Scully shot my horse and put me a-foot. In that instance the One who watches over me sent three wolves to protect and rescue me."

"Our battle is never against mere flesh and blood."

"Our enemy comes only to kill, steal, and destroy," Daniel answered, head bobbing. "We conquer evil by continuing to do good. I got to Gray Eyes shortly after he passed. Warmth still lingered in his body. He had written the name of his killer in the sand."

"That's it then, Daniel. We will not faint or be weary. We will conquer by continuing or we will be transferred to glory," Deacon said blandly. "Any news from the Weitzels?"

Twosongs chuckled. "Hans and Eliza are fiddling fine. Their farmstead has sheep, goats, chickens, cattle, and horses. The grandson of Gray Eyes works for them now. He is Gray Cloud, which describes him. He is pessimistic to the core, but puts muscle to every task."

"What of Caleb?"

"He is his father's son. A man with a vision for what he wants," Daniel replied, eyebrows rising to crease his brow. "He has made several scouting trips to the Colorado Territory. I rode along with him once. He has his sights set on a parcel of land. He's culling out a prime starter herd with plans to drive them north and build a horse ranch in Colorado."

Contemplative melancholy showed in Coburn's eyes. "Colorado," he whispered, fingering his moustache. "If Caleb Weitzel settles there it'll give me a reason to revisit that country." He closed his Bible and glanced around the barroom. "The day ended too long ago for us to still be here. Come back to my boardinghouse. A room with a soft bed awaits you."

Daniel Twosongs was agreeable. The companions sallied forth together.

On this night, not another word was spoken between them.

Pete Axler was in a foul mood, a rare occurrence to be sure. A toothache had awakened him in the middle of the night and sleep refused to return. He had tossed and turned for over an hour before finally getting up and dressed. There had been no warning; the pain began as a dull throb that became piercing stabs without any rhyme or reason he could fathom.

He had tried picking at it. He had packed a whiskey soaked cloth against it. There had even been stressed out moments when he had his mouth open with a mirror in one hand and a knife in the other. The candlelight was too poor for him to see clearly enough to even scrape it, let alone attempt some haphazard extraction.

Now, with the sun rising on a new day, he headed to the jailhouse with the scent of liquor thick on his breath. Desperate for just a residue of comfort or relief he had taken three shots of bourbon for breakfast. His jaw hurt enough to make his pale eyes watery. Always a slow-mover, he was even more so this morning. Folks out and about doing chores or running errands noticed his gawky look and halting pace.

He entered the office. A fellow deputy was at the desk, his feet propped up on it and his hat pulled low over his eyes. The slumbering man grouched a greeting to him, which Axler brusquely returned. He got the ring of keys and went straight to the cell holding the man who had drawn on him. The lock was contrary. He had to wiggle and jiggle the key for what seemed to him to be several minutes before he could pull the door open.

He leaned a shoulder against the iron doorjamb. "You're free to go."

Jondreau was squatted comfortably on the cot, his legs crossed and his back against the red-brick wall. "So then, you decide I am innocent, eh? No judge, no trial, buddy-boy?"

"Innocent of murder," Pete said, "but guilty of carrying a firearm."

Jondreau didn't move. "I am a bad man. Don't put out a wanted poster on me."

Axler ignored the comment. "I saw to the care of your horse. That's a superb animal."

"The pony's got smarts and spunk, but it's not for sale at any price."

"I already know that," Pete said, eyes flinching edgily.

Jondreau regarded him. He blinked rapidly. "Cloves."

"Let's go," Pete ordered grumpily.

Jondreau stood and smiled. "Whiskey drinks fine, but cloves are better."

"Let's go," Pete repeated, squinting in confusion. "What?"

"Use cloves for the toothache," Charley replied, adjusting his floppy-brimmed hat. "Place a clove on the sore tooth and bite on it for twenty minutes or so. If it don't pain too much chew on the clove until it's mushy. It'll bring numbness to the area."

"Toothache? How'd you know?" Pete asked, befuddled. "Cloves?"

Jondreau held his hands up and gave him an ambivalent shrug. "Any decent general store should have them in stock. By the tautness of your jaw you better lay in a good supply. You're agonizing and sweating like a prostitute at a fire and brimstone meeting."

Axler frowned crookedly. "Cloves, huh? I never heard of such a thing."

"It is medicine that'll help in a pinch," Charley said, taking a step closer to him. "You can always chomp on a second piece if the pain persists, but getting the rotten tooth yanked is likely your only real remedy. It's something for you to consider, Pete Axler."

The lanky lawman was taken aback. He rubbed his bristly chin as he attempted to read and measure the man. "Thank you for the information. I will put it to use." He sidled out of the doorway. "Do you have any plans? Are you leaving town?"

"Maybe," Charley said with a grin. "Maybe not. Am I *free* to go or what?"

"Your revolver will be kept under lock here until you're ready to ride. I got no say in the matter," Pete told him, almost apologetically. "That's how the ordinance works, especially when it has been violated. Do you want your knife?"

"Leave it on the belt," Charley replied indifferently. "I'll return to get the pistol, the holster, and the knife. Keep them safe until then, eh?" He edged past him and exited.

Axler returned the key-ring to its bureau drawer. He then followed Jondreau outside. He watched and waited in the bright sunshine, his right palm rammed against his jaw. The skin on that side of his face was hot and sensitive. Jondreau disappeared around a corner.

Axler shifted his gaze in the opposite direction. He took in details of the street. Though still early there were groups of loiterers and habitués congregating at the usual and customary storefront vantage points to chinwag, speculate, and take in the consequential and insignificant comings and goings. He pushed his hat up and groaned when he stepped off the boardwalk.

Pete Axler headed to Moon's Frontier Store with plans to purchase a load of cloves.

Flora stopped and swayed in her footsteps, but not soon enough. She was distracted by the untamed wanderings of her thoughts. She came out of her daze and gasped when she bumped into a solidly built man hurrying along. He had his hands in his pockets and his head lowered, his face hidden by the drooping brim of his headgear.

"Excuse me, sir," she said, flustered and stuttering a bit. Their eyes connected and locked for an extreme instant. The swarthy man relentlessly probed her with a penetrating scrutiny. She hitched in a startled breath. His eyelids pulsated strangely. She was unnerved.

He pushed a mellow smile at her. "All is well, eh? Hope is always nearby, as sure as thunder follows lightning. Search your heart. Hope is there to lead you onward." He brushed past; as he did so a hand purposefully gave her forearm a firm squeeze.

Her mouth gaped open. She covered it, her eyes on the man as he continued on his way. Her fingers bopped over her lips. She was flabbergasted. Her brain was spinning. She had never experienced such a happenstance and was baffled by it. His words plucked a chord in her soul, but were also disconcerting. Just now she deemed them to be bizarre and meaningless.

She was suddenly aware that others were gawking at her. She had been walking around town since sunrise unable to loosen or be free of the complicated feelings clogging up her mind. Some of those in the roadway audience had been passed more than once on her circuitous route. The eyes currently prying at her held no comfort or sympathy.

Flora intentionally met the stares head-on. The smile that filled her face was impressive in its geniality. "Would any of you care to perambulate with me on this fine morning?" she asked, joyfully inviting. The only response forthcoming was raised eyebrows and condemning daggers tossed at her. "You all be sure to have a lovely day." Her gracious expression enlarged. She dipped her head in a kindly fare thee well, then returned to her stroll.

Her colorful sunbonnet was flowery, as was the conservatively cut dress. The pleats of the skirt were billowy and distinctive. She moved along and sorted through all the clutter in her head. Her right hand cramped. She hadn't realized it but the fingers wrapped around the handle of her purse were stringently compressed. She relaxed her grip. The spasm passed.

She didn't have any particular place to go. She was simply attempting to be brave and keep a clear eye on the changes she intended to embody. She had the notion that putting Deacon Coburn's advice into practice would strengthen her determination: *Don't you duck your head to anyone. Walk these streets with your head held high and your heart bowed low in humility.*

Liam Greer kept popping to the forefront of her mind. The pain she had inflicted on him was enormous; she could easily get inside of it because she had been intimate with abandonment and worse. The idea of reconciliation was not a foreign concept to her. She innately understood that to go forward she first had to repair broken fences, of which there were many. Her past was littered with hurts and failures. She wasn't sure how to proceed.

She was on Texas Street. She had just gone past McInerny's Boot & Saddle Shop. She turned around and saw her son a half block away coming in her direction. Her heart jumped. Heaviness filled her lungs. She wanted to flee. The urge was tremendously tempting; it burned inside her. She squelched it. She seized the moment by directly approaching him.

"May we visit, Liam?" she asked, blocking his path.

Greer shuffled his feet. "Hot, isn't it?" He looked at her with blank-eyed inquisitiveness, as though he didn't even recognize her. "We ain't got nothing to say to each other."

"Indulge me. Please, Liam."

"I got shopping to do." He pointed to the leather goods store.

"Liam, please. There are some things I need to tell you."

He had a large chaw of tobacco in his cheek. He spat a runner of juice that splattered near the hem of her garment. "I ain't interested in anything you have to say to me."

"I'm not the monster you think I am."

"I don't think you're a monster. I know you're a whore."

Her shoulders sagged. She fought to maintain an even emotional keel. "Yes, I *was* a whore. I cannot deny any of what is behind me. I have no excuses. And I do not expect you to forgive me any time soon, but I want you to know that I am sorry for all the wrong I inflicted on you." Her voice was soft and vulnerable. "It was a mistake for me to leave you."

"Why did you?"

"I was lost, Liam."

He sneered and spat another gob of brown gunk at her feet. "What's that mean?"

"I was messed up and confused. It was a dark, dark place to be." She inched closer to him. "In a way I did to you what was done to me by another," she said honestly. "You deserved better than me. Jack Greer was also much worthier of better than I had to offer."

He shifted the wad from one cheek to the other. His head was uncovered, his face tanned and the patches of peach-fuzz bleached by the sun. He seemed to soften. "Until not so many years ago I thought you were dead. Pa told me you died when I was born."

"Perhaps the lie should've been true."

He gave her a cockeyed smirk. "Maybe that would've been best for all concerned."

She exhaled a shaky sigh. "I've thought the same more than once." She looked straight at him. "I floundered in a chaotic maze for a long time. I was lost and afraid, Liam."

He slouched. His eyes narrowed and grew murky. "I know what that's like, I think."

She smiled; it was small and sympathetic. "My feelings were jumbled, my perspective and outlook jangled. I couldn't find my way back to who I was and took so many wrong turns."

He hunched his shoulders. "I suppose that's something, but it don't help me at all."

"I am sorry, Liam," she said openly. "I own all the poor choices and errors in my life. I live with the consequences of them every day. I am ashamed of so much."

"Thanks for saying so, I guess."

She crept closer. Impulsively, in a hesitant and unsteady motion, she put a hand on his shoulder. "I haven't changed all I would like to yet, but I know I'm not the same."

He bolted backwards several steps. "You can't have it!" he shouted, eyes tight and thin. His body was rigid, his hands flexing. "I know what you're up to, woman. You're setting a trap for me, but I wised up. I won't be duped by a whore." He padded around her in a half-crouch, like a starving predator readying for a kill.

"I have no tricks, no wiles . . ."

"Shut up, whore!" His hostility was tangible; a spiked club bludgeoning her again and again. Every word was another blow that struck and sliced sure and true. "I ain't going to let you lead me on. I ain't no green-horn. And you're nothing but a used up harlot looking to score." He was still circling her, hands claw-like and trembling. "You ain't going to get it."

"What?" She was scared and genuinely mystified.

"The silver case is mine. You . . . can't . . . have . . . it!" Each syllable raised an octave higher and came with a spray of sticky spittle. His shallow chest was huffing and puffing. He swirled the chunk of tobacco around his mouth, then discharged it at her. The slick and slobbery slop splashed across the front of her dress, striking bosom high and upward.

Flora was aghast. She backpedaled slowly and held her composure in check. She thumbed a trickle of gluey slime off her chin. "I only wanted to apologize," she said, mild and evenly. She turned and walked away, his curses hurting her ears. She glanced back at him.

He grabbed his crotch, outrageously obscene. She whipped her head around, flushed and bleary-eyed. She quickened her footsteps. That lewd image of him would stay with her. It was the last time she would place eyes on him standing upright. She would weep for him; she would pray for him; she would have nightmares about him, but never again would she see him alive.

Old Blue loped and frolicked beside them. The buggy and unflappable mule, rented for the day from Ed Gaylord's Twin Livery, rolled west of town at an effortless speed. Sam Beadle, an eager-beaver suitor, held the reins loose and acted the part of a tour guide. He regaled the lady with true though slightly aggrandized accounts about the area's history.

Abbey Langton sat cheerful and happy, careful to keep six inches of space between them on the bench. Her golden-brown hair was braided in coils and gathered beneath a tall sunhat with an oval-shaped brim. A matching parasol was balanced on a shoulder. It was fringed by purple ribbons, which fluttered lazily.

The sun was straight above them in a bluer than blue sky that had no end. They had been riding along steadily for two hours, chatting and enjoying the goodness of the day. He was a natural-born storyteller; she a rapt learner and listener. Their buggy-ride across the grassy prairie traversed the territory between strangers and friendship, on its way to becoming something more.

He slowed and halted at the crest of a rise. He extended an arm toward a brushy thicket of willows a few hundred yards below them. "There's a creek in the middle of that grove. It's a tiny tributary of the Saline River." He lifted a barrel-like canteen from under the seat, uncorked it and took a swig. "With the heatwave and lack of rainfall it may be nothing more than a dry bed of gravelly dust, but we can walk and stretch our legs some." He offered her the container.

She accepted it with a grateful smile. She wiped off the spout and drank her fill. "Thank you, Mr. Beadle. The walk is a peachy idea. My bottom could use the rest."

He was grinning as he took another drink. "Mine, too." He returned the canteen to its spot and spoke encouragingly to the mule. Old Blue barked twice and ran on ahead of them.

They rode downhill in silence. He chose a shady place to park. Much of the creek-bed was cracked and parched, but a three-foot or so wide rivulet remained in its middle. It was still and to a certain extent stagnant, but would do. He unhitched the mule and led it to the water. Old Blue was splashing around and making growling noises. He hushed the dog. It obeyed.

Abbey studied the noteworthy willows. Clusters of them lined both banks of the creek. The hollow was secluded and hidden from the grassland by a staggered wall of fifteen-foot high trees. She plucked a few silver-gray leaves and smelled them.

"They call them coyote willows," he said, watching her. "Not sure why."

She whirled around, her face shining brightly and her skirts flowing. "This is so weird. It reminds me of a grove of black willows along Mad River in Ohio. Mom and I picnicked there in the springtime before she got sick. It's a favorite memory of mine."

"Was Deacon with you then?" he asked, rather tentatively. He staked the mule behind the buggy, giving it sufficient line to roam and munch. Old Blue was snuggled in and dozing.

She pinched a bittersweet smile at him. "No," she replied plainly. "He left us during the winter of '64. Mom died early summer '69." She adjusted her angle to search his face with a prolonged look. "You do realize that he's not my biological father, don't you?"

"No," he admitted, "I hadn't put that together yet."

"What kind of newshound are you?" She giggled a laugh as they fell into walking along side by side. "He's the only father figure I've ever had," she said, eyes aimed off in the distance.

He kept his mouth shut, prompting her with a looping wave of a hand.

She sighed and shrugged. "Mom's people were clannish, from some remote hamlet in Kentucky. They disowned her when she ran off and married George Langton. He was a tinker and fixer handyman from the big city. Cincinnati bred and born, an only child and something of an entrepreneurial street urchin, or so I was told." She tilted her head, eyebrows peaked and brow furrowed. "My parents were going to build a kind of paradise farm and raise a bunch of children, but providence or kismet or fluky chance foreordained a whole other deal."

"Life has a way of doing whatsoever it pleases," he said tonelessly. It sounded like some philosophical observation by an academic. They were following the course of the creek, making sure to stay in the relative coolness of the shade. There was considerable distance between them. Each time he edged in closer she subtly but surely took sidesteps away from him.

"Pa died four days before I was born." Her voice broke ever so slightly. "Deacon came along when I was nine. He was kind and gentle and benevolent. Apparently he and Mom fell in love and had something special, but I didn't pick up on any of it. If he is now saying that I am his daughter that's just fine with me. I will gladly receive his guidance and protective influence." She snapped the parasol closed and poked it at him. "What about you, Mr. Beadle?"

"Me? I consider Deacon to be a good friend."

"Don't be a smart aleck."

He stopped. He turned and motioned for them to head back. He again attempted to sidle up to her, but she nimbly evaded his effort. He held his hands out and gave her a wide-eyed shrug. "Not much to tell," he said flippantly. "I read lots, write lots, and have itchy feet."

"How well traveled are you?"

"On a map it'd be a zigzagging line from eastern Pennsylvania to here."

"That line isn't complete, is it?"

"I certainly hope not. Dodge City beckons just now."

"Your plan is to go there before summer ends, correct?"

"That's in my mind, yes."

"So I'm just a summertime conquest? A notch on your belt?"

His hands shot up in surrender. "No, not at all, Miss Langton."

"Then what are your intentions with me, Mr. Beadle?"

He froze in his tracks and eyed her. "What do you really ask?"

She regarded him stiffly. "How many other ladies have you brought to this spot?"

"None," he answered at once.

"You ought not to tell fibs, Mr. Beadle."

"I swear, Miss Langton."

"You've never tried to woo another woman?"

"Not here," he said, his manner growing sad. "I pursued a lady in Pittsburgh. I thought it was serious, but she had some funny ideas about love and life. She had other boyfriends."

"Am I to believe you've never *been* with a woman?"

He went red in the face. "That's inappropriate, Miss Langton."

"Inappropriate or not, Mr. Beadle, it's a question for which I'll have an answer," she said, in a severe and demanding tone. "I only have one heart and will not allow it off its leash for the amusement of someone with the traits of a philanderer."

He swallowed hard, cheeks still ruddy. "I am unsure of what to say."

"The truth is always a good policy," she replied softly. They were coming to where the buggy was parked. She knelt and called Old Blue. The dog rolled over onto its paws and ran to her. She hugged its neck and gave its sides a rubdown as it tried to lick her face.

He pursed his lips. Flecks of agitation showed in his eyes. He rubbed his hands together and nervously surveyed the vicinity, evidently wanting to make sure they were alone. "I am inexperienced, Miss Langton." He crouched to be on eye level with her. "What about you?"

"Beg pardon?" She read his face and feigned shock, fanning herself. "Why, Mr. Beadle, aren't you the impertinent one. How dare you ask a lady such a thing?"

"Sass for sass, ma'am. You know what's said of the goose and the gander."

"I do not play games, mister," she said tartly. "Be assured that I've never given my heart to anyone. As you say, I too am inexperienced and we shall not speak of such matters again."

He nodded and suppressed a grin. He popped up and went to work hitching the mule. It gave a short neigh in complaint at having its feeding time interrupted, but was accommodating. The beast swished its tail and twitched its ears as the harness was secured.

She nudged Old Blue away. The dog yapped and whined contentedly. She stood and looked around. Her face was pensive, eyes soft. "This would be a fabulous location for a picnic."

"Shall we plan on it some time?"

"Yes, let's do." She took an easygoing gait to the passenger side of the buggy and waited. He scooted over and offered to help. She accepted his hand. While balancing the parasol, she boldly placed her other hand on his shoulder as she stepped up and sat. "Thank you, Sam."

His mouth momentarily tightened. His eyes glinted with sparkles and his lips formed an engrossing smile. "You're welcome, Abbey." He fairly skipped around the buggy as if he was on air. He hopped onto the seat. "You do know I'm going to marry you, don't you?"

"Why, Mr. Beadle, you certainly are presumptuous."

"Not presumptuous at all, Miss Langton," he said, peering directly into her pretty eyes.

"What would you call such an audacious statement, Sam?"

"Tell me I'm wrong, Abbey."

She opened the parasol and rolled her eyes at him. "I will not argue or contest the issue at this juncture, Mr. Samuel H. Beadle," she said with prim formality. "I will, however, tell you that I have high standards and expectations, so tread prudently and be watchful." She parted her lips in an exquisite smile that cut to the marrow and did him in. He was finished, love-struck.

On the return to Abilene he noted that she sat a smidgeon closer to him.

Liam Greer was fully provisioned. His swaybacked mule was loaded. Amongst the gear, necessary foodstuffs, and boxes of bullets was what would become the instrument of his trade; a brand new Smith & Wesson Schofield Revolver in a keenly-crafted black leather holster with flashy silver beadwork on the belt. He had intended to ride out of town with the rig on his hip, but the retailer warned him of the city ordinance prohibiting such displays.

He was now perilously close to penniless, having spent the proceeds from the sale of horses on top-drawer items; nothing second-rate or mediocre for him. He didn't care that there were just a few loose coins jingling in his pocket. He had decided that on the trail he planned to set ablaze cash money would be of the easy come easy go variety.

He cut a showy swell in the expensive saddle atop Hero. He wore a fine linen shirt with intricate embroidery across the chest. His beige Stetson, slanted back cockily, had an interlaced rawhide band. The boots in the stirrups were of the thinnest calfskin and had a hand-tooled design carved along the sides. The palomino must have had some peacock in its bloodline for it preened and strutted with the same pride and brashness of its rider.

The sun was sinking. He walked Hero through town, enjoying the feel and movement of the animal against his thighs. He also found fulfillment in the looks and gestures of interest from those busy or lounging on the boardwalks at various popular gathering locales. It was the second go round on the thoroughfares and he was about ready to start tracking south.

He was on Cedar Street. He stopped Hero in the middle of the intersection of Texas Street. He had the reins in his left hand, the lead-line for the pack-mule in his right. He took in all his eyes could see. He had heard much of the lore and seemingly farfetched sagas about the carnival of criminal activity that had been centered here in the wild old days. The whooping it up gunplay and riots of lawlessness intrigued him and pulled tirelessly at his heart.

He spoke a whisper to Hero. The horse neighed and reared back on its hind legs for a mere instant before going forward in a high-stepping prance. The mule heehawed and put up some resistance. He gave the rope attached to its bridle a hard yank and it lumbered along grudgingly. He started chuckling—it soon became a crazed melody of laughter.

He throttled it off, but an arrogant leer remained plastered on his face. He was leaving Abilene a nobody from nowhere. He anticipated returning shortly to begin making his name on these fabled streets. He would force the world to remember him; there would be no mistaking his legend. The ambition to become a feared gunman was fuel on fire inside him.

There were debts to be paid in blood; there was a woman to be won. Abbey Langton had done something delightfully maddening to him. He couldn't get her out of his mind, or more explicitly stated, out of his dungarees. He lusted after her; she ignited a rage in his loins. He equated the feelings with tenderness. It was pleasurable to daydream about her, picturing her disrobing for him. He would impress her; he would make her love him. Or she would die.

In the deepening dimness of twilight he rode south, following Mud Creek out of town. There was no hurry in him. He was content to putter along and sort through a headful of plots and schemes. He expected to make camp by moonlight at a cozy nook beside the stream. He had discovered the outlying shelter of woods with his father on the trip north.

The place would be his hallowed schoolhouse; where he'd learn to shoot and master the art of the fast-draw by dedication and unflinching repetition. He had purchased heaps of ammunition; a dozen cartons of .44 caliber cartridges to practice, practice, practice. His thoughts kept leaping to the future. He rode easy, immersed in dazzling intrigues of glory and fame.

The changeless cast of Pete Axler's face was set in granite. Bafflement dug in around his eyes, which were squinted. "A giant crow? Skinwalker? What the dickens is a skinwalker?"

Deacon Coburn grinned. Daniel Twosongs mirrored that expression. The men were at the Alamo Saloon, having a gabfest about the murder of Yance Rawlins, but the talk had just taken off in a different direction. The establishment was packed, with the only vacant chair being at their table; a collection of drummers and cowboys were lined up two-deep at the bar.

The nighttime cavorters were loud and rambunctious. The buzz of conversation droned on and on, spiking now and again. An acrid stench hung in the hot, sweaty air. Mixed in with cigar smoke and kerosene fumes from oil lamps was the crosscurrent stink of manure drifting in from the Great Western Stockyards.

"It's not a mystery that can be solved, Pete," Deacon said helpfully. "The story of Daniel's experience with that crow shouldn't be impulsively discounted. I've not had a personal encounter with a skinwalker, but have seen much evil demonstrated in various ways, so am not at all skeptical. The world is full of puzzles and teasers I cannot explain or understand."

Twosongs sipped his beer. He sat the mug down and leaned in close. His manner became thoroughly reverent. "Amongst the Navajo, skinwalkers are actual, not imagined. It is taught that a skinwalker is a witch that takes the shape of any animal they desire. The animal state can be enlarged or slightly deformed and the eyes are abstract and scary, unreflective and dull."

Axler was dubious. "You truly believe in skinwalkers?"

"Belief suggests I put faith in skinwalkers," Daniel replied clearly. "My faith is reserved for the Creator who is from everlasting to everlasting." His eyes swept the room, as though he wanted to invite others in on the discussion. "Skinwalkers exist as sure as all of this is real." He unfurled his arms around in large circles, lips bending into a deadly serious smile.

Axler took a swallow of beer. He winced. He crooked an elbow on the table and rested his right cheek on the palm of his hand. "I ain't all that smart, Daniel. Neither am I inclined to sinister or celestial matters, but go ahead, feed my curiosity."

"Your inclination one way or another has no effect on reality," Daniel said, eyes pulled tight on him. "Skinwalkers are not Navajo fairytales. They are fast and cannot be trapped or caught, and are nearly impossible to kill for they are protected by the ancient Serpent."

"I'm just an army brat from Arkansas," Pete countered, "so what do I know? This is new stuff to me. I ain't saying anything against it. I'm still listening because you got my interest snagged so unload whatever you got. I may not grab it all, but will give it a helluva try."

Twosongs sat back, relaxing some. "Skinwalkers are not Navajo fairytales," he said again. He placed a hand over his heart and patted it as he continued, "Here's what I've come to know way down deep inside. The idea of an evil witch taking on the shape and attributes of an animal is only part of it. It surely happens, but much more is astir." His tone was ominous.

"I see ample evidence that fallen angels break into the physical realm to do dastardly deeds. The dark powers and principalities in the heavenlies which the Apostle Paul wrote of will transform into whatever is necessary in efforts to attack and destroy all that is good and righteous."

Axler looked back and forth at his companions, perplexed. "Fallen angels?"

"Demons from the pit of hell," Daniel answered directly. "Scripture tells us that one third of the angels of heaven were aligned with Lucifer when he made war against Almighty God in eternity past before time as we count it. In a cataclysmic battle that unleashed forces we cannot possibly comprehend Lucifer was thrashed and cast out along with his legions."

"Lucifer?" Pete appeared pained and entirely out of his depth.

"The Devil," Deacon interjected, "Satan, the Serpent in the garden, the bastardized father of lies, the cunning enemy of our souls." He fixed his eyes hard on the lawman. "Lucifer is evil incarnate and is set loose upon the earth. He roams to and fro searching for breaches or soft spots to attack and wreak havoc, commanding an army of demons to do likewise."

"Humanity is at war," Daniel said, hands held in a prayerful pose. "And the warfare has no boundaries. It is close quarters combat and infighting. We are persistently engaged in the campaign against those nefarious precincts under the dominion of Satan."

Coburn agreed with a quick bob of his head. "Pete, consider your namesake."

"My namesake? I ain't following you."

Coburn took a deep breath, chuckling. "Simon Peter proclaimed Jesus to be *the Christ, the son of the living God*, but when put under pressure on the night Jesus was arrested, the boisterous fisherman denied even knowing his friend and rabbi. Later in life I suspect Peter was chiding himself when he wrote: *Be sober, be vigilant; because your adversary the devil, as a roaring lion, walketh about, seeking whom he may devour: Whom resist steadfast in the faith, knowing that the same afflictions are accomplished in your brethren that are in the world.*"

Axler slowly rubbed his jaw, thinking and processing. "My folks were good people, but not churchgoers or Bible-readers, so I didn't get much Sunday learning." He sat up straight, knuckles against his right cheek. "But I've had many gospel bull sessions right here at this table. I've even listened to a few of your graveside messages, Deacon. Your talk about love and grace gives me hope and persuades me. I ain't ever heard this bleak doctrine from you."

"Not bleak, Pete. Two sides of the same coin," Deacon responded, giving him a kind smile. "I emphasize love, grace, hope, faith, mercy, goodness because those are elements of light and we all need to hear those truths again and again." His eyes dimmed as his mouth straightened into a no-nonsense line. "The flipside is polar opposite and requires no pronouncements from me for we drudge through the dregs of it every day. Hate, greed, despair, selfishness, vengeance, wickedness are components of darkness. Light and darkness are always at odds."

"And skinwalkers are birthed in the darkness to invade the light?"

Twosongs nodded favorably. "Remove all doubts, Pete. That is well put."

Coburn fingered the edges of his moustache. "We have no clue what transpires in the heavenlies, but we know spiritual warfare is true. Paul defined it in his letter to the church at Ephesus: *For we wrestle not against flesh and blood, but against principalities, against powers, against the rulers of the darkness of this world, against spiritual wickedness in high places.*"

"The battleground is here and now in our hearts and minds," Daniel said staunchly. "We must fight the good fight to stand our ground and keep our faith in faithless circumstances."

Axler groaned a sigh. "I ain't sure I need all this philosophizing. I didn't sleep much last night because a bad tooth flared up on me. Now I won't be able to turn my brain off and will be sitting up all night again." He fumbled in a pocket and pulled out a paper packet. He got a clove and put it on his sore tooth. "I suppose this toothache is spiritual warfare."

Coburn laughed. "Perhaps, but more than likely, a toothache is just a toothache."

With that, the topic shifted to more mundane matters, with the weather worming its way into the dialog. They swiftly reached a consensus; if a downpour of rain didn't soon arrive to cut the heat, the potential for trouble to erupt would multiply. The population was getting more and more cantankerous as each sun-scorched day passed with no reprieve on any horizon.

When the men called it a night, they stood and went outside together. The humid air was wet and sticky; the reek of manure thick and oppressive. A few longhorns could be heard mooing or snorting, but other than that, it was peaceful. They stared up at the star-speckled sky in unison. One by one they pointed or gestured as large smiles flooded their eyes and filled their faces.

The golden yellow moon was shining on them as brightly as a benediction.

~~~

In the southwest, Sally Twosongs gazed upon the moon and took reassurance from its shimmering beams. She moved like a shadow amongst shadows. The soft-soled moccasins were silent as she padded to the stand of aspens she treated as her personal cathedral.

Midnight had come and gone. The ceiling of the world sparkled with glittering lights for as far as she could see. She had slept for a couple hours, but was awakened by a nightmare that was strangely different but somehow the same. Her point of view had been altered.

The flappy frenzy of crows, the odd pillars of colors in the sky, the fair maiden weeping in the lee of a towering tree, the booming fireball fury, and the tumult ending in death were all unchanged, but now she saw what she hadn't seen before: She saw the killer's face; she saw who was spread-eagled in the dirt with a gaping bullet hole in the middle of his back; she saw the jaundice-eyed monster. She also saw another; a bald man with glinting eyes.

Fear had done vile things to her whilst she slept, but now it was gone; she refused to give it any stronghold to hide in her. There was, however, a boiling cauldron of anticipation in her stomach, an eager sense of expectancy that was exciting. She wondered on it as she crept into the woods. She slowly turned round and round, bowing in genuflection to the four directions.

She knelt and prayed a formidable liturgy of blessing in Navajo. When she was finished she stretched out on some grass betwixt and between tall aspens. She arranged her loose-fitting cottony nightgown tight around her legs and sighed contentedly. She reveled in the balmy embrace of stillness; it resonated in her. Her hands were locked behind her head. Through an opening of leafy branches she had an unobstructed view of the moon.

A whispery breeze ruffled the leaves, which was only a prelude for it was soon a rushing wind that was frigid. The air temperature dropped instantaneously. She frowned and propped up on her elbows, startled into an eddy of confusion. It had come so suddenly. A vibrantly alive squirm of goosebumps crawled over her skin. She got to her knees.

A thud-thud of wings and a caw pierced the sky. The blustery arctic wind died. Warmth and stillness returned, but it was frighteningly fragile. *Daniel Twosongs is a dead man.*

She *heard* the words. She scrambled to her feet. "Show yourself."

Daniel Twosongs is a dead man. The voice was hoarse and croaky, as though it was being pushed through thick layers of dirt. Measured, soft, almost imperceptible steps were approaching her through the trees. There was a screech and a flutter of feathers; a hulking crow appeared before her. Its ugliness was pinpointed by an empty and bleeding eye socket.

Sally Twosongs rigidly held her position. "You have no power here. Be gone."

The crow squawked and craned its neck to focus on her. It fully extended its wings; the span was breathtaking. *Daniel Twosongs is a dead man. I will destroy him.*

"Help me, Jesus," she murmured, shoulders stiff. "Help me now."

The crow screamed madly. It clawed at the dirt, crazed and feverish. It stalked forward. The evil simmering in its dull eye was palpable. It brattled low in its throat and charged at her, beating its wings and squealing shrilly. It retreated when she was unmoved.

"I will not fear you," she said fiercely. She held her hands up, palms forward. Gleams of moonlight danced in her eyes. A surreal radiance silhouetted her. Not only did she stand her ground, she advanced one brave step followed by another and another. And another.

The demonic intruder backtracked, spitting and shrieking.

Sally Twosongs kept at it, never slackening in her single-minded action. "You go straight to the bowels of hell from whence you came," she ordered, voice booming mightily.

When the one-eyed crow evaded the cover of the aspen grove it let loose an ear-splitting caterwauling and leapt skyward, wings thumping furiously. It flew in an arcing spiral cawing all the while. She watched until it disappeared into the darkness. Her heart was pounding against her eardrums. She sprinted to the house, surprised to see candlelight in the windows. She entered to find her mother at the kitchen table, running rosary beads through her fingers.

"What was that terrifying noise?" Consuelo asked, obviously fretful.

"Father is in danger," Sally Twosongs replied sharply. "We must go northeast toward Abilene and be ready to rescue him. Can we be prepared to leave as early as tomorrow?"

"Tomorrow? Abilene? Sally Twosongs, what are you saying?"

"It's bad, Mother. Evil has set out to kill Father."

"Oh, sweet Jesus! We must pray for him, harder than ever."

"Yes, Mother," Sally Twosongs said, going to her. She placed her hands firmly on the older woman's shoulders. "But this trouble also requires us to put feet to our prayers."

Consuelo covered her mouth, nodding. "We have supplies enough in the root cellar. We can travel tomorrow." She stood, and as she did so, a shuffle of movement outside frightened her. "Dear God, has that terrible screamer returned?" She swallowed dryly; mother and daughter looked to each other, ears attuned to the night, breath held tensely. Time became long, teasing them into snug bundles of worry. The muffled rustle came again, louder and closer.

Sally Twosongs abruptly giggled. A smile engulfed her face. Her heart did a thrilling pitty-pat. The sound was hoofbeats. Even with the horse walking furtively she recognized its light-footed clip-clop. She now understood the anticipation bubbling in her belly earlier. She remembered the letter on her dresser promising a visit; every word of it came to mind.

She opened the door to see her special friend on Shadrach. The steel-dust stallion nickered a greeting as the rider doffed his hat. Caleb Weitzel was a heavily muscled man of eighteen years who relished hard work the way lollygaggers desire a comfy stool beside the chuck wagon. His physical vigor and endurance was unrivaled, but could not be outdone by the sensitivity of his heart, his willingness to serve others, or the rare integrity of his character.

Weitzel dismounted. "I expected to sneak in here, bed down in your aspens, and surprise you at breakfast," he said, watching her run to him. She stopped short. He frowned and reached out to hug and hold her. She put her palms on his chest and chastely kept him at arm's length, aware of the flimsiness of her nightclothes. Comprehension passed between them. He smiled broadly, eyes swelling with respect. He was sweated. She felt the tacky dampness of his shirt.

Sally Twosongs pecked his cheek. She thanked God for sending help.

Flora was alone in bed. The curtains were drawn shut. The inky darkness was total. It held her in its embrace and she accepted its tender silence. She was conscience-stricken, stewing over her son. She wished he could know her remorse; she longed to change the past, and thereby, derail him from his choices. She had reviewed their set-to on the street numerous times. The pain of it slashed her heart. Her good intentions had become a debacle.

Liam's near violent reaction violated her in ways she could have never predicted. There was no way for her to know that his behavior would initiate a vivid replay of the most horrid memory of all. His vulgarity caused her to relive the seminal brutality of her life; the aggressive cruelty that had ripped apart her senses and put her to wantonness and whoredom.

She couldn't bear it. She pushed it away. In teeth-clenched fury she forced the foulness back beneath lie upon lie; old habits of denial dominated her. She rolled over and pulled the thin blanket up to tuck it around her. For comfort she began thinking about her mother. She pondered a bevy of cheery incidents, but then settled on one of their final conversations.

She had been ten years old, sitting in a rocking chair at her mother's bedside. There were cute pink ribbons intertwined in her pigtails. It was evening. The cozy room was aglow with an assortment of candles. She sat straight and tall, her posture perfect, her hands folded in her lap, fingers clenched around the sterling silver case her mother had just entrusted to her.

"You take care of your grandmother's heirloom, Delores," her mother said weakly. She dabbed a lacey handkerchief to her mouth to wipe away blood-speckled saliva. "It is your birthright from her. It goes back many generations. Treasure it always."

"I will, Mama."

"I know, dear child." She sat up a bit. Her breathing was labored, her face bloated and blotchy. "I won't be here much longer. The Lord is calling me home to heaven and my days are short. I have one more incomparable inheritance for you. An angel appeared to me and gave me words to share with you, Delores." She wheezed and coughed, covering her mouth.

"Should I get Daddy?"

Her mother waved a hand at her. In a few moments she recovered. "Not just yet. I want us to have our time alone." She reached over to the nightstand and carefully picked up a flimsy parchment. She handed it to her daughter. "Store this close to your heart."

The young girl received it and turned it over in her hands. It was a handwritten note on canary-colored onionskin paper. She studied it, her eyes becoming murky and moist.

"Do you understand?"

"I think so, Mama."

"Hold those truths close to your heart, Delores."

Two days later her mother died in a gasping, blood-splattering fit. The doctor said it was consumption; Father Martin referred to it as a mystery of God's plan; her father told the priest he was full of shit. Delores cried until her eyes were raw and there were no more tears.

The memory dissipated into the gloom of nothingness. Flora fisted her right hand and struck the pillow repetitively with anger and frustration that had been accumulated over the years. She cursed herself for losing the sterling silver case; she heaped condemnation on her shoulders because she was unable to recall what had been written in her mother's hand.

She hungered to remember those words. They had been vital to her until the eve of her eighteenth birthday. In the horror of that night her mother's pious wisdom had been blotted out and forgotten. She bit her lip hard enough to taste blood. Pain throbbed behind her eyes.

She tried to talk to God. Over and over she recited prayers learned as a youngster. She fell asleep with the counsel of a stranger revolving in her aching head: *Hope is always nearby, as sure as thunder follows lightning. Search your heart. Hope is there to lead you onward.*

chapter three

Barbed Consequences

*"Be not deceived; God is not mocked: for whatsoever
a man soweth, that shall he also reap."*

~PAUL OF TARSUS~

TWO WEEKS LATER THERE had been no change in the weather. Large streaky clouds had accumulated several times and threatened rain, but passed by without unloading their precious cargo. The heat remained suffocating, the humidity doing its best to dismantle the sensibilities of the citizenry. Commonplace minor disputes often resulted in shouting matches or fistfights.

In recent days Deacon Coburn had successfully mediated several such instances, but was losing his belly for the foolishness. To his way of thinking the weather was the weather; people ought to simply do their best to deal with its quirks and whimsies.

He was unshaven and had been for a week or more. He had a raggedy look about him as he tended to the vegetable garden at the back portion of the boarding house property. His Bible rested on a bench alongside the toolshed. He had finished his morning reading and was now working his prayers out. He hoed and lugged water from the trough. He knelt and inspected the tomato plants, pleased to see them ripening. He pinched off several suckers.

A smile caused his moustache to wiggle as familiar words from the weeping prophet came to mind. He considered them more closely by quoting them aloud: "*Remembering mine affliction and my misery, the wormwood and the gall. My soul hath them still in remembrance, and is humbled in me. This I recall to my mind, therefore have I hope. It is of the Lord's mercies that we are not consumed, because his compassions fail not.*

They are new every morning: great is thy faithfulness. The Lord is my portion, saith my soul; therefore will I hope in him."

Birds were chirping a symphonic melody that engaged him. He listened. He stood and appreciated the rising sun. He put the hoe and bucket away, then sat on the bench and waited for what had become routine. He owned no timepiece, but boasted an inner clock that was incredibly exact. He crossed his legs and as he did so, once again he thanked God for the newness of the day and the mercy that was his to receive.

In less than a minute, Abbey Langton rounded the corner of the building accompanied by Old Blue. She had a metal carafe of coffee in one hand and two earthenware mugs in the other. The utensils belonged to the kitchen of Drovers Cottage, but she had some pull with one of the clerks. The dog romped over to him, eyes alive and full of joy. He patted its head.

"Good morning, Miss Abbey," he said, accepting the offered cup. "It is still Miss Abbey, isn't it? Or did you run off and get married since I saw you yesterday?"

"Stop it, Deacon," she replied, pouring the coffee. It was piping hot. She put the carafe on the ground and settled beside him, her hands encircling the mug. "This isn't funny. Sam and I have spent time together every day since we met." She tried a small sip, smiling at its robust flavor. "I do have warm feelings for him; more than warm feelings, really. And he has made it abundantly clear what's in his heart for me, but it's all happening so fast."

He gave her an exaggerated shrug. "Old Blue there likely understands matters of the heart better than me." The dog plumped down on its buttocks, head cocked sideways. "Your mother taught me much, but those lessons were long ago and I've not had occasion to put them into practice. Nor do I ever expect to have such occasion."

Her face flinched. "You could still meet someone. You're not that old."

"I'm too much of a vagabond."

She lent her ears to the birdsongs. The notes were overlapping. Her mouth pursed and a frown creased her brow. "What lessons did Mom teach you about love?"

He mulled that over for a long while. He took a mouthful of coffee and swished it around before swallowing it. "I suppose that friendship must come first. Being friends and respecting each other has to be foundational." He took a deep breath and whistled a low sigh. "She also taught me that there's no room in my heart for another. She was an extraordinary lady. It's easy to see her courage and character in you. She would be proud of you, as I am."

"Thank you, Deacon. You are too kind," she said, a hitch of emotion in her voice. She finished her coffee. "I'm going to miss our mornings together. I surely did when you rode off with Daniel to where his belongings were hidden."

His forehead knitted deeply. "Seeing an old friend well on his way blessed me, but I have no rambling on my foreseeable calendar. What else will interrupt our mornings together?"

"In the words of Sam Beadle: *Dodge City beckons.*"

"Ah, yes. I forgot about that troublemaker Sam Beadle."

She laughed gleefully. "I haven't. In fact I can't forget him. When we take the big step of marriage, we'll be moving to Dodge City at least for starters."

"*When*, not if?" he asked dryly. "It was *if* yesterday."

"Was it?" She giggled and held her hands wide and shrugged.

He tapped a finger against her knee. "Sam's a solid and reliable man. He's a bit of an embellisher at times, but is trustworthy." He put his hands together, leaned forward and shifted to look straight at her. "He'll be a good provider and do right by you . . ." His voice trailed off.

"Is there a but coming?"

He shook his head. "You have a place in my heart, Abbey. You finding me after all these years reminds me of how short our time can be and how we must cherish what we have." He touched her cheek. "I will not willingly allow you out of my life any time soon."

Alarm showed on her face. "Are you saying I *can't* marry Sam?"

He shook his head even harder. "What I'm trying to tell you is that I've never been to Dodge City," he said firmly. "I'll give you newlyweds some space to get established, but I'll be along shortly." Old Blue got to its feet and barked exuberantly. Coburn placed a finger to his lips to quiet it. The dog shut up; its grin was large, its tail wagging enthusiastically.

Tears filled her eyes. "I am so grateful to hear you say so. I have hoped . . ." She paused and wiped away the moisture. "Ever since Sam and I started getting serious I have hoped." She trembled slightly. "Do you ever worry someone will steal our happiness? After walking through the sickness with Mom I'm wary to be happy about any good thing."

He stiffened. "Have there been more Liam sightings?"

"Not yesterday," she answered swiftly. "It's not every day, but it seems that whenever he's in town he makes sure that I see him. It can be kind of spooky."

"That won't do," he said, using thumb and forefinger to brush aside his moustache. "As soon as I see him again I'll give him a severe lecture. It's unacceptable for him to bother you."

She picked up the carafe and stood. "Thank you. Same time tomorrow?"

"I'll be here." He polished off his coffee in one gulp. He grabbed the scruff of Old Blue's neck. "You keep care of this young lady, you hear me, boy?"

The dog gave a whining yelp. Abbey petted it. "Old Blue is always underfoot so you can be pleased it's following your instructions completely." She started to leave, then turned back and said, "You need a shave and a haircut. You're looking like a dirty ragamuffin."

He winced as he bit off laughter. She and Old Blue were around the building and gone, but the words remained to conjure up pleasant memories of her mother. During their first conversation Angela Langton had chastised him in much the same manner. In his mind he heard her clipped cadence afresh and anew: *You'll find the pump beside the barn. There's likely an old razor round here somewhere. I'll leave it at the water trough. Use it.*

Deacon Coburn rubbed his whiskers and chuckled contentedly.

Daniel Twosongs was freezing in the heat. Fire burned in his veins. He had ridden bareback out of Abilene on a bartered for brindle mare. Deacon Coburn tapped his connections and arranged surety, and Pete Axler spoke in favor of the animal, which sealed the deal.

Twosongs parted company with Coburn at the spot where his saddle and rig were cached. He had been alone on the trail for three days when the fever struck. That was two days ago. At first he thought some medicinal herbs from his saddlebags, a good night's sleep followed by a day of resting would do the trick, but now, he realized he was up against it.

He was camped under a lone tree on the prairie. The bone-deep hurt was so hot it was cold. The frigidity couldn't be shaken; it had a near sadistic hold on him. He was leaning back against the saddle and quivering to the point of chattering teeth. Wrapped up in his bedroll, he had the crusty saddle-blanket tugged around his shoulders in a futile effort to get warm. His canteen was half-full and closeby. He took sips from it time to time.

He hadn't started drifting in and out of consciousness yet, but knew that if his latest attempt at a remedy didn't have any effect at stemming the sickness that he would soon begin doing so. He had blended a concoction of dried sage, bearberry, peppermint and plumajillo to be steadily ingested while singing an obscure sacramental chant gleaned from Gray Eyes. The botanicals were to douse the fever, the ritual to chase away evil spirits.

He put blurry eyes on the brindle tethered on a long rope feeding in the tall grass. The brown horse had distinct yellowish stripes marking its body. It moved with a natural fluidity. He had already developed a kinship with the animal; it was strong, gentle and smart.

His supplications were constantly coursing through his head. Every few minutes a flood of words rushed from his mouth as he assaulted heaven's gates with passionate intensity. He contemplated the meaning of healing, the presence of miracles. It was now all about waiting for the illness to be assuaged or to worsen. He had done all things possible; happenings in the realm of the supernatural would be the determining factor.

His mental faculties were foggy, but he could still force clear thinking; for how much longer he couldn't say. He knew that without any changes the madness of delirium would soon set in. He thought about his wife and daughter.

Consuelo had stolen his heart and never gave it back. She was stubbornly independent and strong-willed, which he admired. She understood him; she accepted his wanderings. The rare disagreements between them were easily arbitrated. Their journey together was marked by the teardrops of both laughter and sorrow; joys and pains had been faced together to weave an unbreakable bond of devoted affection.

Sally Twosongs was God's unexpected gift to their marriage. She came to them out of a horrific trauma, emotionally and physically wounded but not broken by a coldblooded fiend. Her tribulation and suffering could've destroyed her, but there was pure iron in her soul. Love, time, tenderness, patience, and unending prayers had amazingly mended and restored her. Her spiritual eyes were keenly accentuated by unshakeable faith and hope entrenched in her heart.

Daniel shuddered against the burning cold inside him. His cheeks were dripping with tears as he reflected on the women who loved him; his heart ached in love for them. If death were to have its way he would gladly be set free of the ravages of sin and corruption; he lived only for eternity, but even in a fallen world, there was treasured sweetness to be missed.

Never again cuddling Consuelo or hearing her laughter; never again holding her hand and searching the night sky for a falling star; never again learning from her insights into what the Creator was doing in their lives. To not see Sally Twosongs perform a celebration of life in the moonlight;

to not be soothed by the remarkable comfort of her flute; to not hug or be hugged by her; to not savor watching her marvel at the wonders as she grew in grace.

All of these possibilities and so much more were nearly unbearable for him to ponder, yet the scenarios whipped in and out of his thinking. He prayed with more fervor. He looked up and blinked rapidly to focus on the vultures in the bright blueness. There were more gathered than the last time he checked. He shivered bonelessly. The scavenger birds were circling closer.

Caleb Weitzel had learned to value sunrises and sunsets from his mother. She always told him that the simple rhythm of sunup and sundown kept her tuned and in perfect harmony. He had grown to understand exactly what she meant. He sat on Shadrach, eyes locked on the eastern sky, which appeared to be aflame. He was ranging ahead, riding a semi-circular route to scout the sweeping grasslands for any trace of Daniel Twosongs. In terms of getting even an inkling of his location, it had been a fruitless reconnaissance.

He spoke to Shadrach. The stallion's ears twitched. It turned and broke into a straight-line trot toward the campsite. He thought of the task and dangers ahead. Jaunting along with two women across the wide-open plains had its complications. The weather alone—the heat and lack of rainfall—could produce a multitude of problems.

The potential for bad luck was extreme, but there had never been an instant's hesitation in him. He simply shouldered the responsibility. The traveling had been safe so far as they steadily put miles behind them. Each morning he silently left camp before first-light to scout ahead. Upon returning, he found everything as he did now; packed and ready to go.

He patted Shadrach's neck as he swung to the ground. He surveyed the treeless area. A cook-fire had been extinguished and covered with loose dirt. The mules were saddled. All the gear was securely tied down on a sure-footed donkey.

Consuelo approached him, a wrapped tortilla in hand. "Any sign of Daniel?"

"No, ma'am," he replied forthrightly. "I'm sorry." He accepted the offered meal and took a large bite. He smiled as he chewed slowly. It was mutton based pemmican; a nutritious mixture of dried meat and berries. "Tasty as usual, Miss Consuelo. Thank you."

Consuelo's eyes were large and pleading. "Do you think we'll have any favor today?"

Sally Twosongs had mounted her mule; she side-stepped it closer to them. "It will not be today," she said in a curt monotone. "We must hurry. He has been attacked."

Caleb gave her a quizzical look. "Attacked?"

"Evil has assailed him," she explained bluntly. "We must hurry."

Caleb hopped onto Shadrach. "There's a waterhole on the trail ahead. We'll replenish all canteens and give the animals opportunity to fill up. Then it's nonstop until nightfall."

They rode into the rising sun. The air was heavy and humid; and as still as still could be, with no hint or suggestion of a breeze. Caleb Weitzel and Sally Twosongs were side by side, with the pack-animal's lead rope secured to her mule. She was humming softly. He listened as his eyes busily kept scanning back and forth. Consuelo was a fair distance behind them.

Weitzel suddenly stood tall in the stirrups. There was movement off to the right. He squinted. Something was definitely there, fifty or so yards away, concealed in the tall meadow. He watched suspiciously. He pushed the brim of his hat up. A bit of gray came into view and disappeared just as quickly. Another flicker of gray whispered through the grassy hideaway; then another. He withdrew his Spencer rifle from its sheath. He shouldered the carbine.

Sally Twosongs cleared her throat with an abrupt cough. "Those wolves aren't pestering anyone and certainly will not harm us. Leave them be."

"I was just going to shoot at the sky to chase them off."

"Don't waste the bullet."

He frowned hard at her. "Are you sure?"

"I am sure."

His expression deepened, darkened. He lowered the weapon and sat in the saddle. "What do you know about wolves?" There was inexplicable secrecy enveloping her that both captivated and frustrated him. "Are you going to tell me more?" He glanced at her without allowing his eyes to stray far from the course where he had seen the wild animals.

She laughed musically. "I'd rather hear about that land in Colorado."

He balanced the Spencer on his lap. He gave her an easy shrug. "It's over toward Wagon Wheel Gap. I came upon it while exploring and just knew it was the place. It's an isolated valley in some high country, walled in by steep mountains. There's a natural box canyon at one end and a spring fed stream that empties into the Rio Grande."

"I am anxious to see it for myself."

"I staked the claim and filed all the paperwork at the land office," he told her, shifting around. He nudged Shadrach. The horse stepped closer to her. "The acreage will be there for us, Sally Twosongs, but there's much work to be done. The living arrangements are meager just now. A dugout soddy is fine for me, but there's a proper house to be built."

"I do not wish for anything fancy, Caleb."

"Not fancy, but solid shelter."

"Will the house be ready soon?"

He chuckled. "Are you rushing me?"

"What if I am?"

"That's not allowed, Sally Twosongs. We decided all those details already."

"Maybe I want to reopen the particulars."

He pushed a stern smile at her. "The discussion is done and finished."

She stared at him. "No chance of a change?"

"No chance, Sally Twosongs. We talked it through together."

"Three years feels like forever."

"I gave Daniel my word. That settles it."

She sighed in resignation. "Time will take care of itself, I suppose."

"It always does," he said, "especially when we stick to the plan." He stroked Shadrach's mane as he heedfully studied the landscape. He turned around. Nothing affected his attention for as far as he could see in any direction. "What can you tell me about those wolves?"

"We will not be troubled by them, Caleb."

"That's all, Sally Twosongs?"

She grinned; it spread upward and made her dark eyes twinkle. "Indeed it is," she said facetiously. The amusement in her voice caused him to snicker. He nipped it off, his head wagging in good cheer. He relaxed some and slid the rifle into the scabbard. He glanced over a shoulder to see Consuelo knowingly observing them. He tipped his hat to her. She nodded.

The sky was full of sunshine. They rode on together in wordless camaraderie.

Charley Jondreau had just finished shaving his head. His scalp was shiny smooth. He dusted off his hat, then pulled it on tight. He moved away from Mud Creek, drying his hands on his trousers. He had been up and at it since daybreak, enjoying the solitude of the morning. The sun was now above the Flint Hills.

He angled away from the campsite, which was scarcely north of the Smoky Hill River amongst a copse of trees. He went to the roped enclosure where his pinto was corralled along with a palomino stallion and a midnight black gelding. He had fallen in with a pair he regarded as ne'er do wells at best. His associates were still loafing in their bedrolls.

He set the piebald loose. It immediately trotted to the water's edge and drank thirstily. When its belly was satisfied, it ran off into the pasture and began chomping on breakfast. He walked to it and spoke kindly. The horse raised its head and gave him an approving look; the demonstrative sort that passes between old friends.

Jondreau spent a few moments hunting around to find suitable tufts of grass that could be woven together. With his selections gathered, his fingers nimbly constructed what would serve well as a brush. He began giving the pinto a thorough rubdown. The horse stopped munching and stood perfectly still, listening to the man talk in a soothing voice.

When the grooming task was completed, the pinto trod off to a fresh patch to continue feeding. Jondreau backed up some. He picked a spot where he could look out for the pony and also keep the encampment in sight. He sat cross-legged on the ground, his hands together in his lap, his thumbs unthinkingly commencing to twiddle.

He evaluated the men slumbering. Jackson Scully was a sad-sack bag of bones, a ruthless and coldblooded killer who was not to be trusted. Jondreau barely tolerated the man; he did so out of a sense of duty to win over and guide the other man. Liam Greer was a browbeaten runt bowing to evil and being bent into a quarrelsome bully. Jondreau didn't hold much hope for success in influencing him onto a positive path, but had decided he would try.

He was calm and at ease. Suddenly there was an abrupt change that would've frightened a passerby, but there were no eyewitnesses. His hands clenched, his spine stiffened, his nostrils flared, his eyes rolled back in his head, his eyelids vibrated in rapid flutters. The smell of the skunk was strikingly on him, its odor clogging up his nose.

Inside his head, he *saw* Greer—brassy and wild-eyed—prowling along on the streets of Abilene. An idiot's smirk was plastered on his face and he walked with a swagger, shoulders thrust back and chin pointed upward. His fists were flexing spasmodically. There was a flurry of action. Greer went down hard, landing in a crumpled heap. He grunted and groaned. He was bleeding profusely and badly wounded; maimed, even. Blood was everywhere.

Jondreau inhaled sharply. A shiver of relaxation came over him. The episode was over. It had only lasted a handful of seconds, but from his perspective, it was much more prolonged. The lucidity of the smell of the skunk never ceased to startle or amaze him, but the foreknowledge was problematic. Over the years he had kicked against a difficult reality. *Knowing* the future and having any capacity to alter or impact it were enormously different propositions.

He withdrew his pistol and expertly checked it over. He clicked it open and spun the cylinder several times. He removed each bullet and rolled it between his thumb and forefinger to examine it before returning it to its chamber. Satisfied with its workings and loads, he twirled the six-shooter and slipped it into the holster.

He noticed that Liam Greer was rousing. Jondreau stewed over what he could do to influence him. The young man flaunted foolishness as he prepared to sow destruction. He had seen Greer practice with his Smith & Wesson; hour after hour, day after day for more than a week. Greer demonstrated an intense determination that was noteworthy in its folly.

Box after box of cartridges were shot at various targets until he was accurate and hell-for-leather quick. Fence posts, tree trunks, boards, tin cans, and the occasional songbird had served well for his repetitive training. Jondreau figured it was only a matter of time and circumstance until Greer would test his prowess with a handgun against an armed opponent.

Jondreau saw that Greer had the reflexes and eye-hand coordination to be a gunslinger, but not the cool-minded temperament; he had no respect or restraint. It was blindingly evident that Liam Greer lacked quality and character. An overstated bravado was the framework that shaped him; delusions of greatness slinked through his skull and oozed off him.

Greer's attitude toward his education was obviously about using the revolver to generate fear and wield power. Jondreau, however, understood that a gun was a tool, nothing more and nothing less. In the hands of someone who had a high regard for its function, a firearm was not unlike a hammer in the tool-box of a skilled carpenter.

Jondreau stood. He gave a low-pitched two-note whistle. The pinto reared up and immediately cantered over to him. He put it inside the roped in area with the palomino and the gelding. He went to where Greer had a fire going and was fixing coffee.

"You got a choice, kid," Charley said, squatting on his heels.

"I surely do," Liam replied as he placed the soot-smeared pot on a flat rock in the flames. "I can have my coffee black and bitter. Or I can have it black and syrupy with sugar."

"The path you are choosing will end in tragedy."

Greer grinned, crooked and eerily. "Only for those who get in my way."

Jondreau dropped onto his backside and stretched his legs out straight. "Shooting cans or birds ain't the same as popping a man who's shooting back at you."

"I doubt there ain't much difference."

"You know so much, eh?"

"Some men need killing."

"You get no argument from me, but killing a man is bad for your soul."

A surly grumble announced that Jackson Scully had awakened. He stirred in his bedroll.

Greer poured himself a cup of coffee. "How many men have you shot, Charley?"

"Not a one, kid," Charley answered flatly. "You got a choice to make."

Greer had skepticism in his eyes. "You ain't never killed nobody?"

"I've never shot anyone," Charley said, offering a wide-armed shrug. "A man becomes good with a gun so he never has to use it, but my hands ain't clean. I've done butchery. My knife has slit throats and stabbed hearts in skirmishes with turncoats." He shifted around and pulled his knees up to rest his elbows on them. "And once I did have reason to beat a Frenchman to death. He took something from my sister that she wasn't willing to give."

Jackson Scully swore loudly. "Will you two shut the hell up!" He heaved himself to his feet and cursed again. "I'm sick of listening to your crappola. *Killing a man is bad for your soul?* Where did that crappola come from?" He wobbled three steps away from where he'd slept and relieved his bladder; all the while creaking murmurs uttered from his throat.

Jondreau had no time or patience for Scully. He simply ignored him.

Scully buttoned his pants. "I've killed plenty of men. Ain't anything wrong with my soul." He cussed and clutched his left leg. He hitched along to the coffee pot. "You go whole hog with that pistol, kid. I'll be proud and happy to ride to hell and back at your side."

Greer beamed. His chest puffed up, eyes full of satisfaction and delight.

"Fact is, I got a killing that needs doing," Jackson said, grinning. He hunkered down, his left leg slanted out clumsily. "Maybe you could help me with getting that done."

Greer brightened even more. "Nothing would please me more, sir."

Jondreau increased his level of disregarding Scully. He was on his feet in an instant and walking to the makeshift pen for the horses. He released the pinto and went with it off into the tall grass. The horse bucked happily and ran circles around him. He spoke softly.

The animal came close and nuzzled his chest. He stroked its neck and engaged it in an intense conversation. His voice was a mere whisper, but the words carried troubling weight. The pony was a trustworthy sound-board; it could always be depended on to listen to his thinking.

An hour later, Jondreau eyeballed Greer as he went to saddle up the palomino.

Naomi Engle was in her room at Drovers Cottage. Fear had drilled so deep into her heart that she was nearly incapacitated by it. She was dressed and ready to embark, but the bravery to face-down the challenges of new beginnings had abandoned her.

She kept gazing out the window, somewhat amazed that she had actually reached her destination. It was a sunshiny morning, peppered by dusty wisps of floating grime. The noise and activity of horses and wagons on the street below was unruly and overexcited in comparison to the pastoral stillness of the rolling green countryside of her upbringing. She had been in Abilene for twenty-four hours, and just now, was having a crisis of courage.

The day was getting away from her. She paced, her hands held tightly together at her waist. An interior monolog of a pep talk kept chattering encouragement. She stopped in front of the mirror and was mostly appreciative of her reflection. She was tall and slim, with large circular eyes that were cheerful and inviting. Her late husband had privately and sweetly referred to her as his brown-eyed daisy. The memory warmed her heart. She smiled tenderly.

She turned sideways. The dress was modest and utilitarian; the somber gray fabric cut roomy and layered. The garment was in no way pretty; she had brought along three exact replicas. Shopping to refurbish her trousseau was high atop her to-do list. A newfound life required multicolored apparel. She stared at herself. Something was drastically wrong.

She pondered on it. Her eyes spread wide as enlightenment came over her. The black bonnet was dismally funereal. It had to go posthaste. She removed it and tossed it aside. The top of her head was a good place to initiate changing her attire. She went to her suitcase. It took all of ten seconds for her to put her hands on a silk navy blue scarf.

She held it against her cheek. She shook its creases free. Its softness fluttered. She made two lengthwise folds and positioned it over the knotted bun of her dark hair. She loosely looped the ends under her chin and arranged them nicely on the bodice. She turned a slow pirouette to regard herself once more in the mirror. She decided she'd delayed long enough.

She took a hefty breath and said aloud, "How can you expect to have a fresh start without making new friends? Get going and have at it, lady." She left her room. When she closed the door, she actually thought that doing so was symbolic of her putting the past behind her.

Naomi Engle went down the stairs in a brisk rush. She took long strides across the lobby and paused in the doorway of the dining room. The place was busy and purring with social discourse. Only one table had a single individual, which she took as an open invitation. A woman with gorgeous red hair beneath a feathery hat sat alone at the back of the room.

Naomi walked directly to her. "Would you care for some company?"

The woman was startled or surprised. She looked up from some documents she was studying. Her eyes narrowed and her brow wrinkled. She glanced around, evidently aware of and put off by the attention coming from others. "You'd be most welcome. I'm Flora."

"Naomi Engle." She took a seat across from her.

"You're new to Abilene."

"I arrived on the train early yesterday morning. How could you tell?"

"You have that newcomer look to you. Not hardened yet," Flora said, shuffling legal papers into a file. "Plus you chose to sit down with me in a respectable establishment."

Naomi tilted her head oddly. "Why wouldn't I?" A waitress approached their table. Naomi politely declined a menu or to hear the specials. She asked for fruit juice.

Flora sat back. Her lips pinched into a vague smile.

Naomi was insistent. "Why wouldn't I?"

Flora's smile broke; it became sad. "Folks judge me harshly and perhaps rightly so."

"What people do is their affair," Naomi said solemnly. "I try to offer to others the grace which I wish extended to me. The world's too big and life's too short to do otherwise."

Flora lifted a finger and wagged it. "You are familiar to me in some way."

"You are kind to say so, Flora. I like you just fine."

Flora eased forward. "What brings you to Abilene?"

A glass of pulpy orange juice arrived. Naomi sipped it. She wanted to be straightforward and honest. "Priority one is to make a niche for myself, to know and live the dream God has for my life; to have a second chance to somehow make a difference and find fulfillment." She took another drink. "There's a secondary purpose that has to do with finding a man."

Flora laughed. "Be careful. Men can be dream breakers."

Naomi shook her head and dismissed the idea with a sly grin. "Not this one. He left our community when I was ten years old. It was upsetting. At some juncture he came west. The only letter we had come from Abilene. That was two years ago."

"Maybe I can help. What's his name?"

"Deacon Coburn."

Flora gasped audibly. She covered her mouth. "How do *you* know Deacon Coburn?"

"My maiden name is Coburn. Deacon is my big brother."

"That explains the familiarity," Flora said, eyes wide and radiant. "You have his manner and bearing. You carry yourself with his certainty, and believe me, that's a huge compliment."

"When I was a child I thought he could walk on water."

"I've had that same impression more than once, Naomi."

"I haven't seen him since before the war."

"That's a long time."

"How do you know him?"

Flora's expression toughened to the point of being brittle. "Not in the way I've known most men." She sighed and softened some. She absently fingered the file folder. "He's a gentleman and a true friend. He's always treated me with the utmost deference."

"I wouldn't expect him to do otherwise."

"You don't understand. I have a rather checkered past."

Naomi pooh-poohed the notion. "If a checkered past was the end of the matter, then a whole lot of pages would have to be ripped out of the Bible I read. Those character's stories are all about hope and redemption. The past is the past. Each day is a new opportunity."

"I've heard those sentiments from Deacon."

"Thank you for telling me so, Flora. It reveals much," Naomi said merrily. "I'm learning again and again that we often require truth affirmations day by day."

"A conversation with your brother is a dose of reassurance to me."

Naomi tented her eyebrows flippantly. "Perchance he *does* walk on water."

Flora giggled. Her cheeks were rosy. "His ears must be burning."

"He's had worse happen to him, I'm sure."

"I suspect so, though he seldom mentions his past."

Naomi finished her orange juice. "Where could I find him?"

Flora thought for a few moments. "It's too early for him to be at the Alamo Saloon. He might be at the Merchants Hotel doing business for Big Bull Wallace. I'd try there first." Her eyes lit up with laughter. "If no luck's to be had there, then if I were you, I'd go hang around the barbershop for a spell because Whitey has the bulge on everyone in town. If Deacon's not there, you can bet Whitey will know his whereabouts. Whitey probably has his entire itinerary."

"Whitey?"

"Whitey Fitzgerald," Flora replied, smiling broadly. "He's an enchanting fellow, as fine as cream gravy. He's a true friend of mine. Would you like me to accompany you?"

"Yes and no," Naomi answered swiftly. "I appreciate the offer, but feel as though I must make acquaintances and discover these streets for myself. Another time?"

Flora nodded. "Definitely. Take in the whole kit and caboodle, Naomi. Stay on the boardwalk when you can and when you can't, keep an eye peeled for horse patties."

Naomi pushed her chair back and stood. "This has been lovely. I'm so happy to have you as a friend, Flora," She started to leave, but turned back. "Would you be willing to take me shopping some time? I only have dreary dresses and must liven up my wardrobe."

"Yes, I would enjoy an outing with you."

"We'll plan on it," Naomi said, then departed. She moved determinedly. She loitered on the veranda of Drovers Cottage for a few moments, taking in the air. It was hot and sticky. An outgoing blue-ticked cattle-dog came over to give her an exhaustive sniffing. Its approval of her could be seen in the vigorous wag of its tail and meaningful glimmer showing in its eyes.

Naomi Engle gave its head a pat before scurrying off to find her brother.

<center>~~~</center>

Liam Greer was straddled on Hero, riding lazily toward town. His eyes were glassy and inattentive. He was in a trancelike fantasyland, wedged between harking back to Jackson Scully and looking ahead to the murderous exploits they'd undertake together. The horse picked its way along the trail beside Mud Creek without any prodding or tugs on the reins by its owner.

Scully had been with Sweet Flora the night Greer first met her. There was no mistaking the man's crippled gait. Greer had seen him teeter totter across the side yard to his horse. Of that, Greer had no doubt or illusions; neither did he care. From the moment Scully had ridden into camp and declared that he had a previous claim on the site, Greer had taken a liking to him.

That initial partiality now bordered on deification. Scully had shown interest in Greer's efforts to master the handgun; he had provided tips and pointers that steered him in the direction he wanted to go. Scully was a counterweight to Jondreau's cautionary counsel. Whereas, Jondreau spoke about morality and principles, Scully emphasized techniques and trickeries. Greer took fanatical pleasure in the ex-soldier's advocacy and words of affirmation.

He arched his back and stretched in the saddle. The palomino whinnied, but remained steady. He wondered about the killing that Scully said needed doing. He thought about the thrill of partnering with Scully to do murder. To be mentored by such a battle-scarred veteran of combat appealed to him; where would the trail take them and to what heights of glory?

He conjured newspaper headlines that featured his name. The bold letters detailing his daring filled him with excitement and pride. He was famous far and wide. A sketched picture was prominently displayed on wanted posters and in tabloids across the country; it showcased him as handsome and steely-eyed, with a jutting granite jaw and dashing moustache.

In his make-believe he was a near perfect caricature of a highwayman with a golden heart, plundering the rich and a champion of the poor. The violence and murders were glossed over; only bad men and unscrupulous robber barons tasted lead from his pistol. Ballads were written about him and pretty girls fawned over him in parlors.

The smile on his face as he rode was vacuous. He removed his Stetson and palmed sweat off his forehead. The sun was high above him, torturous and pitiless; the horizon in front of him shimmered with heat waves. He put his hat back on. He began picking at the front of his linen shirt and fanning it against the wetness trickling down his chest.

He reached for a plug of tobacco. His supply of it was dwindling because he had been excessively indulgent. He bit off a hunk and chewed it open-mouthed for a few minutes, his jaw laboring almost mechanically. The flavor of molasses was sweet-smelling and gratifying.

When he finally had it soaked and softened, he tucked pieces into each cheek, which gave him the unappealing appearance of a chipmunk eating. He began thinking about his plans for the hours ahead; a glorious scheme of gallant banditry. The day was destined to be momentous. By sundown his woman would be at his side, affirming her love and loyalty.

He intended to go straight to Drovers Cottage and find Abbey Langton. He would give her a kissing to sweep her off her feet. If she refused to be swept, then he was prepared to have her by force if necessary. He expected no problems, but just in case, his gunbelt was hidden in his saddlebags. The city ordinance made a mockery of his self-image, but he would adhere to it for now. If, however, need or opportunity arose, the weapon would be within reach.

He spat a streamer of juice that dribbled down his chin. He cussed and backhanded it away. He felt a chill pass over him. He was suddenly antsy. His skin crinkled as the sheen of perspiration momentarily dried. He glanced over his shoulder, but could see nothing or no one. He twisted in the saddle to study his back trail. It was clear for as far as he could see.

Greer grimaced and rode on. Edginess lingered in him.

Sam Beadle was in a bit of a tizzy. His emotions were loose and spinning out of control. He was walking aimlessly, attempting to make plans, but hindered by a critical urgency spiraling downward inside him. He had been on his own and making his way in the world since leaving home at seventeen—almost half his life and now, big changes were coming at him.

He couldn't stop thinking about consequences and responsibilities. Marriage meant being answerable for the welfare and well-being of a woman. He was realizing that the ramifications of those obligations were infinite. To him, until Abbey Langton breezed into Abilene, matrimony had only been a vague notion that would occur in the natural passage of time.

He was endeavoring to keep his mind focused while maintaining a disengaged heart; a herculean task that had impossible properties. No matter how hard he tried, his brain refused to function with its normal discipline. There was not enough oxygen in his bloodstream. The blood pumping through his heart had been permeated by Abbey Langton; the promise sparkling in her eyes and hiding behind her smile overwhelmed his sensibilities. Love had done him in.

His hands were in his pockets; head lowered and shoulders hunched forward in a physical manifestation to the heaviness of the word responsibility. He couldn't parse or deconstruct it; the magnitude of it was endlessly inescapable. He had circled town twice, but was making no advances at all in his mental machinations.

He spotted Pete Axler and ran over to him. "You got a minute, Pete?"

The lawman wasn't wearing his gun or badge. He looked haggard. "Suppose so."

"Let's sit a stint," Sam said, jabbing a thumb at a bench. It was on the boardwalk on the shady side of the street, not far from the Merchants Hotel. He took a seat and leaned forward, elbows on his knees, hands clenched into tight balls.

"I got no new information, Sam."

Beadle was nonplussed. "About what?"

"Regarding Jackson Scully and the investigation," Pete replied, sitting down. He jostled his hat up his forehead. His face was more deeply lined than usual; pain showed in his pale eyes. "I figure Scully's in the wind or hanging around somewhere on the outskirts. Our office ain't putting in time or manpower into tracking him down. I sent out a flier on Scully, but the murder of a drifter like Rawlins ain't going to generate much interest or sympathy."

"Thanks for the update, I guess. But the topic wasn't even in my mind."

Axler raised an eyebrow, dubious. "What? Why are we gabbing here?"

Beadle frowned. He rubbed his hands together and let go a slow rush of air that came out as a sad sounding sigh. "I got a tough nut to crack and would appreciate your input."

"I ain't all that wise, Sam. Maybe you ought to talk to Deacon."

"I can't talk to Deacon on this one."

"Sounds like the jig is up."

"What's that supposed to mean?"

Axler chuckled thinly. "If you can't talk to Deacon, then this is about his daughter." He fisted a hand against his sore jaw. "Miss Abbey has got you stumped, doesn't she?"

"I'm down for the count, Pete. She knocked my lights out."

Axler slouched back and crossed his arms. "The way you been mooning over that girl I ain't surprised. A one-eyed blind man looking the other way could've seen that coming." His mouth puckered into a wince as he let out a low groan. He deposited a slobber of saliva on the walkway. He immediately covered the splat with his boot and squished it.

"Have you ever been in love, Pete?"

Axler reddened. "When are you going to drop the punch line?"

"No joke," Sam said quietly. "I'm serious."

Axler pondered on it. He kept pressing his palm against his right cheek. When he spoke it was in a confessional tone. "I ain't ever been one who had a way with women, Sam. I can hardly talk to them. I can't seem to understand ladies. I had a chance once, but no more." A small smile bent his lips. "When I was still in Fort Smith I lived with a grass widow for a couple years, but then, she decided I wasn't a money maker or didn't move fast enough or something. She got her fancy on for a banker, made her move on him and that was the end of us."

"That's too bad, Pete. Was she worth it?"

"When it was good it was *real* good," Pete answered wistfully. "We had us a time, but could've never made the long haul. There were too many differences and I was too wet behind the ears to know any better. I'll tell you this, Sam. There ain't nothing like waking up in a soft bed beside a woman every morning; her warmth, her smell, her smile."

Beadle waggled his fingers. "I fear failing her."

"You fear stupidity," Pete said sharply. "A case of cold feet is all you got. If you had the sense God gave an ox you'd quit whining and marry that gal." He stood. "I'm off-duty, which more and more seems to be the norm, but I've got to go. I have an appointment to keep."

"Thanks for your time and counsel, Pete. Both are appreciated."

Axler gave him a nod of a shrug. He ambled off in his usual dragging gait.

Beadle exhaled wearily. Unless he lost his nerve, today would be *the* day. With his mind elsewhere, he jumped up so quickly that he almost slammed into a woman in a plain gray dress. He mumbled a hasty apology and headed toward Drovers Cottage. There was a locket pendant that needed to be retrieved before he took care of business at Ed Gaylord's Twin Livery.

All the due diligence had been done. Sam Beadle now had to be a man about it.

～～～

Charley Jondreau was in the saddle, trailing a mile or so behind Liam Greer. He wasn't in any particular hurry; neither did he care if his presence was known. He had nothing to hide, therefore no reason to put forth any effort to be undetected, though it was evident that Greer had not seen him. He knew Greer's destination, and was tagging along only to witness the young man's objective, or if necessary and doable, to prevent him from his self-destructive designs.

A dot appeared in the boundless blue sky. The instant Jondreau saw it, he kept it in view. It was high and far ahead, but dropping and coming toward him fast. The space was speedily gobbled up. When Jondreau recognized it, his eyes squinted into skinny slits because of the force and fullness of his smile. The bird was a mature hawk, large and inspiring.

He felt peaceful watching it draw near. His heart was as free as the bird of prey sailing across the cloudless expanse. Sunlight reflected off its feathers, giving it a radiant aura. Its breast was white and speckled by markings of rust, its tail the color of dried blood. The raptor flew effortlessly, its wings angled to soar on the heat-charged currents of air.

He glided with it; his body on horseback, his mind faraway in the heavens above. His eyes closed. A deep-pitched chant whispered from his throat. It became strong and loud, ancient phrases of admiration and thanksgiving rooted in the spirituality of his maternal ancestors. His hands released the reins. He leaned back, arms stretching wide in full surrender.

A hoarse rasp of a scream brought him back. The hawk was less than twenty feet directly above. He bowed his head for a moment. It dipped low to the ground behind him and swooped into a one hundred and eighty degree turn. Its wings flapped mightily in a rushing burst of energy as it climbed higher and higher, flying off in the direction of Abilene.

Charley Jondreau followed obediently. Any bits and bobs of doubt haunting him scattered and disintegrated in a heartbeat. There could be no mistaking his purpose. He was where the Great Spirit wanted him to be; he was doing what the Great Spirit wanted him to do. He spoke to the pinto and patted its neck. The pony snorted and leapt forward, running in long strides.

~~~

"Is it going to hurt?"

"Of course it's going to hurt," Whitey replied, eyes lively and flashing. "Do I look like some snake charming, tent revival miracle worker? Take another good swig of whiskey."

Axler balked. "I've already had three."

Fitzgerald poured the liquor. "Have another or I'll bust your head and bash you loopy with a mallet." He handed him the glass and said, "I swear, you're being such a sissy."

Axler tossed off the drink, swallowing it slowly. "I ain't a sissy." He put the glass on the counter and sat back in the barber chair, hands gripping the armrests. "You can call me a sissy or crazy if you like, but I just don't happen to be a fan of pain. That's all there is to it."

"Well, you won't see me shedding any tears for you," Whitey replied, grinning happily. "You only got yourself to blame for the sorry condition of that tooth." He opened up his canvas dentistry toolkit. "You've been playing doctor with it for how long?"

"A couple weeks maybe," Pete said, flinching uneasily.

Fitzgerald made his click-click noise, eyes rolling in disgust. "Glory be," he exclaimed, poking a finger at him. "You ought to have come seen me when it first started aching." He began laying out forceps and pliers, sickle probes, and a dental mirror.

Axler gulped. "What are you going to do with those things?"

"Would you like me to be all chummy and tell you a big story?" Whitey asked, arranging each tool in a specific order. His voice was dripping with sarcasm as he went on. "It could go like this: Pete, these fine instruments here be magical. If you'll just open your trap and let me put them to use, a spell will be cast and you'll be healed. No fuss, no muss, no blood."

"I ain't an idiot or feeble-minded, Whitey."

Fitzgerald held his hands up and pressed a contrite smile at him. "There ain't no easy way to do what's got to be done here. I'll be as quick as I can be, but you're going to experience pain. I'm going to examine that rotting molar by picking at and around it. In all likelihood I'll have to rip it out by the roots and you're going to bleed like a stuck pig."

"Okay. Stop yammering and do it."

"You want more whiskey?"

"No. I already got my load half-on."

"You want a blindfold?"

"No blindfold, Whitey. Just get it done, will you please?"

Fitzgerald got the dental mirror and a probe. "Lean your head back and open wide."

Axler complied. The man born into chattel servitude went to work, his hands deft and agile. He scratched the tooth and gently prodded the inflamed gums on the lower right jaw, all the while click-clicking in staccato fashion. His patient stiffened as rigid as an oak plank.

Fitzgerald took a step back. "There ain't no way to save that molar, Pete. It has to be extracted." He returned the probe to its spot and selected the largest pliers available.

Axler's eyes bulged, then immediately squeezed shut.

Fitzgerald positioned himself, feet firmly secured on the floor. He inserted the mirror with one hand, the pliers with the other. Getting a grip on the bad tooth presented no difficulties. He clamped the handles as tight as possible and began applying lateral pressure. It was at that precise moment that his lanky customer began squirming and kicking.

The nappy-haired barber turned dentist held on with a fierceness that belied his pintsize physique. He yanked hard and leaned one way. He tugged and vehemently inclined to the opposite slant. A sickening suction sound erupted, but was muffled and drowned into silence by the moaning scream emanating from the rock-bottom of Axler's lungs. It was a shrill rumble that bounced off the walls of the barbershop and rebounded into the street.

Fitzgerald stretched up, tugging and wrenching and sweating. His grasp on the pliers, which remained firmly clinched on the noxious molar, was fixed and braced. He kept pulling and heaving with strength and smoothness; there was no jerking or twisting involved in his exertions. His hands were slickly lathered with blood-flecked saliva. He was almost on top of the lawman's chest. The rolling wails of his discomfort were gaining volume. Axler was twitching seizure-like, but abruptly, when the task was mercifully accomplished, he collapsed into stillness.

"Oh, my! Could I be of some service?"

Fitzgerald spun around to see a woman standing in the doorway. His feet hit the floor with a thud, his right fist clinging to the pliers, which held the bloody culprit in its jaws. It was a hellish eyesore, dripping with glutinous globs of mucous and tissue.

She whipped past him and grabbed a hand towel to begin tending to and tidying up the man sprawled limply in the barber chair. He was no longer shrieking. He had passed out and was groaning. He started to regain consciousness, gagging and choking on blood and pus. She dabbed the wretched goo off his bristly chin and cheeks.

Fitzgerald was blabbering incessantly. His words gushed out in an animated flood of emotion. He gave her instructions on what to do next, his click-click furious and seemingly out of control in the excitement. The only flaw with his directives was that he was consistently one step behind her. She was efficient, effectively deploying practical nursing skills.

Axler's eyelids flickered. His eyes popped open with a jolt. He straightaway pulled back from her touch, startled and ill at ease. He tried to sit up, but wobbled and slumped back.

"Stay put, Pete." Fitzgerald nudged her. She stepped out of his way. He handed Axler a glass with a shot of whiskey in it. "Hold this in your mouth and swish it around for as long as you can. It'll kill the germs and impurities. *Don't* swallow it! Spit it out."

Axler did as he was told. His eyes narrowed on the stranger watching him. As his lips puckered and pursed, he blinked rapidly as though he was clearing his focus. The confusion in his distressed expression was distinct and well-defined. He spat with a grunt.

Fitzgerald took the tumbler from him. He dumped the swill into the bucket where he'd dropped the decayed tooth. He handed him some whiskey soaked cotton batting. "Wad this up and tuck it into the hole. Scrunch your teeth around it. Sit back and rest awhile."

Axler fidgeted clumsily for a bit. His fingers were shaking, his eyes watery. He finally managed to get the compress in place. His breathing thickened as his eyes winked closed.

Fitzgerald turned to the woman. "I be Whitey, ma'am." His smile expanded and fluttered into a bright-eyed and welcoming look. "That suffering soul is Pete Axler. We're both grateful for your assistance. You came along when you was most needed."

"I'm Naomi Engle," she said pleasantly. "I'm happy to meet you and glad that I could help." She offered him a large smile; it creased her eyes and cast her cheeks into a rosy hue. She gave him the towel she had used and brushed her hands against the sides of her skirt. "I was told you would know where my brother, Deacon Coburn, might be just now."

"Say what?" Whitey huffed in air and lurched in his footsteps as though someone had stuck a darning needle in his backside. "You be Deacon's sister? I'll be a hornswoggled old huckleberry. Lord Almighty, first his daughter comes to town, now his sister."

Her smile faded into uncertainty. "His daughter?"

"She be a pretty young thing. A real go-getter."

"This is interesting news to me."

"Deacon and Abbey get along as right as rain. Lots of kindness between them."

Axler snorted and moaned, then was still again. Fitzgerald studied him, nodding.

"Where could I find my brother, Whitey?"

Fitzgerald scratched at the underside of his jaw. His head was trembling back and forth in a fitful shake. "That man be an enigma, ma'am." He shook his head more energetically. "He's mostly on the move during daylight hours. Sometimes he's in here every day and then I won't see him for weeks. It's been that way lately." His brow wrinkled deeply. "Your best bet this morning might be the stockyards. All you got to do is follow your nose."

"Thank you. I'll go there now." She started to leave.

"Miss Naomi."

She turned back. "Yes, Whitey."

"It sure be fine making your acquaintance, ma'am."

"I count you as my friend, Whitey," she said sincerely. "You take care of Mr. Axler. Tell him for the next few days he ought to regularly rinse out his mouth with salt water." She adjusted the loose loop of the navy blue scarf. When she departed, a glowing smile graced her face.

Fitzgerald watched her walk away. He moved over to his patient, who was snoring. "Lord Almighty, did you hear that, Pete? You got pampered by Deacon's sister." He busily began cleaning and putting away his dental instruments. His chitchat was continuous and laced with humorous observations as he click-clicked and marveled over recent events and revelations.

The afternoon solitude at Willows Rest, so christened by infatuated sweethearts, was endearing and tranquil. An intermittent breeze eased through the grove of coyote willows along an insignificant offshoot draining into the Saline River; the leaves riffled so slightly as to be indifferent to the irregular swirls of hot air.

Abbey Langton had arranged a thick blanket on a level spot beneath the branches of one of the largest trees. She sat leaning back a bit; her legs folded beneath her skirt and off to the side. She had been asked to stay put, which she did with feigned reluctance.

The meal—fried chicken, potato salad, and apples for dessert—had been enjoyed, but Sam assured her that the picnic wasn't over yet. He'd strapped the basket on the back of the buggy, and was now moving the mule to a fresh patch of grass. Her eyes didn't stray far from him. The potent vitality of her feelings stirred her deeply; if a flurry of desperation to deny them lashed her, she knew there could be no contradicting the status of her heart.

She was anxious. She had no idea how to sift through the grains of her emotions. So far the day's conversation had avoided those depths. She and Sam had come to the verge more than once, but in each instance, diverted to superficial matters. She wondered how much longer their discussion could be about the drought and other weather related issues.

Old Blue had dug a hollow in the shade. It was stretched out there on its belly, motionless except for an occasional swish of its tail. The dog's ears were perked up, its eyes dutifully fixed on Abbey, monitoring every shift in facial expression or change of posture.

Sam Beadle was chaffing his hands together as he returned to the blanket. He sat across from her, hesitation in his manner. He took a quick look in the direction of the western horizon and announced, "We'll need to leave in no later than an hour or so to get back before dark."

"I'm ready whenever you are, Sam. You're the one driving."

He fidgeted. "That's true. I'm also the one who has something important to say."

She lowered her eyes. "I'm listening."

He stared past her. He reached inside his vest and fumbled with a velvet covered box. His eyes settled on her face. "I hope you will accept this gift as a token of my affection."

She tried to suppress a smile. She held her lips in a threadlike line, but the sparkle showing in her eyes exposed her delight. "Thank you," she said, taking it. She turned it over in her hands. It was a long rectangular container, with a snap centered on its topside. She clicked it and hitched in a surprised breath when she saw what was inside. "Oh, Sam . . ."

She lifted the adornment out. The glimmer in her eyes dropped down and lifted her lips into a spectacular smile. She held the circular gold locket in a palm, fingering the intricate floral design around its edges. She touched a tiny clasp. The top of the locket popped open to reveal his picture framed inside. She compared it to the man staring longingly at her. "Thank you, Sam. I will treasure this always." She handed it to him. "Will you please help me put it on?"

He took hold of the spindly gold chain. Her auburn hair was an orderly collection of large ringlets resting on her shoulders. She gathered the curls together and pulled them aside. He knelt behind her, mishandling the fastener for several seconds. He managed to get it working. She guided the pendant as his hands skimmed the sides of her neck. She sighed and shivered. His scent filled her nostrils; it was a pleasurable mix of perspiration and bayberry.

He completed the task, remaining on a knee. "Abbey," he said, reaching around to touch her chin. She didn't protest as he turned her face to him. Their eyes dovetailed together; hers were wide and dreamy, his pulled tight and burning intensely. "Will you marry me?"

Her lips quivered. "Sam . . ."

"Is that a yes?"

She pushed his hand off her chin. Old Blue was up and barking at her. She slid a couple feet away from him. "I'm flattered and thrilled by your request, but I'm afraid."

He squatted on the blanket across from her. "Afraid of what, Abbey?"

"Afraid that we're moving too fast. Are we really ready for marriage?" Old Blue came over and nuzzled her hard. She grabbed the scruff of its neck. "It's a forever step, Sam."

"I'm aware of that, Abbey."

"I know you are, Sam. I'm sorry. I'm not saying no. I'm saying wait."

"Wait for what? My heart is full of love for you, Abbey."

She cast her eyes downward. Tears dripped onto her cheeks. Her right hand caressed the gold locket. "My heart is overflowing with joy and love, Sam, but I'm scared," she said, voice tense and muted. "I know how short and fragile life can be. What has happened between us seems too good to be true." She gave Old Blue a shove. It whined and pawed the ground. She persisted in thrusting it away. The dog flopped down, staring at her with definite sadness.

He gave her a whacky grin. "You should listen to Old Blue."

She wiped moisture from the corners of her eyes. "Maybe so, but I need to think all this through, Sam. I want to imagine what our life together will look like. I'm not saying no."

He smiled. "*The lady doth protest too much, methinks.*"

She sat bolt upright, eyes broadening in surprise. "What do you know of Hamlet?"

He regarded her, obviously caught off guard by her reaction and tone. "Just a few lines from Hamlet, but I can recite several passages of Macbeth." He stood unexpectedly and made a big production of striking a theatrical pose, extending a hand toward an unseen object. "*Is this a dagger which I see before me, the handle toward my hand? Come, let me clutch thee. I have thee not, and yet I see thee still. Art thou not, fatal vision, sensible to feeling as to sight? Or art thou but a dagger of the mind, a false creation, proceeding from the heat-oppressed brain?*" He broke off the soliloquy, clapped his hands and started laughing uproariously.

She was grinning at him. "What's so funny?"

"Come now, good lady," he replied, bowing at the waist. "You must see the irony. Given the heatwave, it occurred to me that perhaps my *heat-oppressed brain* misheard you."

"Ha-ha-ha, Mr. Beadle." She batted her eyes. "Where did you learn Shakespeare?"

He sat down, close to her. "Back in Souderton," he said, crossing his legs. "Miss Pringle taught me to love words and language. The rhythm of Shakespeare got inside my head."

She was absentmindedly cuddling the pendant in her right hand. "My mother used the Bible and Shakespeare to teach me mostly everything. I learned reading and writing, and a multitude of different lessons about human nature to be applied in real life situations."

"We have much in common, Abbey."

"I know, Sam."

"So what's the holdup?"

She raised her eyebrows. "Don't consider it a holdup. I only mean to take this step once. Allow me the opportunity to weigh and cherish these moments." Her eyes were pleading, tender, inviting. He cautiously leaned in to kiss her. She angled back and placed three fingers against his lips. "Not quite yet, Samuel Beadle. We can wait until our engagement is official."

He chuckled throatily. "When can your decision be expected?"

"Tomorrow, I promise. I'll give you my answer tomorrow, Sam."

He rolled to his feet. "I intend to hold you to that, Miss Langton."

"That's fine, Mr. Beadle. I'm a woman of my word."

He offered her his hands. She accepted with a demure nod. She appreciated the strength of his grip when he pulled her up. As she rose, she twisted just enough for her right shoulder to brush against his chest for a fleeting instant. He haltingly reached to wrap her in a hug, but she scampered free and wiggled a no-no finger at him. Bantering laughter passed between them.

Old Blue howled and rollicked as they folded the blanket together.

Liam Greer was steamed. Anger boiled in his veins. He had gotten to town early in the afternoon and dropped into Drovers Cottage, only to find that Abbey Langton was nowhere to be found. He decided that he would wait for her to return. He hung around the Merchants Hotel and struck up an argument with some horse traders. When that fizzled out, he walked the streets alone for several hours, growing madder with each swaggering footstep.

His plan might need some adjusting, but in his mind, the outcome was all that mattered. He would make such a big splash of impressing Abbey Langton that she would declare her undying love and adoration.

When dusk began its descent, Greer was sitting on Hero, biding his time by replaying imagery of his woman fussing over him.

He had been so preoccupied in his fictional delusion that he never noticed Deacon Coburn sitting on the veranda of the Alamo Saloon. Neither was he ever once aware that Charley Jondreau had kept tabs on him all day. Just now, Jondreau was easing along the shadowy boardwalk, staying twenty yards behind his quarry.

Greer rode in an identifiable pattern. Along Cedar Street, then back to Texas Street; he would patrol up and down Texas Street before revisiting Cedar Street. His elaborate turns at the intersection were displays that involved Hero doing a high-stepping prance for several yards. To and fro he went, his demeanor proud and cocksure, his Stetson low on his forehead.

Thick swatches of gray were blending the blue out of the sky. He ignored the activity going on all around him. He alternated between the role-playing scenario trolling through his mind and scanning the surroundings with eyes to see only Abbey Langton. He was so obsessed and fixated on her—in and outside his head—that no one else even registered.

When he saw her, it was from a distance. He stood in the stirrups. His heart jumped. She was sitting beside the hotel clerk in a mule-drawn carriage, which was traveling at a rapid clip. They were smiling and expressing amusement. Their evident contentment and closeness enraged him; in his state of thinking their laughter was directed at him.

His ire escalated off any conceivable scale. A hot-flash seared through him. His blood pressure soared, his eyes bugged open. A buzz began ringing loudly in his ears. The pulse-points in his temples throbbed. A dizzy wave of vertigo struck him. He wobbled and grabbed the saddle horn. All color drained from his face as his teeth gritted into a hate-filled sneer.

In that instant, Liam Greer detoured to a place that was entirely beyond the realm of reality. He began screaming a string of unintelligible phrases that were slurred and slobbery. The bellowing braggadocio shocked bystanders. Every person within earshot whirled about, looked out a window, or ran toward the shrieking noise. Clusters of onlookers knotted together, lining the streets to watch what appeared to have the makings of an exciting spectacle.

Greer was too absorbed elsewhere to notice the audience. All he saw was Abbey Langton in the company of another man. His protruding eyes zoomed in on them. He dug his heels into Hero's flanks and jerked its head back. The stallion exploded into a gallop straight at the buggy, gaining speed and gobbling up ground.

A raging obscenity blistered the air; it was a terrifying oath birthed inside some craterous trench of Greer's madness. He rode upright, one hand working above his head as though he had an invisible lasso. He yanked on the reins, spewing profane gibberish directed at the woman who inhabited his pretend world. Dirt flew and splattered the air as yells erupted from all corners.

The palomino pounded to a thumping stop, but not before slamming into the mule and knocking it sideways; it reared up and writhed wildly. Sam Beadle fought to control the animal and balance the buggy, which was tilted backwards at a precarious angle. Abbey Langton, alarmed and infuriated, hung onto him fiercely, hands intertwined around his waist.

Old Blue reacted in pure instinct. The woman it had chosen to befriend and protect was in danger. It hunkered low and raced toward the palomino. The strapping cattle-dog remembered all its training with longhorns; it also recalled that the broad-shouldered man who helped everyone and fed it hambones for breakfast had given it the challenge to care for the young lady.

It catapulted its body at the horse, striking full force in its chest. The stallion backed up, pawed the air and attempted to hoof its attacker, but was no match for the bluish-black bundle of ferocity. The dog never hesitated. It dipped and darted, nipping at the palomino's heels as the panicky horse kicked, snorted and rotated around in a frenzy to escape.

Old Blue subdued the horse in a rapid sequence of herding; the stallion stood still, eyes wary. Then, without pausing, the dog turned its attention to the rider, who it understood to be the real threat to the woman. The man was unnerved and intimidated. He gasped wetly as he reached and rummaged in the saddlebags. The dog snarled and leapt, its jaws locking on a shirt sleeve.

Greer yelped and squealed like a frightened child. The linen material ripped free, which caused Old Blue to plunge headlong into the dusty avenue. It toppled into a skid, immediately crouched and stalked the man, its hackles ruffled into spikey thickets of hair. The dog spat and growled. Greer's complexion was ghostly. He wheeled the horse around and took off south.

Old Blue was not yet satisfied. It chased after him for a half-mile or more.

~~~

When Old Blue launched its body at the palomino, the scene was bedlam. The mule was heehawing and thrashing about in a berserk ruckus. Its hindquarters were lunging in the opposite direction of its front, straining against the harness. Sam was shouting commands and nearly standing as he tugged on the reins; Abbey was silent as she clung to him.

Deacon Coburn, along with several other men, ran full-speed to the buggy. They latched onto the backside of it and heaved their muscles against it to prevent the vehicle from tipping over. Charley Jondreau arrived at the same time. He grabbed the mule by the bridle and wrestled it. He murmured soft words in a soothing voice and held tight to the leather straps. The animal soon settled and became docile. He rubbed its sweat-lathered neck and stayed beside it.

Jondreau spoke quietly to Coburn. "I told you he was unredeemable."

Coburn grimaced. There was bitterness in his face, which was set as unbreakable as a brickwork wall. He pursed his lips as he stepped close to him. In a stringent rasp meant only for Jondreau's ears, he said, "Don't ever tell me I told you so again. *No one's* unredeemable."

Jondreau smiled grimly. His mouth took on its bulldog appearance. "Time is not contrary to truth, preacher-man. I can wait it out to see who's right and who's wrong on this one."

Coburn's expression hardened even more. He lifted a hand and acted as if he was going to reply, but then, his jawline constricted and his head shook tremulously. He sidled to where his daughter was standing beside Sam Beadle. They were both red-faced and livid. He had vaulted to safety in a sweeping fluid motion, with her securely in his arms.

"I'm going after him, Deacon."

"That'd be a mistake, Sam."

Beadle scowled. "This ends now."

Abbey laughed nervously. "Leave him be, Sam. He's twitchy in the head."

"Letting him be doesn't set right with me, Abbey."

Coburn put an arm around her shoulders and held her in a firm embrace. She was seething, trembling with emotion. He noted the pendant hanging on a chain around her neck because she kept tapping it as though she was checking to make sure it was real. With the excitement over, the crowd had dispersed and gotten back to their activities.

Jondreau loitered over and took up a spot in front of Beadle. "Greer is a coward. He will get his due," he said in a tone that was sharp and edgy with authority. He pressed in even closer and placed a hand over Beadle's heart. "You are a much bigger man, eh." His smile was shrewd and perceptive as he tipped a nod at the woman. "You have a better life to live."

Beadle was inflexible. "Someone has to end it. If Greer ever crosses me again . . ."

Abbey stopped him by giving his hand a squeeze. "Take the buggy to the livery, Sam. Get some sleep. I will see you tomorrow. I have a promise to keep. Remember?"

Beadle blushed and lowered his eyes. He shuffled toward the mule.

"I'll come along." Jondreau fell in behind him. "My pony's stabled there."

Coburn gave them a wave that was almost a salute. A barking accompanied their departure. Old Blue came loping back, grinning and breathing hard. It went directly to Abbey Langton and sat at her feet. The dog's eyes were forlorn. It started sniffing her as if to determine her condition. She knelt and hugged its neck. She gave its sides a kneading and allowed it to lick her cheeks. When she stood, its tail was thumping enough to make a puffy dust cloud.

"You done good, Old Blue," Deacon said, patting its head. "Let's go, Abbey." He took her by the hand and led her away. The dog kept close to her. She momentarily cast her eyes back. Then she relaxed against her escort's shoulder. She could feel the tension in him and was sad for it, but grateful for his concern and compassion. She looked up. Her lips curled happily.

An ever-growing number of stars were twinkling in the darkening sky.

An hour later, when Deacon Coburn was sure his daughter had no lingering hurts, he said his goodnights and closed her door at Drovers Cottage. He had one more stop to make. It wasn't far, but he was nearly emotionally rudderless. Memories and regrets were unhinged inside him. He paced along the second floor hallway, conflicted and disbelieving.

He bucked up and knocked on the designated door. He waited, holding his breath.

A minute passed. Then a voice tentatively asked, "Who is it?"

"Deacon." The door swung open. He gasped and shuddered. His heart swelled. He felt moisture gathering in his eyes. In his mind, he hurtled into the past. The highs and lows of his upbringing came from nowhere, along with the loneliness of blunders and misadventures. He was flummoxed by the sentiments cascading through him, but remained stoic.

The lady staring at him had their mother's lean and gentle beauty, but like him, she possessed their father's black hair and tawny complexion. She wore the drab garb of the River Brethren and her tresses were tied up in a bun. She had only been a child when he'd left home to be involved in righting wrongs and making a mark for justice in the abolitionist movement; he easily recognized the little girl inside the woman.

"Please come in, Deacon."

He did so. His posture was reticent, his face expressionless. "All day long, everywhere I went, people told me my sister was looking for me. I thought they were crazy. I see that they were correct. How are you, Naomi? More to the point, what are you doing here?"

"Will you sit and visit awhile?"

He took a wide circuit around her and sat in a wing-back chair. She moved purposefully. There was one oil lamp burning on a bedside table beside a Bible. She adjusted the wick to its optimal height. The room brightened, but she wasn't finished. She lit another lamp, tinkered with the flame until it shone radiantly, then placed it on the chest of drawers.

She sat on the edge of the bed, facing him with an earnest smile. "My husband died. We were childless. I decided to put that pain behind me and search for a new beginning."

Empathy filled his eyes. His voice was low as he quoted a Proverb of Solomon: "*Hope deferred maketh the heart sick: but when the desire cometh, it is a tree of life.*"

"I stand on that assurance, Deacon," she said, somewhat brusquely. "I'm angry at God and occupied by turmoil, but my everyday prayer is for the faith to believe."

"God greets your anger with grace, Naomi."

Her mouth flinched. "I want to hold onto that with all my heart."

"The Lord can take whatever we puny humans dish out," he said emphatically. "God has seen and heard it all before; the hurts, the failings, the guilt, the blame, the shame, the rage, the times we shake an awful fist at him. Nothing we say or do can ever take him by surprise." He crossed his legs comfortably and folded his hands together. "God is omnipotent. Shouldering your anger won't hinder his everlasting love for you, Naomi."

She stood. "Mother would be uplifted to hear your words." She sidestepped to the bedside table and picked up her Bible. She removed an envelope and handed it to him. "When my decision to travel west was final, she wrote this in hopes that I would find you."

He took it. There was no name or address on it. He jostled the envelope against his knee for several moments before unsealing it. He shook
the single sheet out and unfolded it. The first thing that occurred to him
was that the flowing scroll of the penmanship was fine-looking and artis-
tic. He was breathing evenly as he held the letter close and began to read it.

May, 1872

*Dear Son: It has now been more than a decade since we last laid eyes
on each other. We cried and prayed together. I have often remembered our
tears in my prayers for you. On that day I gave you my blessing; I renew the
sanctity of that benediction to you here and now.*

*You belong to God utterly. Your path, though far different than what I
had planned, is the one ordained for you by the Maker of heaven and earth.
My understandings are frail and tarnished by fallible human reasoning, but
in faith, I know your steps were shaped whilst I carried you in my womb.
Walk them with integrity and righteousness. When hard-pressed by evil,
embrace the deliverance of God. He will not fail or forsake you.*

*I must share news on behalf of Father. I beseech you to receive it with an
open heart. Shortly before he passed from time to eternity, Father repented
of his wrongness in withholding the right hand of fellowship from you. He
sought your forgiveness and reconciliation. His sorrow broke his spirit. He
longed to express his remorse to you personally, Deacon. He wanted to be at
peace with you. May the Lord grant you much goodwill and harmony with
the information.*

*I am well, thank the Lord. I pray this finds you strong and centered. I
was grateful for your letter. I will not ask you to return, but I do request a
regular correspondence, so as I can know how best to present your needs to
our Heavenly Father, to whom all glory belongs.*

Blessings Always,
Your Loving Mother

He was teary-eyed and his chest was heaving as he took in gulps of
air. He returned the letter to its envelope and laid it on his lap. The feelings
running loose in him were sentimental and nostalgic; there was also an
undercurrent of mourning and an abiding sense of loss. He shifted in the
chair and rubbed his eyes with the heels of his hands.

"Mother has never wavered in her love and prayers for you," Naomi
said in a sympathetic tone. She was sitting on the bed. "There was tension and confusion after you left. Elders came to talk with Father and

Mother. The children were hustled out of the room, but we heard. Our family life changed and very soon our standing amongst the brethren was different too."

"I'm sorry, Naomi. I had to follow my conscience."

"You have no reason to apologize to me, Deacon."

He shrugged. "Often personal choices have wide-ranging consequences for others."

"When I learned what led you away I was proud of you. I thought of you as a knight on a white steed doing battle against evil." She gave him a raised eyebrows smile. "Father became severely strict, demanding that we follow his leadership. Martha and our brothers did so, but not me and not Mother. We secretly rebelled. In our quiet times together we always wondered about where you were and what you were doing. Our prayers for you were fervent."

"Only eternity will reveal how those prayers sustained me."

"We refused to take the shunning to heart," she said, "though it wasn't officially referred to as shunning. You had been disciplined and disfellowshipped for your waywardness."

"Perhaps it was best. After all, I did take some wayward turns."

"Aren't wayward turns places to learn lessons and make course corrections?"

"If grace and wisdom prevail," he replied gravely.

"Grace and wisdom must have prevailed in your case."

"I was fortunate, Naomi. I was lost for a long while."

"You're not lost anymore. All the folks I met today have enormous respect for you, which speaks to the vitality of your upright moral fiber. I gleaned much." Her brown eyes were full of warmth and good cheer. "I felt like royalty being Deacon Coburn's sister."

His moustache twitched as his lips tightened. "You are too kind."

"I was at the window earlier," she said, soft and cautious. "I saw you walking protectively with a young lady. She had her head resting on your shoulder. I believe her name is Abbey."

"She's my daughter. Her mother passed."

"I'm anxious to meet my niece."

"Maybe tomorrow." He rose to his feet, stretching as he did so. "It's late."

She came off the bed as though spontaneous combustion had put it aflame. She was on him with a suddenness that was startling. Tightly wound emotions became unmoored as she encircled him in an enthusiastic hug. She wept against his chest. He was speechless. He held her, guardedly at first, but then, as her sobbing increased, he strengthened his grip. When she had cried herself dry, she disentangled and promptly turned her back to him.

"I'm sorry. I had not wanted to make such a scene," she said in a faint murmur.

He was at a loss for words. He glanced upward to the ceiling, examined the envelope in his hands, then took some time to have a good look at the floorboards. He stiffly shifted weight from one foot to the other for several prickly moments before he walked toward the door.

"Deacon," she called, snuffling.

He had a hand on the doorknob. His eyes were downcast.

She took a step toward him, grinning slyly. "You should visit Whitey tomorrow. You need a haircut and some trimming. Underneath that scruff, I think you favor Father."

His face wrinkled and reddened into a shiny smile as a chuckle rolled from deep within. He thumbed aside the edges of his bushy moustache and wagged a finger at her. "I'm glad you're here, Naomi." He slipped out and set off down the corridor. He stopped near one of the oil lamps on the wall at the top of the stairway. He peered at the envelope. He was content and at ease. A lump of gratitude crystallized in his throat. He was in silent awe of the richness of his life.

When he jogged down the stairs, thanksgiving governed his perception.

Caleb Weitzel turned Shadrach around in a big arc until the sunrise was at his back. The eastern horizon was pinkish-orange hues scaling the slate wall of the blue-gray sky. He lifted his canteen and took a short slug from it. Long ago he had developed the habit of conserving water because it was always best to be prepared for worse case contingencies.

He had been up and on horseback for an hour or more. He had ranged purposefully over the plains far ahead, eyes and gut intuition straining to spot any clue of Daniel Twosongs, but once more, the scouting expedition proved unsuccessful. There were particles of discouragement and concern germinating in him as he returned to the campsite.

Shadrach must have sensed his consternation; the steeldust whinnied softly and moved slowly, its face expressive and animated. The bond of communication between horse and master was uncanny. He shushed it with a nudge and slight tickling of its right ear. It was an established signal that Weitzel knew would assure Shadrach. The stallion, which had already sired a dozen colts, began cantering at an anxious pace, as though there was a ready mare waiting.

Weitzel had much thinking to do. There were possibilities to be weighed and considered. He had to evaluate duty and the task ahead with the Twosongs women. What options remained for them; were they on the right track or had the rescue caravan drifted too far to the north? He gave Shadrach the reins and rode easy in the saddle. The horse took a straight-line route over the grassland, taking dips in and out of rolling hollows in stride.

Sunlight was swiftly burning away the shadows of dawn. The rays were warm on the back of his neck. He had about decided that they would tack south-easterly when an icicle chill slid down his spine. He sat upright and without delay surveyed the surroundings. There was nothing out of the ordinary, but then, at the top of a rise he hastily halted Shadrach.

Weitzel reacted deliberately. Every nerve ending snapped to attention. He retrieved his Spencer from its scabbard and flexed his knees tensely against the saddle. He aimed the carbine. His heart was in his throat; his mouth was cottony. A hundred yards below, still far away from camp, Sally Twosongs was dashing in a hurry and three wolves were round about her.

The beasts were moving fleetly, but he suddenly realized the animals weren't hostile or threatening. He was perplexed by what he saw; what was unfolding didn't make any sense. He had what appeared to be the dominant wolf in the rifle's sights when it occurred to him that she wasn't running or being chased. Sally Twosongs was dancing with carefree abandon, twirling and whirling. Her arms were outstretched, swaying effortlessly in willowy motions.

His finger trembled on the trigger. Shadrach stood completely still. She stopped and knelt. He bit the inside of his lip hard enough to taste blood. Helpless indecision roiled through him. His eyes spread wide in disbelief as one by one the wolves approached her, tails wagging. She rubbed and interacted with the feral beasts. She was laughing as the wolves played and squirmed with the easy friendliness of mollycoddled lapdogs.

It was obvious that she was talking to them; and more weirdly, listening. He watched and waited in amazement. He was dumbfounded. He reluctantly lowered the Spencer. His eyes were seeping a mix of astonishment and doubt. The wolves had relaxed completely and were sitting in a semicircle in front of Sally Twosongs.

Shadrach snorted and pawed the ground. The wolves were instantaneously up and sprinting, darting this way and that until disappearing in tall waves of grass. Weitzel rode down the slope. Sally Twosongs walked toward him, cheeks flushed and eyes smiling gleefully. Her hair was plaited in one thick pigtail that just now lay on her shoulder and across her bosom.

He dismounted, rifle in hand. "What was that, Sally Twosongs?"

She went near to him. "It will be today, but we must hurry." She touched the gun's barrel and gently but unquestionably pushed it downward. "We are to go directly east from here."

He studied her suspiciously. "What did I just witness?"

"Nothing to be concerned about, Caleb. What do you think you witnessed?"

"Sally Twosongs, please. I want to understand."

She inched past him and started caressing the horse's hindquarters. "Do you talk to Shadrach? Does Shadrach understand what you say?"

His mouth pursed and his shoulders pressed back at what she was insinuating. "No, no, no. That's different. Shadrach has been trained. We've spent years and miles together learning from each other. What I saw here is way, way, way different, Sally Twosongs."

"Is it really?"

"You *must* explain yourself," he replied, agitation showing.

"What can I tell you to take away your distress and calm you, Caleb?" she asked, continuing to pay attention to Shadrach. "It's an unknown that I cannot explain. The Creator has his ways which are not our ways. It is his world and all who walk the earth are subject to him."

"I have faith in God, Sally Twosongs."

"Place this occurrence on him. The wolves are a gift to us."

"I am baffled."

She giggled. "Me, too. I'm often baffled, but I've come to know that I must trust the mystery because we do not have the right to tell the Creator how he has to function in his creation. He does whatsoever pleases him. He uses whomever he desires. He communicates with us in nature all the time, though we are often preoccupied or too blind to see, too deaf to hear."

He took hold of her hands. "I saw what I saw. It puzzles me."

"You saw miraculous beauty. Accept it."

"I suppose I must."

"Embrace it, Caleb."

"Not sure I can get there just yet."

She flipped her hair back. The pigtail came to rest between her shoulder blades. "If you are open to the Creator, acceptance will lead you to embrace the wonder." She reached over and pushed his hat up his forehead. "We have limitations when it comes to our understandings of the Creator's methods and means. Try not to be hardhearted about it, Caleb."

He was shaking his head. "Your spirituality is so deep that sometimes I worry on you."

"Care for me, but don't worry on me. Ever," she answered with a decisive certainty. "Those three wolves are our allies, Caleb. Messengers the Creator sent to lead us to Father. And now we must hurry. Mother will be waiting for us, packed and ready."

He took a protracted look in the vicinity where the wolves had vanished. He checked the load and action on the Spencer, then returned it to its sheath. He stepped into the saddle and hoisted her up behind him. She shifted around some, her arms under his, her hands together over his chest. She leaned her head against his back as Shadrach trotted toward the campsite.

The day had only just begun, but the heat was already taxing and blistery.

Naomi Engle could hardly contain her excitement, so she was on the go before sunup. The thrills of the previous day and the heartening reunion with her brother had her restless and ready to set out to see new sights and make her way. She'd been the first customer in the dining room, where she had enjoyed a scrumptious breakfast of bacon and eggs. She then ordered a half-dozen muffins, which she intended to pick up later.

She was now on the broad veranda of Drovers Cottage trying to decide which direction to explore. The streets were mostly vacant, with only a few early risers out and about, but even so, noise and a bouquet of stink unsettled the morning. The continuous bawling of cattle from the stockyards filled the air, along with constant whiffs of manure.

She noticed a lanky fellow moving sluggishly. He was fifty or so yards away. He had a pistol holstered low on his right thigh. He came to a full stop every few steps to look here and there; his pattern included turning to reassess where he'd just been. His hat was high on his brow. His head seemed to be on a swivel for it steadily rotated to and fro.

Naomi watched him with interest. She wondered about what he was doing and for what reason was he toting a gun? Why was he so engrossed in scrutinizing the area and what was so fascinating about whatever was behind him? She thought that he had a dodgy manner, as though he was up to no good. Was he involved in some nefarious criminal activity?

It was obvious that there was no urgency in him. His posture and body language gave her the impression of an elderly gentleman whose faculties were a bit scattered. As he got close enough for her to see his face, surprise unexpectedly nipped at her. She recognized him. A bright and breezy smile engulfed her face and she rapidly walked toward him.

"How are you on this fine morning, Mr. Axler?" she asked as she stopped a few paces from him. "Is your jaw still sore? Do you have a headache from yesterday's ordeal?"

He blinked and eyed her apprehensively. "Excuse me, ma'am?"

"It's a grand day to be alive and well, isn't it, Mr. Axler?"

His face was blotchy, his expression as blank as a clean leaf of paper. The silence between them was immediate and substantial; it thickened and grew louder as the seconds passed. His hands fidgeted at his sides as he glanced around nervously.

She regarded him closely. She was put off by his manner, but not deterred. "I came upon you in your hour of need, sir," she said briskly. "And now you act as if we've never met. How do you suppose that makes a lady feel? You're not much of a boost to my ego, Mr. Axler."

"Um, I . . ." Pete had his eyes everywhere except on her. He scratched at his permanent crop of whiskery stubble. "I'm not sure I can suppose much of anything, ma'am."

Her eyes showed confusion. It was then that she noted the tin star pinned on his shirt. He must not have been on the job on the previous day because he hadn't been wearing the badge. She now thought she understood and proceeded with her assumption. "I didn't know you were a lawman, Mr. Axler. If you want me to let on to others that I never saw you when you were hurting and in a compromised position, that's just fine with me."

"Compromised position?" He gawked at her as though she had just slapped him across the face. "I'm sorry, but I don't recall ever meeting you, ma'am."

She took a step back. "I will do or say nothing to damage your civic standing, so please don't playact as though you've never made my acquaintance."

"Civic standing?" He shook his head. "I don't recall *ever* meeting you, ma'am."

"Mr. Axler, I am somewhat appalled by your mulish stubbornness."

"You got me again, ma'am. I have no clue here."

"Let me tell you something, sir. I don't appreciate your pretend insistence," she said in a tone that was becoming increasingly perturbed. "When a woman rushes to a man's side to aid him, she expects the common courtesy of being remembered. Perhaps I should've simply ignored the cries of pain coming from the barbershop yesterday and just walked on by."

He gave her a squinty-eyed grimace. Realization and his grasp on the circumstances showed in his pale eyes as bright flecks of light. His right hand covered his mouth, fingers drumming against his cheek. Red streaks of embarrassment colored his complexion.

She tilted her head. "Are you recalling it now, sir?"

"I do apologize, ma'am. I don't have much of an excuse," he replied, shrugging.

"An explanation is better than an excuse."

He hooked his thumbs in the gunbelt and tried on a grin, but it wouldn't stay in place. His lips were tight and thin. "I'd poured down a lot of whiskey and was half-drunk. When my tooth got yanked by those pliers, I passed out. I was stupefied when I came to and saw you nursing me. I thought I was dreaming or something. Afterwards, I figured Whitey was pulling my leg for sure. I do appreciate you caring for me the way you did, ma'am."

"I was gratified to be of some small service, Mr. Axler."

"Can I ask you something without getting in trouble with you again, ma'am?"

"You never were, nor are you now in trouble with me, sir."

"It surely felt like trouble, ma'am."

She smiled self-effacingly. "What's your question, Mr. Axler?"

"Are you *really* Deacon's sister?"

"Of course I am. Why do you ask with such incredulity?"

"Whitey is a grand master spinner of fibs and yarns," he answered unequivocally. "He has been known to fabricate outlandish whoppers just to get my goat, ma'am."

"Not on this occasion, Mr. Axler. Deacon is indeed my big brother."

He lifted his chin and for the first time mustered the wherewithal to actually look at her. The corners of his mouth twitched. His eyes connected with hers for a moment or two; just long enough to fluster him into stammering awkwardness. "I must be on my way."

She stopped him by raising a hand. "Perhaps you can assist me before you leave."

He appeared extremely rattled. "I will if I can, ma'am."

"Do you know a woman named Flora?" she asked easily. She was unsure of how to react to his jumpiness around her. "I didn't get her surname, but I'd like to know where she lives."

His discomfort increased; the proof was in the frown that dug deep grooves around his eyes, which were strained almost shut. His head was bent low and his mouth was open, as though he was diligently forming the words to say. He stuttered as he provided succinct directions. He then gave her a nod and tapped the brim of his hat as he dawdled past and went on his way.

She felt sheepish observing him, but did so until he turned a corner.

Jackson Scully was feeling loose and lucky. His mind was riveted on the task that had brought him to Abilene. He was gleefully hidden in a nowhere alley off Cedar Street. The gelding was surreally silent. His eyes were alert, his intentions soon to be realized. He had an unblocked view of the Alamo Saloon. The dawn's early light was adequate for his purposes.

Liam Greer was at his side on the palomino. Mentor and student were both giddy with eagerness. The plot had been repetitiously hashed over. All was as it should be; every aspect of the proposal had come together without any hitches or delays. The breakout escape called for them to split up and ride like greased lightning; one would go east, the other west, then both would loop around and reconnect down the trail toward Wichita.

Scully was sure that it was flawless. It had been thought through and weighed out; the daylight foray, which was to culminate in an assassination, had no margin for error. The kill-shot was to be a single squeeze of his Henry rifle's trigger. Then, in the ensuing pandemonium, two gunmen would vamoose into the wind, but for now, it was merely a waiting game.

Whilst he sat in the saddle, nasal mucous flowed in rivulets from his bulbous nose. He pinched or thumbed the ooze away and maintained focus. The chronic pain birthed on a long ago battlefield was presently inflamed and severe. The fiery misery began at the ankle of his game leg and threaded its way all the way up his left side and along his spine, like red-hot wire stitches being sewn and wrenched into place by some inhuman mad doctor.

Scully inhaled an excited breath and a sloppy grin formed when his target came into view. Deacon Coburn exited the Alamo Saloon, alone and ambling slowly. He stopped on the boardwalk and stretched his arms out. His hair was shaggy on his tree-branch shoulders. He stepped into the street and chatted with a passerby for a moment. He appeared carefree and unburdened. He paused and made a gradual turn, apparently looking for someone.

In that instant, Jackson Scully cramped low in his belly. His kidneys screamed a complaint. A trickle of urine dribbled out. He didn't give a damn. Snot was running like water from both nostrils, dripping over his lips and congealing in his moustache. He didn't give a roaring rip about that either. His concentration elevated. His eyes bulged.

The Henry rifle was at his shoulder. He aimed it at the center of Coburn's back. He made an adjustment and lifted the barrel slightly. He exhaled purposefully; his lungs emptied. A wave of warm relaxation surged through him. His finger put incremental pressure on the trigger. The weapon boomed in his hands. Laughter burst out as his bladder released its contents.

The bullet struck at the base of Coburn's skull. Blood and brains sprayed as his head jerked violently backward, then flopped forward. He was dead on his feet, slack-jawed and convulsing like some spineless scarecrow. His arms flailed, hands grasping and flexing spasmodically. Yells of alarm and shouted expletives scorched the air.

Liam Greer giggled jubilantly. He rocked back in the saddle and slapped a thigh.

Jackson Scully was far beyond ecstatic. He was frozen in a state of euphoria. "Killing a man ain't bad for *my* soul," he said in a growling whoop. He watched the crowd congregating around the bloody, broken body crumpled in the dirt.

Fingers began pointing straight at Scully. He sneered at them. He cussed a blue streak and dug his heels into the horse's flanks. The animal twisted its body and shrieked hideously. The colors of morning light lengthened and warped into funny patterns.

Then he woke up to the bellowing blare of his voice. Lunatic hilarity was slashing from his throat. It shattered the stillness. He gasped and almost choked on the merriment spilling out of him. His eyes fluttered rapidly. He sat up on the hard ground. His bedroll was a bundled mess at his feet. His head bent around and around. He oriented his senses.

The campsite had no other occupants; his two cohorts were gone, along with their mounts. He caught his breath and calmed down. His smile was huge; his eyes were bleary and bloodshot, but still full of mirth. There were gooey runners of yellow gunk caked on his upper lip and around his mouth, and all the while additional fluid discharged, which he ignored.

The sun was at high noon. He was awake, but a night spent chasing laudanum down with shots of rotgut whiskey kept him in a hazy stupor. His head throbbed so loudly in his ears that it felt like it would explode. He staggered to his feet and wobbled for several lopsided steps. When he gained his balance, he saw that his trousers were soaked across the crotch.

He swore as he hobbled to the edge of Mud Creek. He leaned over and tweaked his fingers across his nostrils to blow his nose. He waded into the slow moving stream and plopped down. He squirmed around until he was comfortably settled on the mucky bottom. The water was up to his chest. He splashed handfuls over his face. It was all good and cleansing.

The dream, with its vividly successful homicide, remained imprinted on his mind like some multifaceted tattoo. Its thrill had his brainpower scheming in the throes of enthusiasm. The simplicity of the strategy and its triumphant outcome fascinated and compelled him. He retained the imagery and struggled to cling to the specifics of the scenario.

There in the middle of Mud Creek, while taking a bath and doing his laundry, he arrived at the conclusion that the risk-reward factor in the dream's sequence of events was enticing. He would make a nighttime ride into Abilene, hideout and wait until daybreak to attain the ultimate payback. The killing of Deacon Coburn would be a rousing slice of gratification. There was danger involved to be sure, but given the potential prize, it was tolerable.

The getaway maneuver in the dream would need to be partially modified. He would definitely recruit Liam Greer to be at his side; and when the bloody deed was accomplished, he'd send him to the west hooting noisily all the way out of town. Greer would dutifully follow instructions and track south; however, there would be no rendezvous on the way to Wichita.

Scully had other intentions. While the law scampered after Greer, he would lay low, sneak away and soundlessly skulk off to the east. In his figuring, Greer had no chance of ever outfoxing a posse, so the braggart kid would be the patsy. By the time the authorities realized their error, Jackson Scully expected to be more than halfway to Kansas City.

He sloshed around in the water. He dunked his head and came up with a mouthful, which he squirted between his teeth, chuckling optimistically. He ran the ideas through his head again and again. And again. He was convinced that all that mattered now was bold implementation.

Tomorrow, if he sobered up long enough to do so, the plan would be carried out.

The day, as experienced by Naomi Engle, had a pristine beauty that spoke to her deepest inclinations. She walked along, her heart full of singing as she gaped at the sky, which was cloudless and bluer than anything she had ever seen. There was a bit of hurry in her steps because lunchtime was imminent and she wanted to arrive a tad early.

She was on the far north edge of town. Numerous stately oak trees provided large pockets of shade, which she enjoyed immensely. She came to a quaint clapboard bungalow that caught her attention for it fit the description she'd been given. It was white and trimmed by a fetching tint of green that accentuated its picturesque charm.

She hesitated temporarily, a woman in gray wearing a silk blue scarf and holding a small wicker basket by its loop handle. The contents were covered by a red-checked linen napkin. She took a look left and right, seemingly verifying that she had the correct residence. Satisfied, she went up the laneway, strode onto the porch and rapped lightly on the front door.

It soon opened. Flora smiled, reserved and careful. "Naomi. This is a surprise."

"I've brought apple fritter muffins for our lunch. Fresh baked this morning." She held the basket up, eyebrows raised. "Tea or coffee would go well with them."

Flora stepped back. "No tea, but I do have Arbuckle's. I serve it hot and as black as sin, which may not sound nice or be too ladylike, but it's the way all the cowboys like it."

Naomi entered and closed the door. "If that's how it is in these wonderful western lands, then please pour me a cup and I'll give it a whirl." Her manner was chirpy and buoyant.

"To the kitchen we shall go," Flora said, taking the basket from her. She carried it to the round wooden table and got busy. "Pull up a chair while I get the coffee ready."

Naomi glanced around. The room was decorated in varying hues of pink and green; flowers and butterflies were the dominant themes. She saw the glass-door china cupboard and went over to admire it more closely. She ran a finger over the woodwork and popped a door open. She took the liberty of setting two places at the table. "You have a lovely home."

Flora turned from her labors. "Thank you. It won't be mine for much longer."

"Why is that?" Naomi asked, taking a seat.

"It's a long and a short story." Flora finished putting the coffee on the boil. She had used splinters of maple and cedar to kindle a small fire in the cook-stove; the air was becoming sweet with the wood's aromatic scent. There were two sets of windows in the spacious kitchen, which were wide open, but there was no breeze or freshness stirring.

"Then I'm glad I ordered six muffins," Naomi said cheerily. "That's three apiece, which ought to keep us munching for both the long and the short particulars." She took the red-checked napkin off the basket and placed a muffin on each of their plates. She sat tall, her shoulders back, her backbone straight and stiff. "I've been told that I'm an excellent listener. I have time and a friendship to build, unless of course, you think I'm intruding or being pushy."

Flora sat across from her guest. "You're not intruding. I welcome the opportunity to chat." She broke her muffin in half. "Did you find your brother yesterday?"

"Yes. We visited last night. I haven't met his daughter yet, but hope to soon."

"I'm not quite sure what the story is there because Deacon can be as closemouthed as a clam." Flora tossed her hair back; its scarlet waves crested on her shoulders. "He did introduce her to me one day last week. She's young and pretty, and has her whole life ahead of her," she said, sounding reflective and rueful. "I was like that once, but no more."

Naomi smiled knowingly. "I was young once too. For you and me, our future may not be stretched out as far as it is for Abbey, but we still got some dreaming and kicking to do."

"That's a nice thought to hold onto." The aroma of coffee was getting robust enough to smother the lingering maple and cedar. She poured two cups and placed the pot back on the stove. "This kind of brings me to the long and short of it about my house." She returned to her seat, tentative and unsure of where to begin. "Have you heard any rumors about me?"

"I take no stock in gossip and have little regard for those who partake in it."

Flora narrowed her eyes and hitched in a deep breath. "Never mind how it happened to be because that's ugly and hurtful, but I was in a lucrative business for many years." Her attention was centered on her hands, which were gripped around the cup of coffee. "I had contacts with lots of respectable and influential men, bankers and lawyers and such. With their tips and tutoring I invested much of my profits. I was a quick study. I thought that if I could be rich, I'd be happy, so I convinced myself that what I was doing to earn money made no difference."

"What business was it?"

Flora waited. Her face was stony and blanched. "At first I was just a woman of easy virtue. Then I became a whore mistress. I recruited and turned out women into the trade. I operated my own houses with red doors, which involved me in lots of illicit deals."

Naomi was blank-faced, but compassion brimmed in her large eyes.

"I have much to atone for," Flora said sorrowfully. "I ruined women's lives by taking advantage of their circumstances." She took a bite of muffin and talked while she chewed. "Two years ago a switch clicked inside my head or heart and I realized that all the money in the world could never provide contentment or goodwill. Neither could riches ever buy back what I stole from all those women or what was ripped away from me."

"Ripped away from you?" Naomi tilted her head, forehead furrowed

Flora sloughed it off with a backhanded wave, but enormous sadness filled her eyes. "It matters not now. I'm selling my house and leaving Abilene. The legal papers await my signature. I'm packing a few belongings and getting on a train to start over anew somewhere."

Naomi took a sip of coffee. Her face flinched in a pleasurable smile. She had a much larger drink. "I am well acquainted with making a new beginning. It's what brought me here. Maybe we met just so as I could encourage you to take the step and follow your heart."

"Follow my heart," Flora murmured wistfully. "I had dreams once, Naomi. So many mistakes have messed with my mind that those dreams all disappeared. I only know that now I want to help others and in kindness, perhaps I can pay penance for all my wrongdoing."

"I understand. Really, I do."

Flora snickered bleakly. "I'm glad you do because I'm not sure I do."

Naomi held up a finger in explanation. "What I mean is that I understand what you're saying and why, but truth is, God's grace is free. We can't pay for it by being good deed doers or any other perceived acts of penance. Grace is free and it's for everyone."

Flora's brow darkened. She appeared to be bemused or in disbelief. "It was in some distant long ago when Father Martin taught me, so maybe my understandings are skewed, but I thought that receiving absolution from sins required confession and penance."

"Confession of our faults and failings is always good for our souls," Naomi said with empathic conviction. "In first John 1:9, the Bible tells us that *if we confess our sins, he is faithful and just to forgive us our sins, and to cleanse us from all unrighteousness.*"

Flora's eyebrows dipped low in confusion. "Confession, forgiveness, penance, absolution; none of it matters much in my case, Naomi. I have too many skeletons in my past. I'm terribly afraid that no amount of confession and penance will bring about forgiveness or absolution. There will never be enough good for me to do to outweigh the evil I've done."

"*That's* why Jesus died, Flora. At the cross he took our penalty on his shoulders."

"I try to pray, I try to accept God's forgiveness and grace," Flora answered, "but it gets clogged up or something." Her head was shaking and her shoulders were scrunched. "Even if it came to me clearly, I cannot forgive myself. I have destroyed people's lives. Now all I can do is to keep trying to pray and endeavor to be a better person . . . a different person."

"God's grace is free and it's for everyone. Even for you, Flora."

Flora shrugged heavily. She gave her a grim-faced smile. "That's the sum and substance of the state of my affairs, Naomi. Whoever told you that you were a good listener was right. Thank you. You have been a godsend to me. I pray *your* new beginning will be hopeful."

"And I promise to pray for your fresh start, Flora."

"With that all settled, what about our shopping outing?" Flora asked perkily. "The day has plenty left to it. Is there any reason why we can't get to it as soon as we finish lunch?"

Naomi beamed. "None comes to mind."

The kindred spirits ate jauntily as their relationship continued to be cultivated. There was transparency that included teasing and jocularity. They each had two muffins. Naomi also drank a second cup of coffee. She savored its flavor. While they were cleaning up together, Flora invited Naomi to a home cooked dinner the next evening. Naomi cordially accepted.

Then they were on their way, strolling along blissfully in the vibrant sunshine.

~~~

"Who's this darkening my doorway?"

"Knock it off."

Fitzgerald mimicked him. "*Knock it off.*"

Coburn scowled. "Yes, please do, Whitey."

"Well, glory be!" Whitey exclaimed with a click-click and a handclap. "At least the man with all the secrets remembers my name. I suppose I ought to be thankful for that crumb."

"Is this the way it's going to be?"

"I be clueless as to your meaning, Deacon."

"Can I get a haircut, or what?"

"Give me a minute to check," Whitey replied, grinning. With a fussy flair of drama and histrionics, he paced around the shop, his eyes checking every corner of it. Then he went outside and leaned one way and the other, perusing up and down the street. He returned and stood beside the barber chair. "I do believe you be the next customer in line, Deacon."

Coburn sat and folded his hands over his midsection. "Are you going to be a grumpy old gus the whole while or are we going to get past your miseryitis?"

"I still be clueless as to your meaning. Besides I'm barely talking to you."

"Now what did I do to tick you off?" Deacon asked good-naturedly.

Fitzgerald draped a sheet around his neck and fastidiously tucked it under the collar of his shirt. "I'll tell you straight. I be your friend, ain't I? And yet, you be a walking riddle to me. I've been making you look fine and handsome for years, but you don't tell me nothing."

"Hang on a minute, Whitey. What do I know about you?"

Fitzgerald balked. "That be different. I ain't got no story."

"Everyone's got a story."

"I ain't got no daughter. Nor a sister," Whitey fired back, click-clicking furiously. "I won't be having no parade of people coming out of the woodwork looking for me."

Coburn chuckled. "Let's do some horse trading here."

"Whatcha saying?"

"I'll swap some of my story for some of yours."

Fitzgerald had scissors and comb in hand, but hadn't started cutting yet. "That be a dandy idea. You flap your gums while I do my level best to get rid of your sheepdog look."

"It seems everybody has a joke or comment about my hair."

"Skip that and get a yakking," Whitey said, beginning the job.

Beneath the sheet, Coburn folded his arms over his chest. "Naomi is my youngest sister. She was a spunky tadpole when I went off on my own. I have another sister and two brothers back in Pennsylvania. I was the oldest. Until last night I hadn't seen any of them since before the Confederates fired on Fort Sumter. My mother's still alive, but my father passed."

"They raised you up fine."

"Sure enough," Deacon agreed, smiling thinly. "I left the farm in '53 and been mostly a traveling man since then. In the war, I was attached to the Army of the Potomac . . ."

"Whew doggies," Whitey interrupted, punctuating it with a loud click-click. "The Army of the Potomac, you say. That surely has a ring to it for a mighty fighting outfit."

"Yes, sir," Deacon said, eyes flashing. "There was much blood-soaked carnage, I can tell you that for sure. I saw the gory horrors of slaughter. I wandered off the battlefield at Gettysburg, addle-brained and soul scarred. I came west and found some measure of healing while learning the ins and outs of cattle ranching in East Texas. And that's about it."

"That's about it?" Whitey protested excitedly. The scissors never stopped clipping and the comb kept the same tempo. "You ain't hardly told me nothing about nothing."

Coburn sighed; it was weary, inching close to exasperation. "My life's my life, Whitey. It ain't no dime store novel for sale to the highest bidder. I ain't a seer or mind reader. It ain't like I can figure what others might find interesting about it. Ask me what you want to know."

Fitzgerald's jaw tightened. "Daughters tend to have mothers."

"I reckon that's a hundred percent fact."

"So?"

"Her name was Angela. She's gone to glory," Deacon answered flatly. "We loved each other, but didn't even know it. And it still hurts, so I'm done talking. Your turn."

Fitzgerald kept snip-snipping with the scissors, never easing up at all as he turned on his chatterbox. "Ain't much to tell, but I'll give you the best I got. I'm just a good-timing jester who ran into a streak of fortune. I was a house nigger on the Fitzgerald plantation, which was a big estate north of Mobile, Alabama. My people labored there for several generations.

"Master Fitzgerald was a drinker and gambler who didn't need much of a reason to throw a party. He was kindly enough, I suppose, though I got me some stripes for not stepping and fetching quick enough for him.

I polished and shined the big house. Did some butler and barber work; learned cooking skills and put my hand to the art of dentistry. An old pappy taught me all he knew about the care and pulling of teeth."

Coburn laughed loudly. "Pete told me you almost killed him."

"He be an exaggerating complainer. You think yanking a sick molar ain't a-gonna set-off shooting pain? I ain't a magic man with my pliers," Whitey said, mockingly defensive. "I be near the end of my story. You want to hear it or tell me all you know about doctoring teeth?"

"Sorry I side-railed you, Whitey."

"Well, you should be," Whitey quipped, eyes twinkling mischievously. "I was rolling along and gathering steam." He put the scissors and comb on the shelf beneath the mirror. He picked up the brush and soap-cup, then started whipping up lather. "After the war I fell in with a bunch of other emancipated slaves leaving Alabama to come to the promised land of Kansas. Some smarty-pants wisecracker called us Exodusters in a dang newspaper and it stuck."

"I remember reading an account of that migration. The imagery made me smile."

"You liked the Bible reference, did you? Imagine that," Whitey said, snickering. He began dabbing and swishing soap onto his cheeks. "You do lots of reading, don't you?"

"Use to, I did," Deacon replied nonchalantly. "I read every book and periodical I could get my hands on. Nowadays keeping up with the Bible and newspapers is about all I do."

"I done told my tale. You won't read it in no Bible or newspaper."

"I do have a question, Whitey. What's your true first name?"

Fitzgerald frowned, startled. His eyes squinted as he took a step back. "I don't rightly know, Deacon. I was surely given a real name but I been Whitey for as long as I can recall. My hair sprouted snow-white before I was knee-high to a mule. I can't say it's the reason, but my mammy told me I got scared by a polecat when I was just a wee pickaninny." He began rapidly stropping the straight-razor. "Now hush your mouth so as I can shave you shiny."

Coburn's face wrinkled into a broad smile. He relaxed, shifted back and closed his eyes.

Fitzgerald attacked the beard with a cool efficiency, hands swift and sure. He effectively manipulated the blade while nattering on and on about this, that and other things. Satisfaction gripped him when he took note that his client's lips remained creased wide in contentment.

~~~

While Deacon Coburn was at the barbershop, Naomi Engle and Flora were having a fabulous time picking out fabric and looking through catalogs at the mercantile; Sam Beadle was watching Liam Greer. Beadle was at a window in the lobby of Drovers Cottage; Greer was staked out in a spot across the street and had been lounging there for the past hour.

Beadle wasn't angry. His annoyance was in check, his mind clear. He had noticed Charley Jondreau squatting on his haunches in some shade less than twenty yards behind Greer. His droopy-brimmed hat was pulled low, his back resting against a corner of a building. As far as Beadle could tell, Greer was completely unaware of Jondreau's presence.

The sun was a whitish ball of fire midway across the western sky. There was considerable wagon traffic back and forth, with drummers and teamsters hard at it hauling freight and goods. Every time a buckboard creakily passed, Beadle heightened his attentiveness. He changed his angle or popped up on the balls of his feet. His eyes never strayed; he had no intention of letting Greer out of his sight even for a second.

He had no idea or even an inkling regarding what was in Greer's mind. There could be no comprehension, but after the spectacular madness on horseback, Beadle knew that nothing was outside the realm of possibility. The good news was that his surveillance of Greer had revealed that there was no gun or knife; the man was unarmed.

Greer was on the move. Beadle lurched in his footsteps, jumped away from the window and ran to the door. His blood was getting hot and he felt a burst of adrenaline rising. There was a rustling movement and a voice behind him, but he was too zoned in on happenings outside to take the time to look or respond. Old Blue was blocking the doorway, on its feet and growling. He crept past and paused long enough to speak to the cattle-dog.

"Sit and stay, Old Blue. I've got it covered."

Old Blue eyed him doubtfully. It whined, laid its ears back and sat.

Greer came steadily forward. His slouchy gait had swagger, shoulders shoved back and head slanted upward in a show of determination. His fingers were fluttering intermittently against his thighs. He was still wearing the shirt off which Old Blue had torn a chunk of the sleeve. His Stetson was listing to one side and perched high on his forehead. A cocky smirk prevailed on his shallow-cheeked face; it was disconnected and eerie.

He waggled his legs and stopped in his tracks as Beadle confronted him. "You best stay out of my way, mister," Liam said in a snarl. "I got a date with my woman." He pointed a finger toward Drovers Cottage. "Are you going to give me clearance or do I get mean and ornery?"

Beadle stood rigid and unbending in front of him, hands on his hips. His eyes were tight, his countenance set as buffed and rigid as burnished steel. He never said a word. The men were face to face in the middle of the thoroughfare. Greer hooked his thumbs in the waistband of his trousers for a casual moment, then without warning threw a punch, cursing as he did so.

The blow caught Beadle on the chin, but not squarely. At the instant before impact, he faded backward and turned his head to the side. Greer acted triumphantly, as though he was sure the blow had injured the man. He was emboldened and plowed forward, wading in with an untamed fierceness. He danced and lunged at him in a flurry of fakery and flying fists.

Beadle reacted as instinct and training demanded. There would be no restraint on this go around. His hands were up in the classic style, knotted in tight balls. He was on his toes, slipping and sliding as nimbly as a topnotch ballerina. He ducked beneath one fist and blocked another, patient and methodical. He waited patiently, anticipating an opening.

When the opportunity presented itself, he feinted to the left and unleashed a straight right that was blinding in its quick ferocity. He turned his hips and rolled his shoulders, driving the sledge-like blow through the target. The pummeling fist struck firm and fast between the eyes. Beadle remained perfectly balanced and prepared for follow-up, but in the whisper of a breath, he realized any further action was unnecessary.

Greer's nose exploded as his head cranked back at a weird skyward angle. His body was airborne, arms flailing as he slammed to the ground splayed on his back. His frenzied momentum carried him into an awkward reverse somersault. He crash landed on his belly and like a beached carp, flopped over onto his butt, clutching his face and crying.

His nose was shattered and mashed flat; it was a saggy mess of flesh and cartilage. Both nostrils were spewing blood like some bizarre fountain; the crimson flow blotched out the linen shirt's fancy embroidery across the chest and pooled into coagulated muck in the dirt.

Beadle stepped back, hands returning to his hips. A sense of thankfulness came over him when he saw Charley Jondreau scuttling to Liam Greer's assistance. Jondreau's manner was one of regret; his face was pained, his eyes narrow and teeming with sorrow.

He removed his hat and took a handkerchief from the lining of its crown. He folded and put it to use, clasping it tight around the broken nose in an attempt to stanch the bleeding. He struggled to help Greer to his feet, nearly having to lift his wobbly body off the ground.

"I'll do what I can, eh," Charley said earnestly. His expression became wrinkly and he jerked a thumb toward Drovers Cottage. "You got a better life to live. Go live it." He put his shoulder to the task of balancing Greer. He half-carried him in the direction of the livery.

Beadle frowned. He stayed put. He sensed the looks from those who'd gathered and witnessed the one-punch affair, but he refused to acknowledge the audience. When he turned around, his mouth went dry and his heart acted like a mushroom, sprouting up his throat. The attractive lady he had picnicked with on the previous day had her attention glued to him.

His cheeks blushed. He hung his head. He shuffled along slowly, dragging his feet.

Abbey Langton was on the veranda, Old Blue at her side. Her hands were clenched and white-knuckled. She had seen the encounter from beginning to end. She'd been coming down the stairs when Sam was in a race to get to the street. She had called his name, but evidently he was either too far gone or too engaged in choleric emotions; or he had simply ignored her. She didn't know for sure one way or the other and neither did she care a single iota.

As he approached, her heart was thrilled, beating like the fluttering wings of a caged butterfly. He had a hangdog look of shame, but she was overawed by pride and gratification. He was her man, her protector; a thinker and dreamer who had the resolve and character to carry himself with sureness and authenticity. A distinct wave of candor and clarity washed over her. She grasped the fleeting wonder of all the jumbled feelings soaring through her.

He halted in front of her. "He didn't give me any option, Abbey."

"I love you, Sam." She took hold of his right hand. She held it close to examine it for any injuries. She pressed her lips against the knuckles, then lashed her arms around him and hugged for all she was worth. He melted against her. She pressed up and kissed his mouth. He responded, softly and tenderly at first, but swiftly passion was inflamed.

She felt his strength and enjoyed all the wildness set loose in her. She broke off the kiss, leaned back and peered directly into his eyes. "I'll marry you, Sam. I'll love you and be a good wife. We'll have adventures together, but I won't take your name. I never knew my father. He was buried the day I was born. Langton was his name and I intend to take it to *my* grave."

He was staggered; discombobulated, even. His eyes enlarged as his senses absorbed all that she had said and done. "I love you, Abbey Langton. I will always respect your wishes. Though, if truth be known, I'll likely take some ribbing and be called a milksop or worse."

"You are no milksop, Sam Beadle. You're my gallant and dashing champion," she said brightly. "The wedding ceremony will be tomorrow at noon right here in the lobby. Afterwards, we'll be ready and leave immediately for Dodge City. We have much to do."

"We can't be packed and tie up loose ends here that quick, Abbey."

"Says who?"

"Says me."

She disregarded his objection and repeated the agenda with undiluted emphasis. She was smiling persuasively as she added, "Shall we go to the dining room to have some supper and make lists to get things done?" She grabbed hold of her fiancée's hand and led him inside.

Old Blue craned its head back and let out a yap-yapping howl.

Vultures. Dozens of the ugly cusses dotted the gray sky.

Daylight was burning out when Caleb Weitzel came to the top of a rolling ridge. He was a few hundred yards ahead of the women, eyes fixed on the flock of vultures circling low. At the crest of the rise he saw many more of the scavenger birds roosted in a lone tree in the middle of miles of grassland. Beneath its spread of branches was the bundled form of a man. A short distance away, a horse with yellowish stripes was picketed and grazing.

He shouted and waved to Consuelo and Sally Twosongs, then urged speed from Shadrach. The stallion complied. It bolted and loped into a gallop, causing the expanse to disappear in humungous strides. The vultures in the air squawked and rose in a spiral pattern; the red-hooded carrion-eaters in the tree took flight, screeching and flapping furiously.

Weitzel reined in Shadrach near the tree, and canteen in hand, hit the ground running before the powerful horse was completely stopped. He took a careening tumble, but was instantaneously on his feet and scampering. A jittery unease went through him when he took a knee beside the man and tried lifting his head to get him to sip some water.

Daniel Twosongs was in a ravaged condition, unresponsive and co-matose. His heartbeat was thin and thready, and he was barely breathing. His lips were blistered raw from dehydration. His face was sallow, his skin clammy. There were gobs of dried vomit on his shirt and saddle, which he was using as a pillow. Death had a pigeonhole lined up for him; the grim reaper, with its sickle at the ready, was an invisible specter hanging in the humid air.

Weitzel examined him as thoroughly as he could, his hands steady. He loosened the collar of the man's shirt and wiped his brow, palming away slimy droplets of sick sweat. He heard the clopping hoofbeats of the mules and looked around, knowing that Sally Twosongs would arrive first. She dismounted and rushed toward him. Consuelo was riding hard close behind her.

Weitzel was on his feet. "He's in a bad way."

Sally Twosongs hurriedly took the canteen from him and knelt be-side her father.

Weitzel went and helped Consuelo down, then took her by the hand to her husband. He hovered near them for a few moments before he real-ized that the women had the situation under control and he needed to get out of their way. He took several steps back and squatted on his heels to be ready if needed. Mother and daughter silently nursed and cleaned the ill man.

Sally Twosongs rummaged through Daniel's saddlebags and came out with three pouches of medicinal herbs. She opened them one at a time to determine the contents. A tiny smile curled her lips. Murmuring ancient words of supplication, she took a pinch from each sack and mixed it all together in her cupped palm. She stood and bowed her head respectfully.

With hallowed reverence and awe-inspiring protocol, she paid hom-age to the One who transcends time and space; the Sovereign One who had spoken creation into existence. She genuflected in the four directions and as she did, ceremoniously tossed the cuttings in her hand into the still air; north, south, east, west. Her voice kept increasing in volume as she prayed in Navajo—strong, deep, demanding phrases that originated in a holy sanctuary of her soul.

Weitzel observed it all. He listened closely and shivered despite the heat. Though he was endeavoring to learn her native language, it was a lengthy and laborious process, and he did not comprehend most of what he was hearing. He only understood that she was speaking directly to the Creator, and thought that no Deity could ever deny the urgency or power of her petitions.

Sally Twosongs suddenly ran to her mule. The pigtail dangling down her back jumped and swung with her jerky motions. She retrieved her flute and returned. She gently kissed her mother's cheek and did the same to her father's forehead. She positioned herself at his feet, sitting cross-legged. She shut her eyes and lowered her head. Moments later, prayers in the form of a courageous, high-spirited melody contested the gathering gloom of nightfall.

As the music went heavenward, Consuelo took a spot at his side and kept dabbing his face with a wet cloth as she zealously prayed the rosary. "Our Father, who art in heaven, hallowed be thy name; thy kingdom come; thy will be done on earth as it is in heaven. Give us this day our daily bread; and forgive us our trespasses as we forgive those who trespass against us; and lead us not into temptation; but deliver us from evil. Amen.

"Hail Mary, full of grace, the Lord is with thee; blessed art thou among women, and blessed is the fruit of thy womb, Jesus. Holy Mary, Mother of God, pray for us sinners, now and at the hour of our death. Amen. Glory be to the Father, and to the Son, and to the Holy Spirit. As it was in the beginning, is now, and ever shall be, world without end. Amen."

Over and over she prayed, but no dullness or monotony crept into her voice. Each word had its own meaning and influence, imbued by the force of her faith as she carefully enunciated clearly and confidently. Her upper body swayed to the rhythm of the song; the notes of the flute rose and fell, harmoniously matching the cadence of the rosary.

After more than a half-hour passed, the tune climbed the steps of the sky and culminated in a conquering crescendo. An echo lingered momentarily, followed by the lonesome yowl of a wolf from some far off locale; its cry was insistent and inspiring. The sound of it drifted away and all that remained in the stillness of night was Consuelo's continuing appeals.

Sally Twosongs went to Caleb. He stood. "What can I do?"

"We will stay here a time," she replied, eyes wide and watchful.

"Can Daniel recover?"

"Jesus is good medicine."

Weitzel nodded at the dire hope of her pronouncement. She returned to her spot at her father's feet and began playing another song. It was hymn-like and melancholy, a lament calling upon the Maker of heaven and earth for his intervention in the midst of sorrows.

He listened and said a prayer as gooseflesh crawled across his back. He shook off the tingling sensation and got busy seeing to the care of the donkey, horses and mules. He was thorough. He removed the tackle and gear, and systematically set it in order. He rubbed down each animal, gave them an even serving of water and set them on long tether lines to feed. Shadrach was acting frisky, neighing and pawing the ground. Weitzel easily recognized the behavior. He made sure to secure the steeldust stallion out of reach of the brindle mare.

After the animals were tended to, he set up camp and dug a small fire pit. He then sidled off to search for whatever possible fuel could be found. He took along a burlap sack because, as was the case the last several nights, he suspected the only material available would be dried dung. A mile or so away, he came upon a supply and loaded the bag with buffalo chips.

The stars and the warbling of the flute led him back to the campsite.

It was long past midnight, but Flora was wide awake. Her brain would not switch off. She had been studying legal documents, but put them away; she could no longer concentrate on the papers because of other concerns and in all honesty, she was wholly satisfied with the business matters. All the arrangements were coming together for her to make a new way in the world.

Even so, worry and trepidation were part and parcel of her outlook. Regardless of how pragmatically she spun the possibilities, she couldn't shed the fear that the past would tag along with her. There was no escaping the notion that the apparition of Sweet Flora would forever follow her; she agonized over always being known as a woman of ill repute.

Her faith—tenuous and rickety—on most days, was persistently at odds with doubt. She had come to accept the spiritual tussle within as customary and normal. There were the briefest of instants when it appeared as though faith might gain the upper hand, but then, in quicksilver mode, doubt would rise up and have the advantage. She was full of faith and full of doubt; it was an endless tug of war within that burdened her day and night.

She was being intentional about making every effort to hold onto the light of optimism. Her bedroom was dazzling and radiant, with collections of large round candles arrayed at various places. The flames were formidable and luminous, chasing away the darkness. She was on her knees beside her bed, mutely thinking and praying on all the choices, decisions and changes.

There was substantial heaviness in her heart; the massive weight of bygone iniquities and consequences sank through her. She wondered if she could ever be free; her mind was turbulent and mixed up with thoughts about sin and redemption. Those were not new concepts to her. Sin was the stain of her life; redemption a broken-winged hummingbird dying in a barren desert. Her sins were too many, her immorality too depraved for her to ever reach redemption.

She sighed; it came out as a grief-stricken groan. Thoughts of her emerging friendship leapt to the forefront. It had been a surprise and delight to meet Naomi Engle. She was a natural encourager and without question, Flora was in extreme need of encouragement. Talking to her had been beneficial; the confession had provided some soothing balm.

However, Flora wasn't kidding herself; she had never really told Naomi anything that wasn't already common knowledge amongst the townspeople. Everyone knew that not so long ago she had been Sweet Flora, a whore and brothel madam. There remained a secret that no one knew about; abomination so dastardly in its sinfulness that it had never been uttered aloud.

Yes, Naomi had received the information about her prostitution with a generous measure of grace, but what of the reprehensible episode in Flora's life; the one that scarred her past, traumatized her present and threatened to terminate all hopes for an altered future? Naomi had told her that *confession of our faults and failings is always good for our souls.* She then quoted the Bible: *If we confess our sins, he is faithful and just to forgive us our sins, and to cleanse us from all unrighteousness.* All of it was a spinning gyroscope inside Flora's brain.

She wanted to believe in the cleansing power of God; she yearned to trust and have confidence in the prospect of being washed spotless. If it could be true for her, then there was a chance that she could once again be Delores. She trembled when the whirl of Naomi's thoughts on confession suddenly slammed to a stop and connected together with a soul-chilling thud.

The inference upset her; for Flora to be remade into the image dreamed of by a child, then confession of her crime was a necessity. She would never gain the freedom to be Delores without laying the truth bare before God by sharing it verbally to a willing listener. She had to tell some-one the truth; the wicked ugliness had to be spoken of for healing and purification to be realized. Denial could be no more; denial had to go the way of dinosaurs.

She squeezed her eyes shut and desperately attempted to give voice to her prayers. Her mouth opened and closed soundlessly in dismay and frustration, her lips forming words that never found expression. She refused to quit. Her hands clamped together and she kept at it, applying all the patient endurance she could muster.

Finally her heartfelt cries shakily whimpered out in fearful weakness. "Dear God, please help me. I'm not worthy. I am but a poor supplicant begging for your merciful kindness. Forgive me. Give me courage to do right. Grant me the strength to make confession . . ." She shuddered and gasped breathlessly. The rest of her prayers were overwhelmed by wretched sobbing.

As guilt and anguish wept out, purpose and willpower entered. A mystifying warmth and comfort flooded her senses. She stood. She went around the room snuffing out all the candles. She crawled into bed, scrunched around and consciously worked to brace up her resolve.

When sleep came, her backbone had been forged into a chain of steely grit.

chapter four

Trails & Byways

"The name of the Lord is a strong tower: the righteous runneth into it, and is safe. Before destruction the heart of man is haughty, and before honor is humility. The spirit of a man will sustain his infirmity; but a wounded spirit who can bear?"

~SOLOMON~

DANIEL TWOSONGS HAD NEVER seen an ocean. Much of his life had been spent traveling hither and yon across the country, but on no occasion had he ever reached either coast. He had never tasted or felt the spray of salt water. Until now, that is; now he was adrift on a raft in the middle of a vast immensity of choppy waves. The width and breadth of it was incalculable.

A queer-colored darkness covered the sea. The blackened firmament was starless and there was no moon showing anywhere, yet streaky green columns of bluish-yellow shone upwards in the sky, and a luminous glow stretched forth on the horizon in front of him. He was astonished by the mysterious wonder of his surroundings and circumstance.

There was peace beneath the astonishment, but also mixed in was an undercurrent of anxiety. The gentle rocking of the ride was pleasurable and pacifying, but couldn't dispel the tinge of disquiet in him. He studied the craft; it was sturdily constructed, with a plank platform across two grooved log pontoons. A simple sail propelled it forward and though there was no breeze that he could feel, the sheet of canvas billowed and ruffled rhythmically.

He had no idea how he had gotten here. One moment he was elsewhere, in some dusky and feverish abyss, and the next, he was afloat and not bound by any sickness, making trails in the water. For the third time, he leaned backwards to look straight above. His eyes strained to find a familiar constellation to enlighten him as to his position in relation to the heavenlies, but there were still none to see, identifiable or otherwise. Not a solitary star was visible.

The bluish-yellow rays were shimmering up and down in a flickering pattern that was fascinating and intense. He watched, almost mesmerized, and speculated on the inexplicable phenomenon, in which he was completely alone, at the mercy of the destiny within the swells and upsurges of the surf. The lock, stock and barrel of the happenings had his absolute attention, bewildering and thrilling him. He had much to ruminate on. His mind began to race.

There was no pain or sorrow in him; no tiredness or thirst; no hunger or anticipation of food; no heartaches or fears; no regrets or perception of loss. The anxious unrest was gradually ebbing away; he could feel the difference in him. Tranquility was amassing force, and it felt safe and gratifying; he desired more of it. All the struggles of life on earth were leaving him.

The breakers were becoming whitecaps, pitching the craft side to side. He was on his hands and knees, pressing hard against the floorboards so as to not be tossed beneath the waves. The air was cool with mist, which refreshed and invigorated him. He jumped up and set his feet wide apart, clinging to the roughhewn mast to stabilize and maintain balance.

His heartbeat had increased significantly. It was rising and falling inside his ribcage in the exact cadence of the currents splashing all around him; the oneness of it enchanted him. The radiant gleaming in front of him was getting brighter and brighter. There was unearthly warmth arising from it that enraptured and beckoned him. It called in sweet-sounding thunder, speaking the language of angels and he understood; the words soothed and echoed to his core.

The tide pool of his heart was being inextricably drawn toward the commanding light. He *wanted* the raft to go faster. He longed to reach the brilliance of the horizon. He knelt and humbled himself before the mightiness of the majestic unknown. In a tangible act, he gave himself to the illumination of the great beyond by extending his arms in surrender.

His eyes were closed. He was blanketed by tender and loving feelings that made his flesh prickle and crawl in such an extraordinarily wondrous manner that it was impossible to resist. He was dying and it was beautiful. Fragments of memories fluttered before him as he soared higher and higher. He gloried in the cocoon of emotional excess. He cried out in ecstasy and sought to be free, to fully abandon the constraints of being confined inside of human skin.

When his voice reached the apex of its volume, his vocal cords ceased to work. Silence tore from his throat; it was enormous and overpowering, present everywhere. He was falling and falling. Then, from outside the vacuum of soundlessness, a knifelike vibration stabbed his eardrums. He clapped his hands over his ears as he dropped onto his backside.

Far away behind him, there was music and muttering. He listened. The melody was loud and piercing, carrying his name in its notes. It had a bizarre leverage over him. He crawled and turned around to examine the bleakness from which he had already come. The green-streaked beams of light followed where his eyes settled. His head throbbed.

Tears poured out of him. A mighty struggle ensued, in which he thrashed around in helpless desperation. He was sinking deeper and deeper. The shining luminosity of the skyline that mere moments earlier had been appealing and captivating, was rapidly being gobbled up by outrageous darkness. He lay down on his back, breathing shallowly. A gasp wrenched out and he jerked into a sitting posture. His eyes flashed open to the leaden sunlight of dawn.

His head pivoted crazily up and down, as though he was a marionette and the puppeteer pulling his strings was in the travails of an epileptic seizure. His arms were reaching and grasping to grab hold of some invisible reward. His mouth was working furiously. He was chewing chunks of air and attempting to speak, but all efforts to communicate failed.

He saw Sally Twosongs sitting at his feet with her flute and Consuelo beside him, her hands clutching rosary beads. His wife was talking to him, but he closed his ears. His eyes were pleading and earnest. His lips twisted downward in an expression that was the epitome of mournful sorrow. He wanted to return to the ocean; he ached to reach the glittering horizon.

He groaned. Aromatic smoke tickled his nostrils; a smudge of dried botanicals—sage and lavender—was burning in an abalone shell on the ground near his saddle. Slowly and haltingly, he collected his bearings. There was much discomfort involved in the process for his joints all felt bloated and inflamed. He looked upward. There were no vultures anywhere to be seen.

His eyes blinked and flinched as he searched the area. His heart leapt in his chest cavity. Less than twenty yards away, the three wolves that had been his companions on his journey to Abilene were pacing and circling. He moaned in resignation. He unstopped his ears. He laid back. His eyes were open as he stared vacantly at the branches of the tree.

"He saw the other side, Mother," Sally Twosongs said, awe in her tone. "He was gone and lost to us in the domain halfway between life and death."

"Daniel," Consuelo whispered, wiping his brow. She leaned over him, putting her face close to his. "Stay with us. Please stay with us, Daniel."

Daniel Twosongs nodded weakly. He was aware of the frailty of his body; the illness had skinned his strength down to feebleness. The incident upon the waters remained real inside him. He knew that he had been approaching the barrier in front of the infinite unseen. He had traversed the passage that separated the physical and spiritual realms.

The gateway giving entrance to the beginnings of eternity had been within reach. He had come so close to crossing over the threshold. The taste of his rapture and elation was still on his tongue; the peculiar warmth lingered in his bloodstream. In some deep inner chasm a bonfire of yearning crackled and raged; he wished to return and complete the mystical odyssey.

He heard his wife praying, his daughter playing a song of worship and thanksgiving. There was a rush of reluctance in him, but he pushed it away. He realized he had no choice, for the Creator was the author of life and death. He said goodbye to the miracle of the future. The present demanded his concentration. He recalibrated his mind to the chore of recuperating.

In the east, the sun had terminated the reign of night.

At Drovers Cottage in Abilene, Abbey Langton was in the dining room having an early breakfast on her wedding day. There was a lot to be done before noontime. Excitement was in her, but not so much for the ceremony. That would be short and sincere. It was the afterwards that had her eager with anticipation; the living and doing together, the dreaming and loving.

She nibbled on scrambled eggs and took an occasional bite of toast. Mostly she moved the food around the plate, absently rearranging it while her mind vaulted from one item to the next as she pondered or finalized details on a mental checklist.

She glanced up. A tall woman was in the doorway watching her, a small smile on her lips. She wore a flower-patterned dress that was pretty and eye-catching. Her ensemble was topped off by a complimentary pinkish hat that had a frilly maroon ribbon around its brim. Abbey stood and motioned to her. She drew near, her deportment straight and graceful.

"You must be Naomi."

"I am. And you're Abbey."

"Indeed I am." She sat and motioned for her to do the same. "Our paths have finally crossed. I have been anxious to meet you. May I call you Aunt Naomi?"

Naomi Engle smiled largely. Moisture dribbled from the corners of her big brown eyes as she settled on the chair and adjusted her bottom. "That would be pleasing to me, Abbey."

They bantered about everything and nothing for several minutes. There was an instant easiness between them. A waitress, who had to cover her mouth to stifle a yawn, took Naomi's order, which consisted of black coffee, along with a serving of toast and fruit preserves.

When it was delivered, Abbey asked, "Did you enjoy the train ride across country?"

"Yes, I found it congenial and somewhat therapeutic for me," Naomi answered briskly. "I had a lovely time visiting St. Louis. It was all hustle and bustle. I am so glad to have arrived in Abilene in time for your special day. You must be exhilarated beyond measure."

Abbey set aside her plate, dabbed a napkin to her lips and tried to subdue a grin. It refused to be restrained. Her eyes sparkled. "You can't imagine the angst and worry in me. It's difficult to explain because it gets all mixed up with an eagerness that makes me giddy."

"I can surely do better than imagine, Abbey. I can remember," Naomi replied, a crease knitting itself across her brow. "When I woke up on the day I was to marry Adam Engle, I put my feet on the floor and sat on the edge of my bed and cried."

"Cried?"

"Yes, cried. All by myself, I sat there and cried." She shrugged and gave her head a little shake. "Not because I was sad. On the contrary, I loved Adam and he loved me, and we had all these exciting plans for our lives. Big ideas and high hopes. I was about your age, maybe a little younger. I couldn't have been happier and yet I was crying."

"Why?"

Naomi rolled her eyes ever so slightly. "I was afraid. I didn't know what to expect. Sitting on my bed that morning I knew that by nightfall I would be alone in a bedroom with a man and there would be expectations put upon me. I had seen barnyard animals copulate, so I'd made some observant guesses on how all of that would happen, but I wasn't sure on any of it. To me there was something frightening about the whole idea.

Whenever I queried Mother on such matters, she simply told me that I would find out on my wedding night."

"And did you?" Abbey asked slyly.

"Yes, I did, young lady," Naomi said, lips curling contentedly. She took a bite of toast and sip of coffee. Her eyes narrowed as she looked around, evidently checking to see if anyone was in earshot. "It turns out that the basics are not much different than horses, except there's much more tenderness involved for us. I don't think mares have near the enjoyment."

Abbey giggled. "Do you have any advice for me?"

"About tonight? Heavens, no!"

"Why not?"

Naomi raised her eyebrows prudishly. "You'll find out soon enough."

Abbey pouted in mock complaint. "Thank you, Aunt Naomi."

"You're embarking on a partnership," Naomi said, stern and serious. "It will grow or wither according to the energy and affection you apply to it. Adam and I had twelve blissful years together before his accident. We cherished each other. We made allowances for each other. We always had time for each other. Adam was my best friend from the morning we first woke up together. That friendship only became more intense and complex as the years passed."

Abbey was smiling and nodding. "Sam and I have so much in common. We have all the raw materials to build something special between us."

"Dream your dreams together."

"We've expressed those exact sentiments, Aunt Naomi."

"That's wonderful. Don't ever take your dreams or each other for granted."

"I don't foresee that ever happening."

"Be careful, Abbey. Love and friendship has to be nurtured," Naomi counseled, concern pooling in her eyes. "Dreams can die or be snatched away without warning."

"My mother taught me that lesson well."

"She was wise to do so, Abbey. Life is hard; harder for some than for others, but hard for us all." Naomi finished her coffee. Sorrow crept across her face. "We always have to be prepared for when life doesn't get into alignment with our dreams. Adam and I wanted a passel of children and we tried—believe me we tried—but it was not to be. That disappointment still causes me to grieve, but one way or another life goes on according to God's purposes."

"I'm so sorry for you, Aunt Naomi. I didn't know."

"No reason for you to know about my discontents or to be sorry for them, dear," Naomi said, softly and sympathetically. "Life is what it is and it has no guarantees. I used to think I could tell God what to do and how to do it, but no more. I've learned that it's how we react and what we do with the brokenness and loss that define our contentment and character."

Abbey folded her hands together. "I seek God's protection and guidance, but I know that life's going to do what it does. I haven't got any say or control over what it throws at me, so mostly I find myself praying for strength and wisdom. Courage, too."

Naomi quickly bobbed her head in agreement. "Deacon told me that you possessed a rare maturity. I suggest that he grossly understated the facts."

"He's always too kind and generous," Abbey said, color rising in her cheeks.

"Don't be bashful, young lady," Naomi countered breezily. "You are thorough and efficient, but I have to ask; is there anything I can do to assist you on this day?"

"Just one thing, Aunt Naomi," Abbey replied, without hesitation. "You'd honor me if you would consent to stand with me at the service. It really is going to be a simple affair."

"Honor *you*?" Naomi said in a squeal. "It would be my delight and *my* honor."

In a rush, they simultaneously reached across the table. Respect and warmth passed between them as their hands linked together along with their eyes. The pithy moment was fully charged with poignancy. No more words were spoken to solidify or seal the tight connection. The joyful emotions flowed freely, forming droplets that glistened on their cheeks.

~~~

"You got a choice, kid."

Liam Greer grunted. He was lounging on the ground against his saddle.

Charley Jondreau fed sticks into the campfire, then sat back and picked up his tin cup of coffee. It was his second of the new day. He crossed his legs, eyes squinting to the east where the sun resembled a gigantic orange ball suspended on a rim of the Flint Hills. He shifted around and scowled at the hurting young man across from him, as though demanding an answer.

"I heard that before from you," Liam said, all smarmy. "I ain't got nothing to say to it."

A groaning moan of a gulp came from the ex-cavalryman sleeping off his drunk. Jackson Scully was a short ways from the fire, sprawled on a bed of patchy grass beneath the saggy branches of a willow. He was unconscious and inert, entirely out of it. His limbs were askew and as stiff as a corpse. The only sign of life was the irregular gasps of his loud snoring.

Jondreau angled a thumb at him. "You want to end up a souse like him, eh?"

Greer scoffed with a flippant wave of a hand. "I ain't ever going to be no drunk." A wince caused his jaw to clench. He was black-eyed and swollen-faced, the rainbow colors ranging from pink to yellowish-red to an ugly purple. The bridge of his nose was flattened; the nostrils turned up and distended. "I only drink beer. I don't touch hard liquor."

"People make choices, kid. Choices make paths."

"I ain't going to be a drunk like my old man."

"No? That might be the best end for you."

"Best end?"

"A boozer ain't likely to get hung."

"Hung?"

"Killers and thieves get hung, kid."

Greer chuckled glibly. "I don't intend on being a drunk or getting hung."

"Intentions ain't choices. You're on a reckless path."

"You're wrong, Charley."

"Am I? You fancy being a gunman, eh?"

"I'm going to be somebody, yeah."

"No. You be just another nobody deceived into believing lies."

Greer scowled and flinched in anger and pain. "Lies? What lies?"

"You reject good counsel to follow bad counsel," Charley replied flatly. "We all have two directions within, good and evil. There are lots of gray pathways in the middle ground between the white and black of good and evil. We choose which way we go, which way we lean."

"Lies? What lies?" Liam reiterated, sitting up a bit straighter.

"Each day we choose. You choose evil, always. I watch. I *see*, eh."

"Evil?" Liam was chuckling. "You mean pointy-horned, long-tailed devil evil?"

Jondreau brushed off his levity by saying, "Evil wins when it gets portrayed as some cartoon prankster. That clown character you describe is pure deception. Evil is real and it ain't no joke. Evil will kill your soul dead, then prance and preen in victory."

"I ain't buying none of it, Charley."

"I ain't selling anything, kid."

"You ain't? It seems like you're giving evil the old hard sell."

"I'm telling you truth. You choose what to do with it."

"Truth? Good? Evil? Ain't nothing to any of it."

"And therein is the diabolical falsehood that deceives you," Charley said, mouth drawn tight. "Ain't no one can force you to believe anything, but know this; truth doesn't require your belief or permission to exist. Neither does good and evil." His tone was calmly adamant. "Every choice has a consequence, kid. *Each* day we choose. *You* choose evil, *always*. And like a sapling that can be bent and shaped, you are bent and shaped by the evil you choose."

Just then, Jackson Scully snorted and sat upright. His head twisted and jerked, bloodshot eyes protruding with such force that it appeared as though they were going to dislodge from the sockets. It was clear that none of the circumstances were registering; his expression was vacant and insipidly dull. His arms thrashed and wind-milled illogically. He slurred a yelp and collapsed backwards, tossing and twitching in a spasm of tremors. The dry heave convulsions lasted for a full minute before ending to leave him rigid and lifeless once more.

Greer had observed the fitful outburst, alarmed and on guard. He took the opportunity to purposefully withdraw from Jondreau and ignore him. Lines of apprehension began sketching in around the colors of his battered face. He rolled onto his hands and knees to dig around in his saddlebags. He ferreted through them until he took hold of the sterling silver case his father had carried as a treasure for as long as could be remembered.

He held it over his heart. He altered his position, wiggling his keester to get comfortable against the saddle. He unsnapped the lid and studied the tintype. The eyes, lively and engaging, stared back at him. He timidly and with pronounced care fingered the outlines of her face. It was as if he was seeing her for the first time and wondering; what had she been like way back then when she was young and impressively beautiful? Tears fell down his puffy cheeks.

"What have you got there?" Charley asked, standing near the fire.

Greer gawked at him. "Nothing."

"Nothing, eh?" Charley stepped closer to him. "Let me see nothing."

Greer frowned doubtfully. "It's just a photograph."

In a swift instant, Jondreau snatched it from him. He immediately smiled as he focused on the likeness. "I saw this woman. She's older now, but still a fine looking lady."

"Everyone has seen that woman. And she ain't no lady. She's a whore."

"No," Charley said tersely. "She was once, but not now. I know for I've *seen*."

"Once a whore, always a whore."

"You got a lot to learn, kid." Jondreau's eyes curved from what was in his hands to the inebriated old horse-soldier, who remained wasted in a cadaverous condition. Jondreau edged around the dwindling flames. His eyelids flickered. Veins in his neck bulged and pulsed as his nostrils flared. He shuddered and the condensed moment of epiphany passed. He tossed the silver case back to Greer. "It's not yours. It belongs to the woman pictured, your mother."

Greer recoiled, then jerked forward. "Screw her. She's a whore."

Jondreau exhaled slowly. "You got a choice, kid. The byways of change are in front of you. Your convergence at the crossroads is now. It is for you as it was for your mother, not so long ago. She made a wise choice, eh." He wiped his palms together in a down-to-earth washing motion and said, "I will walk with you until I will walk with you no more."

He clapped once and held his hands up shoulder high as he backed away. He brusquely spun around and sidled to the rope corral. He spoke to the piebald pinto and set the animal loose. It neighed and burst into a run. He followed, strolling to the sloping bank of Mud Creek. His hands were tucked in the side pockets of his trousers and he was whistling softly.

The orange ball of the sun had climbed above the Flint Hills.

Caleb Weitzel was returning to the campsite. Tiredness crept across his shoulder blades. The sunshine on his back was already hot and steamy even though it was still early morning. He had been on a hunt to put fresh meat in the cook-pot. A small pronghorn antelope, already gutted, was balanced in front of the saddle as Shadrach trotted effortlessly.

The tree, under which Daniel Twosongs was being nursed, came into view as he rode out of a low hollow. He slowed the steeldust to a walk. Weitzel surveyed the grassy landscape in front of him, eyes wide open and senses on alert. Thin tapers of smoke were rising beneath the tree. The distinctive odor of sage and lavender reached him.

After a few moments, the horse's ears pricked and it whinnied; there was no anxiousness in its conduct, but rather, calmness rippled through the stallion's body. Weitzel felt its muscles relax. He was wary. He pushed his hat up his furrowed forehead. He studied the scene. Nothing seemed out of the ordinary. Consuelo and Sally Twosongs were sitting near Daniel. The mules, donkey and brindle mare were standing quietly where he had picketed them last night.

He wondered on Shadrach's manner. He squinted hard. Then there was the briefest of movement not far from Daniel and the women—in between them and the tethered animals. He pushed up in the stirrups. His heart jumped as his eyes identified what was nearly hidden in the shadowy shade of the tree. Amazement leapfrogged in him. He shivered. Three wolves were lying flat in a swatch of deep grass, still and silent, heads on paws.

Shadrach reared up slightly and whinnied again; it was its typical friendly greeting. The horse started high-stepping, its head bobbing, its ears flicking. Weitzel reached forward to stroke its mane and spoke quietly. He wasn't quite sure what to make of his mount's actions; nor did he have much comprehension of what was going on at the encampment. The wolves were up and stretching, necks craning up and down. There was no panic or urgency that could be discerned in the animals; neither was there any apparent alarm or worry in the women.

The noble beasts—each with a silvery collar of hair—formed a line, acting with the precision of a team following orders of a drill master. In single file the feral canines padded along in a definite pattern, encircling the people and the tree. Three times the wolves went around, each circle creeping tighter and closer.

Weitzel observed as astonishment dried all his saliva; his tongue felt furry. His eyes, as blue as the sky above, were fixated on the wolves, full of disbelief at what was happening. His backbone was straight and unbending; knots were cramping in his shoulders. Though his hands were flexing anxiously, he never once reached for his rifle.

Suddenly the wild animals stopped, heads tilted upward to howl as one. The wolf-song was full and throaty; when it peaked, Shadrach shook its hindquarters and blew noisily. Each wolf barked in reply, then together dashed across the meadow past the mules, donkey and brindle mare—the livestock reacted by neighing or bucking happily.

Weitzel stepped out of the saddle. He had the shakes, as though a wintry wind from some distant northland had whipped through him. He stood unmoving until the coldness in him eased away and the quivering wobblies passed. He was still a fair piece away from camp. He dropped the reins. His mouth was gaped open and he was breathing shallowly.

His steps were those of a man sneaking through a graveyard at midnight; on his toes, slow and faltering. The steeldust followed at that hesitating pace. Weitzel kept watching the wolves run to the west, then without becoming concealed by the terrain, the creatures were no longer visible. He stopped dead in his footsteps. The wolves were no more; vanished. His eyes flinched and he sucked in a gush of air.

Sally Twosongs was hurrying to him. "Father is on the mend," she reported as she approached. She halted next to him and touched his chin to tenderly close his mouth. "Evil almost succeeded in killing him, but all is well now. The brain fever broke and the sickness is sweating out of him. Time and prayer will complete the healing."

He stared wonderingly at her. He was speechless.

She softly stroked his jawline. "All is now as it should be, Caleb."

He kept gazing at her, uncertainty in him. Her eyes, dark and permeated with secrets, were heavy and blearily fatigued. "Have you or Consuelo gotten any sleep?" he asked gently.

"No, we tended to him and prayed all night. Father is here with us. We are safe," she replied, taking hold of his hands. She squeezed and he reciprocated. A taut smile puckered her lips. "I won't lie. It was fearful. Father came close to death. The shoreline of time without end summoned him, but the Creator still has duties and tasks for him here."

"I won't ask about the wolves."

The Navajo maiden laughed in a musical, upbeat manner. "You just did. We are under the Creator's shelter and security, Caleb. As I told you yesterday; Jesus is good medicine. Much greater is the Christ in us, than our enemy Satan on the prowl in the world."

Shadrach snorted, head bobbing and ears twitching.

"I saw what I saw, Sally Twosongs. I don't understand it, but I saw it."

She whispered another laugh and gave him a strong hug. She promptly pushed back and told him, "You butcher that pronghorn and I'll get a cook-fire going to roast it."

A grin tugged on the corners of his mouth. She turned. He watched her walk away. The grin grew into an extraordinary smile that climbed up his cheeks to transform his eyes into thin slits. Even exhausted and operating on no sleep, Sally Twosongs was beautiful. She moved with a light-footed sway that made his heart churn and caused his love to overwhelm his emotions.

The weariness in his shoulder blades was gone. He got busy prepping the antelope.

~·~·~

Pete Axler was in some kind of a quandary. He sat on a bench in front of Moon's Frontier Store, whittling on a chunk of wood and muttering. Mostly he was yammering under his breath, but every so often he'd glance in the direction of the sun, which was halfway to the top of the sky, then aloud in a raspy voice, ask and answer a question all at the same time.

Deacon Coburn, dressed in his finest outfit and newly shaved, had joined him more than ten minutes ago, but had yet to get a word in edgewise. He was hatless, his naturally curly hair a semi-controlled tumble that came to rest evenly on his broad shoulders. He sat listening, rather amused by the lanky lawman's seeming predicament. Coburn picked through all he could hear in an effort to fathom what it was that had his friend in such a state.

"Heatstroke. That's what I got," Pete blurted gloomily.

Coburn gave him a quizzical look. He held it on him for half a minute or more.

"Ain't you going to say something? Tell me I'm right or wrong."

"I ain't a doctor, Pete. I doubt its heatstroke."

"Heatstroke, I tell you. That's what I got."

"Again, I ain't a doctor, but for land sakes, what are your symptoms?"

"I don't need any doctor, Deacon," Pete answered testily. He stopped carving for a moment, examined the blade, then went back to cutting slivers off the wood. "I require the services of a priest of some kind. I know you ain't a priest, but you're close enough."

Coburn swallowed a chuckle. "A priest?"

"Geez, I don't know, Deacon," Pete said, head shaking like he had palsy. "Ain't a priest supposed to help people with the stuff that's in their head and heart?"

"I suppose so."

"Well, dangit! I need some help here. I can't think straight. My mind is scattered and jumping all over the place like a liquored up jackrabbit." Pete leaned forward, elbows on his knees as he continued using the knife to shape the wood. "And forget about my heart. It's a muddled mess. I need to talk some stuff through to figure things out."

"Tell me what's got you all flustered."

"It ain't that blamed easy, Deacon."

"Grumbling ain't helping, is it?"

"If I could nail it down, I wouldn't be flustered, would I?"

"Let's talk it out, Pete."

Axler paused to inspect his handiwork. He spat a grunt that expressed dissatisfaction with the progress. "Everything's happening way too fast and I'm feeling like it's all getting away from me," he said dejectedly. "Sam is getting married and moving on. It won't be long and you'll be leaving Abilene too. Changes, changes, changes; everywhere I look there's changes. Mix in the fact that the cattle business is waning and I ain't a sodbuster."

"It's called life, Pete." Coburn fingered his moustache, which was neatly clipped along his upper lip. "By the way, did Sam track you down last night or this morning?"

"I ain't seen Sam since early yesterday."

"He's on the lookout for you."

"I ain't going anywhere," Pete proclaimed, giving a backhanded wave. "This block of wood should keep me fixed here for a few more hours." He returned to the task, taking slow strokes with the blade. "I ain't on duty today because there ain't many cowboys around town to whoop it up. I've had lots of days off lately. My time of wearing a badge is coming to an end."

"What are you planning to do when the cattle shipping season is over?"

"That's what's got me confounded."

"Wheat is bringing more and more families and farmers. It wouldn't surprise me none if some River Brethren folks from Pennsylvania migrate out this way. It will be schoolhouses and stability," Deacon said bluntly. "Abilene will be as peaceful as a church next summer."

"Don't I know it? Soon enough I won't be drawing no wages."

"What are your options?"

"That's just it, Deacon. I ain't got any."

"Not true," Deacon replied, laying a pair of fingers alongside his jawline. "You sell yourself way too short, my friend. Whatever you decide to do will result in a measure of success. You're reliable and trustworthy—a man of your word. You put brawn and brain to good use. Where I come from those are significant qualities to be found in a man."

"Where you come from? We ain't where you come from, are we?" Pete blustered, edgy and nervous-like. He sat up. He rubbed his bristly chin with the back of a hand and said, "Tell me something, is Naomi Engle really your sister?"

"She surely is, Pete."

"I made her acquaintance whilst I was half-drunk and bleeding all over the place."

Coburn laughed. "Getting your tooth yanked?"

Axler nodded, deeply chagrined. His cheeks flushed the color of red roses. "She talked to me on the street the next day and befuddled me. She's a handsome woman."

"I reckon she is."

"It doesn't matter," Pete said dully. "I ain't ever been much of a planner. I kind of just go with the wind and take whatever comes along, but lately that doesn't seem so wise."

"Why?"

"I need to get me some ambition."

"To do what?"

"I raised horses back in Fort Smith. Tinkered at it mostly, but made a few dollars."

"That's not surprising to me, Pete."

Axler sat forward again and turned the piece he was making over in his hands. "I'd like to get back to breeding horses again," he said wistfully. He peeled a splinter off the wood and looked at it in an abstract way. "I got a nutty idea of having a paying horse ranch. I got a little capital socked away, but I ain't got the gumption to do the start-up."

Coburn dragged a hand through his hair. He hunched his shoulders. "In all my wanderings, I've only ever known one man who had a finer hand with horses than you. He's a young fella and I hear he's developing a starter herd, looking to build a ranch in Colorado. I should put you in contact with him. He could use a steady man."

"I'd be grateful for the opportunity," Pete responded in a sincere tone that for him signified enthusiasm. "I'd dearly like to have a few years running horses."

"I'll get word to him and make the introductions," Deacon said, giving him a nudge. He got to his feet and took a deep breath. "I can't jaw with you any more just now, Pete. I have to be ready to give my daughter away to Sam Beadle in marriage. Who'da ever thunk it?"

"Not me, Deacon. There are too many changes for me to keep pace."

"Life is always full of surprises, Pete. Never forget it."

"That won't be difficult to remember. The changes and surprises have no end."

"Life ain't going to stand still for you." Deacon smiled and began to good-naturedly shake a finger at him. "Maybe you ought to apply a lesson from your horse wrangling days. Take charge of your feelings and circumstances; rope them in and make them do your bidding. Get a lariat around the neck of life. Break it just like you would a tetchy bronco, Pete. Then you can ride it down easy." He gave him a robust thumbs up as he spun around and rapidly departed.

Axler grinned. The challenge resonated with him. It was real and seemed doable.

Sam Beadle rushed into the barbershop as though something with snarling teeth was chasing him. He had been racing around town doing errands and taking care of details since sunup. He was as harried as he had ever been. Sweat streaked his face as his chest heaved up and down. He was breathing so hastily that he was incapable of getting any words out.

"Step right in and sit on down, Samuel," Whitey said, with a genial half-bow. "I've been watching and waiting for you. I be ready to slick and shine you up."

Beadle struggled to catch his breath as he asked in a gasp, "Have you seen, Pete?"

"Not since I ripped his tooth out. Are you looking for him?"

"Yes," Sam answered, stepping into the barber chair. "But the window's closing on him and time is slipping away from me. I need you to be quick, Whitey."

Fitzgerald smirked. "Quick is relative, Samuel. I can make you look pretty or I can do a hack job on you." He dipped a white hand towel in a basin of water, wrung it out and handed it to him. "Use this on your face and back of your neck. You need to lighten up or you ain't going make it to your wedding night. You want to have a heart attack? Breathe slow and easy now."

"Thanks, Whitey." Sam used the towel thoroughly. The coolness felt good.

"It's just a wee-bit after ten o'clock. You'll get to the lobby by high noon."

Beadle let out a swishing sigh and was still agitated when he said, "I appreciate your confidence, but I still have to find Pete, clean up and change my clothes."

Fitzgerald made his click-click sound as he took the towel from him. "I'll have you out of that chair in fine fiddle, Samuel. Why don't you rant about this tempest you're caught in?"

Beadle laughed, beginning to relax. "Why should I bother? You likely already know more particulars and minutiae than I do. You should have been the reporter, not me."

Fitzgerald rolled his eyes with hammy emphasis. "That's almighty gracious of you to say so." He shook out a sheet, fluttered it over him and slipped it in place. He readied the scissors and comb, and grinning cheekily, began the task of cutting his hair.

"It has been tempest-like to be sure, but it's all good," Sam said calmly. "Once Abbey Langton gets her mind settled there's no slowing or stopping her."

"You be a lucky man."

"The luckiest, Whitey."

"You be leaving right after the ceremony?"

"I won't be the one brave or stupid enough to goof up Abbey's timetable. She has slotted us fifteen minutes to change into our traveling clothes," Sam answered, eyes wide and happy.

"Jumping jiminy, you best toe that mark and walk that line."

"Don't I know it? She's a spitfire."

Fitzgerald's scissors were snapping in a lilting meter. "Is everything set?"

"Deacon and his sister, Naomi . . . have you met her?"

"I be one of the first souls she visited here in Abilene."

"That seems about right," Sam said, chuckling. "Deacon and Naomi are going to coordinate the shipping of our possessions that don't make the trip with us. An hour ago I completed a deal to purchase a buckboard and a pair of seasoned mules. I also hired a couple roustabouts to load it and have it outside Drovers Cottage ready to go."

"Those be fine arrangements."

"With everything else, I've been hopping."

Fitzgerald put scissors and comb away, giving a cheery click-click. He rapidly worked at brushing up lather in the cup. "I'll likely be joining you in Dodge City by and by."

Beadle raised his eyebrows doubtfully. "Really?"

"You think you be the only one who glories in the excitement of a cowtown?"

"I suppose not. You know who else is leaving Abilene?"

"Miss Flora," Whitey replied, soaping up his customer's cheeks. "Her house is for sale."

"I hear Deacon is going to act as her agent."

"You don't say?" Whitey stropped the straight-razor.

"She's leaving forthwith, by week's end, I think. Not sure to where though."

"Hush up now and be still," Whitey said, leaning in with the blade. "You don't want no nicks or gashes on this day." With a slow and steady hand, he sliced away the coarse whiskers. He finished with a flourish, by energetically rubbing on bayberry-scented lotion. "There you be. Go get your Sunday meeting rags on and you'll be looking swell and hunky-dory."

Beadle stood and handed over an expensive cigar. "I want you at the service, Whitey."

"Whew doggies! That's a pricey upgrade above your usual brand."

"I'm getting married. I splurged."

"Glory be! No one or nothing's going to keep me away. I'll be there." Whitey turned the cigar over in his hands. "And I'll enjoy this rolled tobacco for sure. I'll be at a prime spot on the veranda of Drovers Cottage puffing on it as the newlyweds pull out of town. You best prosper as a married man." He was grinning and click-clicking, eyes twinkling. "When I set up shop in Dodge City, I'll expect this fine smoke to be your usual fare."

Beadle laughed easily. "Until then, take care, my good friend."

Fitzgerald's lips puckered tightly. His eyes misted. He nodded and turned away.

A lump of emotion climbed up Beadle's throat. It was hard and prickly. He acted as if he was going to say something; his mouth moved for a few seconds, but no words came forth. In his comings and goings, he'd learned that goodbyes always seemed to be equipped with unspoken feelings. He exhaled a murmuring lament and left Whitey Fitzgerald to his cleaning chores.

Sam Beadle hurried. He was on an eleventh-hour mission to find Pete Axler.

Meanwhile, at the campsite on Mud Creek south of Abilene, Jackson Scully was scuttling along in his gimp-legged gait. After the previous day's impromptu sloshing around in the water, he began sipping from his bottle, then wholeheartedly dove into it. Though he had passed out and slept in a drunken fit, he remained in a stuporous daze. The dream of murdering

Deacon Coburn had met a suffocating end; the intent and objective that'd so invigorated him—to complete the killing scheme—had been drowned beneath whiskey laced laudanum.

He eyeballed the area. Liam Greer was lounging against his saddle near the campfire, which was a mere scattering of smoldering coals. The kid had a silver case open in his hand and was studiously appraising its contents. He looked wrecked; his purplish face was squashed and ugly. Scully grunted a hoarse chuckle for he had no sympathy for him. He regarded him as a brainless punk who had gotten what was coming to him.

He limped around in his lopsided way, eyes squinting tight and head inclining as he searched for the man wearing the floppy-brimmed hat. When he blearily found him, he sneered and a ribald thought sped through his head; it had to do with buggering. He snickered as he watched Charley Jondreau, a ways off in the meadow with his pinto, giving the animal a rubdown. In Scully's thinking, the man had far too much affection for his horse.

He tottered over near Greer and was about to plop down when curiosity got hold of him. He was intrigued by what appeared to be fascinating the kid. He angled his body and strained to have a peek over his shoulder. His eyelids flickered. His neck muscles constricted as he crooked over to get closer. Ever so slowly he began to wag his head back and forth in disbelief.

To see an image of Sweet Flora staring back at him caused him to almost tip over. There was a crazy spinning against the walls of his skull. His arms stretched and waggled frantically as he stumbled and caught his balance. He renewed his focus on the photograph.

The woman who frequently inhabited his bloodstream gave him a jolt in the solar plexus. She was young and beautiful. Her eyes, vibrant pools of sensual promises, demanded his concentration; he got lost inside them. His belly did a memory boosted somersault. His intake of air quickened. Color crawled out from under the bush of his beard to darken his complexion.

"I want it," Jackson said breathlessly. "I want it now."

Greer glanced up, seemingly surprised to see him hanging over him. "What?"

"Give me it," Jackson answered, menacing him. "Where did you come by it?"

"It's mine."

"Where'd you get it?"

Greer scowled at him. He snapped the case shut and drew it tight against his chest. "It ain't none of your business, so why would I tell you? It's mine, all mine."

Scully's eyes popped open; flecks of rage sparkled in the center of them. "It ain't none of my business? That woman wants me to marry her. Now give it to me." With a startling display of nimbleness, he garnered stability and leaned back on his boogered up leg to kick him.

The upward blow struck Greer's chin, slamming his mouth shut in a teeth-rattling grimace. He scrambled and rolled over in time to avoid the follow-up attack, which was another boot that flew past his ear and stomped against the saddle.

"I want it *now*!" Jackson screamed, hopping around him.

Over in the grass, Charley Jondreau had jumped into action, moving doggedly.

Greer scrabbled backwards in an attempt to escape. "Are you crazy?"

"I want it," Jackson repeated adamantly. Sticky spittle matted in his chin-whiskers. "Whatever claim you have on it, I guarantee that mine is larger. I've known Flora for many years. She wants me to run away with her. Give it to me or you're going to die."

Greer clung to the silver case. He cast the impression of a helpless child, alone and forsaken. The tears collecting in his puffed-up eyes dribbled down his discolored face. In a broken voice that had a mix of hatred and shame, he muttered, "She's my mother."

Scully balked, staggering backwards. An acidic gush of bile roiled in the pit of his stomach, then geysered up his throat. It scorched like a kerosene fire. He clutched and clawed at his torso. He folded at the waist and choked out a splatter of rancid puke. He spat and slobbered for several seconds before gaining control.

He stumbled as he teetered toward where he had slept. His blankets were lying in a heap. His saddle was closeby, up against a tree trunk. He was making guttural noises with each afflicted step he took. He withdrew his handgun from the holster, which was looped on the saddle horn. He turned, so slowly that it appeared as though he was going to topple over.

Unseen or undetected by the onetime soldier, Charley Jondreau had been scrambling from the moment trouble began to brew. He rushed the pinto into the rope corral and hurried to get positioned at a strategic spot nearby, without taking the opportunity to retrieve his gunbelt secured in his bedroll. He was unarmed. No gun, no knife.

Greer watched both men, his fraidy-cat eyes flitting back and forth.

Scully stalked toward him. "Give it to me or you're going to die."

Jondreau gruffly cleared his throat. "If anybody dies here, it'll be you, eh."

Scully gasped in shock. He shook his pistol at him. "This ain't your concern."

"I choose what concerns me," Charley said in a calm and hushed voice.

Greer kept sliding farther and farther away, slinking inch by inch like a lizard.

Scully squared off to facedown Jondreau. "You must be bulletproof."

"I don't need to be, eh. Your gun's empty."

Scully blinked rapidly. His tongue did a flickering dance along his upper lip. He tried to think clearly. There was numbness cluttering up his brain. He couldn't remember when or if he'd cleaned his sidearm or checked its loads. His hands flexed. "Empty? How you figure?"

Jondreau was taking small steps toward him. His eyes were firmly locked on the man aiming a revolver at his midsection. He padded steadily forward. "You're so hung-over you have no idea. I know you're empty, but you know nothing, eh?"

Scully was anxious and excitedly nervous. His eyeballs were stretched wide, popping and full of puzzlement. He was panicky to revisit the recent past; was the firearm loaded or not? He had no answer. He licked his lips. His mouth was dry and cottony. Pain from his left hip flared up his backbone to settle at the base of his skull like an ooze of molten lead. His bulging eyes lowered toward the gun. He tilted it slightly in an effort to determine what he couldn't recall.

In that momentary lapse of his attention, Jondreau exploded into action. He leapt at him and covered the space between them as a lynx would pounce upon a lazing prairie dog. His left hand grabbed hold of the weapon while he unleashed a shoulder-rolling right cross that struck Scully high on his cheekbone. He crumpled to the ground and sprawled there, sputtering.

Jondreau loomed over him. He slapped the six-shooter's cylinder open and removed a cartridge from each chamber. He pocketed the bullets and dropped the gun at Scully's feet. "This is the only mistake you get to make with me, eh. Leave the kid be. Go sleep it off."

Scully cursed. He took the Lord's name in vain. He moaned and grumbled a host of obscenities that called into question Jondreau's ancestry going back numerous generations. When he exhausted all invectives to call down damnation, he skulked to the water's edge. He knelt cumbersomely. He washed his face. His breathing remained rapid and shaky.

All Jackson Scully desired was the pacifying companionship of a bottle.

Pete Axler had eased off into his own little world, where every idea he had was good and every intention came to fruition. He was still lodged in front of Moon's Frontier Store, replaying his conversation with Deacon Coburn whilst continuing to chip flakes off the block of wood. It was oak and he had ascertained the token concealed inside it. The memento wasn't what he had expected to find, but he respected the process; he simply had to be faithful in bringing it out.

As he labored away and thought through all that was running amuck in his head, he came to a couple decisions. Both startled him and caused nervousness to rise up, but not enough for him to change his mind. First, he knew exactly what he would do with the craftwork when it was complete. And secondly, no matter the outcome or difficulties involved in his situation, he would roundup his feelings and pursue the possibility of working on a horse ranch.

With those matters settled, he released a hiss of air and sat up straight. He put the knife and wood down on his lap, then stretched and yawned. He removed his hat and briefly finger combed his hair before putting it back on. He heard his name shouted and glanced down the street to see Sam Beadle, looking out of sorts and aggravated, scurrying toward him.

"There you are, Pete!"

"Here I be, Sam. What's got you badgered?"

"Where you been hiding?"

Axler scratched at his stubbly whiskers. "Hiding? I ain't been hiding anywhere."

"I've had an eye out for you all morning."

"I've been planted here since shortly after sunup," Pete said cavalierly. "I saw you racing past a couple hours ago." He frowned at him. "Ain't you getting hitched today?"

"In less than an hour, for crying out loud."

"Shouldn't you ought to be doing something?"

Beadle blustered wordlessly in exasperation. A crooked grin formed. He sat on the edge of the bench. "I am doing something, Pete. I'm asking you to stand with me as my best man."

"What? Who? Me? When? Now?" Each word came out raspier and higher pitched.

"There's no time to banter, Pete."

"I ain't bantering, Sam." He closed the jackknife with a snap and lifted up a mite to slip it into a back pocket. He held onto what would soon become an oak medallion so tightly that the knuckles on his left hand reddened. "Do I have a few minutes to get presentable?"

"Just that, Pete. A few minutes, no more."

The men got up together. Axler turned and thrust his right hand forward. His friend accepted the offer. "Congratulations, Sam. I'm more than proud to stand with you."

The handshake was firm and dead-level; the moment expectant with unspoken warmth and fondness. Beadle broke it off and hurriedly jogged away. Axler went around the corner and up the outside stairs. He was moving faster than a rabid fiend in search of a nest of mischief.

The sun was drawing near to its apex in a crystalline blue sky.

Flora was quiet and introspective; stand-offish, even. Troubling pressure had deposited pain that throbbed behind her eyes. In contrast, her dinner guest had an irrepressible case of the bubblies. The women were finishing their meal. Outside, the violet hues of twilight were shimmering and blending into the streaky gray shades of the gathering darkness.

Naomi Engle was overflowing with news regarding the events of the day. "It really was a wonderful service, sweet and to the point. There was just one brief delay."

"Oh? Was Sam a dragging his feet groom?"

"Not at all. He was ready and waiting," Naomi answered chirpily. "Mr. Axler was the last to arrive and he apologized for his lateness with a joke about not having nimble enough fingers to get the knot centered properly in his string tie, which caused everyone to laugh."

Flora looked up in surprise. "Pete made a wisecrack?"

"Yes, it was quite humorous at the time."

"Pete Axler?"

"Yes."

Flora gave her head a shake. She pressed her thumbs against her temples and rubbed hard. "He wouldn't know funny if it strolled up and gave him a big wet smack on the lips."

Naomi cocked her head, frowning. "Now that you mention it, he wasn't chuckling or even smiling. In fact, he appeared distraught or put off by our merriment."

"That sounds more like the Pete Axler I know."

Naomi leaned forward. "What's Mr. Axler's story?"

Flora shrugged. "He's a nice enough man, to be sure. He's kind and steady, but lackadaisical and a slow-mover in all things. Our paths crossed in Fort Smith. I purchased a splendid stallion from him, which gave me many hours of riding pleasure." She set aside her plate. "Pete gets tongue-tied and easily embarrassed, especially around women."

"That's interesting," Naomi remarked, putting her fork down.

Flora stood and began clearing the table. "Let's do a quick put-away and I'll finish in the morning. I would like to visit in the living room. I need to confess something to you."

Naomi's brow wrinkled. "Confess . . . to me?"

"Yes," Flora replied firmly. She exhaled a rush of tension. "After our talk yesterday, it came to me that I have another step to take on my way to making a new beginning."

The ladies worked together and it wasn't long before the leftovers were stored and dirty dishes scraped and stacked in a basin. They retired to the cozy living room, where Flora lit a bevy of candles, along with several oil lamps. She also scooped up her cloth sack of tobacco, which contained cigarette papers and matches. They sat on either end of the chesterfield, looking like a pair of opposing bookends; one stiff and uneasy, the other open and responsive.

"I haven't really thought through what I need to say," Flora began, jostling the pouch from hand to hand. "I was praying last night. Well, crying more than praying, but in the release of emotions, it was impressed upon me to make confession. If I refuse or fail to do so, then this horrible thing in my past will always torment me." She took the fixings out and began building a ciggy. "To have any hope at all I need to say it aloud for my repentance to be real."

"Each day has a measure of hope for us," Naomi assured in a voice that was inviting and sympathetic. "We can always put the past to rest and start fresh and anew."

"I want to believe that, I want to live that, Naomi."

"Then do so."

Flora smiled, grim and cheerless. "If it was only that easy." She fired up the cigarette and blew a whiff of smoke. She held her hands in her lap and stared at the glowing ember. "I'm a horrible person. I've broken every one of the Ten Commandments, including number six."

Naomi swallowed dryly. She shifted sideways. "*Thou shalt not kill.* How? Why?"

"Mama died when I was ten. She was the best mother ever," Flora said, head bowed and eyes fixed on the smoldering tip of the rollup. "It was just me and Daddy after that, which was fine for a while, but when I started to blossom . . ." Her shame was severe and palpable.

Silence dropped between them. Naomi slipped through it in a murmur, "Incest?"

Flora gave a tiny bob of her head and shivered. She was biting the inside of her bottom lip. "He bribed, cajoled, berated, and finally convinced me that I'd be making Mama happy in heaven if I'd take care of him. I was fourteen when he first took me. It hurt and scared me. I bawled and whimpered the whole while, but it got to be regular. Not every night, but often enough to make me sick. I was mortified. Whenever I complained or tried to end it, he got nasty, real nasty with me. There was no one to safeguard or help me."

Naomi shifted close to her. Her brown eyes were slick and glistening with empathy. She began to slowly stroke her shoulder. "None of what he did to you is your fault, Flora."

"I don't know."

"I do," Naomi said angrily. "You are not responsible for his sin."

Flora turned to flip the butt into the ashtray. She clasped her hands together in her lap. "It stopped after a particularly violent incident in which I almost gouged his eyes out. He reeked of whiskey. For my efforts to defend myself he swore he'd kill me. He battered me until my arms and legs were massive bruises. He never struck my face or anywhere that would show."

Naomi gave her upper arm an encouraging squeeze. "I am so sorry for you."

Flora inhaled a trembling breath. Teardrops were tracking down her cheeks. "I made myself scarce and stayed away from him. He left me alone for more than a year. I thought the nightmare was over." Her lips were quivering. "Then on the eve of my eighteenth birthday he came to my bedroom in the middle of the night and started on me. He was surly and drunk. It was rape. I screamed and fought, kicking and scratching as he violated me."

Naomi was sniffling. And speechless.

"I was in the darkest of places. I became a different person. I went through the next few days figuring an escape," Flora said, detached and toneless. Her eyes were glassy and focused on some far-off distance. "It wasn't long before I was queasy in the mornings and found out I was pregnant. My father's seed had planted a child in me. I put my getaway plans into action.

"I met a weakling of a man I could manipulate. We had a wedding of sorts and I used him to get out of St. Louis. I went into labor near Little Rock. The baby was underweight and scrawny, so it was easy to say it was premature. My dimwitted husband was none the wiser." She took a large breath. "However, before I married Jack Greer and took off with him, I cooked my father a tasty stew spiced with arsenic. I stood beside his bed and watched him die."

Naomi gasped. She wrapped her arms around Flora and pulled her close.

"I killed my father. I killed my son's father. I'm a murderess." Flora's voice was a thin quiver as she buried her face in Naomi's bosom. Flora's composure shattered like a panel of glass. Violent tremors shook her body. She collapsed in a heaving of wretched sobs.

Naomi held onto her fiercely. She cooed comfort while silently praying.

"Oh God . . . oh God . . . forgive me," Flora cried out, her voice manic and infused with ragged desperation. Over and over she repeated the plea for mercy until it became a mantra. The words were punctuated by unintelligible moaning groans that choked up from some unknowable nadir of her soul; it was the pure, undiluted vernacular of grieving and contrition.

"Give her grace, Father," Naomi implored, clinging to her.

"Forgive me . . ." Flora was wheezing and hyperventilating. The deep-rooted mourning surged out of her in uncontrollable convulsions. She twisted and wrestled, fighting to break away from her friend's body-hugging embrace. She did so and slid to the floor. On her knees, she pounded her fists against the cushion of the chesterfield until the strength of her sorrow shattered in one wretched wail. She bent low, hiding her face in the spot she had thumped.

Naomi knelt and laid hands on her. "Our Father who art in heaven, hallowed be thy name," she prayed, weeping intensely. "Flora is humbled before thee. Turn not a deaf ear to her cries. Thou art holy and righteous and just. Thy child was wronged and she did dreadful wrong in return. She seeks to be touched by thy everlasting mercy and compassion. Her iniquity shames her, Lord. Hear the heartfelt agony of her soul. Cleanse her with hyssop. Wash her whiter than snow. Blot out all her sins. Grant her the knowledge that forgiveness is real and reachable. Bless her days ahead with a double portion of thy grace, Lord. Amen."

Flora felt the warmth of peace squeeze her. It radiated from her core outward. Her skin prickled. Though she was dried out, she was still crying. There was no moisture remaining to seep from her sore eyes, but the sounds of her repentance and rebirth kept pouring from the pained depths of her heart. She straightened up and let out a loud utterance.

A dim recollection drifted from under the debris of her subconscious. She gulped several jerky breaths. She couldn't grasp what was floating just beyond the range of her understanding, but discerned that it was lurking within; a piece of the past that she had completely blocked from memory to be forever forgotten was urgently rearing its head. One more secret remained.

Just now, she had no emotional or spiritual energy to set it free.

Night was falling. Stars were beginning to twinkle and spread across the blue-black sky. The air was warm, the humidity substantial and sticky. At Willows Rest, Sam Beadle and his bride were completing the chores of setting up camp. Very few words had been exchanged between them since their arrival, but all the jobs were getting done.

The mules were fed, watered and picketed in a batch of grassy pasture. A small fire was crackling. A supply of wood had been gathered and stacked in preparation for cooking breakfast. Off in the deep shadows beneath a coyote willow, the bed had already been made with care. They had undertaken the unfolding of it together, treating the task to a degree of solemnity.

Old Blue occupied a prime location under the buckboard. The good citizens of Abilene no longer had any claim on the sturdy cattle-dog. It was now exclusively a one-woman animal; its protection and allegiance was reserved for Abbey Langton.

She was sitting on the tailgate of the wagon, swinging her legs while watching the moon rise. It was waning and yellowish, perhaps three-quarters full. She thought about how many times she had passed the best part of an evening doing exactly this, dreaming of the future in the moonlight. The huge difference was that now all those schoolgirl fancies were here for her to experience. She was more than a little anxious, but certainly was not going to show it.

"Abbey," Sam said in a hushed tone. He eased up on her from behind.

She sighed contentedly. "Are we *finally* ready for bed?"

"Not quite yet," he replied, grinning. He put his arms around her and arched his back to peer directly in her eyes. "First our garments must be shed, don't you think?"

"I suppose so." She giggled softly. She placed her hands on his shoulders. She kissed his lips tenderly. "Let's go slow." She pushed him away and stood. She took a knee and casually lifted the edge of her pleated skirt to remove the ankle holster and derringer.

He gawked at her. "Have you been wearing that all day?"

"I wear it every day."

"Even your wedding day?"

"*Every* day," she said, smiling broadly. "I believe it's best to be prepared for any and all necessities, so each morning I check its loads and make sure it's ready for action."

"I don't think you need to continue carrying it."

She gave him a pouty-lipped smile. "Really?" She rose up and handed the pocket pistol in its leather case to him. "You are now responsible for its safe keeping, but I will expect it back in the morning, Mr. Beadle. After all, I may require it to keep you in line."

He wiggled his eyebrows. "For that you'll likely need a larger caliber, Abbey."

"If so, I'll gladly purchase a bigger gun," she said gleefully. She pressed against him. He put his hands on her hips and kissed her hard. She led him past the campfire to the grove of willows. There was hesitancy in their steps, anticipation in their breathing.

They disrobed on either side of the bed, casting awkward glances as every article of clothing was set aside; the longing was mutual. Then, naked before each other and in the sight of the heavens above, they crept beneath a thin blanket to spend their wedding night upon a thick and heavy buffalo robe. Their lovemaking was gentle and tentative, passionate and satisfying.

Sweaty and spent, they fell asleep in each other's arms.

The gunshot was what put her into motion. Until the blast, Sally Twosongs had been still and silent in the midst of chaos. It was as it was before, only she wasn't on a far horizon seeing it all transpire through a vaporous haze; this time she was almost in the line of fire. Crows were flocked together and squawking as the bizarre colors in the sky pounded up and down.

Fear was in her. A precious silver gem spun and glinted as though it was being tossed about by the tumultuous wind. Many hands clutched to grab it, but the prize was elusive. Curses were shouted and threats screamed. A murky-eyed bald man was in the background. She couldn't understand why his presence provided a ration of comfort to her, but it did.

The air became hotter than hot. A noise chugged and churned, louder and louder. It rolled and rumbled with the force of a freight train. Horses were agitated. The animals snorted and bucked and wheeled about, panicked and full of frantic fear. Bloodcurdling shrieks came from the horde of crows. The birds were in a wing-flapping frenzy.

Madness was set loose upon the countryside. The peg-legged monster with furry jowls was raving and slobbering. Spittle foamed on its lips as it prowled toward a man whose face was painted into a grotesque mask. Hate raged as a jagged fireball flash crashed and burned, followed immediately by the boom of a thunderous roar. As the temperature plummeted, a single gunshot blazed; it was then that Sally Twosongs leapt into action.

She ran fast and furious. The dead body, sprawled face down in the dirt, cried out to her. It beckoned and called to her, unleashing a burst of fascination. Suddenly a sense of peace and faith struck her. She stopped cold in her footsteps. She turned ever so slowly.

Her heart jumped as her eyes fell upon the fair maiden, whose gorgeous hair was fluttering in updrafts of the breeze. She was almost hidden in deep shade. Tears of sorrow poured from her, mixed in with perceptible hope. A frown lined her face which was difficult to read. She fiercely held the silver treasure against her bustline.

Sally Twosongs felt a wave of wondrous emotions crash through her. And finally, she saw and comprehended the towering tree that obscured the sad-eyed lady; she was swaddled inside the outlined shadow cast by a cross. She stood secure and safe in front of the Roman instrument of torture on which the king of glory had been crucified.

A thrill sliced at Sally Twosongs. She slowly sidled to where the jaundiced-eyed monster was bleeding from an appalling hole in the middle of its back. She crouched close for a look. As the iron in her soul stiffened, in simple eloquence, she said, "You got what you gave."

Then she woke up. Her eyes flickered open. She sat forward in a startled lurch. A moment of uneasiness passed and she straightaway oriented to her surroundings. The fear that had been within her did not accompany her from the dream. Stars glittered above. Her eyes grew accustomed to the darkness and she took comfort from the night.

She peeled back her covering as though she was unwrapping a gift and slipped from beneath the bedroll. She stood and stretched. Her skin was damp with perspiration. The air felt cool and refreshing. She moved around as gracefully and soundlessly as a panther. The campfire was nothing more than a glow of ashes. She carefully stacked several pieces of buffalo chips around its edges. Flames soon hungrily licked and lapped at the fuel.

She peeked in the direction where Caleb was snoozing. He was on the perimeter in a guarding position. She knew that his rifle would be at his side for he was constantly ready to confront trouble or difficulty and take charge. The vitality of her feelings for him were close to the surface; she murmured a prayer of thanksgiving for the future that awaited them.

Her mother was sleeping deeply and snoring softy. She tiptoed past to take a seat on the ground at her father's side. She stared full in his face and delight wrinkled her brow, for his eyes were wide open and focused on her. She whispered, "You are gathering strength, Father."

"My hour has not yet come."

"I am glad."

"It was a good day to die, but not *my* day."

"I am grateful, Father."

"I, too, child." He raised a finger. "The wolves . . ."

"Yes," she said, "the wolves were heralds that led us to you."

"I'm alive because the Creator is our refuge."

"He is our stronghold. We must remain humble and obedient."

"Yes," he agreed quietly. "His goodness has no end."

"He has shown me mystery."

"You were restless, Sally Twosongs. I heard you muttering in your sleep," Daniel told her in a dry and scratchy tone. "What have you seen?"

"Revenge, I think. Or perhaps, justice," she replied as she varied her posture and crossed her legs. "There was a lady who was hurting bad, then she had hope."

"Hope," Daniel said weakly. "Revenge, no. Justice, yes. Hope, always. Hope arises with each dawn. I have nearly been to the other side and my understandings are enriched. I realize the hope that is ours in this dimension is a glorious necessity." He reached over and gave her hand a gentle squeeze. "The hope experienced here fixes us and spurs us onward, yet it is a frail and fragile figment of the hope that awaits us in the forever land beyond time."

"Tell me of your journey, Father."

"I cannot, Sally Twosongs."

She persisted with a sly grin. "Cannot or will not?"

"Cannot," he answered soberly. "There are no words in human language to describe the marvel of it." He shifted up and pointed. Pale moonlight gleamed in the leaves. "I have been studying this tree. Several branches there on the right side could be cut and used for my travel. We can be on our way home tomorrow before the sun reaches too high."

"Are you strong enough?"

"I'll be fine."

Sally Twosongs placed a hand on his forehead. She smiled. He nodded and gave her a rather hefty poke in the ribs. Her smile cracked into a croaky giggle—his nod became aggressive and obstinate. He took hold of her hand. Father and daughter swapped a knowing look. She accepted the fact that there would be no denying him. Her eyes angled to the east.

The first pinkish gleaming of sunrise was still hours away.

Charley Jondreau was no thief. However, as he rode north through the darkness he had something in his saddlebags that did not belong to him. The right and wrong of it had turned into a filmy pigment of gray in his mind. He had his own yardstick for reasoning through ethical or moral dilemmas, and according to his judgment, he was doing right.

The night had a peculiar stillness that intrigued and disturbed him. He was fixed and alert, examining what lay ahead, then compulsively swiveling in the saddle to check his back trail. The air felt strange to him; he sensed that it carried an ominous harbinger on it. He sniffed and tested it, which told him nothing. His well-founded foreknowledge of the future was no help.

The sky was clear and cloudless. Stars were bright and twinkling for as far as his eyes could see. He had his mind set on where he was going and wouldn't be diverted. He eased the pony around the outskirts of Abilene, enjoying the solitude and silence of the nocturnal hours. Even the stockyards were quiet. Whatever cattle present were bedded down and content.

He rode all the way around town, as though he intended to scoot past Abilene completely, but then turned south to approach his destination from the north. He came upon a row of oak trees. He dismounted and led the pinto. A streak of yellow flashed above. He grinned as he watched the falling star fade into a skinny line and disappear.

When he saw the clapboard bungalow, he stopped and surveyed the area. He spoke to the horse in a gentle voice and ordered the animal to stay put. He had no hesitation as he laid a hand on the possession which he would deliver to its rightful owner. It had been simple enough to acquire without being detected; as proverbially easy as taking candy away from a baby.

He strolled up a laneway to the house, stepped onto the porch and knocked hard on the front door. The pounding fractured the tranquility. He never paused. Seconds turned into minutes. He kept striking the wood with his knuckles until he saw the flare of a match glinting in a window. He waited. The light within grew larger. He heard footfalls creeping.

"Go away," the woman said through the door. "There's nothing for you here. I'm no longer in that business. Go away and leave me alone."

Jondreau responded by hitting the door even harder. Again and again he hammered away. The force of his determined blows caused the doorframe to vibrate and shake.

"Please, Jesus, please," she muttered, desperation in the prayerful pleading.

Jondreau ceased his noise making. He palmed his hat up his forehead and rocked on the balls of his feet. He pushed forward and spoke in a soothing tone. "Hope is always nearby, as sure as thunder follows lightning. Search your heart. Hope is there to lead you onward."

She gasped. The door cracked open and a wedge of light shimmered from the oil lamp in her hand. Her eyes, puffy with sleep, were suddenly wide and shocked. "You? Who are you?"

"Charley Jondreau." He examined the tintype in his hand. He glanced at her and smiled thinly. He snapped the silver case shut, gave it to her and said, "This is a gift from your mother. Heed its counsel." He turned and left her. He walked to his horse and swung into the saddle.

The piebald pinto neighed softly.

Flora was bowled over. Her legs were rubbery. She staggered and nearly toppled to the floor. She set the oil lamp down on a table just inside the door. Exhausted and afraid, she tugged the plain-colored housecoat tighter around her waist and cautiously edged onto the porch. Her mouth was hanging open as she watched her nighttime caller ride away.

She stood, frightened and spellbound, for a long while. She listened until she could no longer hear the hoofbeats. Her brain was sending urgent messages that got entangled in an upheaval of emotions. The air was hot and humid, but coldness covered her. From the soles of her bare feet to the crown of her head, her flesh was shivery with goosepimples.

The heirloom from her maternal grandmother was clutched against her bosom. Her cheeks were wet with tears. She came out of her stunned paralysis and took a handful of tiny steps into the front yard. Her heart was thumping. She tilted her head back and stared in awe at the starry vastness twinkling from one horizon to the other.

Just then, in the quadrant of the sky that engaged her interest, an explosive burst of energy flamed brightly as a star burned up and scorched a path to oblivion. The beauty and wonder of it took her breath away. She was captivated. Her balance was wobbly. She felt something touch her deep inside; something unexplainable, marvelous, miraculous. It was as though warm fingers were cradling her heart in a loving and protective embrace.

It lasted for only a few moments, but the fervency of the sensation galvanized her. The light-headedness passed and she found her equilibrium. She hurried into the house, shut and locked the door. Without delay, she went about the chore of gathering every candle she could find to fully illuminate the living room. When she was finished, the gloom of darkness had been banished to nooks and crannies where it mattered not to her.

She sat on the chesterfield. The sterling silver case was in her right hand, which was pressed over her heart. She was fearful to open it; afraid of what she would see. Or more precisely, afraid that there would be nothing for her to see; perhaps the inheritance was only a high-priced empty shell created by some unknown silversmith. The photograph and what had been painstakingly hidden behind it could be long gone and lost forever.

"Whatever is here, help me, Lord. Meet me at this place and give me wisdom." Her voice was firm, her demeanor steely and stubborn. She steadied and slowed her breathing. She fingered the silver treasure, making circular motions. As she did so, she came into contact with the teeny latch mechanism and the lid popped up. She hitched in a gulp of air.

She held it close to her face. She inspected the edges of the tintype. Her eyes pulled tight and narrow. She wondered if what she had concealed all those years ago endured. There were no marks or scratches to indicate that tampering had occurred, but she was no expert and couldn't be sure. What if the handwritten note from her mother had been discovered by some faceless bandit who stole it? What if all that remained was the photograph?

It was then that she actually looked at the picture; it apprehended her attention. She immediately remembered details of the circumstances of when it was taken. On her eighteenth birthday, she had made arrangements with a studio as an act of defiance against a bitter pill of fate. A short twelve hours earlier, whilst she slept, her father had begun his cruel assault. He was relentlessly unrepentant as he tore her future to shreds by raping her.

In the morning, hurting and all alone, she'd harnessed the fierce anger simmering in her veins by retreating inwardly to a spot where the building blocks of denial were easily accessible. She defied the detestable thing done to her and processed the pain by making believe it never happened. She got gussied up in her finest outfit and fussily brushed her hair until it was just so, then embarked on an outing that concluded with her sitting for a photographer.

Now, gazing at her eighteen year old self, she was preoccupied and saddened by the passage of her youthful beauty. She had wasted all of it. The years had not turned out the way she had dreamed of as a child. How different would her life have been if her mother hadn't died when she was ten years old; could her byways have taken a far different trajectory?

The wreckage in her wake was so difficult to overcome. It was never going to be easy to shed any of it. There would always be something to remind her of the destruction of lives for which she bore responsibility. Receiving God's forgiveness surely gave her a measure of freedom and the grace to stand upon, but it didn't make the consequences go away.

She desperately desired to pry the picture back, but an overpowering fear had her in its paws and wouldn't release her. What if the directive from her mother was forever gone? She yearned to listen to her mother once more. Her guidance had always been kind and wise. Flora closed her eyes and attempted to recall a memory to console and encourage her. There was only blankness. She nibbled on her bottom lip. She tried and tried, but as she probed around the recesses of her mind, she couldn't see or hear her mother.

Then, out from under the ash heap of yesteryear, the lone lingering secret of her life bounded into view. She saw the moment of choice in the past as clearly as though it was happening directly in front of her. She jolted backwards at the force, but didn't resist or fight it. She wouldn't stuff the truth down into its hideaway in the deepest confines of her heart. Her hands began to shake. Her breathing sped up. She wanted a cigarette, but decided against it.

She stood and tucked the silver case in the housecoat's belt. She went to the kitchen, rattled around a drawer and returned with notebook paper and a pencil. She sat and crossed her right leg over her left to use her thigh as a desktop. An almost perfect clarity was piloting her. Once the clandestine deeds came into view she realized that she could unearth the private matter and rectify it; action could be taken to fix and perhaps even bring about healthy reconciliation.

It was within her power to do something. To go forward would require employing investigators. From her days as Sweet Flora she had contacts with the Pinkertons. She considered the proper phrasing, then busily wrote the text. In the morning, before the day got too hectic, she would proceed to the telegraph office to set into motion her plan to repair a disgraceful decision.

The possibilities excited her. There would be no more sleep for her on this night.

A new day was dawning when Charley Jondreau came awake with a jerk. He sat up. No fog of sleep hindered him; his awareness was instantly active. Upon returning from his midnight jaunt to town he had placed his bedroll far off from his campmates. The two rogues were beneath a tree near the fire, still nestled in slumber. Other than their loud snoring, all was quiet.

The sky was muddy gray; the rising sun was a mere glimmer of amber behind a ridgeline of the Flint Hills. Peaceful and content, Jondreau regarded it for an extended interval. He enjoyed the lonesomeness of mornings. He rubbed a hand over his scalp; feeling the stubble, he decided that once again it was time to put his blade to work.

He pulled his knees up and was about to rise, but a potent hunch stopped him cold. His nostrils flared and his eyelids flickered. His eyeballs rolled back in his head so that all that could be seen were the whites. The pulse-points in his temple bulged; veins in his neck swelled. His head lagged listlessly, as though his spine had turned to mush.

The smell of the skunk was concentrated and extreme on him. In an instant of flawless lucidity, he saw a young woman with bronze skin and a twined rope of luxuriant black hair dangling down and swinging free. She was as beautiful as a princess; her carriage poised and commanding. She wore a buckskin skirt and a breezy ribbon-blouse. Her hands were busy, her feet swift and graceful. Her dark eyes were aglow and mystic, and converged on him. He returned the gaze; their eyes locked. He sensed an overwhelming kinship with her.

He gasped in a lungful of air when the powerful vision released its grip. He exhaled a rush through his nose to expel the vestiges of the acidic odor which always accompanied such premonitions. He glanced in the direction of the sleeping men. His eyes fell on Jackson Scully. His head twitched, eyes blinking like shutters. He *saw* and knew that there was a prior connection between the ex-cavalryman and the bronze-skinned woman he had *seen*.

Jondreau was as befuddled as was within the realm of his experience. Queries raced through his head: Who was she? What of the bond of affinity between them? Where could she be located? Was he destined to come alongside her? Did the Great Spirit have a purpose for them to find each other? Was she warning him? How did Jackson Scully factor into her story?

The man from the Great Lakes region stood. He ambled to the makeshift corral and set his pony loose. His usually disciplined mind was cluttered. He couldn't sort things through and think straight. He went to the edge of Mud Creek and knelt. He energetically splashed water on his face and rubbed his eyes. He took several deep breaths.

An irresistible need rose up from some hallowed vault within. The chants of the ancients cried out to him. His eyes closed. His arms were outstretched as he turned his face heavenward and made prayers of supplication in the language of his Iroquois forbears. His voice was quiet and subdued, but the words were insistent as he sought discernment and comprehension.

When his song concluded, he scrutinized the sky. He instantaneously felt the downy hair on the nape of his neck spike and prickle. There was evil afoot. The burgundy hues developing off to the east were strange; ugly, even. He stepped close to the pinto and murmured to it. Then he went to his bedroll, got his gunbelt and strapped it around his waist. He jammed his hat on and pulled it low. Shaving his head would have to wait. Trouble was fast approaching.

When it arrived, Charley Jondreau would be ready and waiting.

It didn't need doing, but by shortly after sunup, Whitey Fitzgerald was sweeping the porch of his shop. In his usual vigorous manner he was making the broom snap and pop. His smile was enormous, his demeanor full of contagious enthusiasm. He was humming an old tune from childhood, signifying the end of each stanza with a click-click.

When he was satisfied that every bit of dust and grit had been removed, he stepped to the edge of the stoop and had a drawn-out look at what he referred to as his hometown. He had in mind the idea of leaving. He worked it through and turned it over and over again. There was no compunction in him demanding that he stay put, but even so, doubts pecked at him.

The eastern sky caught his attention. His breath snagged in his throat. "Mercy me, those are the queerest colors I ever did see," he remarked aloud. "It looks to be the calm before the storm. A bad one's a-coming." He switched directions and saw a lady scurrying on the far side of the street. He tossed her a wave and she altered her angle to come toward him. "Whew doggies, you be a pretty sight for these eyes of mine this morning, Miss Flora."

"Whitey, you are incorrigible, but thank you." She stopped in front of him and did a little curtsy, laughing in a relaxed way. She wore a corduroy skirt with a matching buttoned-up jacket, topped off by a threadwork-trimmed hat. "You're looking just fine yourself."

Fitzgerald slapped a knee and tipped her a wink. "Now who's incorrigible?"

"I suppose it takes one to know one."

"That be a piece of truth," he said, with a peppy click-click. He had a keen look-see up and down the avenue, which was not at all busy. "Where are you running to, Miss Flora?"

She shifted a small cloth carryall from one hand to the other, seemingly distracted. She gave him a half-hearted shrug and acted as though she wanted to say something important, but then lowered her eyes. "I have to attend to some delicate business."

"Taking care of details on selling and moving on?"

"Maybe . . . sort of, but not really, Whitey."

"You ain't going to tell me, are you?"

She gave him a sideways frown. "Why would you say that?" she asked, genuine hurt ringing in her voice. "You're one of the few true friends I have in the whole wide world."

"That's sweet of you to say, Miss Flora."

"I enjoy your company, Whitey."

Fitzgerald exhibited an aw-shucks grin that was boyishly charming. "I'll miss you. I hope you'll stop in and give me a proper farewell before you get on that train."

"You know I will, Whitey."

"I'll be here waiting to give you a big old hug."

She smiled demurely. Her eyes crinkled as she inched in closer and said, "I'll also be praying that our paths will cross again somewhere down the trail."

"That be a peachy prayer. You pray that one real hard."

She took a step back, hands tight on the carryall. "I must be on my way. I have some telegraphs to send. I'm attempting to revisit a mistake I made, in an effort to fix it."

"I wish you nothing but the best of luck with that, Miss Flora." He shooed her with a backward flip of both hands. "You hurry off now and get matters handled, but don't you dare dilly-dally. You'll want to be home before the crabby weather sets in." He gestured to the offbeat hues tarnishing the horizon. "My whiffer says it's going to be a doozy."

She nodded. "Mine, too. Take care." She whirled around and departed at a brisk pace.

Fitzgerald watched for a moment, then went inside and began his daily clean-up.

At Willows Rest, as the sun rose above the eastern skyline, Abbey Langton woke up face to face with her husband. She was breathless. She stared at him. He was handsome and strong. The kindness of good fortune was too much for her to wrap her brain around. She snuggled closer to him. He rolled over on his back, opened his eyes and pulled her into his embrace.

Birds were chirping. The thickly humid air was alive with the twittering melody. Old Blue was stretched out in a patch of sunshine, eyes never straying far from its mistress. She gave the lightweight blanket a gentle tug and arranged it over them. There was no embarrassment or tentativeness between them. They cuddled together in silence for a significant amount of time, listening to the rhythm of each other's heartbeat complement the birdsong.

Abbey unexpectedly lifted up slightly. "What's wrong with the sky?"

Beadle followed her eyes to the sunrise. "Those are peculiar colors."

"Yes, peculiar. It looks eerie to me."

"It's probably just rain coming. Lord knows we surely need it," he said, tightening his hold on her. "We must have more important things to talk about than the weather."

She rested her head in the crook of his arm. "You mean dreaming our dreams?"

"That's exactly what I have in mind."

"I want us to stay on the move," she told him, adamancy in her tone. "Settle in here or there for a spell, then move on to the next spot where its boom and bust and happening. Let's not allow the grass to grow under our feet, Sam."

"I was in Abilene for five years. That's about the limit for my itchy feet."

"That's pleasing to hear."

"There might be a problem, Abbey."

"Problem? Whatever do you mean?"

"Children could change or put a crimp in our plans."

She smiled and giggled girlishly. "I suppose that's always possible."

He hugged her closer. "And natural."

She absently patted his chest as she pondered the topic of conversation. "If the Lord chooses to bless us, then our children will take on our vagabond ways."

"I guess so."

"Our life together is going to be an adventure, Sam," she said confidently. "There won't be any mediocrity tolerated. We are going to see and do and be a part of history."

"And our children will be gypsies."

She laughed happily. "Yes, gypsies."

"Let's be serious here."

"I'm pin-point serious, Sam."

"Do you *want* children?"

She countered, "Do you?"

"I really don't know. Maybe, I guess."

"That's hardly a definitive answer, Sam."

"It's all I got . . ."

"One might even call it evasive or ambiguous."

"Evasive? It's not my intention to be evasive, Abbey."

"Ambiguous?"

"Perhaps," he replied, furrowing his brow. "Ambiguity isn't a bad viewpoint to nurture and keep in place. It often is misconstrued, but there are plenty of unknowns and uncertainties in life for us to roll with or kick against. I choose to roll with ambiguity as much as I can."

"Pragmatic?"

"Yes, I think that's a sensible way to be."

"Me, too. Whatever it takes to get to where we want to go."

"Abbey Langton, I declare that you and I are going to get along just fine." He ran his fingers through her hair and shifted slightly against her. "You do realize that because of our headlong dash to the altar there are several gaps in our knowledge of each other?"

"That's what living and dreaming is for, Sam. Ask me whatsoever you so desire."

"When's your birthday?"

"Next March I'll be nineteen."

He cringed and pulled back a bit. "Oh, my."

"What?"

"I thought you were twenty-five or so. In a few weeks I'll be thirty."

She squeezed him. "I thought *you* were twenty-five."

"What are we going to do?"

"What do you mean?"

"We can't deny the giant age difference, Abbey."

"Deny it? Why on earth would we *ever* want to deny it?" she asked earnestly. "It seems to me that all of this was settled the moment you said, *I do*." Her lips were curled upward and there was a high-level of teasing in her voice. "Are you now recanting, Mr. Beadle?"

"Of course not."

She gave him another forceful squeeze. "Then I propose we love each other until death do us part. We'll grow old together. You'll just reach your dotage before I do . . ."

He jerked up on an elbow. "That's what Deacon meant when he told me you were green." His eyes were wide and bright. "I should've figured he was talking about your age, but my head was all mixed up and wasn't working properly. I was intoxicated by you—still am."

She snickered and touched his cheek. "Was I green last night?"

"No, ma'am. We were ripe together."

She blushed. Her eyes squinted as she tried to stifle a torrent of feelings. She pushed back and slid away from him. "Now I'm going to have to ask you to look the other way."

"Why?"

"Can't you just do as you're told?" She playfully elbowed his shoulder. "I intend to get up and walk over to the water and wash up some before getting dressed."

"So why do I have to look the other way?"

"Do I have to remind you that I'm in my altogether?"

He rolled his eyes and chuckled loudly. "I won't be struck blind, Abbey."

She attempted to be stern. "We want to put some miles behind us today, Sam."

"The miles can wait," he said, kissing her. She responded in kind. The passions of one kiss led to another. And another. Their tenderness gathered momentum as birds flew amongst the coyote willows, singing a serenade to them. Old Blue barked twice, then trotted off.

Three hours later they were finally packed up and on the trail.

Pete Axler was on a mid-morning walkabout, heading toward Drovers Cottage. He was straggling along at his usual dawdling pace, but there was resolve in his step. His tin star and holstered pistol were under lock and key at his closet-sized apartment above Moon's Frontier Store because, as had become the normal turn of events, he was off-duty again.

He took note of the sky. A large buildup of dark clouds was gathering in the southeast. The thunderheads looked to be full and angry, with spider-webs of black tendrils crawling across them like a sick malignancy. He had seen rainclouds with that manifestation before and had a sense of what was coming. He sniffed the air. His mouth pursed into a tense grimace.

He thumbed his hat up his forehead. He kept on task. A woozy feeling squirmed through his belly as he came close to his destination. He halted across the street, eyes peeled and anxious. He jammed his hands in his back pockets and began strolling back and forth in a ten-yard beeline. His fortitude was ebbing away. He shored it up by being deliberately vigilant in his breathing; inhaling through the nose, exhaling out the mouth. His courage soon solidified.

A half-hour passed. He never varied his gait or pattern. There was plenty of traffic, commercial and pedestrian, occurring on the street, but he was unaffected by any of it. Wagons creaked along and some passersby had to take quick sidesteps to not bump into him. He ignored all of it because he had a matter of the heart tumbling around his brain. He was thinking through and quietly practicing what he had to say.

Then, the object of his intentions, stepped onto the broad veranda of Drovers Cottage. He spotted her immediately. In a rapid spurt of speed that was vehemently contrary to his character, he marched directly up to her. His face, shaded by the brim of his hat, was lined by deep grooves of determination around his eyes. There was a spring of boldness in his manner.

Naomi Engle, wearing a flowery dress with a frilly lace collar and cuffs, smiled gaily when she saw him. "Mr. Axler, good morning to you. You appear to be troubled."

"Not troubled at all, ma'am."

"I guess I have misread your demeanor. My apologies, sir."

"I wonder if you'd have a few moments for me, ma'am?"

"Please call me Naomi."

"Huh?" He gave her a puzzled frown. He removed his hat and jiggled it from one hand to the other. "Oh? Yes, that'd be swell. You can call me Pete."

"Fine, Pete," she said, taking a step back. "And the answer is yes."

"Yes?" His discomfort and unease was tangible. His rehearsed speech had gone missing from his memory and he was stammering in an attempt to adapt and press on.

"Yes, I have time just now," she replied, eyebrows tented sympathetically. "Could we go inside and have a cup of coffee together?"

Axler glanced around, as though he was expecting someone to speak on his behalf. He returned his hat to his head, leaving it to rest high on his brow. "That'd be nice, ma'am."

"Naomi."

"Huh?"

"Come along, Pete," she said, lips puckered as she held back a giggle. She turned and entered Drovers Cottage. He followed. She made her way across the lobby and into the dining room, which only had a few occupants. She went to a table at the far end of the room and sat with her back to the wall. He took a seat across from her. After they were settled, a fast-moving waitress took their order and served them. The coffee was black, strong and richly aromatic.

Axler dug around the inside of his cowhide vest and came out with the carved oak medallion he had whittled. It was perfectly round and about the dimension of a pocket watch. He turned it over in his fingers as if it were a large coin, held it toward her and said, "I wanted to thank you properly for coming to my aid, so I made this with you in mind."

She held a hand over her mouth for an instant before accepting it. Her eyes spread wide and flickered joyfully. "This wasn't at all necessary, Pete. It's beautiful!" She cupped it in her palm. The backside of it was flat and as smooth as glossy brass; on the front was an intricate work of art. She marveled at the exquisite detail. It was a seamless replica of a horse's head, with the plume of its mane abundant and flowing, its eyes deep-set and lifelike.

"Do you like horses, ma'am?"

"I don't know what to say, Pete. Thank you."

"Huh?"

"Yes, I do like horses."

He scratched at his bristly chin. "You're welcome, ma-am."

"Naomi. Please."

"I'll try to remember, ma'am."

She laughed; it was soft and gentle. Her eyes were fixed on his gift. She was obviously appreciative of the craftsmanship. "Whatever gave you the idea to do this for me?"

"I'm not sure, ma'am. I just thought I owed you a kind gesture."

"You didn't owe me anything, Pete."

He had a sip of coffee, then took off his hat and placed it on a vacant chair. "Maybe I want to get to know you better and ask if you might care to keep company with me."

She flinched in surprise at his bluntness. Her brown eyes squinched narrowly as her olive complexion grew even darker. "Oh, my. You have knocked me off-stride, Mr. Axler."

"Pete. You're supposed to call me Pete."

"Yes, but you've startled me."

"I'm sorry, ma'am," he said truthfully. "Upsetting you was the farthest thing from my purpose. I'm having a difficult time saying what's in my head because that's the way of it with me. Someone I respect instructed me to rope in my feelings and put a lariat around life, which is what I'm trying to do here. I'm gratified that I ain't mumbling or stumbling."

"I am truly flattered, Pete."

"Is that a good sign? I ain't one who can easily read a lady."

"You seem to be finding your way, Pete."

"So we should chat some and see where it goes?"

"I think that's an excellent approach."

"I like horses, Naomi," he said, nodding. "My granddad raised horses and I learned all there is to know about them from him. He was a strict and thorough teacher."

She was still charmed by the engraving. She kept tracing a finger over the delicate and comprehensive handicraft. Her eyes were lowered, but she was furtively searching the seemingly ceaseless grizzled crinkles of his face. Her lips parted in a contented smile. "Perhaps we could go horseback riding together. Might you show me the scenery some time?"

"I can do that," he answered, rather hurriedly. The enthusiasm of his response gave rise to a flush of ruddy color in his cheeks. He lapsed into hemming and hawing, which she soon discovered could be diverted by making specific inquiries. Sizable segments of silence crept up between them, but they managed to navigate their way through a longwinded conversation.

Noontime came and went before they said their goodbyes for the day.

The black-mottled clouds were irately bumping against each other, alive and kicking with electromagnetic activity. There was an odd scent churning in the hot currents of air. The churlish and turbulent sky was swollen and protruding like a pregnant woman's midsection ready to pop at any moment. Thunder was rolling and reverberating, whilst the wind howled and snapped with the fierce desperation of a coyote caught in the jaws of a steel-trap.

A flock of crows had evidently been infected with insanity, squawking and flying erratically amongst the copse of trees just north of the juncture of Mud Creek and the Smoky Hill River. The distressed cawing was riotous; dozens of the birds were flapping and flitting from branch to branch, swarming like a mad plague of locusts.

Lightning continuously flared in the thunderheads, sparking and flashing to sporadically brighten the gloomy grayness as though crazed imps were playing with matches. Every few minutes a ragged bolt blasted downward and struck the ground, followed by a bullwhip crack of thunder. The blustery squalls trumpeted a waterfalls noise in counterpoint.

The men at the campsite were scrambling around to tie down all that could be secured. Each was aware of the others; when tasks necessitated communication, their voices had to be raised to the shouting level to be heard above the wind. Charley Jondreau was collecting most of the gear, with the intention of lashing it to a tree trunk. Jackson Scully had his hands full as he wrestled and struggled with the stock in a feverish effort to prevent a stampede. The animals were overwrought and lathered with sweat, snorting and bounding wildly.

Liam Greer was frantically rifling through his saddlebags. His Stetson had gone sailing with an early gust of the windstorm and was now flopping and bouncing across the prairie. He was scared. The irrational recklessness of the crows frightened him; the dipping, diving and thumping wings kept him edgily nervous. He was on his knees, teeth clenched and rainbow-encircled eyes stretched as wide as the bruised tissue would allow.

He had been racing about and exerting energy, which restarted an incessant nosebleed. There was stabbing pain behind his eyes, accompanied by a steady drip-drip that invigorated bitter anger in him; he craved revenge on Sam Beadle. The blood trickled from both nostrils and he periodically thumbed it away as though it was snot.

Greer suddenly slammed his saddlebags to the ground, leapt to his feet and uttered a primal scream of rage. His heartbeat was pulsating against his eardrums. Something crackled within and he felt an all-consuming change come over him as fiery strength erupted in his belly. He had taken all the abuse and bullying that could be endured.

There was a clack-clack-clacking rattle of bones inside his skull. He sucked it up and mustered raw courage. His face distorted in a hate-filled grimace. His gunbelt was on and just now, he knotted the holster's thong tautly around his right thigh. He searched the area until he saw the ex-soldier gimping away from the job of hobbling the horses.

Greer stalked toward him, cursing and spitting. "Scully!" he yelled at the top of his lungs. "You scum-sucking maggot. You stole my silver case. Give it back to me now."

"You whelp!" Jackson exclaimed hotly. "Falsely accusing a man is a killing offense. You want to die here and now, say it again." His pistol was low on his hip, his gun-hand opening and closing in a deliberate, methodical rhythm. He took on a peg-legged stance that accentuated the appearance of his bum leg; it stuck out as straight as a length of timber, causing his swagger to tilt precipitously to the right. Not more than ten yards separated them when they halted their approach—a series of swift whirlwinds of dust seethed between them.

Greer had fire in his veins. He could taste the violence in him. He was ready. "I ain't taking back truth, Scully," he bellowed stridently. "If you ain't got it, who does?"

"I ain't your nursemaid or babysitter, kid," Jackson replied, bulgy eyes tight and bleary. He was sweating and red-faced, his voice loud and grating. His shoulders were stiff, but his hands were loose. "If you ain't got the cajones to hold onto it, don't be whining to me."

"You're a low-life loser, Scully."

"I'll live to piss on your grave, punk."

An outburst of wind agitated the heat as a blinding crack of lightning sliced jaggedly and crashed closeby. Both men jumped in their footsteps. In the booming drumbeat of thunder, Charley Jondreau eased over and got in the middle of the combative dispute. His expression was impassive and as impenetrable as stonework, his posture relaxed, almost casual. The force of the storm was intensifying; the crows were caterwauling in an uncontrolled frenzy.

"Get out of the way, Charley," Liam said thickly. "Or you'll be stuck in the crossfire. I ain't backing down. One way or another, I'm shooting that bastard."

Jondreau shook his head. "Why?"

"He stole my property."

"He ain't the one who took what didn't belong to you."

"Who?" Liam asked, glowering.

"I did. You want to draw on me, kid? Pull anytime, eh."

Greer balked in disbelief. "You? Why?"

"I delivered it to its rightful owner."

Greer's body sagged. His shoulders drooped. "Liar!"

Jondreau's face showed no emotion. His eyes were flat and icy cold. "Liar?" He gave a sideways glance at Scully, then dusted off his hands and held them up as he withdrew. He backed up cautiously. When he was clear of any possible straight-line gunfire, he hunkered down on his heels and began twiddling his thumbs as he viewed the unfolding developments.

Greer and Scully eyeballed each other. The temperature increased as a slight change occurred in the pressurized atmosphere. The furious madness screeching among the horde of crows escalated. A weird luminosity shone in the blackened rainclouds; a maelstrom of flaming orange and sickly green pillars was pumping up and down. A funnel cloud began to form with a whooshing roar. The vortex of wind took shape and skittered across the sky.

A terrifying blast of lightning smashed into Mud Creek; the cloying stink of charred ozone soured the air. Less than a second later, an ear-splitting thundercrack made the earth quake. Scully lurched off balance and wrenched around. Greer reacted in cunning coolness. He seized the instant. In one speedy and fluid motion, he drew his Smith & Wesson and crushed the trigger.

The bullet flew true to its mark. It struck dead-center between Scully's shoulder blades, severing his spinal cord. A bawling moan ripped from his throat, which was swallowed by the buzzing din of the tornado. He hit the soil hard, floundering fitfully as the area was bombarded by a barrage of feathered corpses—crows were tumbling out of the sky.

The narrow end of the twister came into contact with the ground a furlong or so to the south. An explosion of dirt and debris belched forth and became airborne. The rotating column of air violently carved a gash out of the grassland and zigged its way unpredictably. There was a deafening crash of lightning and thunder, which ignited a detonation inside the fulminating clouds. The rock-hard shrapnel of hailstones pelted the earth for a thrashing minute before giving way to a torrential wall of rain. The humidity was shattered and the temperature plunged.

In the midst of the mayhem, Liam Greer stared at Charley Jondreau.

~~~

Hundreds of miles to the west, a soft rain was dripping. Caleb Weitzel and Sally Twosongs were riding side by side. He was holding his hat in his hand and had his head tilted skyward, eyes shut and mouth open to receive the blessings of the cleansing shower. He valued and had a connection to rain; he had been told that it drizzled on the day he was born and also, a rainstorm was stirred up on the night when the only dog he ever owned came into the world.

She observed him, a pleased smile encompassing her face. She angled head and shoulders around and gave a tiny nod, then shifted comfortably in the saddle. "Father is doing well."

"At this clip, we have a couple weeks of traveling," Caleb said plainly.

"You'll get us home safely. Thank you for all your hard work."

Weitzel chuckled. "It really is my pleasure. I'm glad we've been together."

"In three years we'll be together always."

"There's much to do, Sally Twosongs. That ranch won't build itself."

"You'll finish it quickly enough, Caleb Weitzel. I know you." She held a finger up to him as a simultaneous burble of agreeable laughter tripped from their lips.

Behind them, Daniel Twosongs was swaddled on a travois that was being pulled by the brindle mare. Caleb had climbed the tree at dawn and heeding Daniel's instructions, chopped the necessary limbs, arranged the pieces and manufactured the vehicle. The horse had chaffed at the task, but after Weitzel gave it a thorough talking to, the animal became resigned to its role.

Consuelo rode to the side of the transport device, carrying on an often one-sided conversation with her husband, who drifted in and out of a slumbering catnap. When he was unresponsive to her chatter, she watched the rain water the earth and quietly lifted up prayers of thanksgiving. The pack-donkey tagged along compliantly, its lead-line attached to her mule.

Weitzel occasionally turned in his saddle and checked on them. He was doing just that when he heard a shrill yelp from Sally Twosongs. His head swiveled toward her.

She was twitching. Her hands were trembling on the reins. She gazed straight at him, her eyes blank and disengaged. "You got what you gave," she said, her voice low and gravelly, sounding as though it was being filtered through a thick blanket. "You got what you gave."

His shoulders stiffened. He gawked at her. "What?"

Sally Twosongs shivered hugely. The spasm ended. She flipped her pigtail back. Her eyes refocused and she pushed an apologetic grin at him. "Sorry. Not you, Caleb. The monster."

"The monster? What do you mean, Sally Twosongs?"

"It's done. The monster got what it gave."

Weitzel dragged a hand over his head. His face screwed itself into a confused frown. He let out an exasperated sigh and put his hat on. "That doesn't help my understanding. You're going to have to explain better or shed more light for me to see."

She wagged her head. "There's nothing more to say," she answered simply. "What's done is done. The monster got what it gave. Be at peace and be assured that we are safe."

"Sure thing, Sally Twosongs."

"Are you being silly?"

"Not at all," he said, shrugging as though he was helplessly at her mercy. "You're my north star, Sally Twosongs. I'll not make myself kooky trying to figure you out."

"Nor should you," she told him, eyes all a-sparkle with teasing sternness. He gave Shadrach's neck a pat and smiled. Without any signal or prompting from them, both mounts side-stepped closer to each other. They laughed together. It was pleasant and cheerful, full of adoration and respect. He took hold of her hand and they rode that way for many miles.

The caravan continued on through the balm-like petals of gentle rain.

In Abilene, a flood-like deluge was gushing from the heavens. The downpour rapidly transformed the dung-festooned streets into mucky quagmires. Big fat raindrops splattered and streamed to wash away the grime of dust and dirt. The sky, which had gone through a bizarre metamorphosis of flamboyant colors, was returning to the bleak gray normalcy of a cloudburst.

A bracing coolness breezed through town. The tormenting heat had released its hold and the fresh fragrance of newness wafted in the air. Deacon Coburn was enjoying the relief immensely. He sat on the porch of the barbershop, elbows on his knees and hands clasped together. The nonstop rat-tat-tat of the rain drumming on the roof and the muddy rivulets slashing across the thoroughfare were entertaining him.

"I be ready for a good visit," Whitey said, stepping outside. He had sidled inside for a match and was now puffing on a newly-lit cigar. He sat on the bench beside his friend. He leaned back and kinked his left ankle over his right knee. "That storm reminded me of one of those gulf coast hurricanes that hit us time to time in Alabama when I was a wee-one."

"I experienced a hurricane in East Texas once. Don't ever wish to see one again."

"No, sirree. They're nasty cusses."

"I was lead hand on the *Double B Ranch*," Deacon said, smiling broadly as he remembered. "I thought Big Bull Wallace was going to have a conniption as we scrabbled and fumbled around to batten down all that could be battened down."

Fitzgerald click-clicked and shook his head with certainty. "Not sure I'd want to be around a man named Big Bull if he was having a conniption."

Coburn chuckled. "It was a sight to behold."

Fitzgerald took a satisfying pull on his cigar. He casually blew a chain of smoke-rings. The final one lingered long enough for him to poke a finger through before it dissipated with the others. He was grinning as he asked, "Are you truly moving on to Dodge City?"

"I gave my daughter my word. Come springtime I intend to keep it."

"April or May?"

"I reckon. It's good riding when the prairie's all green and blooming."

"You might be a grandpappy by then."

Coburn inhaled and considered the possibility. His eyes creased. "I suppose, I guess."

"You care for a companion on the trail?"

"That depends," Deacon said slyly. "Who do you have in mind?"

"Come planting season I be ready to travel with you," Whitey replied, rolling the cigar between thumb and forefinger. "It be time for this Exoduster to see more of the promised land of Kansas. I figure there's barber and dentist work to be found anywhere, so why not?"

Coburn gave one loud and hearty handclap. "That news tickles me down to my socks. As far as I'm concerned, the matter's decided, Whitey. We'll relocate together." Laughter, along with a head-bobbing expression of affirmation and delight, was exchanged between them.

When it passed, the men settled in to savor the rejuvenating purity of the rain.

~~~

Dead crows littered the landscape. The wind had blown itself out and faded into a spooky calmness, but the rain was still pounding like a zillion hammers. Where the cyclone had touched down south of the Smoky Hill River, there was a deep scar a half-mile long. A meandering series of shredded craters were notched on the far side of Mud Creek.

Liam Greer paced warily, surveying the damage. He stepped around like a shell-shocked soul on a battlefield, avoiding broken branches, chunks of sod and deceased birds. He stumbled more than once. The front of his shirt had sticky stains from the nosebleed, but the nostrils had clogged up and ceased the discharge. His pistol remained clutched in his hand as though it was a surgically implanted extension of his arm.

With his first kill under his belt, Greer had a thirsty bloodlust scratching at his core. A restless hunger clawed and clamored to be fed. He intended to saddle up and ride into Abilene to settle all accounts. He eased over to the body spread-eagled face-first in the dirt. He booted several deceased birds out of the way and then, with a prideful grin pulling on his lips and making his eyes gleam, he scrooched down to examine his handiwork.

Scully's neck was contorted at an abnormal tilt, crooked and freakish. A sour stench emanated from the ghastly wound, which was seeping; an ooze of blood was being splashed and sluiced away by the rain. Greer chuckled creepily. He rocked and swayed on his haunches as he used the gun barrel to poke around the gaping hole. The longer he calculated the lifeless results of the gory work of his hands, the brighter the radiant afterglow shone on his face.

Charley Jondreau kept his eyes on the killer as he cared for the livestock. He was ready to use lethal force if that would be required against the wannabe gunslinger. The animals were still skittish, but unharmed. He diligently did what needed to be done. Then, with his face set in a severe and rigid scowl, he walked toward the supposed tough-guy.

"I'm heading to town," Liam announced, rising. He kicked another crow. He holstered his revolver, then stretched and arched his back. He dragged both hands through his soaked hair and shook like a wet dog. "I got stuff that needs doing."

"We'd be wise to pack up and ride south, hoss."

"Not just yet, Charley."

"What's taking you to town, eh?"

"I'm putting Beadle six-feet under for what he done to me," Liam answered, laying a pair of fingers alongside his smashed nose. "I'm going to give more than I got."

"He did for you with his dukes. You intend to use a gun?"

Greer sneered, slouchy and flippant. "Damned straight, I'll be swinging iron."

"You just murdered one man, now you're going after another?"

"Murdered?" Liam queried sharply.

"A coldblooded murder is what I witnessed, eh."

"No chance, Charley. It was a shootout, fair and square."

"You'll be hard pressed to explain that bullet hole in his back."

Greer shrugged dismissively. "He was turning as I drew . . ."

"Bullspit," Charley cut in, "you didn't make your play until he turned."

"You're wrong," Liam insisted, head held up defiantly. "It was a fair showdown."

"No. You killed a man, plain and simple," Charley said as he took a few careful steps backwards. He widened the position of his feet and slackened his posture. "You got a choice and it's clear. Bury him and ride out of here with me. Or go to town and trouble."

"I've lived nothing but trouble. I'm changing all that now."

"You want to draw on me, eh?" Charley asked grimly. The rain was whipping down on a slant. "If you do, tell me how you want to die. I can kill you fast with a bullet between the eyes or put one in your gut and let you bleed out in agony. It makes no never-mind to me."

Greer sagged and staggered to one side. The portions of his face not discolored by bruises became pale and pasty. He raised his open-palmed hands in surrender. "You'd kill me?"

"You'd be doing yourself in, eh."

Greer felt dizzy and nauseous. "I don't want to die, Charley," he said shakily. He spun around and collapsed onto his hands and knees. He heaved and vomited, gagging on the gusher of bile. The retching and coughing sounds were horrid. When the contents of his stomach were emptied, he spat repeatedly and wiped his mouth. He flipped over onto his backside. He yanked his knees up to his chest and wrapped his arms around his legs in a despairing hug.

Jondreau took it all in. He *saw* the lost little boy inside the youngster attempting to make his way in a world that had done him wrong. He *heard* an irksome echo clanking around his head: *No one's unredeemable.* His jaw clenched as he took a step closer to him. "You have much to learn, kid. I told you before; a man becomes good with a gun so he never has to use it."

Greer was sobbing. "I don't want to die."

"Gird up your loins like a man," Charley said, referencing Old Testament Scripture. There was fierceness in his face. "We ride and head for Texas. I'll tend to the body."

Greer wobbled to his feet. He was sniffling. "You want me to pack up?"

"I will walk with you until I will walk with you no more," Charley replied emphatically. He made a brusque backhanded gesture in the direction of the animals. "Saddle our horses and be ready. Set Scully's gelding loose and leave his gear untouched."

Greer nodded, subdued and amenable. Jondreau watched him get to it for a few moments. He then went about doing what needed to be done. He hoisted Scully's body up, shouldered it and carried it to the bank of Mud Creek. With the rain still hemorrhaging in a furious gale, he put his hands to the grisly task. He made little attempt to actually bury or conceal the carcass. Using sludge and rocks he weighed it down in a shallow hollow.

When he was finished, Jondreau climbed up from the water's edge. He was mucky and soaked. He spoke appeals for purification in a low voice. His eyes were closed. He leaned back, bent his head heavenward and with arms extended, he reveled in the purging drencher. He stayed in that reverential attitude of supplication until serenity gratified him.

The rain lessened, becoming a sprinkling spray. A crack appeared in the concrete crypt of clouds. Rays of sunlight broke through and shone on the campsite. Jondreau could feel the difference in the pit of his stomach. He opened his eyes and had a look around. He saw that Greer had completed the chores and was astride Hero, fidgety and wool-gathering. Without any further ado or conversation, he went to the piebald pinto and stepped into the saddle.

Sunbeams advanced and expanded as the sky began revealing more and more patches of blue. The air was sweet and clean, warm and invigorating. A peaceful draft of wind whispered its dispatch of healing across the traumatized and besieged countryside. As Charley Jondreau and Liam Greer rode south in the misty rain, the shadows of revenge were cast behind them.

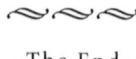

The woman formerly known as Sweet Flora sat stiff-lipped in a private railcar on the first stage of her journey to Santa Fe. The whore extraordinaire, dead and moldering for several seasons, had now, decisively been buried. No songs were sung; no invocations or pious litanies were intoned. There was no fanfare or any guests in attendance at the graveside.

The red-headed woman putting Sweet Flora's place of internment behind her was Delores Solrizo. She would *never* be Flora again. Until she met her Maker she would be Delores. After much grappling with various options, she had settled on her maternal grandmother's maiden name. It seemed appropriate and gave her a large quantity of motivation to be faithful.

A drizzly rain was falling, which she vaguely watched. Her mind was engaged elsewhere. An embroidered handbag was clutched in her lap. Her mouth was dry and cottony, lips pressed together and teeth clenched in determination. Her heart was doing a giddy-up and go urging as she opened the purse to remove the sterling silver case and a small pocket-knife.

She ignored the photograph. Her hands were a-tremble as she gingerly pried the tintype back. It took a long while. She gasped. The canary-colored onionskin paper remained intact. Her fingers barely functioned as she retrieved it. She unfolded the creases to see the final message her mother had written to her. At ten years old, the words were meaningful, but then, as darkness encompassed her life, the guidance had been lost and forgotten. She read the note now.

Delores - Learn to thank God for every situation, believing that God allows it for a purpose. Look for blessings from your trials. Know that your worth is not determined by your physical or mental assets, but by your willingness to be at God's disposal.

Her upper body shook with a huge shudder of breath. A thousand feelings coursed through her. The consistent rocking of the train somehow provided comforting encouragement. She turned to stare outside. The gray-streaked sky was weeping. She silently prayed in hope. The raindrops on the window mirrored the teardrops spilling down her cheeks.

~The End~